I0677573

The White Room...
A Photographic Love Story

Brad Manard

Author's Statement

As a writer, I am cautious in considerations of censorship, yet as an educator and parent I understand the importance of guiding our children and monitoring their learning. *The White Room* was written as a novel for adults with themes that impact families in today's world much too often. Therefore, I would encourage parents to read *The White Room* and make their own decisions regarding the appropriateness for young-adult readers.

Copyright © 2014 Brad Manard
All rights reserved.

ISBN 10: 0692231773
ISBN 13: 9780692231777
www.bradmanard.com

To Mom,
Tim, Claire, and Jana
And to Dad who lived a life that made me believe.

You have been a great sense of support,
inspiration, and laughter throughout life.

Acknowledgement

At seventeen, I set three goals. One, to win a Nebraska High School Gymnastics Championship; two, to own a new Pontiac Firebird; and three, to write a novel. This acknowledgement is in honor of all who helped me achieve those three goals.

To my editor Claire Seely who ensured that every word expressed the vision of Alexandria and Michael's lives. To Deb Cox, who inspired confidence to mold the true character of the novel. And to Tom Cox and Janina Dingeman who gave valuable perspective in the frivolity of the story.

Since my teen years, there have been many who have accompanied me on the journey to Estes Park, driven the winding roads, seen the magnificent elk, hiked the massive hills, climbed the red rock summit of Gem Lake, reached for the indigo sky, and lived the romance of *The White Room*. A special thank you to Denise for her inspiration in writing *The White Room* and sharing the Bristlecone Pine.

To Jim Salestrom whose acoustic magic and friendship carried me from Lincoln, NE to the mountains of his songs. To those who years ago danced on Acoustic Tuesday to Dick Orleans in the dingy romance of Lonigan's. To Brandon Hull and Scott Stasenka, both outstanding gymnasts and individuals. For a time Scott was a bartender in Lonigan's and Brandon is an outstanding Denver attorney. Both inspired characters in *The White Room*. And to waitress, photographer, and long-lost friend Carla.

To my proof and pre-readers who, from my mind undisciplined to the rigors of typography, crafted the details. Special thanks for the keen eyes and insight of Cindy Ballew, Sheila Alspach Mahan, Kathy Mullens, Nancy Wood, Carol Loy, Larry Dawson, Toni Tarracino, Sonja Babcock, and Josie Kohler.

To my sons Wayne, Jonathan, and Benjamin who have trekked upward to the peaks, wandered the deep woods, and shared the incredible journey of nature and wildlife photography. And to my daughter-in-law Lindsay and grandson Jonas for their enthusiasm, laughter, and love.

Finally, special love and thanks to my wife, Carolyn for her encouragement, enthusiasm and personal belief that *The White Room* is a novel that must be shared. Her push, excitement, and the mystic blue in her eyes were an inspiration of beauty and determination to complete *The White Room* and sing the song.

The White Room

A journey is like a marriage.
The certain way to be wrong is to thing you control it.
                                    John Steinbeck

Part 1: Summer
Chapter 1

Dangling in midair, even with his solid build, the wind swayed him precariously. Seeing the world in a 360 degrees revolution, like a yo-yo at the end of the string, he took in the spectacular view.

Glancing skyward, the overhanging ledge separated him from safety while eighty feet below the treetop spires waited to impale. Clinching tighter, his laughter echoed through the canyon as he felt the surge of freedom in this solitary adventure into the wilds.

Somewhere down there in the forest was what he searched for. Off the trails beyond the black peaks of the eastern ridges in Rocky Mountain National Park was a place where man had failed to descend. It was the place Michael was determined to find.

Rappelling, his legs bounced downward to the base of the cliff absorbed the solid ground. He was alone in the wilderness, beyond the park trails and isolated from both tourists and rangers. Removing his cap, he pulled his black hair back into a ponytail and wiped sweat from his forehead.

Michael checked his pack. Both cameras were secure. Testing the grip of his hiking boots, he worked his way down the crevice through the maze of lodge pole pine.

With no trails to follow, no signs for the recreational hiker, Michael edged along the wall. The rock pattern turned from black to white, and he began to sense the dampness. Stopping at the bottom of the small cliff, he stood listening, his head tilted for the sound.

Faintly, Michael could hear it. Like soft wind through a narrow tunnel, the sound of falling water was a remote rain on a blue-sky morning. His face upward, he could feel the slight mist brushing gently over his eyes. Michael stood for a moment, taking in what he was about to discover.

Stepping onto a boulder above the reflecting pool, he stood quietly, his lips separated as the colors filled his eyes. Listening, he gazed spellbound as the waterfall proved mystical.

The pool's depth showed white pebbles beneath the water. Across stood rows of pines stretching upward, sunlight penetrating each needle. Wildflowers grew in abundance with exaggerated hues of reds, purples, and yellows flourishing in the dew-dropped blossoms defining the hillside, and the waterfall was a steady, soothing rhythm.

The purity of the flowing snowmelt allowed him to see the light passing through to the shallow sand and white cliffs behind the falls. A cloud passed overhead reflecting in the calm waters at the far edge. This was serenity where nature rested undisturbed. This was Michael's discovery.

Colors filled his eyes, shades of brilliance in green and bright wildflowers. Energized, this was the moment when the ultimate photographer's find stirred his senses. All the off-trail hiking, the blisters and bruises, the chilly winds and icy waters, and the days of muscle aches were now rewarded.

Finally, he lifted his 35mm SLR camera from his pack. Circling the pool checking the angles and light, he pushed the shutter to the sound of the camera's motor. He would take digital test shots tight in and from a distance, estimate the time and impact of morning light, and return another day prepared to capture the untouched image. With his keen eye, he understood that light in the angles of the sun would highlight perfection.

Chapter 2

Alexandria stood beside the Mercedes in the no parking lane of Denver's International Airport. Anxious, she tried to block the guilt she was hiding. Normally William would have had the limousine drop him off, and they wouldn't be standing face-to-face. But Josephine was flying with him as far as Kansas City, and Alexandria had insisted on driving them.

Both parents masked their discomfort. Instead they shared their daughter's excitement about flying to visit her grandparents. At Alexandria's insistence, William had arranged his flight through Kansas City. There he would see Josephine to the gate where Alexandria's parents would meet them. Still, Alexandria worried.

"Mommy." Josephine's silk blouse hinted of her little girl growing up. "Don't fuss, okay." She looked around at the passing people, hiding her all-too-grown-up embarrassment. "I can do this."

"I know you can, Baby." She reached for Josephine's hair where a deep black strand shone out of place. "You'll be fine." She smoothed it into a perfect wave.

"Daddy will be with me until Gramps and Grammy pick me up." She opened her eyes wider, mocking her mother's smile. "You've only told me that a hundred times in the last two days. Gramps and Grammy pick me up, and we drive to Lawrence. It's simple, Mom."

"I'll check in with you throughout the week. We'll be able to talk."

"If I had my own cell phone, you could call me instead of Gramps."

"Not this again," she smiled at Josephine's pretend pout.

"Grandmother Chadwick said she'd buy me one."

"I'll buy you one when the time is right." Alexandria corrected.

William cleared his throat. "If my mother wants to buy her a cell phone, I don't see a problem."

Alexandria's eyes cast downward.

"Really!" The excitement shrilled in Josephine's voice.

Alexandria chose to move on, not to fight what inevitably would be a chastising she didn't deserve.

"We'll talk when you get back from Kansas." Her voice was firm. "Now, let's see. Number one, don't talk to strangers." Her eyes were intent with instruction.

William reached his hand to Alexandria, and she flinched involuntarily. With her eyes cast downward, she could not see the glare in his eyes.

"Alexandria, you know she'll be fine. She's traveled enough that she could handle herself even if I wasn't there to meet your parents."

"You will be with her?" Her eyes searched for reassurance.

"Every minute. There's an hour and forty-five minute layover. Plenty of time."

William gripped her arm firmly, controlling, and she did as expected, formally kissing on each other's cheeks. He half expected to see a tear in Alexandria's eyes, her emotional pattern lately, and one he had little tolerance for. Instead, she looked past him.

Regaining her composure, Alexandria pressed her hand over the lapel of William's suit. Forcing a smile, she glanced toward the airport entryway. "Have a good trip." Her eyes softened. "I'll see you in a few days."

She stooped, and Josephine wrapped her arms around her. The hug was a mother's security. "I love you, Baby."

"Love you too," she whispered back.

As Alexandria stood, William leaned forward as if to kiss her. Instead, his words were nearly silent. "Go straight home. Your life could use some attention." Her husband's dark voice penetrated her conscience. "Whatever the hell's been going on with you, I want it straightened out by the time I get back."

As they parted, Alexandria did not look at him. She stared at the speckles in the concrete, reflective of her own thoughts. When she looked up, Josephine had turned to wave one last time before walking into the crowded line at security.

Watching them, Alexandria's pain had become numbing. William's back was strong and distant, revealing none of the calloused manipulation he brutally used. He placed his arm on Josephine's shoulder as if he was protecting, and she realized they were the convoluted image of a perfect family. The handsome father in tailored gray, William was a man of influence and power standing beside their daughter. Beautiful even at a young age, her hair was black like her father's yet her eyes revealed her mother's crystal blues. Alexandria stood in all of her silk and satin, hair pulled tightly into a perfect blond bun except for the slight wave hanging across her cheek.

As her husband and child disappeared into the mass of travelers, Alexandria breathed deeply, allowing air to fill her chest. Slowly exhaling, the anger grew to near tears. She turned and looked at the Mercedes idling at the curb.

The luxury car looked so stuffy and *William-like* with the rich smell of new leather. She wondered what directive he would have given had he checked the workout bag in the trunk. He would be furious if he knew what she was about to do, and if he found out afterwards more than furious, brutal. *Straighten out by the time I get back.* That was exactly what she hoped she was doing.

Alexandria looked over the hood of the car at the mountains towering as a western backdrop to Denver. There was a sense of absolution with his departure, and she could already feel the tension easing from the strain of their relationship.

Maneuvering the car and into the flow of taxis and returning travelers, the airport lanes led directly to the freeway going northwest. Before long, she took the exit driving through Boulder and past the University of Colorado campus. At the north edge of town, she stopped at a service station, went to the trunk, and pulled out her bag. Her silk jacket waved in the wind as she walked, her hair still pulled up tight and unburdened by the breeze, and her high heels clicked across the concrete parking area.

The women's restroom was gas station clean, and the slight grime in the creases where the floor met the wall made her somehow feel real again. She pulled paper towels from the dispenser and covered the floor before placing the overnight bag on top. Looking above the soap splatters in the mirror, her smile was nervous and tension showed in the unnatural wrinkles of her forehead. She breathed deeply, striving to relax. This was her time. She had made a choice. She knew that being in this restroom was freer than she'd felt in years, and she willed herself to go on.

Alexandria glared at her image. As she stared, her eyes turned from blue to shades of red. Stepping away slightly off balance, she leaned back against the paint chipped door as her legs seemed to lose their strength. Dropping to the floor, Alexandria's eyes caught the motion of a cockroach scooting into a crevice in the bathroom tile. That is when she cried, growing uncontrolled with stifling sobs.

When she emerged, the sun energized her tired eyes. Purposefully, Alexandria put a bounce in her step. Her silk suit lay crumpled in the bag she carried, discarded as an unnecessary prim and proper facade. Now, a ponytail slipped through the gap in the back of the cap that advertised *Rocky Mountain National Park*. The silk had been replaced with a deep green denim shirt tied at the midriff. Her khaki shorts were complimented by the freedom of light tan and wintergreen hiking boots yearning for the scrapes and dust of a long hike. For just a moment, she breathed in the air to feel the sense of freedom again. In so many ways, she was going home.

Chapter 3

Michael had crested the curve where Fall River Road opened to the summit above tree line when he saw them. Six magnificent bull elk stood grazing at the switchback. Five were fully mature with velvet antlers stretching toward the middle of their thick, brown shoulders. One was a Royal, larger and stronger with a rack beyond proportion presenting an image of unquestioned power. Michael eased the yellow Jeep upward along the one-lane dirt road. As he glanced back, scattered rays of sunlight broke over the stone peak.

Man did not intimidate these park elk, yet Michael knew he would have to work quickly. As the sunrise peaked, he would have exceptional light for only about twenty minutes. Then the tourists would begin finding their way up Fall River Road. With the noise of cars and people, the elk would lift their heads as they sniffed the hint of intruders. With subtle caution, they would meander down the hillside, away from the invaders, and disappear among the willow bushes as silly people with point-and-shoot cameras tried to get closer, chasing the elk farther away.

He pulled the tripod from the back seat, one camera over his shoulder and the other in his waist pack. Traversing easily from the edge of the road, he moved to a range where the telephoto lens would fully frame the animal's head and antlers. Today was a play day, testing to see the impact of a full headshot, the huge antlers extending off beyond the edges of the image.

She saw the yellow Jeep just above the tree line. Beyond the Jeep were elk, and she gasped at their size, having forgotten the impact from years before. Lifting the binoculars, Alexandria peered through the Mercedes windshield. There were six of them, all in velvet with shining brown summer coats.

He wasn't more than fifty feet from them, yet they seemed not to notice the photographer. He was broad at the shoulders where a wool sweater shielded him from the wind. His hat turned backward with the bill away from the camera, hair hung black reaching well over his collar.

He was irritated to hear the car's engine. When he glanced backward he was even more aggravated. The Mercedes stopped behind his Jeep. Not only was it a tourist, but a rich, arrogant tourist unknowledgeable of their impact. He turned back to the camera, knowing his opportunity was nearly gone.

Focusing on the grazing Royal, he barely heard the door shut quietly in the thin air. Still, three of the elk looked in the direction of the Mercedes. At least the rich fool hadn't slammed the door. Maybe he would get lucky. Maybe they wouldn't walk right past him into the view of his camera, blocking the shot in ignorant tourist fashion, while chasing the elk down the mountain.

The steps behind him were faint, and he turned to see her avoiding the vegetation. She could see his frown and froze. He felt relief that there was no instamatic camera in her hand. Instead, she held binoculars. He pointed toward the ground at her feet, and traced a path for her to just behind him. If he could guide her, the elk might not disappear so quickly into the valley.

Stepping easily, she followed the imaginary path. Her path was chosen to avoid the moss and bits of grass, protecting the delicate alpine tundra. As a rock tilted under her foot, the elk came alert. She too froze. For so long nothing moved. She balanced behind him, and his eyes did not leave the camera. The elk watched, anticipating a need to flee.

Soon the trust returned, and one at a time the full brown-coated animals began grazing while edging a few steps farther away. Feeling her behind him, he turned and reached out his hand. She grasped it for balance, and he guided her the two steps onto the rocky mound.

With a serious look, he stared directly into her eyes and whispered. "Just watch. Appreciate and respect. Don't move. Don't talk."

Through the viewfinder, the large elk lifted his head, stretching. His full brown eyes tilted upward as the velvet antlers disappeared from the top of the defined image. Returning on the other side of the frame, the antlers touched the sun-tipped strength of his shoulders. The camera shutter clicked in a whirl of multiple shots as Michael captured the image.

Then the grazing bull began moving away. Michael watched knowing what was happening. One at a time each bull followed. Wandering a few feet, nibbling a bush, some greens, and then a few steps farther. Grazing as they moved, it would not be long until they disappeared over the ridge to rest lazily through the morning.

Remembering her eyes, he leaned back closer to her, whispering. "In a moment they'll be gone. People will drive by all morning and never know elk are a hundred feet off this road, just out of sight." He pointed at the Alpine Visitor Center visible where the original mountain passage met Trail Ridge Road. "With your binoculars, you can watch them from there."

Her voice was apologetic. "I'm sorry if I interrupted you. It's incredible. I've never been this close, not for years."

He was still watching the elk, now just heads and antlers silhouetted above the ridge. "You have to respect them; patience, appreciation, and respect with a calming distance." He slipped the camera strap down upon his shoulder and folded the tripod legs to become a third the size. Turning, for the first time he saw her.

She was stunning and fit in a hat and boots. While her clothes seemed new, she dressed for the mountains. Smiling, he glanced upward to see eyes nearly as blue as the pond he'd discovered the morning before. Deeply tanned skin complimented the flow of her blond hair, softened his irritation, and he surrendered a smile.

She pointed shyly at his camera. "I'd love to see your pictures."

Knowing he did not share his images, he smiled politely. "Have a nice day. And please, be cautious. It's rough up here." His grin grew, half teasing her. "Rich tourists can get themselves in trouble thinking they know what they're doing."

She stood half irritated, half intrigued, with her mouth agape as she watched him stride toward the Jeep. His muscles flexed firmly as he set the tripod in the back, and he lifted his body easily into the driver's seat. Turning his hat around, he gripped the bill tilting a nod toward her, started the engine, and drove away.

When he had disappeared above at the visitor's center, she turned back to where they'd stood, but there was no sign of the elk. Her eyes cast sadly downward, and she wondered what would happen if she left. Would William ever glance away from his work long enough to notice? Would it matter to him or would it be an embarrassment? He'd have to control to protect his image.

She hated her life of elite society, expectations, and the demands of a name and his family image; detested her mother-in-law's piercing sarcasm that Alexandria lacked the proper social background. Most of all, she hated her manipulated life. The threats he imposed were an intense mind game she was losing and wondered when she had lost herself to fear?

In the beginning she had been naive, believing in the power of money to contain happiness. She remembered when they'd become engaged and her roommates had been so excited. Late that night in the three-bedroom college apartment, they'd drunk strawberry daiquiris and teased her wishing they could wear clothes that wrinkled and have the help do the ironing.

Now the elk and the young man with the camera were gone, and she shivered away who she had become. No one needed to know that at night they slept back to back without words. And in the morning William would be gone, and she would have a vast house, breakfast waiting for her, and dread. How could she ever be free from the dread of living with everything while feeling completely alone?

Chapter 4

"I'll be damned." Standing in front of the Church Shops in downtown Estes Park, Michael was looking past Jimmy.

"Of course you will, you who dangles from mountain tops by a rope?" Jimmy laughed.

Michael elbowed his friend, pointing. "That's her."

Jimmy's eyes followed Michael's arm. "That's who?"

Michael grinned. "The rich tourist from this morning."

"Damn," Jimmy pointed too. "The blonde. Blue jeans, boots, bouncy fringe vest?"

"Yes."

"Damn," he repeated himself. "Mountain chic and hot." Then Jimmy sang, *"And then I knew…I knew, I knew, I knew, she could make me happy, happy, happy."*

Michael turned to his goofy friend.

Jimmy shrugged, "The Cowsills. The fringe on her vest reminded me of 60's music." He shrugged again, "What can I say?"

Michael put one hand on Jimmy's shoulder. "Usual time tonight?"

"Eight o'clock." Jimmy still watched her as she stopped and visited with the hostess at the Grubsteak.

"See you at eight." His hand left Jimmy's shoulder as he jogged off down the street.

"You're going the wrong way," Jimmy called after him. Michael waved him away, and Jimmy sang, *"I love the flower girl, oh, I don't know just why, she simply caught my eye."*

Michael's Jeep was parked a block away on a narrow street. Uncovering the bag on floor, he swirled the combination lock to free it, and pulled his camera from the padded slot. While there were thirty descent shots, seven pushed spectacular, and he grinned at the blending of creativity and morning light. Moving through them a second time, he deleted the unspectacular and kept the seven growing more impressive with each frame.

Camera in hand, he walked against the light toward the Grubsteak.

Stopping against the cast-iron railing, his early morning acquaintance sat studying the menu. Squatting down, his arm rested inches from her bare shoulder. Surprised, she brightened with recognition.

That morning, through his irritation, he had not realized the impact. It was only later, driving down Trail Ridge Road that his mind had wandered to her.

"I brought the elk pictures." He held up the camera.

Her smile grew. "Wonderful. I've thought about them all day." She gestured to the empty wrought iron chair. "Please sit. Show me."

"I have to apologize." He offered, pushing a strand of hair back up under his sweat-stained hat.

She shook her head and the lines in the high, soft cheeks revealed confidence. Her tanned skin accentuated sleek muscles, and the vest was perfect, fringe and all. From her neck, a black, slender cord held the blue stone image of Kokopelli.

She hesitated, her eyes captivating. "I'm the one who should apologize."

"No, I was too impatient."

She shook her head. "And what did you teach me? Patience, appreciation, respect, I believe those were your words."

The hostess sat a beer in front of Michael. He returned her smile, thanking her by name.

Alexandria lifted one eyebrow. "Come here often?"

"Not really. I just make friends easily." He glanced into her eyes. "Which is why I want to apologize. And as an apology, I brought the images you asked to see."

He set the camera between them, instructing her where to push to advance the images and took a deep breath. He knew the images were good, but doubt crept into his mind. It was why he did not share his images. Despite his personal belief, he was always haunted by the question *Are they good enough?*

Tapping the camera, he instructed. "Push here."

Slowly, she pressed the button. The image lit, and she stared at an elk eye-to-eye. Even on this smaller screen, she could see the detail of the velvet antlers lit by the morning sun. She sat back from the screen, still staring, searching the details careful. Without a word, she moved through the images, and with each another attribute appeared, more drawing and more intense.

The elk's head reached toward a touch of unbroken blue sky beyond the mountain backdrop. The antler's thickness showed an animal of power detailed in the morning light. Reaching, the antlers reappeared to stretch onto the shoulders of the magnificent animal.

He sat watching her, the brightness of her eyes and hints of appreciation. She was rare, slipping naturally into the surroundings as if she too were a part of the sunlight cresting the mountain.

Lifting her eyes, she took his hand in hers. "I'm Alexandria. So happy to meet you."

Michael returned the handshake, and he saw that she was not an Alexandria. "Alex," his smile grew, "so nice to meet you. My name is Michael."

She laughed at being called Alex. Never had such informality seemed so right, so fun.

"Mickey," she grinned, "you have an extraordinary talent."

He leaned back in the iron chair. Their hands separated, and he pressed his fingers over his temples and drew his hair back into a ponytail. "I see things, and I try to capture them. I don't know, Alex. Talent? I have a passion, but I don't know if I have the talent. That's what I'm working to discover."

Leaning forward, her chin resting in her hands. "Trust me. You have talent. These pictures are incredible."

Michael laughed. "Okay, so you've made some decisions about me. I have to ask you, Alex, what are you escaping from?"

She hadn't expected it, the way he read her. Looking away, her chest rose and fell until she felt control. With the manufactured laughter she had expertly crafted as William's wife, she asked casually, "Why in the world would you think I'm escaping?"

He reached and touched her hand, and she felt disappointment, believing this was just a cheap hustle with a line to go with it.

"Because extraordinary people, especially beautiful women who drive Mercedes, are never alone."

Hating the car and the image it evoked, Alexandria watched the people strolling past on the sidewalk. He had used the word *extraordinary*. There was a time in her life when she'd believed that hidden deep inside her, there might be something extraordinary. Back in college she had believed she could make a difference, but marriage had changed it all.

"But you're alone." She diverted the question.

He sidestepped the diversion. "No. I was by myself until I sat down with you. Then the waitress brought me a beer. At Lonigan's people are expecting me. It's Tuesday, and they know I love Acoustic Tuesday. But you, Alex, you stand alone in a town where everybody is with somebody."

The waitress set a salad before her, rich with lettuce, cherry tomatoes, and a variety of peppers topped with a fillet of salmon. Mickey smiled at his waitress friend thanking her. She returned the smile, switching out his beer, and winked.

It was not unnoticed and Alexandria found herself feeling like a pawn in a bad chess game. She lifted her napkin, folding it perfectly across her lap. Moving a cherry tomato with her fork, she looked again at Mickey.

"This morning, I went from Fall River Road and drove to the Grand Lake side of the park, discovered a three-mile trail and hiked to a giant meadow where I found a peaceful rock and sat down to think. There I was, all alone when a moose came wandering from the woods. A bull with the largest antlers you've ever seen. I didn't know what to do or think, trapped in the middle of the meadow on a rock, so I sat and watched." She grinned at the photographer across from her. "It was a moment of *patience, appreciation, and respect.*"

He smiled, "These mountains can surprise us."

Then she reached, her fingers lightly resting upon his camera. "Now you've shared these photos with me, and I thank you for the perfect ending to a spectacular day."

"Ending? Not on Acoustic Tuesday. They're expecting us."

Her eyes mocked seriousness. It was time to stop this flirtatious game. "There is no *us* in Acoustic Tuesday." Her eyes stared as sure as they could be.

He raised his beer, and the golden liquid swirled in his glass. "I believe, Alex, you've escaped to these mountains." Quickly, he raised his hand stopping her interruption. "I know I'm being presumptuous. I apologize, but Acoustic Tuesday is great fun with fantastic music, really good people, and plenty of beer. So tonight, be exactly who you want to be. Tonight, escape by joining us."

As she stepped through the door into Lonigan's, he rested his hand on the curve of her back. Thin, she was gentle to his touch. Feeling his hand against her, despite the guilt, she allowed it to stay. At the stairs leading to the sunken bar, he guided her through the tables and people to the old rounded bar with the overstuffed vinyl railing.

"Michael," Scooter waved a greeting from behind the bar.

Michael raised his hand, two fingers ordering beer.

Alex looked around the bar at the locals dressed in work clothes of holey jeans and muscle shirts filled with muscles. The women all looked naturally healthy, quite capable of handling themselves.

From the moment she had stepped down toward the bar, she'd felt different. The memory had escaped her for a time, but now flashed back like a photograph. On her 21st birthday, her father and her, he had brought her here, brought her to Lonigan's in Estes Park, and they had sat at the bar where they had shared their first beer together.

How the memory had escaped her, she did not know. He was an insightful father who had proven to know his daughter better than she knew herself. From that had grown a special relationship. They had always been able to talk, talk about anything and everything with a trust she had never known with anyone else. He had been open and compassionate but honest that evening. Alex remembered her enthusiasm about William, telling her father about his family, his wealth and drive to succeed, and her respect for William's business mind and determination.

That is when her father had turned to her in this bar, likely on one of those red vinyl stools with the high backs, and asked her if she was happy, truly happy in her heart. Questions had always been his way of drawing her out, but she had turned the tables that day and asked him *Why in the world would you think I'm not happy?* Her father had tilted his beer with a hint of sorrow in his eyes and asked *I'm just wondering why you think you are?*

Now here she sat understanding her father's insight with his question echoing in her thoughts *I'm just wondering why you think you are?* She found little intimacy and a degree of contempt for William's manipulations away from the life she had dreamed of. From the family she had grown up in, to the one she lived in now, she had seen the full spectrum of what a marriage could be. Happiness had faded so many years ago. Thinking of her father, she was glad Josephine was with him, with him and her mother back home in Kansas where life was a little more understandable and a lot less pretentious.

Michael was staring at her as her thoughts turned back to the present, and she saw two beers on the bar.

"I don't suppose they have wine?" She asked not even remembering the taste of beer.

Mickey leaned on his elbow. "I told you, no Alexandrias here." His eyes watched hers with the confidence of a man either not tested or one who had passed all his tests.

At that instant, she decided if this were a game, she would enjoy playing. Charming in a rugged way, she had handled boys like him before he had developed such cockiness. She stepped toward him and spoke with her own confidence. "I'll take the beer."

"Scooter," he handed the bottle to her. "This is my friend, Alex."

The bartender reached his hand toward her.

"What does Scooter stand for?" She asked.

"I'm a rock climber." Scooter smiled.

The waitress, tall and lean with a mane of brilliant red hair, set her bar tray on the other side of Mickey. Scooter winked, his ponytail swinging behind him. "I can scoot up the rocks as fast as anyone."

The waitress's hand rested on Mickey's arm. On her pinky was a small silver ring with turquoise inset. Dressed in a body suit, navy skirt, and hiking boots, she leaned toward Alex.

"Wrong version," she winked. "As a baby he never crawled. He scooted around on his diaper." Michael choked on his beer, foam spilling from his laughter. The waitress shrugged, "Scooter? Couldn't climb a damn rock until I taught him. Now he's making up stories to match the image he really wants."

The laughter was free and fun without being measured. Alex pointed at Mickey's face, and he wiped the beer foam from his lip. As he did, she laughed again. Maybe it was the way Mickey held his beer or the slight tilt in his grin. He had optimism, a quality she had seen in her dad.

For so many years her family had come to Estes Park. Every summer when he was not teaching, her father would bring the family for two weeks to stay in the little cabin on Bighorn Drive. She would sleep nights in her sleeping bag on the screened-in porch. It had never bothered her, the cold mountain air.

She was six when she first started watching Long's Peak. Evenings, after a cookout, she would sit on her father's lap, and he would feed her graham crackers, marshmallows, and melted Hershey bars. As she ate, giggled, and felt protected with her Daddy, he would tell her stories of the legendary Enos Mills and the park before people. The stories were of the one room log cabin at the base of Long's Peak, back when man didn't drive but walked into the elements of snow and wind and narrow impassible mountain ridges, back when the bighorn sheep were thicker than the elk, back before man began taking pieces of land for himself.

Every summer her dad would take her on hikes, longer and more challenging hikes each year. Together, they would stride, up the mountain trail past phlox, giant red Indian paintbrush, and alpine blue columbine into the pines and over rocks with little chipmunks sitting on top. For her sixteenth birthday they'd climbed Long's Peak. Altitude weary through the boulder field and on with slow breathless steps, they had climbed the backside of Long's Peak. On her sixteenth birthday she had stood on the top and through binoculars spotted the little cabin on Bighorn Drive.

She hadn't hiked since her last visit to Estes Park, since her 21st birthday over ten years ago. William didn't hike. His family didn't hike because hiking created sweat that collected grime making the body less presentable. It was unseemly for a Chadwick to do such things. Instead, they all went to The Club. The men golfed, and the women lay by the pool with the children while lathered in oil. It was a simple role for the Chadwick banking family, purchased fun with strict rules captured in a vision of the elitism. That was her world now.

Alex looked at Mickey who was looking past her. The sound of guitar strumming came from beyond her and heads turned toward the stage. It was a beautiful sound, the sound of an acoustic guitar played with enthusiasm. Instantly, music filled the room in the full volume of a talented player. Mickey's smile showed a slight dimple on his left cheek as his head began to sway rhythmically.

For a moment it was surreal. What was she doing acting as if it was okay to be here tonight, looking at Mickey and thinking the thoughts she was thinking. She shook her head, shuddering with the surety that a man of her husband's resources would certainly discover any indiscretion. What was she thinking?

The music grew as people sang with the singer causing Alex to look away from the bar. The door was across the room. This game had gone on too long. She was not free to play, for to win she would have to cheat. She turned back to Mickey who was watching the singer, his body still swayed to the music. Alexandria leaned into the young man to tell him she had to go. It was time to walk across the room, step outside, and disappear into the night.

"He's a friend of mine." Mickey's words were barely heard. "Great musician, great song writer. Jimmy and Acoustic Tuesday."

"I have to go." She called out above the music.

His hand moved to her back drawing her attention. "Here's someone you should meet."

Did he not hear her? She had to go. He had to take his hand from her back. The touch, she needed the touch to go away. Thank you for sharing the pictures, thank you for the laugh, for making me feel desirable. Thank you for having long black waves of hair that no self-respecting banker would ever consider. Thank you for the beer and allowing me to feel a hint of myself again. Thank you, Mickey, but I must go.

"Alex," he stepped back as a grubby man with a beard and tattoos stopped before them. "Alex, this is Ralph. Ralph lays concrete and rides a Harley."

"Shit, Alex. You are one god damn beautiful lady. Hell yes, you are."

Mickey laughed. "Be nice to her, Ralph."

Before Alex could move toward the door, Mickey disappeared into the crowd.

Immediately, Ralph made her uncomfortable. His hair was long, straight and stringy, pulled back and held together with a red rubber band. An untrimmed beard with a little braided length from the middle of his chin surrounded his toothy smile.

"You one of our welcome tourists, Alex?" Ralph took a long neck swig and smiled toothy.

Alex looked past Ralph. The bar was full of people. People like Ralph, people like Mickey, but no people like her. No designer jeans with creamy blue denim and a slim fit. When she had put these on, she'd believed she was dressing down. Still, there was no one like her.

"You all right, Alex?"

"Yes." She smiled, and his grin returned with a softness that surprised her. "I'm fine, Ralph."

"You like this music?" he asked.

Alex turned back toward the stage. Jimmy sang songs from the heart, songs her heart had forgotten along the way. Somewhere hidden by the Denver Symphony, she had let acoustic guitar and songs from the heart disappear.

"Love songs, Alex. That's what they are." Alex smiled at Ralph, his eyes bright despite the hard wrinkles. He lifted one of two beers from the bar, took her near empty from her hand, and replaced it with the full one.

She handed the beer back. "No, thank you. I'm sure I've had enough."

"Loosen up, Alex. This is supposed to be fun." He swept his hand over the packed room. His left arm was a collage of blacks, reds, and blue-greens with animals, emblems, and symbols of a rough life. He looked back to see her watching him. "My body is an art museum in one format. Ink to skin."

She wrinkled her forehead, sensing the pain the needles. "May I ask a personal question, Ralph?" Always so formal, even in the presence of disturbing body art. "Why the fascination with tattoos?"

Ralph's toothy grin reappeared. "See this one?" He pointed at the demon on his right shoulder. "When I was fifteen, I fell in love. Oh man, was I in love. Hot 18-year-old, older woman with chubby boobs, and when I touched her boobs, love seemed to spurt out all over."

Alex laughed and took a sip to hide her embarrassment.

"Her name was Maureen. Maureen wore tube tops with a whole bunch of cleavage. Boobs were pressing out everywhere. Damn if I didn't want Maureen." Ralph tipped his beer. "She promised me her boobs and more. All I had to do was prove my love to her."

Alex caught a glimpse of Mickey, laughing with friends up by the pool table. She glanced back at Ralph. "This was a tattoo question, right?"

"That it was. Had to prove my love." Ralph pointed at his right shoulder. "All I had to do was tattoo her name right here." He pointed at the twisted demon. "So I tattooed *Maureen* across my shoulder using a sewing needle and blue ink from a Bic pen, and Maureen gave me her boobs and her body, and I became a man."

Alex chuckled. "A man?"

"Hey." Ralph tipped the beer and took three huge gulps. "That tattoo hurt like hell."

They both laughed as Alex eyed his demon shoulder. She had never seen a tattoo up close, and reached her hand rubbing. The contrast was crimson nails against the blood red tattoo. "So where's Maureen now?"

Ralph shrugged. "Just a memory hidden under the demon."

"Hidden."

"When Maureen went away other girls weren't too excited about my home grown tattoo. I had to get rid of the *Maureen* or I might not ever feel the tender love of a woman again. My first professional tattoo was to cover *Maureen* forever."

"You covered her with a demon?"

Ralph lifted his bottle to toast. Alex tapped her long neck to his, and he rubbed the tattoo fondly. "Maureen was a demon in the sack, chubby boobs and all. Never had another like her. It was heaven and hell all at once."

Alex had never toasted with a long neck or shared such a story, nor had she found a tattooed biker man with rough skin from a hard life so endearing. She laughed at the irony, reaching over and rubbing Ralph's demon again, a hint of sorrow sweeping through her.

"Can't be sad here, Alex," Ralph grinned. "It's the law."

"The law?"

"Acoustic Tuesday. People come here to be happy, to free themselves. Nothing frees you more than the sound of an acoustic guitar. So let the music make you happy."

She looked back at Jimmy, the happy singer changing to a 12-string with more freedom to come. Fear ran through her and shuddered a chill across her shoulders.

"Thank you for the beer, Ralph." She gave him a warm smile. "You're a nice man of devilish fun." Tapping his shoulder. "Unfortunately, I must go."

Without waiting, she moved past him, squeezing herself through a group of construction workers. Mickey stood beyond the bar at the top of three stairs, and the thought of a *Mickey* tattoo flashed in her mind. Startled, she knew she had to leave now.

The sounds of the 12-string filled the room, full and powerful. Jimmy's voice was of the mountains, and the words *Colorado Canyon girl that set me free*. It was a *Pure Prairie League* classic in this place that seemed to draw her while she wanted to run. She remembered the song – *Boulder Skies*. Mickey saw her, moving closer with his hips swaying as Jimmy sang *Searching for some other place to be*. She reached her hand to say good-bye, and he took her fingers in his.

She nearly laughed as his hips swayed. "Nice moves, dancing man?"

"There's always a reason to dance," he answered.

"No," she turned sad again. "It's time for me to go."

Still not listening, Mickey walked past, his shoulder brushing against hers, and led her through the crowd to the middle of the dance floor. His hips moved before her not meaning to be seductive but incapable of being otherwise. Embarrassed to be standing still, she moved her own hips to blend in. The mixed feelings seemed to overwhelm her. She wanted to stay yet run in panic. This was too good, too much fun. Dancing. She was laughing again and forgetting, dancing to the acoustic music. She was back in Estes, the one place she felt she had truly been herself.

The rhythm returned quickly, her moves from the dances at the Lawrence YMCA after high school football games. She lifted her arms over her head, and Mickey moved with her. She ran her fingers through her hair as if the freedom had never escaped her. The stress and fear easing from her, she was liberated.

Jimmy played determined, each stroke of the 12-string beating freedom. *Take it so you'll feel it, take it so you'll know.* For an instant, she was feeling again. Dancing to music forgotten in a place she'd loved all her life. *Take one long last look before I go. More than anyone can try, I'll hope you'll see that I belong standing right before your eyes.*

The dancing went on, songs to sing as they moved. How long since she had laughed without thinking, without feeling the eyes of the room? Soon she'd forgotten to think about how good she felt, and she just felt. Before her, Mickey moved with smooth power. Alex leaned toward him, together in the sounds of the song. He reached for her, taking her hand, spinning her into his arms. Her hair flying, Alex swirled until she was staring up into his eyes.

The music stopped, and Alex's laughter burst unconstrained.

Mickey looked down, laughing back. "Welcome to Acoustic Tuesday." Then he lifted her to stand. "Alex," he said. "I have to apologize. I would love to spend the entire night dancing with you." His eyes were sincere disappointment. "I have an important day tomorrow. I have to take pictures early."

"Elk pictures?" Her fingers rested on his chest.

"Something different. Something special." He explained. "It's physically challenging, so, unfortunately, I have to call it a night."

She tried to hide the shock. Just when she had released herself, just when…and now he was going? She wanted to argue, to convince him to stay. This was important to her, to feel this, just for a moment. But now the game was ending, and she realized it had not been a game at all. His intentions had been honorable.

"I'm sorry," he repeated, "but I have to go, Alex."

The music began again, and she leaned in for him to hear her whisper. "Will you walk me to my car?"

Together they turned toward the doors as Mickey waved to Jimmy. Playing a Rocky Mountain ballad, Jimmy's head nodded his goodbye. Alex smiled shyly, then turned toward the waving tattooed arm extending from the middle of the crowd and returned a wave.

Stepping from the door, the music began to fade, and as it disappeared, sadness returned to Alex. The air was cool and stars shown from between the black of the mountains as they walked toward her car.

"Do you hike?" he asked.

"A long time ago." She thought of her father.

"Tomorrow, it's a challenge…where I'm taking pictures. Would you go with me?"

The Mercedes was in the now nearly empty lot behind Lonigan's. It was pure white like her life. Her husband had given her the car for her thirty-second birthday just months before.

Mickey persisted. "It's quite a hike, and I have to be there when the sun is right. So, I have to be at the trailhead by four, in six hours. But where I'm going, it's spectacular."

She wanted the freedom to say yes. To hike again would be liberating. Standing beside the car, she reached for her keys, the key chain her daughter had given her, the key chain with the Mercedes emblem.

"Alex. I'll show you some incredible things hidden in the mountains. Just up the hill from Bear Lake."

The key chain felt sharp in her hand. She turned and unlocked the door. Slipping into the seat, she looked back at Mickey.

"I'm sorry." She pressed the key into the ignition. "Thank you for a wonderful evening."

Mickey nodded and closed the door for her. As he stepped away with a final wave, he wondered what was wrong with Alex's life that she was here but still so afraid.

Chapter 5

William sat in the private room, cigar smoke hovering like hot fog on a humid evening. In the back of Hagarity's, the home restaurant of New York Senator Clayton, Chairperson of the Senate Committee on Banking, Housing and Urban Affairs, he relished the secrecy.

This was William's third meeting with Clayton, a man he had determined was the key to the merger of three banking empires owned by the last independent banking families in the United States. Each could trace their lineage to small town western banks. Hell, William's father liked to proclaim one of his family's original banks in Genevieve, MO was robbed in 1873 by Jesse James himself.

William was drinking scotch, a taste acquired from late nights strategizing to expanding the empire. It was the way he and his father were, driven to work and grow beyond their need of power and financial immortality. This was his father's legacy, but William knew with the merger and his father's pending retirement, his own legacy was being born.

Along with 30-year old scotch, Senator Clayton had an acquired taste he had bestowed upon William during their first visit to this restaurant known for its discretion. Tonight, the business had been conducted, a chef's special consumed, and private understandings confirmed.

William glanced around the room of white linen and elegant but outdated velvet drapes. On the center table, candles flickered on the candelabra as if seducing them into the night. Now was time for excess. With fine liquor leading the way, William produced his American Express Gold Card then laid an additional stack of large bills on the table.

"Very good, sir." The restaurant owner nodded, lifting the tray with the credit card as he slipped the bills into his pocket. "The limousines will be here momentarily."

William rolled his Arturo Fuente cigar along the corner of the ashtray, the cinders tumbling into the clear bowl. Lifting the cigar, he sucked hard to see the glowing red tip brighten. He felt powerful, controlling the destiny of so much money knowing that volumes would end up in his own family's hands. This was his legacy. This would elevate him to the same legendary status his father owned in the world of finance.

"So," he asked curiously, "does Mrs. Clayton ever question your whereabouts?"

The Senator winked from behind his cigar smoke. "I have a unique job that requires unique hours. She has grown to appreciate the demands of my service to our country."

"Understood." William returned a sly smile.

"Yours?"

"Mine has not yet recognized the value of business, still entrenched in life whittled out in small town Kansas." William's eyebrows bounced upward. "She still has visions of a perfect world where we do family picnics, and there's a picket fence surrounding our meager bungalow."

"An idealist," Senator Clayton laughed. "Can't see the fuckin' world for the stars in their eyes."

William shrugged. "I wish she'd just be a mother and keep spending her weekends looking good by my side. That's a role she should relish."

The restaurateur interrupted. "The limousines are here, gentlemen."

Extinguishing their Arturo Fuentes, the two men rose, buttoned their charcoal tailored suits, and stepped to the door. Senator Clayton patted William on the shoulder in a moment of secret camaraderie.

"I'll contact you when I have all the votes lined up."

Then they moved across the flowing pedestrian traffic of the mid-town Manhattan street.

Separate limousines, the Senator moved to the first black stretch, William the second. Hesitating at the door, William placed his hand on the cell phone in his breast suit pocket. He thought about calling Alexandria, to play the part of a caring husband, and let her know he was watching. His other hand on the door, a slight wave of guilt rolled through him, and he thought of the cathedral two blocks from his hotel. William put the phone back in his pocket and reminded himself that tomorrow, before dinner, he would go to confession, something he had done following each of the two previous visits to New York.

William opened the door, and glanced inside as if unwrapping a gift at a bachelor party. Draped on the shining black leather was a beautiful young girl with flowing auburn hair and full, claret lips. Nearly twenty with a cleavage that enticed, her legs were long with one crossed over the other showing black nylons and toeless stilettos.

She was not Alexandria, not even close to Alexandria, but there were also no expectations of caring, romance, or awkward cuddling afterwards. He had no time for such intimacy. Life was moving fast and like this girl, negotiations were completed upfront. That's what he liked, all the pretending to care, yet in the end she walked out the door and disappeared, another business transaction completed. Tomorrow, he would wake refreshed and ready for the intensity of a day's negotiations.

She slid her hand over the shear black of her thigh, and with one long ruby tipped finger the familiar seductress drew him into the limo.

Chapter 6

As she stepped into the Park River West Condo, she shuddered realizing how accustomed she had become to controlled luxury. Alex walked to the sliding glass door, slid it open, and stepped into the night air. The sky seemed closer here than in Denver, closer to the stars that sprinkled the blackness. She had three more days in the mountains, time to clear her head and once again find herself.

The bull elk had been magnificent, their rich colors and velvet antlers reflecting the sun above tree line. He had stood so close to them doing the magic he does with his camera. What freedom Mickey had, and he had integrity, letting a game end that had not been a game at all. Smiling to herself, she thought of the evening and being held in strong, protecting arms. It was what she yearned for from William.

William was somewhere in New York at some five-star restaurant being served an incredible meal that he would hardly notice, deep in a business conversation. Ten years before he had been her shining knight, but now she only felt anger. He had kept her emotionally locked up like some Guinevere with a distant view of a life she was not allowed to touch. Somewhere between marriage and the family's banking corporation, he had abandoned their love leaving only harsh manipulation. Damn, he had no right.

Alexandria felt the tears rolling down to her chin. Sometimes it just happened; in the car, over breakfast, or standing in a boutique tears would appear. Wiping her eyes, she looked out from the balcony. Stars glistened in the beautiful night sky.

Alexandria knew she needed a night of sleep; long, deep, recovering sleep, yet night's illumination only intensified her other thought. Alex would have gone to Bear Lake.

Chapter 7

It was still dark when Michael turned his Jeep into the parking area at Bear Lake. A few cars sat scattered in the lot, backpackers spending the night deep in the backcountry. Michael turned the wheel parking the Jeep up against the hillside. From the back, he lifted his pack, tripod, climbing rope and helmet. By dawn he would be at Sky Pond, and from there, over the top and down to the secret falls before the morning light crested the mountain.

A single light showed at the end of the parking lot near the trailhead. As he stepped on to the dirt path leading to Bear Lake, she sat quietly on a rock just a few feet before him.

Alex smiled and shrugged.

In the hours since, the idea of hiking once again into the depths of Rocky Mountain National Park had filled her thoughts. It was some of her best memories, hiking with her father miles along the trails to roaring waterfalls and vista views, passing wildflowers along the path. That beauty and the return, the hike down when your legs ache and thighs burn giving you a sense of accomplishment. She missed that freedom and the discovery that came with it.

Mickey nodded to her. Awake or dreaming, she had not left his thoughts. Her khaki shorts and hiking boots proved she was ready. The blond ponytail flowing from under the baseball cap gave her face a slender, capable look. Somehow through the night she had become more intriguing.

He stood before her, pleased, but not wanting to act so. "You ready to go?" He said matter-of-factly as if he'd expected her.

"You lead, I'll follow." She tried to sound confident.

"I'm glad you came." His smile warmed. "Surprised but glad."

"Me too." Her voice was nearly silent. "I need to hike."

She reached her hand forward, and he helped her to stand, leading her the first few steps up the trail toward Sky Pond.

The moonlight provided just enough brightness to follow the trail. Around the edge of Bear Lake, they began the walk toward Alberta Falls, The Loch and beyond to Sky Pond.

Years ago with her father, Alex thought of how she had followed him the first mile through the tall, dark trees. She had loved that birthday hiking Long's Peak. She suddenly realized that for months her father had been running, lost weight. Three miles a day, five days a week, he ran for four months. She now understood he had done it so he could achieve the physical demand of a seven mile, 4,800 feet climb to the 14,000 feet summit of Longs. Her father had run for months so he could share one-day with his daughter.

Mickey reached his hand backward, and she froze. Something was on the trail up ahead. Eyes flashed in the moonlight, three sets close to the ground, and then there was movement through the shadows and into the trees. Raccoons. Nocturnal.

Mickey smiled back at her. "It's a different world at night. How you doing? Boots okay?"

She watched the youth in his smile. "My feet love these boots. They've been solitary for ten years."

"So, does that mean *I'm fine?*"

She grinned, trudging past. "I'm fine," she said, taking the lead.

He followed her up the hill toward Alberta Falls, passing stopping points where flatlanders catch the breath that has deserted them.

At Lock Lake they stopped for a moment to watch the moon reflecting off the black water. She sat on a boulder, her knees pulled up to her chest. He rested his pack against another rock.

Suddenly, Mickey pointed toward the southern sky over the lake. Alex's stare followed his hand to see the slight tail end of the bright light flashing in the sky.

"Did you see it?"

"Soosh!" She whispered, "I'm making a wish."

Mickey smiled, looking to where the falling star had been.

"What'd you wish for?"

Alex flipped her hand toward him. "You know I can't tell, so let's just say I hope I'm not walking into a deep dark forest."

"No worries." Michael pointed back up the trail. "The morning light will begin to show itself soon."

"Okay." She stood, adding, "It's so quiet here without people."

He nodded. "Have you been here before?"

"I remember one time, years ago with my dad." She pointed at a large boulder set out into the lake. "Ate lunch on that boulder. I was a kid hiking in boots, shorts, and a bikini top. Got a terrible sunburn, but it was never like this, never dark and quiet." Then she asked, "Mickey, where are you taking me?"

"Have you been to Sky Pond?"

"Maybe, but I don't think so."

"It's another two miles from here, nearly five from the trailhead. We'll be there by 6:30. You'll like it, the light of morning. But we have to be over the other side before the sun peaks the ridge about 7:15. At 8:15 we will be where we need to be. It's a special place. No trails to it. People don't go beyond Sky Pond because the trail dead-ends. Where we're going, the sun will peak over the ridge about 8:30. There are few places that provide a photographer a chance to be an artist. That's where we're going."

"If it's so private, why me?" She asked.

He swung the pack back over his shoulder. "Like this place we're going, I believe you're someone that, if I can know you well…Well, some people make your life better. My instincts tell me you're that kind of person."

For an instant she stood staring at his back before she smiled, nodded, and followed on.

An hour later the light had begun to show itself. Mickey led her through an Aspen grove with a small stream running clear among the trees. Bunches of wild flowers, purple and yellow grew where the water did not run. A slight morning fog rose from the stream creating a mystical image of some fantasy in the making.

Up ahead the trees cleared to show a steep wall with water cascading from Sky Pond. Mickey did not hesitate. At the cascade, he simply began to climb the wall, hands and feet reaching and stepping, searching for the hand holds.

Leaning forward, she pressed her hands against the damp rocks, gripped, shifted and pulled. One step and then another, an awkward ladder of short, damp jagged rock steps. She kept climbing, gaining confidence that this scary looking wall offered little to fear. Nearing the top, she reached to feel his hand grasp hers. With little effort he pulled, lifting her over the edge and on to her feet beside him.

Sky Pond spread out before them, a perfect mountain lake amphitheatered by the steeples of black rock beyond the acres of water. The sky above the steeples began to hint of the deep morning blue. For a moment, she closed her eyes, inhaling.

"Alex," Mickey spoke. "This might be enough for most people, but we're going further. Time's important. We've got to push on."

That little waterfall climb had been a warm-up, both a teaser and a tester. The steeples were just sloped enough, just rugged enough to allow them to climb. Time and again, she hesitated wondering if she could make it. Their hike had shifted from the stair-stepping trail to a rock wall that was a ladder of rungs from one misshaped rock to another. Challenging to a point of fear, she was cautious yet determined, so she climbed on undeterred.

It was the most dangerous thing she had done, climbing to the top of the rock steeple. What would they think? Killed in a climb at sunrise with a young male companion.

Mickey looked down from above. "Do you trust me, Alex?" Something in his smile made her nervous.

She held tightly against the cliff, her hands gripping the sharp black rock. "Do I have a choice?"

"Not really, but I want you to trust me. I wouldn't take you anywhere you aren't capable of going?"

Alex continued to climb, her hands reaching up to grasp the rock next to Mickey's foot. She pulled as he watched.

"You know you're capable, don't you Alex?"

She stopped again, catching her breath as she hugged the wall, looking upward toward his voice. "I know I'm capable. And if you know I can do it, I believe I can do it."

"Good."

Alex groaned with the last push of her weary legs reaching the top only to see a shear cliff eighty feet down the other side.

Below her were the spires of a towering pine forest. Silhouetted, Mickey and Alex stood alone on top of the black steeples looking over the western expanse of Rocky Mountain National Park. Behind her was the magnificent amphitheater of Sky Pond, and to the west she could see the morning light beginning to reach Granby and Grand Lake. It was the same feeling she'd had summitting Long's Peak years before, that feeling of standing on top of the world as if it were hers to have.

"Where do we go from here?" She asked.

Mickey pointed down.

"How do we get there?" Alex looked to her left and right searching for the trail.

Mickey pointed down again. He took the nylon rope from his pack.

Fear shot through Alex, realizing his mad intentions.

"Have you ever rappelled?" He asked without looking.

"Absolutely not." Her eyes stared down the cliff at the tiny trees and rocks below, and instinctively she backed away.

Mickey laughed.

Without moving her eyes from the cliff, she said, "Mickey, I can't do this."

"Have you ever rappelled?"

"Hell no, I've never rappelled. I'm an uptight proper rich lady."

"Time to get over that shit," Mickey laughed.

"I can't do this." Alex's face was filled with the fear and the thought that she might.

"You said *If you know I can do it, I believe I can do it*. Alex, I wouldn't have brought you here if I had any doubt." His hand gripped the back of her arm. "If you'll do what I say, let the ropes and equipment do their job, it's easy. But Alex, I need you to decide now. I'm in a race with the sun."

It was Josephine's smile that filled her mind, a flash of the joy in her innocence. Laughter, always there was laughter with Josephine. Josephine was her reward, the salvation in her life, the one thing that gave her meaning. Motherhood makes you mortal, and you do not risk yourself at the expense of an innocent child.

"I can't." Her face was in panic. Mickey had no idea what he was asking her to risk. "This is so far beyond anything I've done."

"Then it's time to stretch yourself." He reached into the pack, and placed the harness on the rock before her. "One foot in here." He touched the skin of her right calf.

"Mickey, you don't understand. It's complicated." She avoided his eyes "I can't risk myself. People rely on me."

Mickey stood, his eyes intent. "This appears dangerous, but I know what I'm doing. Consider it my elevator. Your risk is no greater then driving back down the mountains to wherever you live."

"She's young. I can't risk something that might hurt her." Her eyes became moist. "I have a daughter."

Mickey's eyes softened, and he looked up to her with understanding. He knew she feared this, but the danger was only in her fear. Technology and his experience had taken the risk away. She was in shape, strength evident in her arms and legs, and she was smart. This was something she could easily do.

"When we get back, I want you to tell me about her, your daughter. I bet she's amazing like her mother." He glanced out over her shoulder toward the valley. "Someday you can tell her about rappelling down a mountain, the exhilaration and sense of accomplishment. Until then it will make you stronger. Eighty feet down, and you'll be as healthy as you are now. Stronger, more capable with greater confidence and still quite healthy." His hand lifted her leg into the harness.

Oh God, she was going to die alone with some young stud, high in the mountains. They would find her remains years from now, identification by dental records. How long would her family go without knowing? She had just disappeared, her car found mysteriously in a parking lot at Bear Lake in Rocky Mountain National Park. No other signs. She had simply vanished.

Kneeling, he looked up at her, his eyes understanding. "The world is full of people living safe, content lives," he said. "They have no idea how their life can grow, the exhilaration of taking the first step."

She was so afraid, and he was so confident. "Alex, I promise your life will change if you trust me. If you don't, your life will change too. It will go back to whatever it is you came here to escape. You will be the same forever, and you will always regret not doing this."

Alex bit into her lip, closed her eyes and turned her face to the sky. The sun was peaking in the horizon. She could go down either side of the peak, back or forward. He was right. It was a choice that would either change her or stop her. Her choice.

He was on one knee, attaching the line with the three locking carabiners to the anchor points secured the day before. He looped the anchor webbing through and attached the rappelling ring to the anchor carabiner checking it three times. Taking the empty pack, he filled it with the extra length and tossed the 60 meter doubled rope outward. It fell and fell until disappearing below the jagged black rocks. He yanked twice, stood up, gripped it, and leaned backward, bouncing with all of his strength. The rope was secure.

"Ready."

"How far is it?" She was pale.

"Doesn't matter." He lifted the harness. "One foot or a hundred feet, the rope and harness control everything. Just do what I tell you."

"You're sure." Tears had built in her eyes.

"You'll be fine."

She nodded with a terrified smile.

"Ready?"

"No. Yes, no. Okay."

"Okay." He was technical now, serious. "You'll go first so if we have any problems I can help." He pulled on the harness, tightened it, securing it firmly around her hips. As if reading her mind, he added, "but we won't have any problems."

He showed her the ATC device looped into the harness carabiner with the rope. "Here's how it works. You lean back over the ledge. You're right handed?"

She nodded.

"Okay, so you lean back with your right hand below the ATC and pressed against your hip. Your right hand and the ATC control your descent. All you do is squeeze and loosen your hand on the rope allowing a bit to slip through as your right hand presses to your hip. Whenever you want to stop and rest, just pull the rope. Your left hand helps guide, but the right hand has all of the control. Does that make sense?"

She nodded, and he picked up the helmet, adjusting the straps, and slipped it over her head, attaching it snuggly with the chinstrap.

"Now, take a few steps backward down the slope, just start walking. You can walk all the way down if you want to. When you get more comfortable, you can ease the grip with your right hand and you'll fall about three or four feet before you grip again and stop descending. This causes you to swing back into the wall."

He smiled at her, his own confidence strong. "Let the rope slide loosely through your hands until tightening it again and the ATC stops you from moving. Hold tightly to the rope until you've reached the wall." He handed her a pair of firm leather gloves. "Allow your legs to bend into the wall, just like jumping up and down. Land on the wall, bend your legs, and give it another little jump. The release of pressure will free the rope, and when you push off, you'll fall another few feet or so."

Alex pulled the sizeable gloves over her hands, using the Velcro to tighten them snuggly at the wrist. "I've seen this done. Is it as easy as it looks?" Mentally, she made the decision.

"It is." Mickey checked the ATC and rope on her harness. "What people can't do is lean back over the ledge, hang out over the cliff and push. But you can do this. You'll be in complete control. Just walk backwards down the wall, and whenever you want to stop, tighten your grip on the rope."

Her laugh was quiet and nervous. He did not laugh.

"If you believe me and believe in the equipment, if you walk or push back and pretend you're doing repeated standing broad jumps backward…" He looked at her. "You aren't afraid to broad jump are you?"

She shook her head.

"Then broad jump backward down this little embankment, and whenever you want to stop pull the rope. At the bottom, step out of the harness, tie the gloves and helmet on, and I'll pull them back up."

He checked the harness again, pulled on the rope. "Okay, now repeat what I just told you."

Alex answered with a specific description, detailing his instructions. Mickey nodded, clarified, and nodded again at what she had just learned.

"Okay," his hand held the rope between them. "You're going to lean straight back, and it's going to scare the shit out of you. No matter how frightening it is, know that when you're ready to stop, pull the rope behind you. Concentrate and you'll do fine."

Staring at his face, she gripped the rope feeling it catch behind her as she leaned backward over thin air. She shifted her feet. Tears were running over her cheeks. Her mind was pounding rhythmic encouragement repeating walk backward, grip the rope, feet into the wall, grip tightly. When she gained confidence, she told herself, she would jump…absorb, flex, and push again. Confidence. Determination. Push, fall, pull, absorb. The dampness on her cheeks turned cold.

She flexed her legs, repeated her mother's prayer, and began the backward journey. Edging parallel to the ground below, she was taking baby steps. Mickey nodded encouragement, dropped to his chest, and leaned over to watch her.

If he asked himself truthfully, he'd expected to leave her sitting at the top, waiting for him, a bit afraid and disappointed in her fears. But there she was, arms flexed, eyes intent, legs strong against the rock as she walked backward down the side of a shear cliff.

She was only about twenty feet down the cliff when she tested herself more. With a tentative jump, she fell maybe two feet, but it was a jump, freeing. She did it, a little stronger, a little further. Gripping, the rope tightened, and she swung hard back in toward the rock.

Flex and push, his mind repeated. Stay with it Alex, stay with it. She pushed harder, swinging back toward the black wall, unable to breathe, coming so fast. She could only react to save herself from crashing against the rocks. Her legs hit with a powerful force and only time to react. She sprang backward and fell again, the rock jetting back at her before she could think. Absorb, push, fall, pull, absorb. Mickey watched as she dropped, not smoothly, but controlled by the rope, ATC and her determination.

Each fall was less terrifying, and her breathing returned. On the fifth jump she felt almost in control. Every jump had become bigger, stronger pushes, falling further in rhythm.

She glanced downward to see the trees behind her, the ground approaching. She could feel the bottom closing in. A quick glimpse again, one more push. She jumped backward and swung down, reaching her feet under her to absorb the bottom and fell sideways onto the ground.

Mickey watched in relief. She had not panicked. She had trusted and believed in herself. From eighty feet above, he watched her stand, arms almost frenzied pulling at the harness. Forcing it down her legs, she jumped one leg at a time, freeing herself.

Alex shot her arms in the air. The adrenaline rushed uncontrolled through her body. Her knees marched high and fast as she danced, letting out a scream of power. She had never been so strong. She looked up, waving frantically. Mickey waved back from above. Her fist clinched as she screamed to him. Echoes of *I did it, I did it* reverberated though out the canyon.

When Mickey reached the bottom, she threw her arms around him in triumph.

"My God, Mickey. What a rush!" Her face was flush with red blotches covering her cheeks. "I thought I was going to die. When I first jumped, I was sure I was going to die."

She was laughing now, hanging from him with a surge of accomplishment pounding into her muscles.

"Never, never, never have I felt like this." She set her feet back on the ground. They were face to face as she tried to control her exhilaration. She laughed in surprise. "I didn't lose it, Mickey. I thought I was going to wet my pants, but I didn't. When I first jumped, I was terrified. But I didn't panic. I held my own, didn't I? I was in control." He too was laughing now. "God, what a rush."

Calmly, he reached up touching her arms, her hands still holding firmly to the back of his neck.

"You were amazing," he said. Her eyes were clearer, bluer, and brighter than before.

She laughed. "Yes I was, wasn't I?" Stepping back, her hands moved firmly to her narrow hips.

"You were," he laughed. "And I'd love to celebrate more, but the sun." He pointed toward the sky above the cliff. "We have to move quickly."

He freed the rope, stuffing it, the harness, gloves, and helmet back into the worn daypack, and swung it over his shoulders. She had grabbed the tripod bag, heading down into the crevice. Jumping sideways, Mickey bounced forward until he caught her and took the lead back.

It wasn't long, maybe ten minutes when he stopped her. "When we get there, I need you to give me room," he explained.

The adrenaline still flowed, and her nod was animated.

"Give me time to get set up and take the photographs. I only have twenty minutes of sunlight." He was instructing again. "Once I'm done, I'll let you know. Then we can explore. You can have the whole day if you want it, but I need the first twenty minutes."

It was the vision that calmed her. As he motioned for her to wait, she could see what he had come to photograph. There were no signs of man, no trails, no paths, no structures, only the lake, clear to the bottom with sand and white pebbles. And wildflowers; one hillside was covered with wildflowers. A rainbow of colors, intermixed bunches of orange, purples, reds, and yellows. The waterfall was not roaring, but spread evenly over the wide ledge of white rock. The far side was a thick growth of pines, spruce and fir, and below her was a sand beach.

He was at the far end of the lake now, the tripod set. From his pack, he lifted a camera. A high end SLR she assumed. Everything was digital, and Mickey would know the capabilities. She sensed that in him. He was curious and detailed, and would have the same capabilities in his camera. He worked to place it on the tripod, his movements deliberate, racing to beat the sun.

From where she stood, away from his vision, a smattering of clouds drifted lazily against the morning sky. Mickey watched behind him, searching the mountain peaks for the sun to break over the steeples. Again, he looked through the camera, slightly adjusting the tripod. He glanced back over his shoulder, and Alex saw the sharp hint of light crest between two mountain peaks.

She now understood what he was waiting for. With the direct sunlight, the magic of the falls turned to crystals of light, and sunrays shimmered in the dew on the wildflowers. Suddenly, the lake reflected the white Aspens and pink edges of the soft drifting clouds, multiplying the beauty of the summit peaks.

As she watched him work, Alex knew something had changed. He had somehow guided her, and silently she thanked him. As the reflection came alive with white light and deep, rich colors, she felt pure, and the sensation overwhelming her. Never had she experienced a sense of calm and exhilaration all in one overwhelming moment. This was her place, her moment, their discovery, and she was a part of it.

He moved quickly, his hands and eyes, his mind working for the angles and images. His movements were intricate, his glances from behind the camera purposeful. He worked with speed and precision, creating multiple images in the most spectacular light. Light seemed to turn the wall by the falls a golden radiance as if a prospector's greatest discovery.

As the sun moved behind the edge of the second peak, the falls and lake turned to merely magnificent. A sense of quiet purpose overwhelmed her, and she was freed from inhibitions. Looking the length of the lake, Mickey motioned for her to join him, but her thoughts were captured in her own personal meaning of the waterfall.

Mickey watched her graceful movements as she traversed down the hill to the sand beach. At the edge, separated by bushes and red flowers, she was only slightly visible as she stopped and pulled her hat away, shaking her blond hair freely over her shoulders. From the opposite end of the lake, he could only imagine what he was seeing. Then her back became bare, and he could see the soft lines of her shoulders. He watched unsure until she emerged from the foliage onto the sand.

The image jolted him, and instinctively he stepped behind the camera. She did not look his way, instead walking exposed across the fine granules of white sand. With a sculptured silhouette, she moved unaffected to the lake's edge. Stooping slightly, the length of her golden hair protected her breasts, and the sinewy musculature of her slender legs. Unconsciously, his finger pressed the shutter button and the camera reacted.

For an instant she had forgotten him. Her world had never allowed her this freedom, never allowed her to walk naked where beauty simply existed. As she touched the mirrored reflection, pure water drew her into the lake. Moving forward, the incredible cold needled cleansing harshness with each step deeper over the sand bottom. The water ripples cresting outward until she stood waist deep in the purifying cold. Easily she lifted her hands, water falling over her shoulders with a frigid chill, and she shivered as a slight giggle escaped her.

Mickey continued to snap images, the zoom lens allowing him nearer to her. She was a vision across the lake, and the lens expanded his imagination allowing him to see her reaction to the chill and her precise smile. Again, the shutter reacted.

Alex moved farther, slipping deeper into the mountain lake. The water slid above her ribs as the chill covered her. The cold was overwhelming, and she broke with laughter, tipping her face to the sun, her hair lying over the water's surface. She rose on her tiptoes, then joyfully, she stepped, reached, and dove, disappearing below the surface.

Moments later, reappearing at the edge of the waterfall, she lifted herself to stand in the mist. Mickey reached into the backpack and quickly switched lenses bringing the falls full frame into the viewfinder, and the camera purred into action.

Her strides were seductive as she walked uninhibited toward the falling water. Through the lens her image became reality. Then, as she stepped into the falls her head fell back as long blond hair flowed with the water, and the light broke from behind the second mountain. Sun rained over the waterfalls, and her image became a translucent silhouette against the white rock. Astonished, Mickey pressed the shutter as it reacted over and over again.

Chapter 8

Moving down the winding road from Bear Lake, exhaustion and limpness was all she felt. Her mind could not think. The morning had been a total challenge of exhilaration. She had rediscovered adventure, and it had awakened the person she missed - herself.

Secretly, she laughed wishing someone had filmed the day. She wanted to have a guest showing for all of the ladies at The Club. Sitting in the movie theater, she would watch their envy and thoughts of being naked and swimming in his lake. Cleansing themselves from high society's expectations, they would shiver in the imagined chill of the waterfall. She ran her fingers though her hair and remembered the cold, the tightness expanding her chest, and the constant rain of falling water.

It was mid-afternoon when she arrived back at Park River West. Waving at a gray-haired gentleman who was loading luggage in his Suburban, she took the eight steps upward gingerly feeling the burn deep in her thighs. Stepping inside, she pulled the denim shirt from her shorts, tossing it on the arm of a chair. The white tank top followed. She walked into the bedroom and fell lifeless on the down comforter. For a moment she lay still, smiling. Then she lifted her feet above her, loosened one boot at a time, and flipped them back over the bed where they bounced across the floor.

The hike back had taken longer, walking miles on the treeless plateau around Hallett Peak and back down Flattop Mountain to reach Bear Lake. Time consuming to go this way, Mickey had explained, but much easier than scaling the eighty-foot rock face. As they descended, passing hikers struggled with the altitude and the barren terrain. She and Mickey must have appeared the vision of health, envied in their enthusiastic descent.

Wrapped in a towel, she discovered the condo refrigerator was fully stocked. Sweet treats and wine, champagne, soda, and beer. Smiling, she silently thanked the owner, pulled out a Coors Light, popped the top, and took a deep gulp. Again, she smiled at the forgotten taste of beer.

Opening the deck door, Alex stepped out and stretched. Sitting, she relaxed with her feet propped on the footrest and allowed the towel to fall loose, drinking beer in the late summer's warmth.

When she woke, the sun had dipped below the western range. Wrapping herself, she walked back into the condo. 6:03 p.m. Shocked at the time, she hesitated before realizing there was still plenty of time. She had told Mickey he could pick her up at Lonigan's at 7:00 p.m.

Rushing into the shower, she rinsed her body and hair free of the well-earned grunge. She did her makeup first, light, and fresh, then removed the chipped red from her nails, leaving them natural. At 6:45 p.m. she was dressed in blue jeans and a red silk tank top. When was the last time she had gone braless? She jumped up landing on her toes and her breasts bounced firmly up and down. She liked it.

Now, if she walked fast, she would be in front of Lonigan's in fifteen minutes.

Mickey had not rested since he got home. From the vague details of his mother's magic, he had made Caesar salad using her special dressing recipe, steamed vegetables, and sautéed mushroom on chicken kabobs. He had showered then shaved against the grain for a softer face. His hair dried in the wind as he raced the Jeep down Elkhorn Drive toward Lonigan's.

She stood watching taffy turn on the candy maker in a store window. Seeing her, he tapped the horn. When she stepped into the Jeep smiling, he felt a sense of relief.

She reached up, rubbing his cheek affectionately. "Do you always have this affect on women?"

"What affect is that?" he grinned.

"Women who hardly know you? Do they often take off their clothes and go polar bear swimming while you're behind the camera."

"Actually," he laughed, driving the Jeep out of Estes past the Elk Horn Lodge. "That was the first time. What's my secret?"

She shook her hair in the breeze. "Not sure? Maybe it was the adrenaline rush. After all, I did jump backward off a cliff."

The Jeep turned down an asphalt side road, and they fell silent. She hesitated to ask, but she had to know. "So, the pictures? This is awkward, Mickey, but the pictures..."

For the first time, he saw vulnerability. Her eyes turned away. No, he realized, it was fear.

She spoke without looking. "You have no idea the damage they could do."

He chose his words carefully, "What I'd like to do with your polar bear images is keep them as something private and special between us."

She let the twang pass through her, the harsh, hated guilt of questioning his intentions. "I'd like them to be private and special." Her voice was barely audible. "That is something important to me. No one can ever know I did that."

"Do you trust me?"

"Jeez, Mickey." The laughter burst from her. "I let you pick me up and lead me into the wilderness where I jumped off a cliff."

"Okay, you trust me. It's our secret." He said reassuring her. "This is my promise to you. I will never reveal our secret. The images may be incredible, but I promise. I will never reveal your name or any recognizable image. Your identity is our secret and any of the identifiable images will remain something private and special between us." Then, to make sure she understood, he added, "You can trust that, absolutely."

Her voice was quiet. "You don't know how much trust you're asking me to give."

Mickey nodded. When he looked at her, his words were simple. "Trust is my promise. I'll never display any recognizable images. Your identity will never be revealed."

"Thank you." Her voice was only a trace as she looked away.

When the Jeep slowed, he said, "I don't know what's going on, Alex. For whatever's bad in your life, I'm sorry. But I promise, you don't have to fear me."

He turned into the driveway of a log cabin with a big front porch, large windows, and a sun deck on the second level overlooking Fall River.

"So," Mickey reached forward and turned off the ignition. "I picked you up?"

She still looked away. "What?" Damn tears, they made her feel so weak.

"A moment ago," his words seemed lame, "you said I picked you up."

Taking a deep breath, she realized she had experienced more in this escape then she had ever imagined. As she stepped from the Jeep, Alex fought between the conflicting guilt and the great relief of being somewhere else with someone else and feeling like the person she'd been ten years before.

"It was, the whole day and last night, out-of-character." She forced herself to say. "So, this is your cabin?"

Shrugging, he opened the screen door. "A friend of my father's. The guy never uses it. I moved in for the summer and kind of took over. My temporary home."

"And after the summer?"

"I'm still working on that."

The cabin opened into a grand room with a large rock wall fireplace on one end. At the opposite end was a roomy kitchen with a giant cutting block in the middle and a bar with three stools separating the living room. The couches were big and fluffy near white, sitting on a thick oval rag rug. Double French doors opened to a patio that sat a stone's throw from Fall River.

Mickey walked into the kitchen. In the refrigerator was his effort at dinner, the salad, veggies, and kabobs. He had bought a bottle of inexpensive wine, all he could afford. He glanced back through the living room to see her sitting on the couch.

"I've got wine."

She rested comfortably, her chin on the back of the couch. "That Alexandria lady is more of a wine person. I prefer beer."

Good choice, he thought, taking two domestics from the second shelf. Walking to her, he wondered how she had transformed into casually elegant. Squatting down eye to eye, he watched her hands take the beer. Despite the rugged day, they were gentle hands, and he sensed their softness.

"So why are you here, Alex?"

She looked back in his eyes. "Have you ever lived for the moment?"

"Up until now, that's all I've lived for."

"I don't live that way, Mickey." Her grip tightened on the beer. "Do you trust me?"

"Can we get past that?" he laughed.

"For today and tomorrow, let's just trust," she said. "I have two days and two nights."

"And after two nights?" he asked.

"Then this becomes a special and private memory between us."

The quiet rested in the air as neither looked at the other.

Mickey looked back toward the kitchen. So those were the limits. This woman he desired. Two nights. He had wished for more knowing such a wish was unlikely. Someone this secretive had many, many complications, and she was simplifying everything within a timeframe.

"What's for dinner?" She tried to move on.

"Mom's special?" he answered flatly.

"Mom's?"

"Yep." Mickey walked around the couch to the old phonograph. "Mom makes it all the time."

It had been so long since Alex had thought in such terms.

"What do you like?" He asked, pulling a stack of classic albums from the shelf. "This guy has a music treasure."

"Your choice."

"How about C,S,N,&Y?"

"Who?" She asked before she could think.

"Crosby, Stills, Nash, & Young."

Her mind relaxed. "Great," she answered, "any acoustic music would be perfect."

"So you liked Acoustic Tuesday?" He pulled the album from the jacket.

"I'd forgotten," was all she said.

As she stood, her thighs whimpered in pain. She stretched, forcing her body to ease the stiffness. With a slight scratchy sound, *Suite: Judy Blue Eyes* filled the room.

Watching him walk into the kitchen, she smiled, remembering the thought of *Mickey* tattooed across her shoulder. A bit of guilt rushed through her, and she decided to ignore it.

"Kabobs," he said as he pushed the handle on the patio door. It edged open, and he slipped his foot against it swinging it wide. She walked across the living room and followed him out onto the rock-patterned patio where the sounds of Fall River soothed the evening. At the grill, he set the meat aside, pushing the button to light the flame.

"So, what do you do?"

"Do?" he asked.

She walked across the patio, watching the ripples of water in the flowing river. "Is photography how you make your living?"

"I just graduated in May."

The beer she was drinking stopped solid in her throat. She quickly did her math. Twenty-two, maybe twenty-three, ten years younger than she was.

"So you graduated from college?" praying that was the answer.

He was watching the kabobs, moving with the breeze to avoid the smoke. "Bachelor's degree is in photography. The University of Chicago."

The hard, nervous pounding of her heart eased.

"Most of my friends, those in photography dreamed of a job with CNN or National Geographic. They want to be directed where to go and what to take pictures of, to be foreign correspondent dodging bullets and capturing history. The violence they want to capture, it's not what I want to see every day of my life, so a friend of the family allowed me to live here short- term. I committed the summer to shoot nature and wildlife, then I go back home September one, and start my own portrait studio. It's a way to make a living and avoid the starving artist route, while, on the side, I pursue this dream of becoming of photographic artist."

She watched his graceful movements as he talked and barbecued. "So, are you getting the pictures you want?"

"Looks like the portrait studio is my future. I did have a job offer from the AP, but this is my dream." He continued turning the kabobs. "I've got several shots I'm excited about, but not enough to make a living."

"I'd like to see your work." She grinned at the way he dodged the grill's smoke floating past.

"Nobody has seen my work." He looked up, apologizing. "I'm very conscious of my images and what is ready to share."

"But you showed me the elk?"

"An exception," he turned toward her. "I'm sorry. I've only got a few images worth showing. I need more to prepare my portfolio and market it, but for this summer anyway, time is running out."

She walked over to stand next to him, looking at the kabobs. "What do you mean? The elk pictures were fantastic."

He lifted the meat and mushrooms onto a platter, shrugging matter-of-factly. "That's the point, Alex. I'm seeking more than pictures. I want to be an artist, and there's an incredible difference between art and pictures of elk." He put the last kabob onto the platter. "So, you ready to test my cooking. I can guarantee it's not a work of art."

Without thought, she rubbed her hand gently over his strong shoulder. "Looks fantastic."

Dinner was fantastic, and then they did the dishes together, their hips swaying back and forth to the classic sounds of *Four Way Street*. As she put the last plate in the cupboard, he went into the living room, adding three albums to the stack on the antique console. He was sitting on the pillowed couch when Alex joined him a body length away. His arm reached outward to rest on the back of the couch, reducing the distance between them. Alex shifted slightly a bit further away. It was done without thinking, a reaction before emotions could tell her otherwise.

She whispered, "Thank you, Mickey," and her hand reached up rubbing the back of his before she moved it once again a few inches away.

He heard the sadness in her voice, something in her eyes. "How can I help?" he asked.

"Let's not get too serious." She avoided going deeper. "Will you show me your photography?"

For a time, the room held their silence. The night had taken over, and the only light came from the candles on the kitchen counter. He knew his photographs were good, but he wanted more. They were his gift, but he wanted his gift to be perfect. His confidence waivered, and stillness surrounded them. So far he had only trusted himself with his photography.

"I've got this room."

She held still.

"One room that I've transformed." He could feel tension in his chest. "I call it *The White Room*."

It was quiet again, the words *The White Room* hanging silently in the air. Avoiding her eyes, he could see the light of the candle flicker against the rocks of the fireplace.

"I've not shared it with anybody, *The White Room*," he said. "Twelve photographs I call art. My life's work, you might say. Twelve images that I've deemed worthy."

She did not speak.

"Wow." His breath left him. "I can't believe I'm saying this." He sucked the air back in filling his lungs. "Would you like to see *The White Room*?"

When Alex lifted her eyes, she was surprised to see his confidence masked by slight fear. Not the fear of the college boy that she had expected, but the confidence of an artist anxious with anticipation at his first opening – hoping his art would be received well by the critics.

"Thank you, Mickey." She reached her hand to rub gently over his. "I'd like that very much."

He took her hand and led her through the living room. Without a word, she followed up the stairs, her arm brushing against the pine walls. The hallway was narrow, and he stopped at a closed door. Placing his hand on the brass knob, he hesitated, taking a deep breath.

"This is *The White Room*. Something private and special between you and me."

They both smiled, and he turned the knob. The room was dark as he led her in, his hand gentle over the small of her back. Easily, he closed the door behind them, leading her to the center of the room where he whispered, "In a moment I'll turn on the lights. Look at the floor until your eyes have adjusted. When you are comfortable with the light, look up."

She felt him move away and for a moment stood quietly. Slowly, she opened her eyes. The floor was fine oak with a fresh coat of finish. She stared down, listening yet hearing nothing. She waited until she was sure her eyes were ready.

In perfect track lighting, on the wall before her was the large image of a hillside blanketed in orange poppies, each blossom in detailed perfection. Stems of purple flowers highlighted the orange under a hint of bright blue sky. She wondered if he had heard her slight gasp as her hand came to her chest. Framed in a white matting and molding against a stark white wall, the colors stood remarkably vivid and clear.

Without realizing it, she whispered, "Oh, Mickey."

He waited patiently until she eased from the first picture to the next. This image too was encased in white. In this image, the sunshine reflected off the ancient wood of a rustic barn, the Tetons towering in the background with the golden peaks at morning's first light. In the third, the grays and blacks of three wild mustangs sprinted freely across of mountaintop of green and purple wildflowers. Full frame, in the next the elk were surrounded by the summer shades of spruce as the calf, still wobbly legged, nursed from her mother. The images floated through her mind as she experienced the feeling of nature's gracefulness and the scent in the flowers on the hillside.

Each image presented a different emotion. She giggled aloud at the rump of the raccoon, dangling unmoving from the hole in the oak, then gasped with the awesome understanding of the bald eagle's powerful flight across the crest of snow-topped mountains. There was the fresh snowfall upon the Aspen limbs in a vision of the slender forest disappearing into the morning sky. Another showed the strength and power of the majestic moose striding through the shallows of a calm lake about to disturb a flock of pelicans watching him wearily. In each, light was the common factor, bursting details accentuated in the sun's rays.

She took his hand, holding firmly as she studied the details of the black bear sow, sitting like a sofa chair for her two cubs as they suckled their evening nourishment. These were not pictures, for pictures do not enrapture the need to know each detail. A feeling, an emotion, each image possessed its own striking personality. She had been unprepared for what he was sharing. She had not imagined the intensity of his talent or the gentleness of his touch.

In the quiet she barely heard the door close behind her or sense that he had left her alone in *The White Room*. Near where she stood in the middle of the room sat a carved rocking chair, a comforter draped over the back. She sat easily feeling the softness of the comforter in the slight movement of the rocker.

Again, she appreciated the unique beauty of each image. How had he captured such contrast, such depth in the sunlight against the details? For the longest time she experienced the tranquility of the poppies in full bloom. She noticed the hints of dew brightening the petals and the stillness of the flowers, absent the breeze.

With the viewing, she felt emotions she had not felt in years. Never again would she see wildflowers in the same simple way. And she knew that the waterfall, the sunlight from their morning together would be his next amazing image. Once again, he had worked his magic, and she desired him for his unselfishness. He was sharing his world with her.

Time had not existed as she sat in the white of the room. It had not passed when she thought of how important it was for her daughter to know nature. Josephine had never hiked to Dream Lake or Sky Pond. She had never seen the elk grazing at the top of Fall River Road. Her daughter had never awakened to the sun striking the face of Long's Peak, welcoming another mountain morning. Josephine had not seen the images as Mickey had captured them.

For a time, she rocked gently closing her eyes to remember the images. Envisioning her life in hiking boots and jeans, she felt herself captured in the cool of the waterfall caressing her body, and her mind allowed him to hold her in a way she had never been held before. She felt the moisture in her eyes.

The day's emotions swept through her, her eyes once again scanning the twelve images. She walked slowly to the door. A dim light shown from the end of the hallway, yet she could not find him. Moving away in the opposite direction of the steps, his scent filled the room as she brushed past his bed to the balcony sun porch. She found him laying in a deep sleep on the wicker lounger, comforted by the greens of the down cushion. She listened to the night sounds, the breeze through the trees, and the softness of his steady breathing.

In the bedroom, Alex took a quilt from the chair and laid it gently over him. The dim light of the moon reflected, and his cheeks still showed the strength of his youth. He was a beautiful boy destined to be an amazing man. Easily, she pulled the quilt to cover his shoulders and protect him from the cold night.

In his room, she saw the clock and stopped, knowing this was where he slept. Drawn, she leaned over, pressing her hands against the sheets, and caressed them to smoothness. Slowly, she rested her head on the pillow and his scent surrounded her. Pulling it closely over her face, she breathed deeply.

Happy and tired from the emotions that swirled in her cautious mind, she stood. Removing her blouse, she hung it over the post at the end of his bed. Her jeans went over the other post. Still inhibited, she tucked her panties into the jeans pocket. The night air hardened her nipples, and she smiled at the thought of his touch as she moved to lie in his bed.

Chapter 9

When she awoke the sun was already warming the room. She rubbed her hand over her breast and down to the softness of her stomach. Her eyes closed as she realized she was still there. Breathing deeply, excitement filled her mind with tantalizing thoughts that Alex couldn't believe she was having. The night before had ended innocently, as it should have yet she awoke to find herself rejuvenated by thoughts of what couldn't be.

The sudden flash of William's face froze her thoughts. He was an image of authority in his charcoal suit, white cotton shirt, and silk tie. She shuddered, angered at his invasion. Startled, she reached for her pants, pulling her cell phone from the pocket. It had been years since William had checked in while on his trips. He always called the office, but rarely did he call home. Still, she was relieved to see that there were no missed calls.

The phone showed 9:30. When had she last slept in such comfort or so late into the morning? The sunlight now revealed a surprisingly clean bedroom. Mickey was everywhere. Hiking boots outside the closet, a tee shirt and worn jeans lay across a brown overstuffed chair in the corner. A hiking stick leaned against the wall, *Michael* and a date were carved into the dried Aspen branch. She breathed deeply and still the air hinted of his scent.

In the mirror over the dresser, she had taken on a different appearance. Without the accents of deep blush and lipstick, she appeared softer. Her skin seemed youthful, her eyes a whiter blue reminding her of years before in college. Slightly tousled, her hair appeared more golden then blond. When had she become young again?

Then she looked deep into her eyes and questioned where she was and what she had done. Why was there not the feeling of guilt, and why was she relieved to still be here? It surely was something she hadn't expected, and told her something she needed to know about her self, her life, and her relationship with William.

Alex turned from the mirror, walked to the chair, and picked-up his white tee shirt. Extra large, it covered her completely.

He was sitting on the patio listening to the river, his right hand holding a ceramic mug, steam floating above it. She looked back into the kitchen where a kettle rested on the stove. It pleased her that he was drinking hot tea. Filling a cup, she dipped a tea bag watching for the exact color.

Embarrassed in only his shirt, Alex pulled the Afghan from the couch and wrapped it around her.

"Good morning," he turned as she walked onto the patio.

"I didn't plan on spending the night," she apologized, lifting the Afghan and sitting in the chair beside him. "But I was so tired and your bed was so tempting."

"No, I'm sorry for falling asleep. Yesterday had it's challenges. I guess it took more out of me than I realized." He took a drink of steaming tea. "I was glad to see you this morning," he caught himself, "to see that you were here."

She blushed, looking into her tea mug. She knew he must have covered her. How long had he watched her? Had he stood over her as she slept naked in his bed?

She was acting contrary to her expectations, or maybe this was a part of her rediscovery, the person she felt most comfortable being had she not met William and become someone else. She felt a slight shudder, and in her own thoughts, she looked away listening to the mountain sounds.

"Mickey?" Breaking the silence, she sounded composed again. "Tell me where you're going with this."

"With us?" he asked.

A wave of sadness swept over her. He didn't truly understand.

"No," she responded with bluntness. "I mean with your photography. I can't tell you how impressed I was with *The White Room*. Your images are incredible. They took me places, touched my emotions. Where do you want to go with it?" she asked. "The dream you talked about last night, making a living with your art."

His eyes scanned up the river toward Rocky Mountain National Park. "I want twenty-five images that I believe are worthy. I have twelve. With twenty-five I want to open a gallery of limited edition prints. Each print will be unique, capturing the appreciation of nature in its own light. I want to make my art special so those who share it have an intimacy with the image. My work will combine a teaching of respect for the wild with the serenity of the image and the personality of the creator. When people view it, my photography will have a subtle uniqueness that will cause them to step back and say *Cabelli.*"

It caught her unaware. "Cabelli?"

And they burst out laughing.

"Michael Cabelli, huh."

"Mickey to you," he reached, playfully pointing toward her.

"So what's this portrait studio silliness?" she asked.

Mickey rolled his eyes. "Stable and profitable, it's not the dream. My plan is to return home in September to begin a life taking pictures of pimply high school seniors, slobbering babies, and pure white brides while supplementing my income doing freelance and advertising photography. Friends think I'd be wasting my talents, but I see it as a way to fund the dream." Mickey's smile lifted. "I can make a good living while having control of my time, turning profits and flexibility to trips into the wilderness. Eventually, *The White Room* will expand into a gallery." His grin broadened. "Picture it. *Nature's Way by Cabelli.* The dream will slowly come to life."

She smiled into her teacup. "Sounds like a slow moving plan."

Laughing, he grinned, "Dreams do not come easy."

For a moment they both smiled, watching the water flow from the mountains down through the valley of Fall River.

"So," she watched Mickey, " you'll go back when the summer ends?"

"Yep. The end is clear, but the journey is just beginning."

She tipped her head toward him to see his eyes. "What do others say about *The White Room?*"

"Alex and Mickey have seen *The White Room.*"

Ever so slightly, her breath escaped her, special and private between them.

"Mickey, you have to share this with others."

Mickey laughed, standing. "In time."

"No. Now." She insisted. "Your images are spectacular. Don't ever question your talent. You're an amazing artist, and your art should not be hidden."

"Thank you." He answered, a smile of confidence growing as he watched Alex's eyes.

As he walked from the patio into the kitchen, her mind worked fast. He was proud, talented, but he could not be a part of her life. She would leave tomorrow, but she would never be the same. William would see a difference; even Josephine would sense it. He had changed her, but she had to separate herself from him. While that saddened her, she knew with money comes the power to do things. That, she had learned from William.

As he handed her the fresh steaming cup, the Afghan fell from her shoulder, and he reached, lifting it back into place.

Alex smiled. "Have you ever thought of applying for grants?"

He shook his head thoughtfully. "No, I mean I've thought of it, but how much money is out there for photographers, particular a guy with twelve images."

"You might be surprised." The tea cooled to sipable. "Before I leave, I want to give you the contact information of a foundation. This foundation works with new artists providing grants to help get started, complete work, or whatever their needs might be. I'm sure you would meet their qualifications."

Mickey was sitting, listening now. "What kind of money are we talking about?"

Alex shrugged. "I suppose it depends on the projects." She thought quickly. "Why? What do you think you need?"

"I've looked into it," he said. "If I could have the winter to travel. Nothing major, but to have time in Yellowstone, Glacier National Park, maybe up to Banff and back here in Estes to take fall and winter pictures. The twelve I have were all taken during the past four years, except the raccoon, and almost always in the summer." He smiled, adding, "I took the raccoon when I was fifteen. Anyway, they were all taken on short one or two week trips. If I could have six months to focus on photography, to be at the right place at the right time emphasizing North American wildlife; add that to what I've done this summer, and I'd have the images to open a gallery. Estes Park is a tourists' mecca. People spend their summers here looking for exactly what my photographs give. Word of my work could spread pretty quickly."

He looked down the river again, his smile confident.

"It's a dream," he tapped the side of his mug, "and when I talk about it, I get excited."

"You should," she watched the lines lifting from the smile in the face. "So, what's the price tag?"

"Oh, I don't know. I'm pretty basic." He smiled. "Me camping, staying in cheap motels? The biggest cost would be additional digital equipment and gas for the Jeep. I could probably do it on the same salary I'd make shooting screaming babies."

"And to open the gallery?" she asked.

"There's a place downtown, just west of Lonigan's. It's an old log building, historical to the downtown area. They want to close the business, but won't sell the building. I think we could work out a lease."

"Okay. From what I know, this might be a grant possibility. So after six months of photography, for gallery start up you'd need first year production and operation costs? Does that sound right?"

"Sure. There'd be remodeling, lighting, the images, business costs, everything you need to get operational plus some promotional materials, advertising to get your name out there."

Her mind was racing, and she took a sip to calm herself. Matter-of-factly, she told him, "If you write a grant, ask for it all, everything you need. Be detailed, but don't be afraid to ask."

"Really?" His eyes were incredulous. "You're talking craziness for a guy with twelve images."

"Twelve amazing images," she corrected him. "You've got to think big, Mickey. You've got to believe in your talent. I'll get you the contact information for the foundation." She had pushed this too far, and it was time to move on. "So what are your plans for today, and am I included?"

He had a gentle laugh. "Fact is you're my plans."

She felt herself embarrassed, feeling schoolgirl silly.

"We're meet Jimmy for lunch. By the way," he asked, "how are your legs holding up."

"Wobbly at best." She kicked out from under the Afghan, dancing her legs before him. "But I can handle whatever you've got in mind." Blushing at the unintended double mantra, Alex pulled the Afghan together at mid thigh, glancing in through the glass doors. The mantle clock showed 10:45.

"Can I borrow your Jeep? I need to get a change of clothes."

"Keys are on the counter," he motioned. "We need to leave here at 12:15 to meet Jimmy by one."

As she stood, the Afghan fully wrapped around her, she bent to kiss him on the cheek. So natural, it was not until her lips met his skin that she realized what she was doing.

Smiling, he told her, "Drive careful, and I'll see you in a bit."

Alex felt the guilt hang there for a moment. "I'll be back in a few." As she stepped into the cabin, she allowed it to drift away.

He was waiting on the porch swing swaying back and forth. When she stopped the Jeep, he sat still forcing her to walk to him.

"You ready?"

"Of course I'm ready," he watched her. "I just wanted to watch you walk."

Blushing like a teenager, she waved him away, "I've been practicing for years, just for you."

"Years?" he asked. "So, how many years?"

"Only a woman knows."

"That's scary."

"What's scary?" She took his hand, pulling him up off the swing.

Dancing ahead of him, they moved toward the Jeep as Mickey answered, "A woman who won't tell her age."

Alex glanced sideways with a slight grin. "So is age an issue?"

He shrugged, seeking more. "Age isn't an issue as long as we have time together."

She stopped suddenly causing the gravel at her feet to roll forward. Despite her feelings, boundaries needed to be understood.

"Please know there's a private side of me that must remain private." She stared at the gravel. "I will leave in another day. That's it. Please accept that. This is a wonderful friendship, and you've taken me on a great journey, but that is the limit. One more day."

The finality of her statement struck him hard. "Tomorrow?"

"Tomorrow," she whispered, looking up, "and then I leave."

He smiled into her blue eyes. "There's got to be another way."

The softness left her eyes. "There's no other way." She said flatly. "I leave tomorrow."

As they approached the gate, he took his National Park Pass from the visor clip, waving it at the attendant who waved him through with a knowing smile. Alex drove on up the curve to Horseshoe Park where Mickey pointed ahead into the meadow.

"The sheep are down."

She slowed to see a large herd of bighorns gathering around a small pond.

"They come down for about an hour each day to feed at the pond," he explained. "There's potassium in the water. It strengthens their bones. They're being repopulated, the sheep. Used to roam all over this area. Then we came along and killed them off. Now we feel bad, and we're bring them back."

Alex turned the Jeep into the parking area and took the last spot among the tourists. They sat and watched. Lambs jumped and played, ewes fed, and the rams watched over them with nervous glances at the distant crowd of people.

Mickey pulled a pair of binoculars from under the seat, handed them to her, and pointed across the meadow at an unnatural clump on top of a large tree.

"Do you see them?" She looked adjusting the binoculars, then suddenly gasp. "Eagles, bald eagles, two of them in a nest."

"In *The White Room*," he said. "The image of the eagle soaring? I was watching them when suddenly one took to flight, coming right at me. I had my camera up, ready, flipped the stabilizer button on my 400 lens, and focused. He turned with this majestic glide that took him into the blue above the mountaintop. The sun struck his wings detailing the feathers, and I captured the image."

She suddenly realized, "That's him, one of those two?" She pointed toward the nest.

"Eagles mate for life. Either the male or female, I'm not sure which, but yes, one of those two."

They sat for a moment and while she stared through the binoculars, he wondered how he'd lost control. Sharing the elk shots was nothing more than flirtation, but it'd all changed. At the moment he woke and found her lying in his bed, so incredibly beautiful and sleeping peacefully, it had changed. He had sat on the bed's edge watching her, her softness, the gentle pink of her lips and checks, the flow of her blond hair upon his pillow, and the way her waist curved deeply. Too beautiful to hide, yet the mountain morning chill filled the room, so he had pulled the cover over her to warm and protect.

"Why the big smile?"

"I was just thinking about you in my bed."

"And I suppose I gave you quite the show." She backed the Jeep out.

Mickey put his foot up on the dash, the imprint disturbing the dust. "Showing might be a better word. You are a work of art, you know."

She set the binoculars aside, shifting into drive. "Nice line, Mickey."

"I try," he grinned, his long, wavy hair blowing in the breeze.

Jimmy was sitting on the ledge at the Rock Cut watching old ladies and little kids laugh at the marmots playing.

As they both stepped from the Jeep, he grinned at his friend, "It appears you've done well in the last couple of days."

Mickey raised his eyebrows, while Alex watched the marmots animated among the rock jungle gyms. He knew the innuendo but was not sure how to describe the reality.

"Actually," Alex turned, "he's had an exceptional time."

Mickey had to laugh. She shrugged as if enjoying the game, and Jimmy stood envious of Alex's devious grin.

"Jimmy," she reached out her hand, "I don't think we've been formally introduced. My name is Alex, and I loved dancing to your music Tuesday night. You're very talented."

"Thank you." He took her gentle hand. "It's nice to finally meet you. I was with Michael as he ogled you the other night. He's quite the smooth ogler, you know."

"I know that now." She bumped her shoulder against Mickey's. "So Mr. Ogle, what's the plan?" She was staring to the south across massive Forest Canyon and the rock hard ice lakes buried in the shadows of Mount Ida and the Continental Divide.

"Just follow us." Jimmy reached into his pick-up and opened his guitar case. It was a guitar of scratches with a deep worn spots where the wood had been shaved to a thin layer just below the pick guard. He put the guitar over his shoulder and swung it around backpack like.

The Rock Cut was along Trail Ridge Road, above the timberline where the road could not pass without going through the rock. So a huge cut had been made to allow a narrow crevice for the road. It was a stopping place to view the distant peaks and the wildflowers that grew on the wind swept tundra.

Jimmy led them through the Rock Cut to a point just beyond where the stone plateaued over the valley, dropping thousands of feet to a river that looked like a line on a map. He stepped onto the first rock, and they followed to where a three-foot crevice divided them from the cliff beyond. She took a breath, a slight jumping step over the crevice, and Jimmy caught her for balance.

Jimmy stepped forward, lowering himself to sit on a flat rock, and dangled his legs thousands of feet above the valley. Alex leaned forward a touch, looking. So far down, only Long's Peak appeared to be higher. Mickey bent down to join Jimmy, and Alex, more cautiously, sat between them.

Jimmy reached into his pack. "I've got a delicious buffet of cauliflower and carrots, cucumber sandwiches, and some granola mix I made myself."

"Health nut," Mickey said. "When Jimmy brings lunch, you eat like the marmots."

They all laughed, and Jimmy handed them a cucumber sandwich adding, "Look how fat and healthy the marmots are."

"Vegetarian?" Alex asked.

"For the most part, but they'll eat anything." Jimmy grinned. "Oh, me? No, just particular."

They ate their lunch while watching the clouds pass high above the valley. In her life she lived with this sense of pressure always invading her, knowing that something felt wrong, but accepted the tension as a natural part of each day. Her body felt strange with no pain in her lower back, and she realized the tension was gone.

Jimmy was older than Mickey, and she smiled, appreciating that he was probably her age. His hair was a nice sandy color and straight like hers, falling over his forehead with a John Denver look. He had a bit of a baby face and this wonderfully sensitive smile that made you want to hug him like a teddy bear. Nibbling on carrots, he looked out over the mountains. She smiled at this strange *Lady Antebellum* scene. The huggable musician, confident young adventurer, and Hillary Scott running away from her comfortable lifestyle to join them on the road.

Mickey laid back to look at the sky, and Jimmy picked his guitar strings, stroking different cords and tuning.

"You going to help?" he asked.

Alex looked confused. "Help do what?"

"Write a song, for gosh sakes. We're on a mountaintop with a guitar."

"A song?" She looked from Jimmy to Mickey. Mickey nodded casually as he lay on the solid bed of rock.

"Listen," Jimmy said. "It's a phrase I've been working on but can't quite put words to."

Jimmy began strumming the guitar and a melody filled the air, a beautiful blending of chords and notes.

"Describe the sound," he said, playing it again.

She searched for words. "It has a deep melody. Soulful? No, *mystical* is my first thought."

"Go on," he kept repeating the sound.

"Like dreaming, something unexpected. Something like *The mystery of....*

What are the words for the feelings?" she thought out loud. "*...an intimate night*"

"I like it," Jimmy nodded. "Repeat it for me."

She felt herself blushing, the thoughts too obvious as she looked across the canyon.

He began to repeat the chords, and Alex's words fell into place among them. "It's a reawaking song like someone discovering new possibilities." Alex drifted back to the image of the blazing trail in the sky. "*A falling star.*"

From beside her, Mickey echoed, "*A falling star flashes bright.*"

Again Jimmy played and Alex sang the words softly adding Mickey's thoughts.

"Go on," she said. "This is too cool. Play some more."

Jimmy repeated the music phrase. "Here's a line I wrote years ago that I've always liked but never found the right home for." He sang with the melody, "*Alone in the night, a song about rain. A guitar player's pain fills our hearts.*"

Jimmy played with the chords as she added. "*As poems of love...poems of love and quiet reflection...*"

Mickey sang softly, shyly. "*As poems of love in quiet reflection brought the stars.*"

Alex closed her eyes and hummed the tune.

"*As poems of love in quiet reflection brought the stars,*" Jimmy played the chords.

"*And the mystic blue in your eyes,*" Michael added wondering if she was looking his way.

Jimmy repeated the words, glancing from one to the other with this goofy look of recognition. "*The mystic blue in your eyes...* How do we bring the falling star into this? *The mystic blue in your eyes... as the sun dips from the sky.*"

Alex sang again, and imagined his touch moving across her chest. "*Lighting the night.*" She felt the redness in her face. "*Lighting the night, a falling star flashes bright.*"

"I like it," Jimmy said, "And what does it flash bright?" He repeated the chords, singing, "*The mystic blue in your eyes.*"

Jimmy continued to play, the song filling the thin mountain air.

Mickey interrupted Jimmy, speaking toward the sky. "It's a song of rediscovery, new chances, and intimacy. *Where have you been, my beautiful friend. Walking to this moment in time.*" He repeated the words again, "*Where have you been, my beautiful friend. Walking to this moment in time. Where have you been, my amazing friend.*"

And Jimmy sang, "*Smiling mystic blue eyes.*"

"Oh, I like that..." Alex spoke before she thought. "It has to have mountains and pine trees touching the sky. It has to have magic and the quiet of a mountain night."

Jimmy suggested, "It's about dreams discovered in two hearts." He strummed new chords. "Something like this..." For a moment he fiddled with the chords, adjusting, moving his fingers with the rhythm of his thoughts. "*The rhythm of the pine tree sings. The song of a lover's new chance.*" He repeated the words and chords, adding, "*Where life and dreams and dances to be....*"

"Yes, yes..." Alex interrupted, talking with her hands. "*Where life and dreams and dances to be...touch the sky.*"

"Perfect." Jimmy played and sang it back.

Mickey's eyes did not leave the sky. "*And the mystic blue in your eyes.*"

Inhaling the words, Alex looked away from both men, unsure what to think, what she felt, and afraid of what she would see in Mickey's eyes, more afraid of what he would see reflected in hers. They were describing what she wanted to experience, the adventure and the passion of a woman unafraid. *Lighting the night, a falling star flashes bright.* She wanted to be *bright* again.

As the melody continued, Alex took the last carrot, stood, and walked along the plateau to the east. The soft music of Mickey and Jimmy refining the song drifted around her. It wasn't such a bad life, the one she lived. Most people dreamed of her life, envied her, all the finest clothes, best restaurants, and the house. She laughed at her own absurdity, thinking of that monstrosity as a house. It was so massive, so cold and impersonal.

She heard Jimmy singing a chorus again.

Every social engagement was of guests, not friends, and served as a business obligation. It was like one Halloween Party after another where they all dressed alike.

He was a well-intended man, William. Committed to their wealth, he lived his work and viciously controlled his image. They were the large family portrait above a too big fireplace in a grand room defined by its massive proportions, cold and disconnected. Did the image really matter? It was completely loveless, and when she thought of the image, she felt the loneliest.

Alex stared at Long's Peak, the 14,000 foot summit where she had stood years before with her father. He was a gentle man, never raising a hand or saying a cruel word, and always holding her tight and protected.

William had never hit her, yet the hidden temper was nearly as devastating. She never knew when or what would set him off, but she lived with the constant fear of his sudden, directed anger abusing her sense of dignity. His words cut deep, harsh and were meant to hurt, inflicting pain in deep emotional wounds.

Josephine was the salvation of her life, Josephine and the Foundation.

Josephine would be the joy tomorrow when she met them up at the airport. She would hold Josephine close then share a welcome home kiss with her husband, where their lips touched but did not feel. William, full of power in his dark suit would be back directing her life.

Alex could feel Mickey's presence behind her. Smiling, it allowed her thoughts to float into the thin air. She fell backward, her arms flopping sideways on the rocks as if surrendering.

"What have you done to me?" She stared up at him, his image a reverse reflection surrounded by the sky above.

"What-have-I-done-to-you."

"Oh Mickey," she was laughing upside down. "I came here to get away, not change."

He squatted down, his knees beside her, their faces not far apart. "Is this a complaint?"

"Yes." She felt teased. "Look what we've done. Danced, jumped, swam, slept; and now I'm writing a love song."

"So what's wrong with jumping, swimming, sleeping, and writing love songs."

They were laughing now in a comfortable way that seemed without expectations.

"Okay," she said, "picture this. Dancing with a sexy boy in a bar of tattooed men, jumping off a skyscraper cliff, swimming naked in an icy mountain lake, sleeping naked in the bed of a man I hardly know. Did you notice the two *nakeds* in there? Then writing the lyrics to a beautiful love song." She closed her eyes but did not add *and thinking of you*. "This from an uptight, rich lady."

"Sounds like a perfect day to me." A slight dimple showed with his smile as she shook her head in disbelief.

"It's a story you're writing. A special and private story." He reassuring. "You're the author, and you control the ending."

He crossed his arms and reached out above for her hands. She grasped upwards, and his hands felt strong. He stood lifting, and she felt herself standing as he untwisted his arms, and she twirled to face him.

"I'm sorry about this," Alex spoke to him, a slight altitude chill shivered through her. "This isn't fair to you, but you have to understand. There's a lot in my life that's wrong right now. Yes, I am running, but it's temporary. You're an amazing person, and this has all been an incredible couple of days. I thank you for that." Looking down, she spoke to the ground between them. "Please understand; I have to go home tomorrow." When she looked up, his eyes stared compassion. "I'm sorry I've involved you in my emotional turmoil."

Somewhere out there William was oblivious to her, Josephine was with her grandparents feeling their unconditional love, and she was here feeling cared for and protected. Reacting, she wrapped her arms around him holding tight as the tears ran down her cheek.

Tomorrow she would be Alexandria again, back in her real life while her heart and soul were lost somewhere in the mountains she'd loved all her life.

They came down off the mountain together, a song written and an understanding neither wanted.

"This is Artie's place," Jimmy stated. They were sitting under the umbrella in the outdoor bar behind the main street shops.

"Who's Artie?" She asked.

"Great barbecue cook." Jimmy raised his eyebrows, emphasizing great. "He's also burned out from too much pot."

Mickey grinned. "I think that's the secret to his barbecue. He only cooks when he's loaded."

A weathered man, unattractive with oily hair that seemed to be torn, not cut, acknowledged them with a nod, his eyes red and glassy. You could tell that somewhere along the line the braces his teeth badly needed had been completely ignored, as had normal hygiene. Leaning on the table, his frame had the familiar pose of a body distraught from too many drugs.

"Boys," like a man who had peaked at Woodstock, Artie welcomed them. "Write any good songs today?"

"Maybe," answered Jimmy. "Kind of a mountain love song about a woman with *mystic blue eyes*. Still working on the details, but the possibility is pretty damn exciting."

"What's the special today?" Mickey pointed toward the kitchen.

"Whatever you like." Artie tapped a tooth marked pencil against the order pad. "Got a fresh delivery of Rocky Mountain Oysters ready for the fryer."

Mickey and Jimmy looked at Alex waiting for a reaction. She looked at them thinking something about Rocky Mountain Oysters sounded familiar.

All three men smiled at each other.

"Bring us an order." Mickey and Artie still smiled, though avoided eye contact.

Alex turned white, suddenly remembering. "No," she said emphatically with her hands pushing them away.

Mickey eyed her. "Alex, you've been so daring until now."

"No way," she blurted, hand firmly between them.

Mickey shook his head dismayed. "Where has your sense of adventure gone, that spirit of discovery?"

"No way, Mickey."

"It's the adventure every woman secretly wants." Jimmy placed his palms between them. "You are one pathetic adventurer."

"Some adventurers," she explained, "have a sense of taste – and I mean both definitions of taste. Besides, Jimmy, you won't really eat them. A cucumber sandwich guy wouldn't eat them."

"I said I was particular, not a vegetarian," he smiled. "Rocky Mountain Oysters are particularly delicious."

"No." Alex was emphatic. "Not for me."

Mickey pointed at the ketchup stained menu. "Then order as you please, something boring and traditional."

Bratwurst was the first thing she saw, started to order, and then stopped herself. She had no idea why she was blushing. She moved down the list to Barbecued Beef Brisket, familiar and safe.

"I'll take the Brisket." She looked up at the three men staring at her. "It's beef, its barbecue, it works." Mickey just laughed. "Okay," she looked directly at Artie, "and a large beer!" Sneering the words *large beer* at the three boys.

The oysters actually looked like overgrown oysters. They sat in a brown, crispy pile between them. Artie set a plate before her. Her oversized sandwich was barely visible under the mountain of French fries. Artie rested one hand on the table, the other patting her back. "An order of oysters usually comes with six. I threw on a seventh." His grin was crooked and mischievous. "Just in case you want to try one."

The boys burst out laughing, and Alex turned pale again. A cold breeze blew down from the mountains and the sun disappeared behind a late afternoon cloud drifting isolated in the sky.

She tried not to watch them eating the brown round slivers. She focused on eating her brisket in peace, but the slow motion and over dramatic moans of pleasure kept drawing her eyes.

Taking a swallow of beer, she waved them off. "How can you guys eat that?"

"You mean *eat those*, don't you?"

Alex stared at Jimmy, the pale returning. "How can you guys eat those?"

"Alex." Jimmy stabbed an oyster with his fork and lifted it between their stare. "You just pop it in." He pushed the steer testicle into his mouth, chewed with deliberate motions, smiled, and swallowed. "It slides right down."

She rolled her eyes and looked away disgusted, her head shaking involuntarily.

Mickey took the last oyster with his fork, pressing down into it. He lifted his knife and gently sliced. When he finished, three fleshy pieces lay on the plate.

"A toast," he stated. "To daring and changing and new discoveries."

Jimmy grinned directly at her, singing. "To *falling stars flashing bright.*"

They were both looking at her. Daring, changing, discovering, she wanted to, but it was repulsive.

Mickey and Jimmy looked seriously upon her, waiting for her to surrender. She fought her skin and the overwhelming paleness. Mickey gently raised his fork, placing it on one piece, and pushed. He lifted it before them, never taking his eyes from Alex. Jimmy followed, the same slow motion intentness. Their forks stood tall in front of her, waiting for the joining of the third musketeer with a jab of her fork into the bull's testicle.

Alex looked straight through both men, pressing her lips tightly against each other. She took her fork in her right hand as if to stab, moved it downward, and stuck the third piece with a fierce jab. Slowly, she lifted the beefy severed maleness to the middle above the plate. In unison, Mickey and Jimmy tapped their forks to hers, toasting. They nodded and each took their piece to their mouths. Alex rested it before her lips, sensing the smell of roasted meat and quickly popped it into her mouth.

She couldn't chew, wouldn't chew; and quickly gulped. The testicle slid down her throat, and her face twisted with disgusted distortion. Mickey and Jimmy roared with laughter. She could hear Artie doing the same from the kitchen. Alex grabbed for her beer, rushing it to her lips, and chugged. Beer rolled down her throat and out over her mouth. Down her neck and between her breasts, the beer streamed as she continued gulping. She nearly emptied the 16 ounces before the taste disappeared, and she slammed the mug back down on the picnic table.

Mickey and Jimmy burst into applause.

She looked at them as if violated. "Augh," her eyes watered. "That sucked."

Her words only made them laugh louder.

At Lonigan's she asked for a large glass of water, drank it immediately, and asked for another. The boys had been laughing continuously, and she was ready to free herself from the joke. She drank half of the second glass, gave them a look, and then finished the water. Scooter reached over the bar and refilled her glass then set a beer before each one of them. Mickey thanked him with a tip of the long neck, and then led the group to the nearest table.

"So," Jimmy asked, "was it that bad?"

"It's more the thought than the taste." She glared at him. "You are boys, you know. Silly, peer pressure driven, gross little boys."

Mickey's beer tapped hard on the table, his eyes watching her over the bottle tilted in his hand. "You forgot to be Alex back there at the restaurant. Alexandria is the frightened conservative. Alex, well, she's not afraid of new adventures."

"I am Alex." Driving a glare of cold blue eyes into him. "Alexandria never would have eaten that dam cow's ball, not in a million."

"Bull's balls." Jimmy corrected.

"What?"

"Cows are female. Bulls are the males. They are all cattle." He shrugged uncommitted. "You ate bull's balls."

"Okay, whatever. Bulls, cows, or cattle, it was gross" she defined. "So Alex ate bull's balls."

Jimmy's eyes danced while Mickey waved her off, laughing as he did. Glancing around the bar for friends, silence suddenly seemed to fall into place. With a hint of distance in his deep brown eyes, Alex watched Mickey. It was a strange feeling of emotions that she could not have, while for Mickey it was an emotion he wanted.

In the silence, he steadied the beer before straightening in his bar chair. "Excuse me," he said suddenly, "I'm about to say too much." He pushed the chair back and walked toward the bar.

When she turned from Mickey, Jimmy was staring at her. "What was that all about?"

"I'm guessing it's about me leaving?"

Her words to Jimmy weren't measured. She told him that she had laughed more and lived more in the last two days than in the past ten years. At this moment, her heart had been freed from years of rigidity. Her sacrifice was the commitment she dreaded returning to. Mickey sensed that. He also knew that she would leave.

Explaining, she told him, "I like myself right now. Very much I like being Alex, but tomorrow I'm Alexandria again. She's different and she's sad. He's angry that I've accepted being sad, but life is not always what we make it. Sometimes circumstances direct us, as unfair and empty as that life might be. Mickey's angry about it, but he doesn't understand the circumstances. If he did, he wouldn't be angry."

"I wouldn't count that out yet," Jimmy answered. "He's something special. He sees things, feels things, and he understands compassion."

She immediately quieted. "Yes, he's very special."

"You're going to hurt him, aren't you?"

Alex looked away. "I should have never come to Lonigan's."

They sat in silence, Alex gripping the wet beer bottle, sitting tall as if she had practiced the pose.

Escaping the awkwardness, Jimmy changed the subject, though his words were clumsy. "I can't believe, well, that he showed you that room, *The White Room.*"

"He told you?"

Jimmy smiled. "Up at the Rock Cut."

"He's such an amazing talent, yet he doesn't believe it."

"Is he really that good?" Jimmy asked.

She had not actually believed that she was the only one. "You really haven't seen it?"

"The room?" he shook his head. "Haven't even seen a picture. He's very private with his work. We all know he takes a lot of pictures, works hard at photography, but no one here has ever seen his work. Ed, over at the camera shop tells us he does incredible work, but he hasn't shared it with anybody. That is until you."

She winked at Jimmy. "I believe that's about to change."

"Oh."

"Enough said." Alex looked back to find Mickey and Scooter deep in conversation. "So, Jimmy is music what you do?"

Alex heard Scooter burst out laughing. "She really ate it."

Glaring, she gave them both her best hate look, but knew Mickey didn't believe it. He was leaning on the bar, one foot up with his hiking boot resting on the bar railing. His legs were tanned with the ridges of impressive muscles. His hips were amazingly small, and a hint of jealousy caused her to smile. The t-shirt fit him loosely but could not hide the narrow waist, full chest, or toned biceps so strong they appeared always to be flexed. But nothing matched his brown eyes, the way they looked across the bar at her, framed by a thick fullness of long and wavy black hair. He lifted his beer, tilting it toward her.

Smiling, she turned back to Jimmy. His eyes were cast downward yet looking at her. "Careful," he said.

Alex nodded understanding, then looked away. "So, tell me about your music."

"Music?" The word brought a smile. "Music is my life. What I do is teach."

She was surprised.

"Vocal music." He pointed toward the east. "At the high school. It's great fun, and the kids love it. I've got this knack. We've built an outstanding program since I came here ten years ago."

"So how does Acoustic Tuesday fit in?"

The beer bottle tipped high, then back down from his mouth. "Very nicely. I play and write songs, a local celebrity by night, mild-mannered teacher by day, and I spend my summer's performing. Heck, a lot of the locals that were in here Tuesday were former students. Sometimes they come up and sing, and many of them have grown up to become friends. It's a nice life I live in this mountain town."

"Super singer," she stated.

"Got a giant 'S' tattooed right here." He thumped his chest. "Evenings and summers, I live my music. Days during the school year, I teach kids to love the music." He grinned self-assured. "And you, what do you do

Alex?"

She sat up straighter. "I'm the mystery woman, destined to disappear tomorrow."

"Sorry to hear that." He tilted his bottle toward the bar. "He's nuts about you," Jimmy winked. "No Rocky Mountain Oyster pun intended."

"Enough about testicles!" She demanded, causing her to smile.

Her eyes glanced down at the table. It was a brown Formica top table that brought people together around it. Day after day people sat around this table talking, sharing, and laughing. It was a great bar table, and she was happy to be sitting at it with Jimmy.

"We make choices in life." Her voice was soft. "Sometimes we have to live with those choices. I made a choice ten years ago. I thought it was a good choice; one I made wearing rose-colored glasses. People, circumstances change, how we see and our lives, so it's certainly not the choice I'd make today. A good choice then, but today, well, it's different."

"How?"

"Jimmy." He could see the wetness pooling in her eyes. "I've said too much already. Can we move on to something else?"

"Sorry." He reached over, patting her hand.

"Michael," Jimmy called toward the bar. "Get your ass back over here."

Over the next hour, they each bought a round of beers, kindly letting her pay for a round without chauvinistic hesitations. They drank and talked, and she had never enjoyed two old friends so much.

"You guys are amazing." She reached her beer to the middle of the table where theirs joined hers.

She took another long, deep swallow, then spoke.

"I have a daughter." Her words were gentle. "I need you to understand." Her eyes met Mickey's. "She's ten and beautiful with an amazing heart and great laugh. She'd love the mountains but has never known them. Thanks to you guys, I know I need to teach her, take her hiking, and allow her to experience nature. In her life today, well, it's limiting, and from the last two days I'm reminded that I need to bring her to the mountains."

"What's her name?" Jimmy asked.

"Josephine." Her smile was motherly.

"Josie." Mickey leaned back repeating the name. "I like that." He smiled. "I really like it. Josie."

"She's amazing and the best part of my life." Hoping this explained her conflict. "I've got to get her into the mountains. I've got to take her on hikes and teach her the things my father gave me." Alex's beamed motherly pride. "She's my light, my life."

Sensing a need to say less, Alex raised her hand, waving. When she left the next day, she needed this to be history. There was a beginning two days before, and there would be an ending tomorrow.

"Beertender," she called out to Scooter. "Another round, please."

When the beers arrived, she raised her bottle to her new friends. "To two amazing men."

They reached their long neck to hers, and Mickey added, "And one incredible women," locking his eyes on hers.

The bottles chimed together, and she smiled, drinking the fourth one with a purpose. The beer provided the comfort she wanted, that she would, just for the night *flash bright.*

Chapter 10

William stood on the balcony overlooking Central Park talking to his secretary in Denver. It had been an exhausting day of negotiations, but he knew he had the upper hand. While the Chadwick Banks were on strong financial ground, the other two family banks were slowly watching their assets being eaten up by large conglomerates, and they needed William more than he needed them. Now the Chadwick family would have its own banking conglomerate competing soundly against the Wells Fargos, Wachovias, and U.S. Banks of the world.

Rolling his cigar in one hand with his cell phone in the other, William relayed several pieces of information. When he arrived back in the office, they would have the basic paperwork put together, and William would be in line to control the largest individually owned bank in America.

Maybe then, he thought, he could get back to those times when he and Alexandria had been close, back at the very beginning of their marriage when they had dreamed of a life that wasn't dominated by the responsibilities of being the President of the Chadwick Banking empire. Until then, business was the obligation of the day, and what a day it had been. He was a man creating power.

"Valerie," William finished with his secretary. "Could you transfer me upstairs to Alexandria's office?"

"Of course."

As the Foundation phone rang, Jennifer stopped at the doorway. She wanted to ignore it, but saw that it was from William's extension.

"Chadwick Foundation," she answered.

"It's William." He sounded short.

"Yes sir." She straightened as she spoke. "I'm afraid Alexandria's not in right now."

"I thought not, but hoped I might catch her." His voice seemed strained. "Do you know what her schedule is tomorrow?"

Searching for what the right answer might be, she shared a vague explanation. "She is in and out all day until she meets you and Josephine at Denver International." Jennifer's eyes searched as she expelled a deep breath. "I know she's missed you both and is looking forward to tomorrow. Is there any message?"

"Nothing important. Besides," he added without serious thought, "if I need her, I can always call her cell. I'll check in with her tomorrow once

I'm with Josephine in Kansas City."

"Sounds like a plan." Jennifer, knew she sounded rushed and unprofessional, a trait not appreciated by William. "I'll tell her you'll call from Kansas City," she added.

"Thanks," he said flatly, and the phone went dead.

Jennifer stared at the phone irritated at both William and Alexandria. Where in the world was she? She'd only left a voice mail that she was taking a few days while William was gone, yet William clearly did not know she was gone.

William closed his cell without thought, and stepped back in from the balcony. As he did, the house phone rang.

"Mr. Chadwick?" the bellman asked.

"Yes," he answered.

"Your limousine has arrived."

Smiling from where the big cigar was clinched between his teeth, he answered, "Send her up."

Chapter 11

When they stepped onto the street from Lonigan's, Mickey's mind was beer fuzz. He knew the best thing to do was offer comfort, yet…Mickey grinned at his mental dramatics.

In her mind, silly, romantic fantasies were being created, and they were all about a desperate need for love. Mickey had made her feel loved. It was silly, she knew, to think of love in such limited time, but this was the most love she had felt in years. Smiling to herself, it would be an amazing adventure into private emotions, and for one night, her star would shine bright.

"What's that smile about?" he asked.

Her laughter was playful. "Last night you said you had wine?"

"Cheap wine," he glanced up and down the empty Estes Park street. "Grocery-store-bought, screw-top bottle cheap wine."

She focused on his lips as she spoke. "Red or white?"

"Blush."

"Perfect. I would love a glass of cheap, grocery-store-bought blush wine." She took his hand, pulling, and led him off in the direction of the Jeep.

Smiling, he knew this night would be about Alex.

As the Jeep rolled along the winding road west of Estes, Alex leaned her head on the seat. The night wind blew through her hair, massaging. Beside her was Mickey, quietly driving toward his cabin. It was like she had transitioned into his comfortable world.

The Jeep rolled to a stop in the cabin drive, but Alex did not move. Her eyes toward the sky, she watched the stars and the clouds drifting over the early moon. Mickey laid his head back on the Jeep seat. It was a coyote moon, a quarter full and bright white.

Mickey released a deep breath, "Cheap wine?"

She reached her hand to touch his. "Perfect."

The cabin was dark save for the moonlight. They left it that way, moving hand-in-hand into the living room. She walked to the stereo and turned on classic acoustic music.

He laughed as he lifted the wine from the refrigerator. Wasn't this supposed to be some wildly expensive French stuff, sitting chilled in a crystal ice vat? Mickey took two wine glasses from the cupboard, blowing on each to remove the dust.

Alex stood in the middle of the room, her hips swaying to the sounds with sensual confidence. Mickey stood with the wine in one hand and glasses in the other as she danced her freedom dance gently in the night. She must have known he was watching, but she was not apprehensive, happy to feel freed.

As she took the glass of wine from his hand, he slowly leaned to her. In that moment he hesitated, she did not. It was a soft kiss, the tenderness that comes from not knowing but wanting and when it finally happens it is gentler than imagined. Her soft, soft lips were touching his.

"So this dream of yours?" Alex grinned, their lips an inch apart.

"Which one?"

"Are there others?"

"Just you and photography," he smiled shyly.

"Well then," her eyes were daring, "maybe tonight one dream will come true, but let's talk about the other."

"To hell with the other." Mickey leaned closer.

She stopped him. "The other is important too." Alex eased away. "The foundation."

He nodded.

"The foundation is in Denver, and they are particularly sensitive to Colorado-based artists, so I would think a nature and wildlife photographer might be right up their alley."

Mickey shook his head. "Listen, I know someday I'll be here, but in three weeks it's back to Bismarck."

"Bismarck?" Surprised she didn't automatically know.

"Yes," he laughed. "I've got to be from somewhere, and Bismarck is somewhere."

"Bismarck, North Dakota?"

"The barren north."

She turned serious again. "So, you're returning home."

"I'm glad to have had the summer. Three of the shots in *The White Room* were taken this summer. I think I have three others that are worthy. And the waterfall, it could be amazing. I've accomplished much."

"But Mickey, you can't stop here. You're too talented. You can't waste your talent on prom pictures."

"I won't," he answered. "The dream won't die in Bismarck. It'll just slow down a bit. In the meantime, I'll make some families very happy taking pictures of their daughters in elegant dresses."

"Just listen to me, will you?"

"Okay?" He questioned her persistence.

"Promise me you'll take a shot at this grant."

Whatever she wanted. "Sure."

"A year's living and start up costs, right?"

He nodded, smiling.

"Ask for that and a second year's living expenses." She winked, seducing and encouraging at the same time. "Don't be shy."

She loved the way the laughter burst from him, the way his head fell back with his hair reaching beyond his shoulders, and that his smile grew as if he might just have the guts to ask.

"Alex, are you crazy." This was getting silly. "Nobody is going to give some guy who has taken a few pictures that kind of money and say *have a good year, hope this gives you your life dream.*"

She reached her hand to his chin, lifting it. "You're not listening. They want to support talent so it can become what it is capable of being. Promise me you'll write and ask, at least send an email."

"If I promise will you let me kiss you again?" He moved his hips, slightly pressing his against hers.

If you'll promise I'll make love with you.

He froze at the sensation of the words, to touch her after three days of wanting her. She had changed, but he wondered if he would ever be the same.

Her lips brushed his, and his hand moved over her thigh and upward, a subtle touch against her breast until his hand was soft over her check. The kiss was gentle at first until the passion grew intense. Her empty wine glass fell onto the couch, and Alex pulled him closer feeling something she had forgotten long ago.

Mickey led her through the living room, up the stairs past *The White Room*, and down the narrow hallway to the bedroom. The bed was still unmade, welcoming her back. Walking to open the doors of the sun porch to feel the quiet breeze, Mickey turned to face her.

Giving her a soft kiss, she felt his hands move over her breast to the button at the V in her sweater. Lips touching, she allowed him to unbutton the first, then second and third.

Pulling his tee shirt from his jeans, her hands felt the raw muscles of his back. His arms moved around her, enveloping her to feel safe and warm, and she released a deep sigh. She had never, not with any other man but William, she had never done this with anyone else.

Mickey kissed her forehead and down to her lips and chin. His hand moved to the last button, and then upward over the Lycra top to her shoulders. He pushed the sweater away, and she straightened her arms behind her, allowing it to fall discarded. His hands pressed over her sides and under the top. His biceps flexing, she could feel the cloth spreading freely out from around her. The top barely touched her as he lifted it away, tossing it over their heads and into the large sofa chair.

Without effort, he laid her upon his bed. Alex felt the warmth of his body, and they shared deep, passionate kisses. At times he was only gentle, yet his intensity brought powerful emotion, and she lay still allowing him to give all she wanted.

She felt the warm sensation, her back arching as the rhythm built inside of her. Why had this never happened? Alex's eyes pressed shut, catapulting her. Finally, her body reacted, and she felt herself shiver and heard her own soft gasps. Over again, and again, she pressed her shoulders downward against his bed, gasping louder for him to go on taking her where she had never been.

As he moved, her body trembled once and then again, and she held him tighter, closer, and unable to stop the surrender. He was so beautiful, his eyes and gentle strength. She could not stop, never wanted to stop.

They lay together in his bed, the scent of summer pines in the breeze as she moved her hand over his chest and thigh, teasing him with the sensation of her lightest touch.

"There are times in your life," her voice was soft, "when everything works. Do you know what I mean?"

She felt Mickey's nod.

"Can I tell you something?"

Mickey's hand rubbed reassuring.

"I have a great life, Mickey. By most standards, I have an incredible life. But what I don't have is someone who has done what you've done."

Sensing her need, he answered, "Don't overestimate this."

"No, I'm not." She turned with one arm on his chest. "Mickey, you believed in me, you taught me, you challenged me, and you never once tried to control me. You just let me be me, and you don't know how wonderful that has felt."

"You like it?"

"Oh, I more than like it," she laughed, kissing him on his nose. "I've discovered this great joy for being naked in the mountains, and I learned about love songs again. See, my life," she thought for a moment, "it's limiting but you devoured my limitations, exposing me. For the first time in so much time, I'm me."

"It's hard for me to understand," Mickey whispered back.

She touched her hand to his lips, quieting. "Don't try to understand. Just know how important you are to me."

Alex moved lying on top of him, her head on his chest. "You gave me life Mickey. Life and laughter, joy and belief, confidence to know that I can go on and my life will be different, but when I go on, it will be my life. You may not have known it, but in such a short time you have given me back to me." She lifted her eyes to his. "I can't thank you enough for giving me my life back."

Mickey stared through the moonlight. "You should know that nothing has happened in the last three days that wasn't in you already. Never doubt yourself, Alex. Never accept limitations."

For so long, she laid in his arms feeling protected. They were in their own private world, and nobody else knew. She thought again about the women at the club. She wondered when they had last truly made love, and she knew it hadn't been with such tenderness.

Smiling, she wishing she could get a tattoo.

Mickey could see her eyes, blue even in the dim light. His hands moved over her thighs to her waist and breast. Alex moved to smile from above him as he reached, her hand holding his. Feeling the fullness of her lips, she kissed each fingertip. Her eyes never left his, and again, they made love in the cool, moonlit mountain night.

She laid thinking about all he had done. No man had ever given her the attention or desired to please her as he had. She now understood that making love was sensual and soothing, enticing and releasing. She had experienced the comfort of being held through the night.

This was the only place she wanted to be, and for that moment all seemed in order. The comfort of being there was interrupted by the thought of leaving, knowing she had a little time left.

She fantasized of a life with him, of taking pictures and making love. Alex wanted to know more, but she knew it was over. This would end with his touch imprinted in her memory.

Still, she felt confident and playful and wanted to leave him with a feeling he would never forget. He was naked on the bed in the early morning light. Carefully, she touched him, moving her fingers around his thighs and the sensual dip in his pelvis. She felt his slight motion, and looked up to see the smile as his hand moved gently rubbing over her back.

This would be one last adventure in three days of great adventures. Smiling, she moved her lips to his chest, frightened but sure. Alexandria had long been afraid while living married to a man clueless of the power and pleasure that could be shared. What had Mickey told Alex last night? Never accept limitations? She giggled then did not hesitate, moving to kiss him, to feel him responding.

With a freedom she had never known, Alex made love to Mickey giving as she had never given.

It was later that Mickey heard the shower, and thought of her and the waterfall. He tried to put all the pieces together. A chance meeting, then there was the hike and comfort of a steady conversation on a three-hour climb. But he had never believed she would jump. That was his first shock, but it was when she walked into the lake that his life had changed. From that moment on he had known that if she stayed, he would stay, but if she left she would leave him with sadness. He now believed things had been too amazing. She would stay. Yes, he tried to convince himself, she would stay.

She came from the bathroom wearing only a towel. Alex laughed again, standing before him and opened the towel for him to see. Then moving to lean over him, her kiss was what he wanted, and she gave him her gentlest. He patted her playfully on the bottom as their bodies touched.

She handed him the towel, laughter always in her voice. "Your turn," she patted him back as he walked past her.

His shower was long and hot. He allowed the water to rush over him, steaming. When he stepped from the warmth, he ignored the dry towel choosing instead the damp one she had used. In the mirror, he combed his wet hair back over his ears to lay damp against his neck. He checked his cheek and chin, decided to shave for her. Soft kisses, he smiled at his reflection. Naked when he stepped from the bathroom, Mickey took a clean pair of jeans from the dresser drawer and pulled them over his hips.

As he walked down the steps, it was mysteriously quiet. She was not in the kitchen, and he glanced through the living room out to the patio. Pain shot through his chest when he saw the small piece of paper on the counter. On a white lined telephone-answering pad, she had left a note. It had his name, the foundation contact information, and one line. *I will always love you - good-bye.*

PART 2: Fall
Chapter 12

Alexandria stood before the floor-to-ceiling, tri-fold mirror. What she saw pleased her. Dressed comfortably in snug, light-blue skinny jeans, she complemented them with a blush-red silk blouse, leather boots, and a suede blazer. The earrings were basic maroon crystals, and she wore a beaded necklace she'd bought in Estes. William walked out of his bathroom dressed for the office save his charcoal gray suit coat. He glanced to see her turning, first right then left.

"Nothing special today?" he asked, clearing his throat.

"Actually," she shook her hair, "I've got a busy day at the office."

William slipped his suit coat on, frowning. He tugged the coat into place for a wrinkleless fit. "What's with the get up?"

"The get up?" Alexandria smiled, not letting him get to her.

A month before, she had gone on a shopping spree. It was part of the intimacy that had evolved over the past five weeks, the private joy of her own life. Free looking and free feeling were her clothes. It was a conscious choice with boundaries defined by her, not others, creating a clear conflict between chic-mountain and international banking.

William stood behind her, looking over her shoulder into the mirror. His glare was one she had grown to loathe. Wrinkled forehead with those thick eyebrows causing him to squint, it was the smirk, the way his lips pierced together with a flat line of righteousness that drove her crazy.

"You can't go to the office in that. For Christ sake Alexandria, the public expects more than jeans and cowboy boots. You look shoddy."

"Shoddy," she allowed a slight laugh to escape. "William, lighten up."

Alexandria turned and patted him gently, her hand sliding from his lapel as she walked past with a self-satisfied smile.

His frown intensified. "I'm serious, Alexandria. Put on something proper, a linen suit at the least." Forceful, his voice deepened, demanding. "Change your clothes. I'm serious!"

Alexandria glanced back giving him eyes that she had seldom dared to show. "I know you're serious, dear." Smiling, she closed the French doors behind her as she left the bedroom.

"Alexandria, I will not allow it." His booming voice followed her.

She stopped halfway down the staircase, turning to look upward over the curve of the white railing. He stood glaring down upon her with gray, despotic eyes.

"You will not allow it?" Her lips pierced controlling her anger. "I will not allow you to degrade yourself. Now get up here and change your clothes." His furor intensified, and she could see the whitening of his knuckles as he clinched his fist.

"William, you are my husband, not my master. How about I stop by at noon, and we go to lunch? We'll have a nice talk like we used to and maybe gain a better understanding of this *get up*. Can you take an hour from your busy schedule today for your wife?"

"I'm committed all day." He shifted slightly. "Now quit acting like a child and change your clothes."

"I've already dressed for the day. Quite amiable, I do believe." She opened her hands as if on a runway, then allowed her arms to fall to her side, speaking with clarity. "William, I know what is respectful and appropriate. If it were an elegant business dinner or the Foundations annual meeting of dignitaries, I'd wear something different, but for work today, trust me, this will be just fine."

"It's not fine, and don't you dare play games with me." His head turned red with anger, pressing his white knuckles into the wooden railing. "Get up here and change into something that doesn't embarrass me."

"Yes, William. What I wear is all about you." She turned, continuing down the staircase. "It's too bad we can't have lunch together. I would have enjoyed the time with you."

Ignoring her words, his were needles, fierce at her back. "I told you to change." His words boomed. "Damn it, Alexandria. Don't you dare wear those jeans to work. I will not allow it."

The door closed leaving William alone at the top of the staircase muttering *disgraceful bitch*.

Chapter 13

This day, he used the company limousine, too many appointments away from the office, and too much wasted time behind the wheel. The black stretch waited in the drive as he exited his estate. He looked at the driver, trying to remember his name. Relatively new, he'd used this driver only once before, two weeks prior. Nice kid. Not nosey, and always responsive. Adam, that was his name.

The driver opened the door, tipping his hat to Mr. Chadwick. "Good morning, sir."

"Good morning, Adam."

William slipped into the back seat, turned on FOX News, and pulled his phone from his inside breast pocket. Before dialing, he pushed the intercom button. "Adam."

"Yes sir."

"The bank first, but only for about twenty minutes. Did my assistant give you my itinerary?" He began punching numbers.

"Yes sir."

"Very good. Some privacy please."

"Of course, sir." Adam pressed a button on the dash causing the window between them to close.

The phone responded. "Bryson-Atwater, how may I help you?"

"William Chadwick for Al Atwater."

"Yes sir. One moment please."

The tall trees along the boulevard passed unnoticed as William stared out the tinted window. She was complicating things. He had no time for it. All she had to do was be his wife and a mother to Josephine. That was his expectation, yet for weeks his patience had lessened. She was like a schoolgirl defying him. Denim at work? If she weren't so damn good at the Foundation, he'd fire her ass and send her back to being a mother and wife.

"William. Good morning."

He turned his attention to the telephone. "Al, how are you?"

"Good, good." His voice filled with artificial enthusiasm. "It's always good to hear from you William, except of course when you're beating me on the links."

William grinned. "Which, unfortunately, isn't often enough."

"You know what they say, even on a bad day you're good." They shared a laugh. "So, what can I help you with?"

He looked back out the window seeing only the dark tint. "It's nothing I'm sure, but I need you to do me a favor."

"Is this personal or is there a problem with bank security?"

"Personal and highly confidential. I want a good man, very discreet and thorough." William took a deep breath. "It's my wife. Something's going on."

"I'm sorry to hear that William." There was a drop in Al's voice, an effort to be sincere. "Of course, confidential and discreet is what our reputation was built on." The voice in the phone turned serious. "You can rely on that, William."

"I don't know what's going on, but something is." His head shook in disbelief. "I need somebody on her for a couple of weeks. Where she's going, who she's seeing. Something's different. I don't know what it is, but I need to know what's causing this."

Al Atwater paused, but did not mention what they were both thinking. "Do you want daily reports?"

"Only if there is pertinent information." William's fist clinched.

Al's voice softened. "If we find anything, I'll call you personally."

"Discreet," William stated.

"The utmost discretion." Al answered.

William hung-up, confident he would get to the bottom of this.

Chapter 14

Alexandria couldn't get the image out of her mind. She drove right by it every day, the big white letters on a giant green road sign hanging high above the freeway. *Boulder.* Every time she passed it, she was tempted to turn. Today, she was particularly tempted to go north through Boulder into the mountains with a sense of freedom that had long been swallowed up by life's expectations.

He had been amazing, and she missed him every day. The little things, a photograph he might have taken, somebody talking about a weekend in the mountains, CSN&Y on the radio. Laughing to herself, she glanced at a billboard beer advertisement. Every little memory from those few days swept over her with subtle reminders. The idea of driving to Boulder repeated in her mind as she realized that not once had Mickey said to her *I will not allow it.*

Every morning she awoke, and William tried to find a way to control her life. Everyday, she drove to work angry yet pleased that she had not succumbed to the tyranny. This was not good, she reminded herself. This is not how a marriage should be.

Alexandria exited the elevator on the fourteenth floor of the Chadwick Building in downtown Denver. At the end of the hallway, she reached for the heavy, hand-carved wooden door emblazoned with the large letters *The Chadwick Foundation.* Before she could pull, the door lunged open, and she stood face-to-chest with her father-in-law.

Alexandria looked up startled. "Robert."

"Good morning, Alexandria." He glanced at her up and down, the slight hint of cigar smoke permeating his suit jacket. "Just stopping for a moment this morning?"

Her father-in-law always made her uneasy with the full body scan. With his thick, gray hair and slightly pouching stomach, it was a weird cross between a boss's expectations and a demented relative's filthy thoughts.

"Several errands to run today, but time in the office is important." She grinned her best daughter-in-law grin. "The Foundation always takes priority." What would honesty matter? He stopped by the Foundation once each month, if that. He had no clue as to her considerable work ethic or commitment.

Robert turned to business. "Your mother-in-law has once again been named honorary chairperson for the Denver Symphony Fund Raiser." He winked. "Sophia wanted me to remind you of her special interest in our increased financial support."

"Of course, Robert." Alexandria gave him the same reassuring lapel pat. "The symphony is always top of our list."

It had been three years since she had become the Chadwick Foundation Director. Overcome with the boredom and possessing a degree in marketing, she had needed something to breath a sense of purpose into her daily pattern. In her mind, she was a natural as the Foundation Director, complimenting her role as Mrs. William Chadwick. William and Robert's struggle had been in letting one of their own women actually hold a job.

But she knew the purpose of the Foundation. Except for their pet projects, the symphony most notably, the Foundation was designed as a tax write off and promotional tool than to actually endow the arts. While they gave big money with a smile as the charitable patriarchs, everything was balanced against the tax line, ensuring that the family benefitted. Other than that, they left her alone to run the Foundation as she saw fit.

The new receptionist, a pleasant young lady with a great ability to talk on the telephone with multi-tasking proficiency, greeted her with a wave as she directed a call to Jennifer.

Jennifer Wilson was Alexandria's assistant and over the past three years had become her best friend. Somehow, William's family had managed to alienate all the previous employees, but Jennifer took their arrogance as something to tolerate in a job she loved.

Alexandria's first objective had been to hire an assistant who could monitor the Foundation's projects. Over the years, she had watched with disbelief as the Foundation had funneled money to projects, publicized their effort, and then, after initial funding, left them dangling for lack of guidance. Jennifer's public relations skills and organizational abilities suited her well as project auditor. Once the project was off and running, it was her responsibility to ensure that the upfront money had a lasting impact.

Much to Robert and William's pleasure, the Foundation had greatly increased its visibility under Alexandria leadership. With the unveiling ceremonies she had initiated, ongoing press releases, and Jennifer's *Celebrations of Artistic Success* campaign, the Chadwick Foundation had brought a much greater public awareness of the money their family bestowed on Denver's society.

Alexandria was sitting at her desk glancing over messages when Jennifer's voice came from the intercom. A few moments later, the door opened. Alexandria always enjoyed Jennifer in the morning. Her bubbly enthusiasm and intensity infected Alexandria with a feeling of youth.

"Need to run some things by you." Jennifer held a list in her hand, and then let it fall casually to her side. "Wait a minute. Stand up pretty lady."

Alexandria gave her a perturbed look.

With hands on her runner's hips, Jennifer scolded, "I said stand up."

Alexandria surrendered, stepping from behind the desk as Jennifer pointed, her hand stopping at her boots.

"I like it," Jennifer approved. "Yes, casual, outdoorsy, and just enough silk for sophistication."

"Thank you for your approval. Now, what's on your all important list?"

Weeks without a word had gnawed at her though she had stopped running for the mail each morning. Whatever Mickey was doing, she wished he'd send a grant request. She envisioned his eyes when he received the Foundation check, saw his right arm shoot triumphantly in the air.

"The list can wait. Now tell me." She waved her hand.

"Tell you what?"

"Don't play dumb, Mrs. Chadwick," her friend teased. "This change."

"Change?" Alex pretended.

"A month ago, you disappear for days, come back, and I'm sworn to secrecy that you never left. No details, nothing from you except these subtle signs of change." Jennifer winked at her friend. "So when I say *this change,* you know what I mean."

Alexandria placed her hands firmly on the desk and allowed the rosiness in her checks to fade. "Jennifer. I took a few days of quiet time for myself. Simple."

"Change?" Jennifer asked the mysterious question. "The family picture is removed from the Foundation website, replaced by Robert and Sophia's portraits. There's a feature on William, minus any mention of his family. Your name is changed everywhere, the website, letterhead, any publication from Alexandria Chadwick to Mrs. William Chadwick." Her stare was intent. "You disappeared from Facebook, and the other day, when we were preparing the press release for the Symphony donation, you replaced your picture with one of Sophia." Jennifer shrugged, "Must I go on?" Then she added emphatically, pointing at her boots. "What's this change?"

"All business decisions in support of the Foundation."

"Okay, okay." She lifted her list. "But I know if I could escape the influence of the Chadwick testosterone, even for a few days, I might sneak off and fool around a little myself."

"Jennifer!" Alexandria reached across the mahogany desk and pulled the list from her hand. "Is that what you think?"

Jennifer watched Alexandria's eyes. "I apologize." Her voice softened. "It's just that a new attitude and new style, and more obvious, a happiness; sometimes it's because of someone else."

"Well, you guessed wrong." She looked at the list, avoiding eye contact. "Now, what are this week's priorities?"

Chapter 15

Alexandria pulled her pearl Mercedes up the ramp from the Chadwick Building parking garage, checking the clock. 2:43 p.m. The mid-afternoon traffic kept the streets busy as she rushed between cars, knowing Josie would be waiting at the academy. This was the one part of her day she had not changed, time with Josephine after school.

She remembered the shock of her mother-in-law, the socially rigid Sophia Chadwick, that Alexandria would even consider detracting from her mothering responsibilities to work. Driving the Denver streets, she laughed out loud at the pretentiousness in their names. Sophia, William, Robert, Alexandria and Josephine. How had they all managed to have such names?

Josie was standing near the curb dressed in her school uniform, looking all grown-up except for the playful way she swung her backpack. Alexandria eased to the curb, and with a smile, Josie bounced playful into the car.

"Hi Mom." Her voice sang. Even with her innocent smile, slender cheeks and alluring eyes had begun to appear.

"Hey baby." Alexandria give her other a big, warm hug. "Good day?"

"Yep," she brightened. "The Guinea Pig in science had babies. They were so, so cute with bald, little bodies."

The Mercedes pulled back into the traffic moving down the tree-lined avenue. The leaves had begun to change with the dry fall. Green tree limbs hung down over the street showing hints of brown, yellow, and red. Josephine continued talking about her day, about the boys chasing them at recess.

Her daughter was the youth Alexandria had forgotten, dancing circles in the wind and laughing at her own dizziness. She had that child's way of looking at life, yet she was determined. Josie had the same thirst for adventure that Alexandria had reawakened in herself. It was a confident feeling she wanted Josie to know.

"Brittney's having an overnight on her birthday."

"That sounds like fun, Josie."

Josie's forehead wrinkled. "Mom? Where'd Josie come from?"

"Is this a where-do-babies-come-from question?"

"Nope," Josie giggled. "It's a name question."

"A name question?"

Josie's head nodded. "You changed my name after I got back from Gramp's and Grammy's. Since then you've called me Josie."

Alexandria hadn't realized it. "Whoops. Just got less formal." She stopped at a streetlight and turned to her daughter. "Sorry, it's back to Josephine."

"Oh," Josephine looked sad. "I like Josie."

"You tell me sweetie. Which will it be?"

"I like Josie." She was giggling again.

Alex reached over and gave her little girl a hug.

"Me too," and then she added, "Josie."

Chapter 16

Through the steamy glass, his body hunched as he reached to turn off the water. Alexandria, naked from her own shower, leaned backward on the marble counter. She watched William reach for the embroidered towel, pull it into the shower, and rub himself dry. The door opened, and he stepped onto the marble floor.

"Alexandria?" Flinching, he pulled the towel up, startled. "What are you doing?"

"I was thinking about when you read me poetry."

He straightened. "Poetry? When did I read you poetry?"

"Twelve years ago you took me on a picnic to Brainard Lake. We ate grapes on a blanket, and you read me poetry."

William stepped forward, holding the towel between them. "Did you like that? The poetry?"

She reached up, putting her arms around his neck. "I loved it."

He looked at her strangely, questioning her erratic behavior. For so many years she had been the perfect wife being by his side and reveling in her role as a mother. Now he found her unpredictable behavior both unnerving and unnecessary.

Blandly, he answered, "Then I should read you poetry again." She felt the pressure of him pulling away as he moved her aside.

The slight stab of disappointment swelled in Alexandria. Suddenly she felt naked. Taking a towel, she wrapped it around her chest with a tuck over to hold it in place.

"William?" she asked flustered. "Why in the world do we have two separate bathrooms? I mean, you have one and I have one, and they're both bigger than either of us would ever need. So why separate bathrooms?"

"Isn't it obvious?" A vain grin broke across his face. "Because we can."

Hosted periodically for The Club's members, this event was a campaign rally for the Republican Party, fighting to gain a senate seat in Washington. A backslapping, hand-clasping formal affair, it was designed to win the support of Denver's wealthy.

As they moved up the walk to the colonnades and carpeted entryway, William actually seemed comfortable with her appearance. Alexandria wore a blue, slim-figured gown. While the sequins were not unusual, the depth of the low-cut front and mid-thigh slit were. She felt daring as the satin blue heels stretched forward with each step.

"A bit revealing, don't you think?" William rested his hand over the slight curve of her back. "Magnificent," he added, "but revealing." Then staring straight ahead, he added, "It reminds me of why I read you poetry."

Stopping before the tall double doors, she reached up and straightened his black bow tie. "Very dapper yourself."

"Yes, but jaws won't drop when I walk into the room."

"Dropping jaws?" She blushed, batting her eyes. "I doubt it."

William gave her a slight smile. "By the way, are you doing these things to aggravate my mother? Her jaw will drop." Uncharacteristically, he was still smiling, and she could feel the gentle rub of his hand across the small of her back.

"Maybe." She winked playfully back. "Or maybe it's just me."

"I must admit I've struggled with this change, Alexandria." He nodded to the doorman.

"I know dear." She squeezed his arm as they entered the ballroom. "But I'm confident you can overcome your insecurities."

A pretty young waiter handed them each a champagne flute as, from behind, the candidate slipped away from a nearby group. He greeted them with a warm handshake, a slap to William's shoulder. He was a man they both knew but Alexandria had avoided, and the artificiality of his smile only reinforced her feelings.

The discussion focusing on the upcoming banking bill New York Senator Clayton had promised to push onto the Senate floor. The candidate could truly help the bill along with William's financial support. Alexandria listened intently to his well-rehearsed campaign speech directed at Chadwick money.

"Besides banking, I'm curious about your thoughts on opening more National Forests to ski developments." Alexandria sipped champagne.

The candidate tilted his head. "We know Colorado thrives on tourism. Another ski area like the one proposed west of Fort Collins could only expand the financial flow into our state."

"But," Alexandria frowned, "isn't that the same area where the concentration of moose re-introduction has taken place?"

"Oh, Alexandria," the dismissing tone irritated her. "We've been co-existing with wild animals for years."

She baited her words. "Which is exactly why we've been forced to reintroduce moose to Colorado."

"A balance," the candidate mumbled, "a balance is always appropriate." He waved at a group of men across the room. "Alexandria, William, maybe we can chat more about the banking bill as the election nears."

"Of course." William reached to clasp his hand.

The candidate nodded. "We'll keep that banking bill in mind."

Alexandria nodded as well. "And you keep the success of the moose reintroduction project in mind."

Smiling, he backed away, lured to others with money.

William turned to his wife. "Moose?" He laughed out loud. "What the hell was that about?"

"Just keeping him on his toes, dear."

"Nicely done."

From across the room, William smiled at his golfing group as two of them waved to him. In uncharacteristic consideration, William resisted until Alexandria encouraged him to go, knowing it was where he wanted to be. He was no sooner off in their direction when two friends from the club besieged her.

"Love the gown, Alexandria." Daisy winked through thick make-up. "Sophia let out a slight gasp when you walked in."

"Sophia is a gasp, though there's nothing slight about her." She laughed, turning to her friend Leslie. "I love the black gowns, both of you, so sleek and formal. Black and blue, you and me, ready to do a little damage."

"Damage? I love it," Daisy acted shocked.

Alexandria leaned in. "I've got an idea, a little mother-daughter thing. Is your Vail house free next weekend?"

Leslie, sharing Alexandria's typical reserve, thought for a moment. "I believe so."

"The Aspen are changing. They should be golden by next week. How about we take the girls after school Friday? On Saturday we could horseback ride at Summerset Ranch."

Daisy's manicured hand touched her chest. "Brittney would love that, though I'll have to think about the horse thing." Her hand moved to Leslie's forearm. "Think Allison would want to go?"

"Horseback riding? Are you kidding? Allison may be packing already." Leslie scanned the room.

"Then it's a date." Alexandria confirmed.

"But do we, us women, have to ride horses." Daisy waved her perfect ruby nails as if the thought was repulsive.

Alexandria waved. "Oh love, get off your high horse."

She could see William across the room, the group having moved to a small balcony where cigar smoke lifted into a cloud. Near them stood Sophia, holding Robert's coattail. As Alexandria approached, her mother-in-law's sneer was unmistakable.

"Good evening, Sophia." Cold shivered up her spine.

Sophia offered a surprised Amway smile. Robert welcomed her warmly, his eyes moving down stopping at her neckline.

"William looks quite handsome tonight, doesn't he?" Curt overtones reverberated from Sophia.

"Your son's a dashing man."

They both looked his direction. "And so successful."

Alexandria moistened her lips. "Driven by riches."

Robert stiffened. "Designer dress? A gift from William?"

With a slight wave, she winked. "Off the rack. Bought it myself." Alexandria could stand no more of this manufactured pleasantness. "Still planning on dinner with Josephine tomorrow?"

"Of course," Robert reassured.

Sophia's smile turned genuine. "How is my little angel?"

"Looking forward to tomorrow night. I'll have her call you after school." Alexandria blew a soft kiss as she escaped politely.

On the terrace, a band played smooth jazz from years before. In the corner, three men were sharing stories. Alexandria seized the moment.

All three men were prominent, and it took her little time. With the skill she'd learned so well, she quickly had their commitment. It was a new venture. A school-to-work cooperative sponsored by the Foundation to support inner city Denver kids in need. Give them a job, guidance with mentors, and keep them off the streets moving toward something after high school. Not too artsy, but in her heart, it was a greater purpose.

As she bid them goodbye, a strong voice came from beside her. "You look so beautiful, I'm afraid to leave you alone. Too many men with leering eyes."

William's words sent a spike of guilt into her chest. "Oh, William, don't be silly."

She could feel William's cold hand against her bare back, his breathe heavy with cigar smoke. He was her husband, she his wife, and they made an appropriate picture for the Post's Sunday Society Section, that is, until she had begun to avoid the camera.

It was eleven o'clock when they exited the club, and stood waiting for the valet to retrieve William's Mercedes.

Staring straight ahead, he spoke without looking. "I'm a bit inattentive sometimes, aren't I?"

Alexandria grinned sadly. "Is that a question you want me to answer or your own personal observation?

"Maybe better left as a personal insight." While his word was disconcerting, his tone was playful. "Poetry, huh?"

"By the lake," she answered, "poetry."

There was a slight melody in his response. "*Nowhere man please listen, You don't know what you're missing, Nowhere man, the world is at your command.*"

The valet pulled the Mercedes next to the curb, and William reached down opening the door for his wife. She turned slightly, lowering into the seat. "The Beatles?"

William smiled appreciation at the slender length of her legs stretching to the driveway. "John Lennon," he answered, watching as she pivoted. "A man of poetry who had money but was always searching for meaning."

Shrugging, he closed her door, and she watched his shadow move around the car.

Alexandria was resting quietly on the soft leather watching the lights of the boulevard boutiques pass by. The champagne felt pleasant in her mind, and she thought of how years before she had enjoyed riding in his car along Interstate 70 across the desert of eastern Colorado into the waves of Kansas wheat.

Her words were a reaction. "Pull in there."

"What?"

"Pull in there?" She pointed at the lights of the neon sign.

"Why?"

"William, our lives are boring. Life should be fun." She laughed. "Just do as I say."

"Our lives aren't boring."

She reached for the steering wheel. "Turn, William!"

Startled, William followed her directions into the parking lot of a neighborhood bar. The Mercedes in park, he turned, and she put her fingers to his lips quieting him. Pulling the end of his bow tie, it fell into two black ribbons. When she tugged at one end, it slid from his neck, and she dropped it on the seat.

"Come on." She stepped from the car.

Before William could protest, she had closed the door and was walking toward the blinking *open* sign. William watched her in the rear view mirror, confused as whether to be irritated at her shenanigans or humored by her playfulness. The answer came as she walked in the slight glow of the parking lot lights.

Still not fully convinced, he opened the car door, calling to her. "Alexandria, let's not go in there."

Without looking back, she waved for him to follow.

"Damn it Alexandria. Let's go home."

Despite his words, she could hear the surrendering tone.

"William," she turned walking backward in her sashaying gown. "Please, just once let's have some fun away from the tuxedo crowd." Then she did a two-step to the entrance with a Moose Drool beer sign in the window.

When William pushed through the door, he felt the discomfort of the gloom. A lanky girl with dishwater hair was draped on a redneck at the end of the bar. Judging from what he saw, it was a place his firm's custodians would frequent. Clearly out-of-place, you could not have guessed it from Alexandria's grin.

When William moved toward her, a wave of self-consciousness swept through him. He slipped his tuxedo jacket down his arms and let it hang fully in one hand. He could handle any situation, yet he was unaccustomed to this feeling, lacking the instantaneous respect always afforded him.

The bartender moved down the wooden rail.

"Two draws?" Alexandria sang.

"Awe, no," William interrupted.

Alexandria stared intently, smiling happily that he was even there. "Beer, William, is what you drink in a bar."

"I'd prefer a scotch."

Alexandria heard a slight scuff from the bartender. She agreed, "Two beers."

"I haven't had a beer in . . ."

Alexandria cut him off, ". . . in too long."

The bartender sat two foamy mugs before them, beer sloshing onto the bar. William patience waned, picking his up as she brought hers to where they joined with a clang.

"To relaxed inhibitions, long deep kisses, and beer buzzes."

She took a hard, full swig, and William grinned at the ridiculous foam mustache left on her lip.

"Long deep kisses and beer buzzes?" William stiffened. "How much champagne have you had?"

"This is a bar, so drink your damn beer." She swatted his shoulder as if killing an arrant mosquito.

She glared over her glass mug. Her eyes would not leave his, blue crystals dancing in a way that made him nervous. Once again, he glanced down the bar where the redneck gave him a nod and two-fingered salute. Conceding, William took his own slight swallow of the fraught tasting liquid.

His face grimaced. "Not fond of it, Alexandria."

"But William," she lifted her glass, "beer is not a taste so much as a feeling. It's the belief that all is good in the world and a cold one makes it perfect. And if all is not good in the world, a beer says *What the hell,* and for a little bit life is better."

William looked at her, puzzled. "It still doesn't taste good."

The redneck and draped lady walked over to the jukebox, dropped some change, and began pushing buttons. The songs were solid but warm, and Alexandria took William by the hand and led him to the small dance floor.

The redneck had on butt-tight jeans and a shirt with the sleeves torn off at his bicep. He showed dance floor smoothness, more athletic than expected. Alexandria led William through a slow informal motion similar to the love-locked dances she remembered from high school. William moved his hand over Alexandria's bare back and the sequins to the slight curve of her hips. Discomfort rose in William with Alexandria's silent sigh.

"William, we've got to have more fun in our lives."

"And this is fun?"

"If you'll let it be."

She squeezed his butt and felt him tighten in resistance. His shoulders rose in an upward tension. Alexandria watched his eyes for a minute. They were dark eyes. Not the shining eyes she'd married, but the troubled eyes of business stress.

"Laugh for a minute, William. Without thinking about money or your position or what your father expects, let's laugh."

As unexpected as the moment, for the first time in so long he laughed, laughed at the absurdity of being in this bar and the realization that he wanted her. William followed her back to the bar and took a drink of beer. His face cringed at the taste, then, once again, he laughed.

Alexandria took a long, deep swallow, her glass nearing empty. "I want our lives to be fun," she told her husband. "I just want us to have fun together. You and me, remember us William?"

He answered with sad eyes, "Vaguely."

Smiling back, a sad but thankful smile, she turned to the bartender, waving her empty mug.

After Alexandria's three beers and William's three quarters of a beer, they thanked the bartender and nodded a good evening. Crossing the parking lot, Alexandria forced him to hold hands. She faced William as they reached the car, turning to give him a warm, long kiss.

As she released, he glanced side-to-side to see if anyone was watching. Alexandria grabbed William's face. Forcing him to look at her. "Take me home, William, and let's have some more fun."

William emerged from his bathroom wrapped in a thick terry cloth robe. Alexandria stood leaning against the pedestal footboard. Still dressed in the blue sequined gown, the glitter reflected the candles she'd lit.

Her eyes seductively staring at him, her hands rose to her shoulders, pushing the narrow straps free. The beautiful blue gown fell to the floor, and he saw her fully naked in a way he had not seen her in many years. Reminding him of another woman, a pang of guilt rushed through his chest. Aroused, William crossed the room.

Alexandria kissed him lightly as she turned him with his back to the bed. Pressing against him, he fell onto the bed, the robe lying open. She leaned forward kissing him as her tongue moved slowly over his chest to his pelvis.

William felt the sensations growing, fighting the discomfort in what she was doing. His mind began to ache as his eyes scanned the ceiling. The feeling of exposure caused fear to consume him. Her lips were here and there. Displeased at his vulnerability and the touch of her kisses, anxiety grew, and his body became rigid.

"Alexandria."

She looked up to see his demand for control. Unimpressed, she whispered, "I want to please you, William. I want you to feel this."

His head shook, glaring intently as her lips moved back down onto his chest and around his navel.

"It's so beautiful. Just let me." She took his hands from her shoulders and rested them on his chest. "For a few minutes, relax and let me make love to you."

She moved to kiss him again, and vulnerability swept over him. Still, there was pleasure, and he fought the guilt. Alexandria pressed gently, her hands against his hips, holding him beneath her. For a moment he saw the ceiling, and wondered why. He had never made love and seen a ceiling. He closed his eyes, feeling her above him. Again, he panicked. Opening his eyes, she was over him, dominating like a New York hooker.

The sensation was overwhelming, that she would be so cheap to do such a thing. In one swift move he grabbed, pulled her up on the bed, and took back the power. William pressed Alexandria backward, forcing himself upon her, and with a driving, demanding thrust he took her for his own.

She stood for a long time in her bathroom, washing as tears silently streamed down her face. When she came back to the bed, he pretended to be asleep, his back already turned from her, but she would not allow it. She eased into the bed, wrapping her arms around him, pressing to his backside. Her head close to his, she breathed softly to allow the comfort to engulf her, but the cold was too dominant.

Eventually, as he slept, she surrendered and turned away.

Chapter 17

It was that wealthy attitude of underemphasizing that allowed Ben to describe it as *The Cabin*. William and Alexandria had visited here last Easter skiing with Leslie and Ben. In actuality, it was a six-bedroom mountain retreat with a wide deck and a redwood Jacuzzi to sit and watch the skiers complete their run at the bottom of the slope that ends in your backyard.

Leslie and Daisy had already slipped into the Jacuzzi with a pitcher of gin gimlets at arm's reach. The cool evening was attracting Alexandria, and she excused herself to walk the bike path through the village. It did not matter that the sun had slipped behind the mountains. Alexandria wore warming layers, a tank top with a tee shirt, under a denim shirt, under a thick, floppy sweater.

Strangely she felt alive, as if her spirit had recovered with her return to the mountains. The stream beside the path was low this time of year, the water reflecting in the lamppost's glow. She wondered what had become of him. No requests to the Foundation. He must be in North Dakota charming brides and prom queens. Why had he not taken her advice? She could have made it easy for him. Sadly, she thought, he'd left the mountains.

She remembered waking alone in his bed only to find him quietly sipping hot tea on the patio. She loved the memory of the way he made her feel, but most of all, she missed the way he listened to her when they talked.

Shivering as the night turned cooler, she wrapped her arms tightly to her body, and turned to begin the pleasant walk back. Friends and lovers, she thought. Never before had she been a friend and lover at the same time.

Stepping from the bridge, she looked up to see the pleasantly dressed man watching her. Something was familiar about him. She thought of asking if they knew each other, but his head dropped, and he turned away. Alexandria watched him walk into the darkness, glancing back once to see her. Strange, she thought.

They were up early, motivated by the silliness of the girls making a breakfast of thick, gooey pancakes. It was mid-morning when they arrived at the ranch where painted ponies and palominos stood chewing on hay. Excited, the girls raced to the corral claiming horses as their own..

A muscular man with slightly bowed legs introduced himself. Bud was a square jawed, tight Levi wearing cowboy with a big, silver belt buckle. He gave them instructions, safety rules, and described the details of the day. They would ride for two hours then break for a cowboy lunch of grub over an open fire.

Alexandria boldly went first, her foot into the stirrup with a swing of her leg up and over onto the hard, leather seat pressing Alexandria's legs out and around the horse's belly.

As the horses moved down the trail, Daisy complained about a broken nail. Alexandria ignored her, watched Josie, and Josie kept turning back and waving to her. To Josie, it was no effort. She moved in the rhythm of the horse's gait. Daisy, on the other hand, had this pained look as if caught in an unnatural act. With each stride, she jolted against the saddle and grimaced.

When the sun had reached mid-sky, the scent and colors of the mountains had become Alexandria's escape. Josie would point to each patch of Aspen or sun-streaked peak, saying how beautiful it was. Her daughter had that look in her eyes, that gazing, absorption of everything around her.

Recently, Josephine had become concerned about things that shouldn't matter. It was the little signs that bothered Alexandria. Alexandria had grown to shudder at the sight of a blue blazer or a white silk blouse with little embroidered anchors on the collar, yet that is what her daughter almost always wore. It matched the subtle attitude she'd developed with her nose in a slight tilt.

To make matters worse, Sophia insisted on taking Josie to little style shows at private boutiques designed to attract women who paid outrageous prices on designer outfits. Such a contrast to her own parents who had bought Josie a new Jayhawk tee shirt and canvas Keds. But now, as she watched Josie riding and pointing, she held out hope that her attitude might change.

As they rode, Alex decided she would buy Josie a pair of hiking boots and a daypack. In the spring they would hike in the snowmelt, water following the trail where it was not still snow-covered.

At an open bed of red rocks scattered like sculptures in a garden, Bud dismounted, directing each to tie their horses to a hitching post. He sent the girls to gather sticks and small logs for the fire while Leslie and Alex helped with the food.

Daisy stood in her studded jeans bending and stretching, rubbing each bun with soothing hands, complaining about how the studs pressed into her backside with every bounce.

Leslie only laughed, whispering to the ladies, "Those aren't the only studs around here." Her eyebrows lifted toward Bud who was squatting down, jeans tight, and beginning to prepare the fire ring.

"I'd trade studs to be back in the Jacuzzi," was all Daisy said.

As the fire began to blaze Josie's eyes grew wide at their lunch bubbling over an open fire. On Monday at the Academy the girls would tell their friends of the discolored tins, the thick black beans, and the sauce that dripped globs from the forks. Somehow, with the distasteful look on the faces of their friends, they would gain hero status.

After a full belly of bean, Bud shared, "If you want, we can take a few minutes to wonder the rock formation just up the gully. They're a maze of tall red rocks, or there's a pretty impressive waterfall about a mile up the trail."

"There's a third option." Daisy didn't wait for a response. "We lay here with our eyes closed and let the sun warm our faces."

"Where's your sense of adventure?" Alexandria nudged her.

She tilted her head back. "I left it in the Jacuzzi last night."

Bud gave his mouth one last wipe with the back of his flannel sleeve. "Hundreds of years of water have molded this canyon. Ain't much water now, but the rocks are pretty dynamic." Bud pointed along the edge of the canyon. "It's very memorable."

Alexandria glanced at Josie. "Bud, is it a clear trail to the waterfall?"

"Can't miss it."

"If Josie and I hike to the falls, will you wait for us?"

Josie looked up startled.

Daisy stopped putting on her lipstick. "Well," she looked puzzled. "I guess we could be sun goddesses while we wait."

"This should be fun." Alexandria exaggerated excitement. "We'll be back in what…about an hour."

Bud shrugged. "Hour fifteen."

Alexandria pushed her hands against her knees, and stood pointing the way. "It's you and me, Baby."

"But can't we stay with the others?" her daughter pleaded.

Alex put an arm around her, squeezing playfully. "Where's your sense of adventure?"

"Is this safe, Mom?"

"What would be unsafe about it, Honey?"

Josie was getting used to questions answered with a question. "Lots of stuff. We're alone in the woods, we don't know where we're going, we could fall, and the animals. Snakes and bears."

"Let's see." Alexandria thought. They were already starting the climb toward the waterfalls. "Wild animals? Too cold for snakes, and if we were lucky enough to see a bear, well, there are only black bears in Colorado, and they're pretty timid." Alexandria wiggled her bottom, and Josie giggling. Then Alexandria added, "You do have to watch out for flying monkeys."

Josie laughed, and Alexandria reached back to take her hand.

"You lead for a while. Just follow the trail."

Josie nodded, skipping ahead in her barely worn Keds.

Half way to the falls, Alexandria stopped on a switch back to rest and offered Josie some water. Scanning the canyon below, they could see the others as only specks. Daisy hadn't moved, but Leslie and the girls were wandering through the red rock maze, the girls dancing as they walked.

Josie sat down on the ground, and took a drink from their water bottle. "How much farther, Mom. I can't breath."

Alexandria squatted next to her. "It's the altitude. You'll get used to it. The higher we get, the thinner the air, less oxygen." She pointed at the mountain. "How many colors can you count?"

"I stopped counting colors in first grade."

"Grumpy when you're tired, aren't you." Alexandria reached, rubbing the back of Josie's neck. "Start from the top."

Josie shrugged. "The top is black."

"That's one. Now, how about the face?"

"What's the face?"

"That flat part, the cliff." Alexandria pointed to the mountain.

"Brown and red." Josie leaned forward. "There's some white or maybe yellow too."

"What kind of trees?"

"Christmas trees and Cottonwoods."

"What kind of Christmas?"

Josie wrinkled her forehead and guessed. "Pines?"

"That's right." Alexandria decided to leave the Aspen for another lesson. "Have you ever seen a waterfall?"

Josie looked irritated. "Sure. Lots on T.V."

Alex corrected. "Have you ever felt a waterfall?"

Josie gave her mother that pre-teenager look, mimicking another despondent lesson from T.V.

"Have you ever sat on the edge of a mountain pond and felt the mist of a waterfall drift over you?"

"Mom, you know I haven't."

"Today you will." Alexandria stood up. "It's a cool massage."

Josie's mouth twisted a bit, her eyes frowning. "Sounds wet."

Hearing the slight rumble of rushing water, she moved ahead of her grumpy daughter confident the hordes of grizzly bears dancing through Josie's imagination would cause her to keep up.

"Your Grampy loves the mountains." Even in his advanced age, Alexandria knew Josie saw her grandfather as a strong man.

"He told me a story this summer."

"About what?"

"A big mountain you guys climbed."

"We hiked a lot of big mountains. Bigger hikes than this when I was your age?"

"Bigger?"

"Much bigger."

"How come Daddy doesn't like the mountains?"

"Oh honey," Alexandria stopped to breathe. "Your Daddy likes the mountains. He just has trouble finding time."

"Sometimes I wish he wouldn't work so much."

Alexandria listened for the water. "Me too, Honey. Me too." She motioned for Josie to listen. "Can you hear the rumble?"

Josie nodded.

"The waterfall," her mother said triumphantly.

"Waterfalls make that train sound?"

Alex nodded, "Yes, they do."

Josie ran off toward the sound, breathing no longer an issue.

When she caught up with Josie, her daughter stood a top a large boulder, reaching her hands toward the falls. From a hundred feet above, a narrow, full stream of water fell. Three ducks played in the water opposite the falls, and Josie giggled as the mist covered her face and cooled her arms.

"It's so cold," she shivered.

"It was snow just minutes ago."

Josie climbed through the mist until she stood above Alexandria on the fallen rocks beside the cliff. Though not that far away, Josie looked small against the cliff. Alex wanted to call out a warning, but held her self back, knowing that Josie needed the confidence to go on. Soon she edged over the wet rocks, reaching her hand into the streaming water of the falls. She shivered again, laughing, and touched her wet fingers to her lips, tasting.

Climbing down to the edge of the pond, Josie squatted to wave her fingers across the water's surface, coaxing the ducks closer. She unzipped her fanny pack and took the cellophane from a graham cracker breaking off little pieces. The ducks were quick scooting over the pond toward her to gobble up the crumbs left floating on the water. Her big wave made sure her mother was watching.

When they were together again, Alexandria said, "Looks like you made a couple of friends."

Josie grinned before her. "When I had food they liked me, and they were so cute. Did you see me touch the waterfall? The water is even colder there."

"Even colder?"

"Really, really cold. Almost as cold as snow."

All they way down the trail, Josie talked until they reached the others. When she ran toward them, she was already shouting her tales of ducks and falling water.

Bud smiled at her excitement. "So you made it to the falls?"

"It was beautiful, Bud." Alexandria said. "Thanks for waiting."

"Only prolonging the inevitable." Daisy still did not open her eyes. "I suppose now I have to wrap my legs around that beast. My butt will never be the same."

"Probably wider." Alexandria smiled as she helped Daisy stand.

Daisy gripped her friend's hand. "My butt is not wide."

"No it's not," Alexandria grinned.

"No," Daisy stood beside her, open-eyed and playful. Her voice quieted. "My butt is sensually full."

"Okay," Alexandria gave a teasing response. "Sensually full."

The evening had turned dark by the time they reached the middle of the village. Leslie and Alexandria were walking arm in arm, talking and warming each other. Daisy was dragging not far behind, both hands pushing firmly against the small of her back.

"Aren't you sore?"

Leslie glanced back. "We aerobercise. You gin gimletercise."

"Yea, yea, make fun, but my ass still hurts."

Leslie squeezed Alexandria's arm tighter. "Thanks lady. I'd forgotten how much fun this stuff could be."

"The girls are having a great time too."

"Horseback riding with Bud was perfect."

The restaurant would have looked elegant had it not been for the turtlenecks, wool sweaters, and the waiter's polo jerseys. From the bar through the cut-glass double doors, the sound of a guitar and soft love songs drifted into the restaurant. The European ambience was an imitation of a century-old Swiss cafe.

"Let's try something new." Alexandria raised her eyebrows, daring them.

Daisy now shook her head. "As long as it doesn't involve a horse."

The waiter appearing beside them was more refined then Bud but just as ruggedly handsome.

Alexandria welcomed him. "I'm Alex. This is Daisy and Leslie." She acknowledged. "We'd like to try something different." She lifted the menu, winking at the waiter. "Could we have a half order of these?" She pointed at the Rocky Mountain Oysters.

"What's that?" Leslie leaned toward them.

Alexandria glanced at the waiter, cutting him off with her look. "Fried oysters. Let's try new things." Her eyes told the waiter not to say a word.

"Fried oysters and your best wheat beer."

"Beer? Augh." Daisy waved. "And a gin gimlet for me, please."

The young waiter nodded politely. "We've got a very tasteful wheat lager that I think you'll appreciate. I'll get these," he pointed at the menu, "and be back for your dinner requests."

When the waiter returned, placing the beers before them and the clear crystal plate in the middle of the table, Alexandria was pleased at how much they looked like breaded oysters. Poking one with her fork, she grinned and lifted it before them.

"I'm guessing the best way to eat this is just plop it in your mouth and chew."

"A delicacy," the waiter encouraged. "Chew slowly and deliberately to fully appreciate the texture and rich flavor."

Alex took a drink of beer to hide her expression, and looked at the oyster. Thinking of Mickey, she took a long, hard, daring swallow, and placed the fried delicacy gently on her tongue. As instructed she chewed slowly and deliberately, knowing both Mickey and Jimmy would be proud. She hadn't remembered the almost pleasant taste, but once the breading was gone the familiar texture felt unnatural in her mouth. She took another drink of beer and swallowed hard.

Alex smiled at the waiter. "My compliments."

The waiter winked, enjoying this, obviously deciding not to leave until all were eaten. He lifted the plate and moved it between Leslie and Daisy. "This is one of our favorite appetizers, a chef's special. Alex, wouldn't you agree it's worthy."

"Absolutely." She took another drink of beer, eyes wide.

Leslie shrugged, "Looks good, and I like oysters."

She pressed her fork into the breading. Daisy did the same. Each slowly examined the oyster as if appreciating its rarity. Leslie bit first, chewing. Daisy followed. She chewed as if in thought, approving of the taste. After a moment, they dabbed the corners of their mouths with a linen napkin then reached for their drinks and sipped. Her two friends actually seemed to enjoy the oysters, finishing the remaining three as Alexandria freely offered her share to Daisy, much to her friend's culinary delight.

The waiter smiled at Alexandria. "May I fully describe the quality of this delicacy to your friends?"

"Please do." Alexandria was hiding behind her beer.

His dark hair hung down over his forehead as he squatted, his toned forearms resting on the white tablecloth. With green eyes slightly below theirs, he looked up smiling.

"Actually ladies, these are called Rocky Mountain Oysters." Both Leslie and Daisy nodded, appreciating the attention. "The strange thing is these oysters aren't from the Rocky Mountain region. We import ours from

Texas. They grow them there, and you know what they say. Everything is bigger in Texas."

Alex's laughter brought beer running down her chin, and she lifted the napkin to her mouth as her friend's queer looks turned back to the waiter.

"You wanted to try something different?" He nodded to her. "Leslie. These aren't actually oysters."

Leslie still smiled, questioning, "Not oysters?"

"Not exactly."

"What type of seafood were they?" Daisy tapped the table.

"Actually Daisy. They aren't even seafood. These are breaded, well . . ." the waiter grinned broadly as Alex smirked. He looked down slightly to regain his composure. "Ladies, what you have just eaten are the breaded testicles of a Texas Longhorn steer."

Leslie's face turned white.

Daisy just looked aghast. "Breaded what!" Blurted from her between her ruby red lips.

"It's a delicacy appreciated by many. Testicles. Calf testicles." The added, "Thick, round, baby bull testicles."

"Oh my God." Daisy reached for her gin gimlet, gulping.

Leslie stared at Alex in disbelief. "What have you done?"

Alex laughed. "They tasted quite good, don't you think?"

"Oh God, yes, they tasted good." Leslie shook her head. "But they were testicles." Her face became distorted. "I ate testicles."

The waiter was controlling his own expression. "Not only did you eat, but you *chewed slowly and deliberately.*"

Leslie reached for her beer, using it like mouthwash.

Daisy reached out her drink glass. "Bring me a double."

"Did you know what these were?" Leslie glared at her friend.

Alexandria's eyebrows rose, her shoulders a playful shrug. "I may have had the pleasure once. Just like oysters, don't you think?"

"I can't believe you did this." Leslie drank more, unsure if she should be angry or laugh.

"It goes right along with the ass-busting horseback riding." Daisy rolled her eyes. "Ass-busting horse and Texas bull testicles. My God, Alexandria, what are you doing to us."

"Isn't life fun!" Alexandria thought about apologizing, but she was having too much fun. "Now, after our meals let's go into the bar, listen to some good acoustic music, drink beer, and talk girl talk."

Leslie stared at Alexandria. "You tricked us into eating balls."

Alexandria shrugged her playful smile. "I ate one too."

"Yes," Leslie answered with a playful irritation. "Then you kindly gave us the rest of your share."

"My God." Daisy's tongue hung from between her lips. "I've thought of biting balls before, but well, they weren't so beefy."

Alex was still laughing, the other two still aghast when the waiter returned. He sat the second round of drinks before each of them and stood formally to take their orders.

"Ladies, our specialty tonight is a wonderful 16 oz. t-bone with a vintage wine sauce. That is, of course, if you're interested in eating the rest of the bull."

The next afternoon, as they drove back down the mountain toward Denver, all was quiet. The girls, having giggled till the wee morning hours, were sleeping in the back seat. Emerging from the Johnson Tunnel, Alexandria stared out the passenger window watching the stream racing by beside them.

Her heart ached leaving the mountains. She was returning to days of going to the office, watching from her window, and wanting to be in the distant high country living a life different from her own. She dreaded, returning.

The night before she had picked a maroon leather booth in the corner where they had privacy yet could see the guitar player. They listened to music, told stories and laughed, things never discussed with their husbands present.

Daisy had surprised them talking about an affair, a cheap, silly thing with the married attorney who had settled her mother's estate. Three important trips to Dallas to close the estate, two trips after the estate was long closed. Meeting him in her hotel suite, there were rambunctious encounters of repetitious sex. Then guilt had gotten to him, and she had come back to Denver to live happily ever after with her ongoing sexual fantasies.

Leslie had asked in disbelief how she could do it. How could Daisy not be wrought with guilt? How could she come home to a husband, talk to him, laugh with him, and make love with him? How did guilt separate itself from her marriage?

Daisy had blown it off, challenging Leslie. Hadn't she ever been tempted? Didn't she have her own fantasies? Sure, like the steamy side of a soap opera but never actions. How could she?

But Alexandria had captured their imaginations with her tale of her own fantasy. A man she said she would create if she could, a man of the mountains, a rugged young man with a solid chest and arms big enough to sweep her off her feet. A man who climbed mountains and drank beer, a man who lived by a stream where he watched the sun set in the cool evening air.

This man would share her life instead of giving it to her and expecting happiness. This man thrived. He was sensitive, caring, and so strong in his sense of himself. This man would know how to love and please a woman.

Alexandria glanced back from watching the scenery to see Leslie looking at her, staring as she had the night before.

"Fantasizing again?"

Alexandria nodded.

"You okay?"

"I'm fine," she answered.

William was coming out the front door when they pulled into the circular drive. He greeted them with a false smile, his eyes darting at Alexandria as he did. Opening the car door, he lifted Josephine from the seat where she fought to wake up.

"Bye, bye Josie." Brittney whispered.

"Bye." Josie was cradled in her father's arms.

By the time they reached the front entryway, Josie was going on about the horses and the waterfall and Bud. William sat her down in the foyer patting her head as he listened.

"We had a wonderful time, didn't we Josie?"

Josie was still talking when William interrupted, "What's this *Josie* stuff?" Suddenly, he became stoic.

"Oh William, I'm not sure. Somewhere it just started and Josie liked it, so we kept using it."

William's glare was unquestionable. He looked first at Alexandria, then at Josephine, and back to Alexandria. "Her name is not Josie. Her name is Josephine. That is her proper name, and that is what we will call her."

"But Daddy, I like Josie." She smiled up at him.

William's glare disappointed her. "I'm sorry Josephine, but it's not your name. Now please go to your room. I want to talk to your mother."

"But Daddy, I like being called Josie." Her blue eyes pleading.

"To your room, please." He was unmoving. "Josephine, now!"

Tears began forming in Josephine's eyes as she turned, running up the stairs. Her little girl anger was obvious as she pounded her feet into each step of the curved staircase.

His glare turned to his wife. "I don't know where this came from or what's gotten into you, but I will not stand for it. I do not want to hear the name Josie. Do you understand me?"

Alexandria stood strong, unmoving. "William, my goodness. What does it hurt?"

He stiffened. "You must understand, Alexandria. We are a proper family without room for triviality. Her name is Josephine. It is what her grandparents expect, it is what I expect, and it is what you should expect. Josephine is her given name, and it is the only name she will be called."

Alexandria was furious. "What is this all about, William? It's just a name, so what's got you so upset?"

William straightened, his back more rigid. "My parents stopped by to see her Saturday afternoon, and here I was alone while you were off roughhousing in the mountains with some guy named Bud. How do I explain?"

"I told you where we were going. "What's wrong, William? We just went up to Vail."

Things had not gone as expected with the merger, and he had left work on Friday to find that he was alone. At first it was good until the phone calls started, lawyers to lawyers, bank presidents to bank presidents, and political manipulations. It had been a nightmare with no one but the help to attend to his needs.

Then on Saturday, while his mother had sat disappointed that Josephine was not there, he and his father had closed the den door spending an hour on a less than productive conference call with Senator Clayton's staff. When he hung up, he had immediately made plans to fly back to New York hoping he wouldn't be spending the week bouncing between New York and Washington fighting for the political control the merger demanded.

"You should have been here to help this weekend. I had banking business to attend to, and you left me stranded."

"William, dear, it was not intended." She was pleading now. "I told you we were going, but it certainly wasn't to strand you."

Unyielding, he pressed her. "This silliness of the nickname Josie is intentional, so it will stop."

"Why must you be so rigid? She likes it."

William's jaw clinched as he leaned into her. She felt the heat of his breath against her forehead.

"It-is-not-a-simple-thing. I will not allow you to play games with family tradition. Her name is Josephine Sophia Chadwick, and she will be called Josephine and nothing else." He pressed against her as his voice lowered. "Somehow you have trivialized our family, and I will not allow it … and quit running off on weekends. What the hell's up there anyway? Rocks and trees. You need to be here, not in the mountains. Do you understand me, Alexandria?"

Alexandria stared straight into his eyes. "Unfortunately, I do, but do you understand that your daughter is a young girl who must some day establish her own identity. She's simply desiring some independence."

Veins pressed outward from William's neck. "She's a Chadwick. It's a blessing, and you better God damn well appreciate it. Honestly, Alexandria, I don't know what the hell's gotten into you."

She dropped her head, afraid she would say *yes, it is a blessing, but at times a curse.* Afraid she'd tell him exactly what had gotten into her, she glared at the floor between them.

"That's better." William turned, striding down the foyer and into his den.

That evening Alexandria and Josephine read together the story by Enos Mills "A Rainy Day at the Stream's Source." Josephine lay in her mother's arms, each reading a page, and enjoying the story of the mountains around Estes before man and the establishment of the national park.

When Josephine fell asleep, Alexandria tucked the covers close around her daughter, kissing her forehead.

"Sleep sweetly, Josie," she whispered.

Chapter 18

It was one of those *I'm-not-in-the-mountains mornings.* Every morning had been like that for the three weeks since they'd returned from Vail. Swiveling in her desk chair, she gazed toward the foothills and distant snowcaps dreaming of where she was not.

Hearing Jennifer's distinguishable knock, Alexandria turned and invited her in faking a cheerful *Good morning.*

"How was Halloween? Spooky?" Jennifer pressed her skirt smoothly under her as she sat in the familiar leather chair.

"A little spooky, a lot of fun." Alexandria mocked a frightened face. "I took Josie to the Halloween Night at the zoo."

"Fun?"

"Grandmamma Sophia was upset that we wouldn't be doing the grand mansion tour to show off her perfect grand-daughter, but Josie and I had talked and decided. The zoo was great fun."

"Lions and tigers and bears, oh my."

Alexandria tapped her heals together. "Giraffes, baboons and penguins, too."

Jennifer waved a piece of paper in the air, her laptop in the other hand. "Got something to show you."

Alexandria reached for the paper as Jennifer handed it to her.

"It's weird," Jennifer pointed. "Out of the blue some guy emails and asks for a grant. I printed this copy and forwarded you the email." Jennifer pointed at the hardcopy. "No references, nothing similar to what we have funded in the past. In fact, it's not even in Denver. The guy has nothing to support his request except some amazing digital photographs he attached. I emailed him for clarification, and he said he was encouraged to apply by a friend. He's under the impression that the Chadwick Foundation supports starving artists."

Jennifer placed the laptop on the table and turned it toward Alexandria. Before her, on the full screen of the computer she stared as the blues, greens, reds, and whites of her mystical mountain waterfall. Despite the smile, her eyes began to water. The ache was incredible, but the image was magnificent. She envisioned herself entering the water, feeling the cold and cleansing chill rush over her body. Closing her eyes, Mickey was at the opposite end, watching and appreciating in his magnificently athletic way, so capable, kind, and gentle.

Alexandria turned to face the mountains, staring into the light, and unable to face Jennifer. "So what does he want?"

"A load of money." Jennifer reached for the computer, and the image changed. "This one's of a deer and a fawn?"

"An elk."

"What?" Jennifer asked.

Alexandria turned and pointed at the image. "It's an elk and a calf. More typical in the mountains. Are there other slides?"

It was as if she were in The White Room, watching each image appear and fill the full screen of the computer. The details were of high resolution, the colors vivid, and the images unique in the way they were captured. Inwardly, her heart ached, yet she felt the joy that he had returned to her life, though he would never know.

Jennifer found herself turning from Alexandria. Whatever it was, it was clear in Alexandria's eyes that a moment of privacy was occurring, and Jennifer, as much as she was confused, tried to respect whatever was happening.

"Quite talented," Alexandria spoke causally though the slight catch in the throat was impossible to ignore. "So what's he want?"

"To travel and build his collection. He's a young, idealistic guy who wants to open a gallery in Estes Park."

Alexandria laughed at Jennifer. "Might I remind you that you too are a bit young and idealistic?"

Jennifer shrugged, "Yes, but I didn't write and ask somebody for six figures based on a few photographs, amazing as they are."

Alexandria glanced at the email. The exact amount she had anticipated. Just like Mickey. What the hell, go for the gold. Brash in his approach, his boldness pleased Alexandria.

"Okay," she tapped her desktop. "I'll glance over what you emailed me and let you know."

"That's it." Jennifer remained puzzled.

"For now," Alexandria answered.

"Okay."

"Okay." Her head down, she waved casually, ending the conversation.

When Jennifer stepped out of the office, closing the door, Alex allowed herself to cry. Softly and intimately, she had not until now. She had come back and tried to put it all behind her. Her resurrected confidence, reborn in the moment of rappelling eighty feet down a cliff had helped her adjust. But now, she just wanted to cry and be happy that Mickey was going to get his dream, so she stood staring out her office window, looking toward the mountains, and released the emotions.

.

Alexandria looked at the clock on the mantle. She pushed the intercom button on, pushed it off. She had to try and control this. Reaching for the phone again, she pushing Jennifer's extension.

"Yes." Jennifer sounded busy.

"Are you busy?" Alexandria half hoped she was.

"Nothing that can't wait. What's up?"

Her boss hesitated. She thought of Mickey standing at the top of Fall River Road, Mickey with his camera and a group of bold bull elk. "Can you come in for a moment?"

"Be right there."

Alexandria had barely hung up when Jennifer appeared in her doorway. She walked to the same chair she had sat in that morning and most days for the past three years.

"So, what's up?" Jennifer's said, sitting quietly and waiting.

Alexandria stepped around the desk, walked across the office, closed the fine oak door, and returned to sit in the other chair.

"I've been thinking about this for some time. The email we received sparked my interest." Alexandria's words were cautious. "There is so much concern over the ecology with the going green thing and global warming, save the whales and such. I have a feeling that we, people in general, are making this outdoor interest more than a trend. Nature and wildlife, you know, those sorts of things. I think it's something we as a society are embracing. Maybe it's time for us to expand beyond the local art scene and do something to support the environment."

Jennifer eyed her warily. "Okay," she spoke slowly. "For instance?"

"This young man who has the gallery plan. From the images he emailed, it's obvious he's talented."

Jennifer interrupted, "Yes, but they were just a few pictures?"

"A few very striking images," Alexandria corrected. "This is something I've been thinking about. Now an opportunity has presented itself."

"An opportunity?" Leaning forward, Jennifer eyed her friend. "What's going on, Alexandria? We've never talked about this." She sat back confused. "It has nothing to do with the strategic plan we've laid out, and you want to give some guy an extremely large amount of money because he sent you a few nice pictures?"

"Actually, no." The point of no return, Alexandria now was the one leaning forward. "I want this to be a very quiet experiment. Robert and William would never support this. Their vision doesn't go beyond the symphony. I, on the other hand, believe in it. This Foundation has been driven too long by their conservative projects. It's time to break out like we're doing with the mentoring project. I just don't want them to know it until we can demonstrate that we've been successful." Alexandria watched the younger woman's eyes, watching for her to bite.

"So," Jennifer's eyes did not waiver. "You're going to strengthen the Foundation by going against our plan and promote some mountain man with a camera?"

"Don't be opposed to new ideas, Jennifer." Alexandria's expression lightened in a weak effort.

Jennifer leaned back against staring past her boss. "I'm not opposed. It's just…you've never shown an interest before. Where's this coming from?"

"Trust me." Alexandria could not look at her. "Let's give him, that is if you agree he's good, let's give him," Alexandria appeared to be thinking, "let's give him twenty-five percent to do six months of photography work, and if you approve the work, we'll advance him, say fifty percent to open a gallery and the final twenty-five percent to carry him the first year."

Jennifer looked long and hard at Alexandria. "Okay, you're the boss. Make the call, set it up, and I'll work it from there." Jennifer reached for the email lying on Alexandria's desk. "He's in Bismarck, North Dakota for God's sake, but he says he'll be in Estes Park over Thanksgiving."

Alex's heart skipped a beat.

"Actually," Alexandria stood and walked over to the window watching the mountains to the west. "I'd prefer you make the call. I don't want to be personally involved in this project. You're ready to take the lead, so I want you to handle the entire project."

Jennifer stood and for a moment they were both quiet. Slowly, she walked to stand beside Alexandria. The quietness was disturbing as Jennifer looked to the same distant mountains.

Alexandria spoke first. "This is my personal effort to expand the Foundation's impact. I want you to work it, but you must be discreet. Nobody else can know."

"Nobody?" Jennifer repeated.

"Nobody," Alexandria reinforced. "You must handle all of the details. I do not want to be directly involved in any way except I will approve written documentation for your files including the grant and check distribution."

"I still don't understand." Jennifer folded her arms. "You want to expand; a new direction for the Foundation. You don't want to be personally connected." She saw Alexandria's slight nod. Something told her she should be quiet, but she pressed on. "You want me to sign some sort of a secret pact to fund this guy but never tell anybody?"

Alexandria did not look at Jennifer as she spoke. "I trust you completely." Her voice quieted, becoming methodical. "He can never know about me, who I am, or that I'm involved in any way."

Jennifer watched her friend staring out the window unable to look at her. For a long moment, neither spoke until Jennifer broke the silence.

"Okay. I'll set up something over Thanksgiving." Then added, "in Estes."

Alexandria stared straight ahead. "Perfect."

"So," Jennifer prodded, her hand reaching up and pressing against her boss's back. "Is this who the change is all about?"

Alexandria spoke in a whisper. "There has been no change."

"Babe, there's been a big change." Jennifer stood next to her rub the back of her arm. "A good change, a change to jeans and mountain hiking and the zoo on Halloween. You've become unstuffy."

Alexandria smiled at the thought. "Unstuffy?"

Jennifer laughed. "Yes, unstuffy. You've started laughing and making different decisions. Good decisions, heart focused decisions. Not decisions you thought Robert and William wanted you to make, but decisions you wanted to make." Then she added, "but this decision, this one is different."

Alexandria turned from the window without looking at Jennifer. "It is a good decision."

"But a private decision."

"Extremely private. I trust your discretion."

Jennifer watched the tears falling from Alexandria's cheeks. Her eyes were red and puffy, but her smile was steady and bright.

"This will make you happy?"

Alexandria nodded. "He cannot know about me."

"He who? Know what?" Jennifer tried to lighten the moment as she took the email copy from Alexandria's desk. When she reached the office door, she stopped, turning back to Alexandria. "He must be something amazing."

Alexandria had already turned back to the distant view.

Chapter 19

William called just as her workday ended. Allowing voicemail to answer, she had no desire to talk in the midst of her emotional roller coaster. It was her ride, and he was not invited.

At home, it was eight o'clock when Josie had gone to her bedroom to read and sleep into a night of innocence. Alexandria looked at the cell phone sitting on the table beside the sofa, and a twinge of guilt ran through her. She had purposefully ignored him.

He was in New York, probably exhausted, fighting to complete the deal of his lifetime. She knew he had scheduled intense meetings filled with political warfare. Things might have delayed his red-eye departure, and she should know if he would be crawling into their bed in the middle of the night.

Ironically, pressing the first favorite on her phone, she waited but quickly got his voicemail. He was either on the plane, she thought, or in a meeting. Maybe, if he had stayed, she could catch him at the hotel. She didn't really want to call, but the guilt kept hanging around, so she put the hotel name into the phone's web-browser and tapped her finger on the number that appeared.

"Esquire Hotel," the young male voice announced. "How can I be of service?

"This is Mrs. William Chadwick?" she said, less than enthusiastic.

"Yes, Mrs. Chadwick," he responded quickly. "It's nice to talk to you again."

Again? Alexandria hesitated, confused by the familiarity. "Is Mr. Chadwick in?" she added quickly.

"No," he spoke as if apologizing. "I'm afraid he's checked out. He left right after you did."

Alexandra stared at the telephone, unable to respond, holding it like a sad letter from a close friend offering shocking news.

"Is there anything I can help you with?"

"Um, no," she managed to say. "I was just hoping to catch him before he left. Thanks."

"We'll see you again soon, I'm sure Mrs. Chadwick." His cheeriness was contrary to her thoughts.

"Yes, soon," she answered flatly. "Soon."

She was still awake in the middle of the night when William came into their bedroom. She listened as he placed his luggage in the expansive closet, slipped into his bathroom, and closed the door. Five minutes later the bathroom door opened to the darkness of their bedroom. As she lay wrapped in sheets and wool blankets, her head deep in the pillow, she watched his shadow cross the room.

Then the bed stirred as he moved the covers away, sat on the edge, and slowly lay back onto the pillow. She listened as his breathing steadied, then quieted, and eventually turned into the slight snore of deep sleep. When it did, she rose, walked over the plush carpet, out onto the cold marble of the hallway, and down the curving staircase. Alexandria walked purposefully to the door leading to the pool, taking a thick fleece blanket from the couch.

She walked across the patio to the lounge chair and pulled the blanket around her seeking the warmth. There she sat, watching the black outline of the western range reflecting off of the glow of nighttime's city lights. In her mind there was anger at one and desire for another, but mostly, she felt guilt.

Chapter 20

Even with the snow touching the mountaintops, the late November morning felt like fall. Jennifer turned her VW convertible into the parking area of the Historic Stanley Hotel built in 1907 by those brothers with the neat little cars. As she parked, she stared at the Estes Park hotel whose fame had been renewed by the ghosts of *The Shining*. Ironically, a small herd of animals grazed lazily on the lawn. Are those elk, she questioned herself?

Her room was larger, unlike today's stop and sleeps yet typical of the early century grand hotels. She could not understand why the nervousness had crept into her stomach like that about-to-go-on-stage feeling. This was just a business meeting. Nothing more. She looked again into the guest room mirror. Heels or flats, and why did it matter. Heels flattered, flats simply provided comfort. She chose the heels.

The carpet on the wide stairway leading the one floor to the lobby was trimmed in bright white highlighting the cream walls. The lobby was empty save for the concierge and an elderly couple admiring the Stanley Steamer with its giant bicycle-type wheels. Jennifer walked the length of the lobby to the Cascades Restaurant where, greeted by the host, she requested a table with a view.

The room was larger than necessary, a grand cabaret of years gone by. Across the garden, the sky was clear with the sun shining on the grazing animals deep tan coats. The waiter brought her hot tea, and Jennifer dabbed the tea bag up and down enjoying that she was in the mountains. Glancing into the lobby, she immediately hoped the man entering the hotel was Michael Cabelli. She reminded herself that this was a Foundation meeting she didn't truly understand but could never reveal.

Jennifer smiled as she stood to greet Michael, a striking man with dark, strong features, realizing immediately what a wonderful secret he must be. Ruggedly handsome with deep eyes matching the waves of his long black hair, his handshake was warm and confident.

"Miss Wilson," he greeted her. "I'm Michael Cabelli."

She felt his hand softly engulf hers. "Very nice to meet you."

"I hope I haven't kept you waiting."

"No, not at all," she smiled sheepishly. "I just arrived."

As he sat, Michael thanked the waiter, requesting coffee.

"So tell me a bit about yourself, Michael."

He nodded, turning to look out over the lawn.

"Graduated last May from the University of Chicago with a B.A. Photography major. I have all of this technical training, could do print or correspondence work, but my love is the outdoors, these mountains and those animals." He pointed toward the elk herd. "Photography is what I want to do, but nature and wildlife photography, that's my creative love. I left here three months ago. Went home to Bismarck, North Dakota. Have set up a portrait photography business to make a living while I develop my portfolio as a naturalist photographer." Michael laughed.

"It isn't working out?"

"Oh, no. It's working out fine." His eyes lifted with optimism. "In fact, I'm surprised at the amount of business in three months. Then a month ago, I was doing a portrait job for a church; one of those deals where I take quick shots of families and kids, and we hope the shot turns out to be a handsome portrait. I was trying to get this rowdy little bugger to smile. He was crying, and I was laughing and giggling, waving a clown doll in front of him, and he puked all over the doll, my hand, and sprayed up my arm. All I could think was mountain landscapes hold still, always smile, and animals do not puke on you. So I threw the soiled clown puppet away."

Jennifer was laughing as she pointed out the window. "You mean you're willing to trade puking kids for all of this?"

"Miss Wilson, I'm willing to trade puking kids, demanding mother's-of-the-bride, and still lives of lawnmowers, office furniture, and ripe produce. I'm also willing to trade security to pursue this creative dream. I have a vision of what my life will become. When I stood in that church with puke all over my arm, well, that isn't my vision. I could do news photography or freelance, but that's not my dream either. The dream is to capture the animals in this majestic mountain setting."

"You've asked our Foundation for quite a sum of money."

"Yes I have." Michael leaned toward Jennifer. "Something changed me a while back, and I now have no doubt, given the opportunity, the dream, as they say, can be realized."

"What changed?"

"Before, it was my private dream, my vision. Then I shared the dream and someone believed in my talent, maybe as much as I privately did. So, I'm here with you, and yes, I'm asking for a good sum of money. I asked because I believe in myself and my work."

She sat quietly watching Michael gazing at the animals between the Stanley Hotel and Estes Park.

"How did you find out about the Chadwick Foundation?"

He took a sip of coffee. "A friend shared the address with me. Actually, I'd never heard of your organization, but I was told I'm typical of the artists you fund. So," he laughed without reservation, "the kid puked on me, and I'm back in the mountains. I want to create my art with my own unique expressions."

Jennifer heard the hints. "As I stated in our emails, I'd like to see more of your work."

"I've prepared that for you. In the cabin where I hope to live, I've prepared a room with fourteen images I believe are worthy as limited editions."

"In a cabin?"

Michael looked at her. She was pretty, about his age, and very business like; conservative business suit cut to flatter her figure. Knowing they lived in the age of distrust, he tried to gain hers.

"I'm sorry. I didn't think." He apologized. "I certainly understand your discomfort of going to a cabin with some long-haired mountain man. Please trust that the presentation is important to the images."

Jennifer found it hard not to trust his smile. "I think we'll be alright, Mr. Cabelli."

"I tell you what. You call me Michael, I'll call you Jennifer."

"Okay Michael. When do I see your work?"

"This evening. I don't want the sunlight to cause reflections and distract from the impact."

"You're very particular."

"In many ways I have extremely high expectations." He was selling himself. "Also, I need to be at Horseshoe Park by four o'clock this afternoon. I heard rumors of a huge bull elk herd moving through. They've just separated themselves from the cows after the rut. Still bold and aggressive, it may be an opportunity for a special shot."

Jennifer motioned out the window. "Are those elk?"

"Yep. Cows."

Jennifer held her chin in her hand. "I thought so."

Michael wondered if he should. He had heard about tourists who didn't have a clue, those uneducated visitors who innocently asked when did deer become elk. He grinned, feeling playful. "It's the metamorphosis." Why was he teasing her so, he wondered?

"A metamorphosis?"

"Sure," he pointed. "The fawns have spots, then become deer. As they grow to maturity, they change. Are you familiar with the metamorphosis of the bald eagle."

"Enlighten me."

"The immature bald eagles grow to full size yet do not get their white head or tail until they're three years old."

Jennifer smirked. "Yes, I've heard that before."

"These animals are the same way. At about five years, the deer hit another growth transition and make their second metamorphosis change from deer to elk."

She grinned at Michael as if believing his ridiculous line, disappointed that she would appear naive. "So these are all fully mature deer." Jennifer pointed innocently at the herd. "Or I guess they're elk now."

"That's true, but they're not fully mature." He turned on his most convincing smile, wide-eyed and knowing. "The most amazing part of the metamorphosis is when they complete the final stage and become moose. They're huge then. Great big thick racks." He put his hands to his head, spreading his fingers like antlers. "That happens at about fifteen years. When they become moose they get old and crotchety, and wander the woods alone."

"Very interesting." She could look gullible when she wanted to. "Until today, I had not seen elk close up."

"Well, you'll see a bunch up here. They wonder all over town this time of year."

"That's pretty neat."

"Yea," Michael agreed. "But the locals act like they're big mosquitoes, eating their shrubs like pesky insects."

"Those beautiful animals?"

"I'll tell you what. Why don't you go with me at four? You can watch me work and see the elk up close and personal. Afterward, I'll give you time alone to view the images at the cabin. You'll see the full process, and all of that should help in your decision."

Despite his ridiculous tale of metamorphosis, Jennifer liked him. If Alexandria had done as Jennifer suspected, she envied her. He was playful with a smile that made you laugh with desire, a free spirit with a dream and the confidence to go after it. "Jeans and a sweater okay?"

"Absolutely. Pick you up at quarter to four."

"I'll be ready."

"See the two Aspen?" He whispered. "In the grass to the left."

Jennifer stood behind Michael on the edge of the meadow. She continued to search, watching the herd of bull elk grazing lazily in the deep golden grass. The sun pushing down the valley as Michael manipulated the 35 mm camera with the telephoto lens, three times the size of the camera itself.

"Did you find him yet?"

Jennifer whispered back. "Which one?"

Quietly he moved the camera, motioning for her to look. "I'm focused right on him."

Jennifer was shocked at the magnification through the camera. What she had not seen was large and magnificent in the camera frame. Hidden in the grass, the unusually large elk laid quietly watching the others graze.

"He's huge." Jennifer stepped back from the camera.

Michael refocused and waited.

She could not resist. "How long until this one becomes a moose?"

Michael watched the bull, anticipating when and where the bull would move? Mentally, he prepared for the possibilities.

"He's an old one." Michael looked through the viewfinder. "Probably in the next year or two."

Three thoughts kept bouncing through her mind. The beauty of the elk on a cool mountain evening, the features of the photographer as dynamic as the giant elk's, and her irritation that he actually believed she bought his tale of metamorphosis.

Then, startled, she stood straight with the sound. Like a fog horn in the night, it seemed to come from nowhere to everywhere. The elk's head stretched forward, its nose pushing upward, forcing his antlers to press the furthest spike down and into his back. The bugle, the dominant mating calls of the bull, echoed throughout the valley, a symphony's full trumpet section.

"Guess he's still horny." As he snapped shots of the uplifted head, a cloud of breath moved eerily with the elk's bugle.

Then she felt her lips separate, her mouth open slightly as the bull rocked forward, pushing its back legs under itself, his rump rising. Then rocking backward and stood. Like a king, dominating the herd of twenty or so bulls, he was an animal of power. Easily, he lowered his head to scuffle with another large bull. Their antlers clattered like a flurry of castanets. Pushing the other backwards, they pressed their bone sharp antlers into an intertwining mix of deadly spears scraping and clacking.

Michael was in full response. Jennifer could hear the motor of the camera's soft whine. With each movement of the elk, Michael was with the animal, oblivious to anything else. Standing behind him, she could feel his intensity and joy. In this moment, she understood his passion.

As he opened the cabin door, Michael explained that it belonged to a family friend, and Michael had taken it over this past summer with permission to make it feel like home. While she waited in the living room, he went to the refrigerator and took out a bottle of wine.

"If you're going to attend a gallery opening, you should at least have a touch of wine." His smiled. "Art world protocol."

She looked directly at him. "Is this seduction Michael?"

"No." His smile softened, but his convincing eyes did not. "And I apologize if it appears that way."

She felt a hint of disappointment.

"This is my important to me," he added, "and I want to make a positive impression. Just trying to set the artistic mood." He pointed, "The White

Room is up the stairs, first room. Take as much time as you like. I'll wait here."

At the top of the stairs she felt a twinge of anxiety. Had Alex been here? Had the change taken place here with Michael?

The light came from the first room. She stopped in the doorway, the glass of wine in her hand. The White Room was not a room with pictures, but a gallery of nature's brightly colored images. Fully white with a hard wood floor and directional lighting, each image had its own illumination.

Jennifer stepped into the room, and slowly she circled taking in each photograph. It occurred to her, if her intuition was right, why Alexandria believed in this man. Jennifer knew little about photography, but immediately she knew Michael had a special talent. The frames and matting were thick white creating a visual focus on the image, the vibrant colors of each photo magnified by the purity of The White Room.

She froze at the beauty of the eagle. She had always loved bald eagles. The eagle was in full flight dominating the surrounding mountains. The power of the rapture was enhanced by the images to each side. To the left was a field of poppies surrounded by purple iris, summer green hills rolling in the background under a bright blue sky of soft cotton clouds. To the right was a fall image. Shades of green and red flowers below, towering pines above with the deep blues of morning, and in the center a waving line of golden Aspen reined.

As she moved, she enjoyed each image with a different feeling. One gave her power, another comforted, and still a third spoke to her forgotten desire to feel a part of nature. She saw the white sand waves of rolling dunes as one powerful ray of light streaked from above to define the contrast of sky and earth.

And there was the waterfall. The colors of the mountains, the trees and sky reflecting in the pond below shared the full solitude in its wide, shallow stream. She looked deeply into the picture, imagining herself alone or escaping into the magic of the falls. She had not expected his images to move her so.

The White Room was a place she wanted to sit and look, listen to soft music, sip her wine peacefully, and feel herself escape into the images surrounding her.

It seemed like an hour, though she knew it had not been nearly that long. At the doorway she stopped for one final look, to see each image in its place surrounded in the white, absorbing light into the colors; warm, spectacular colors.

When Michael heard her on the steps the slight discomfort in his stomach twisted tighter. She walked to where he sat on the couch and stood before him. Nervously, Michael stood.

"Congratulations, Mr. Cabelli." She reached her hand to his. "Your talent is impressive, and I believe you have a tremendous future as a photographer. The Chadwick Foundation would like to help you achieve your dream."

He glanced downward, and then his deep brown eyes met hers. It was an innocence she had not seen, and then the joy spread across his face. It was clear he could barely contain himself.

"I'm very serious, Michael. You have a wonderful talent."

"Thank you, Jennifer." Numb, his thoughts got lost. "I guess I wasn't expecting this. It seemed like such a shot in the dark. I just wasn't absolutely sure you'd like them, my images." He breathed deeply, as he whispered to himself. "She told me they were good."

"She?" Jennifer asked, but Michael simply waved the thought away. "Never doubt your talent again." She reassured him.

"So," Michael beamed. "What now?"

"Well, you and I develop a business plan." Jennifer motioned for Michael to sit. "We are willing to fund six months of work, and upon review, if The White Room is any indication of the quality of work, we propose to support your gallery opening. It's possible, depending on your success, that some additional funds might be available beyond that. The funding all aligns with your request, so we are making a significant commitment to you and your talent. We expect the same from you. Michael, this is the opportunity of a lifetime. Consider it a partnership more than a gift. In order for us to support you, we must believe your commitment. You are the artist. We are simply a mechanism."

Michael's mind was racing, the images already there only to be found and captured with his camera. Yellowstone during the winter, buffalo and wolf dynamic in the harshness of the snow; the massive bison walking single file over the snow patched steaming thermal fields.

He looked off through the glass window toward Fall River. "I love photography, but what you're saying, you're telling me to live my dream, and you'll fund it? To commit myself is the easy part? You have no idea. Those images, The White Room, the images still only in my mind; they are the reality of my dream. It's a shock to have someone so fully believe in you. I will not let you down."

Jennifer gripped Michael's forearm. "I have no doubt."

His eyes locked to hers. Jennifer saw his integrity, and she knew Alexandria was right to do this. Whatever was in their past, she could only imagine, but his future would be amazing.

"So, how do we get this started?" he asked.

"When I return to Denver, I'll complete an agreement for your review." She resumed her business tone. "It will be fairly straight forward. We want you to be able to concentrate on your work without worry about paying the bills. By June 1, we'll expect a private showing of your work, both gallery ready images as well as a gallery design.

When your work and gallery design meet our expectations, we will coordinate to support the development of the gallery. You'll have to trust us to the same degree we're trusting you. You are the artist, and we have the business knowledge."

Michael set his empty glass on the table. "Two questions. One, who is *we*? And two, when do you want me to come to Denver to sign the agreement?"

Jennifer smiled, her mind formulating strategy. "Could I bother you for another glass of wine? After all, this is a bit of a celebration."

"Absolutely." Michael took the glass.

Her mind strategized. *We* was simply the Foundation. He would be working specifically with her. As funding was handled within the Foundation, she would be the account manager who could approve his requests and promote continuation of the project. She would be his Foundation advocate. All calls should come directly to her cell phone. As for the agreement, she had enjoyed Estes Park so much today; she'd drive here. They could spend a couple of days finalizing the business plan then complete the paper work.

Michael handed her the now half-full glass and sat again on the couch. He listened to her explanation, nodding agreement as the adrenaline rush eased from his chest.

"Let me tell you I am very grateful. I will commit my time, energy, and enthusiasm to make this a success. Thank you, Jennifer, and my thanks to the Chadwick Foundation. Someday, we'll look back at The White Room as a beginning. The images and future are infinite. Thank you for opening this door."

So many doorways, she thought. Hidden doors, secret doors. She was the manipulator, the director, the banker, and the discreet inquirer. Alexandria had not prepared her for his talent, charisma or genuineness. He was playful and intense with determined deep eyes, and a mysterious, daring intrigue. Intertwined complexities, she understood her role and the relationship.

"Then Michael, shall we plan on a meeting back here on December 1?" She was ready to conclude the business meeting.

"I have to bring closure to several things back home." He was thoughtful. "But I believe December 1 will work. I'll plan on returning in a week."

"Can we work here, in this cabin?" she asked. "We'll need a couple of days."

"My friends haven't used this cabin much for years." he nodded. "I'm sure I can rent it for the winter."

"Between now and then, if you have ideas, questions, anything, call me.

I'll give you my cell phone number so you can always contact me directly. If I'm not available, leave a message on my cell, and I'll get back to you ASAP." She drank the last sip of wine. "For your purposes, consider me the Foundation. I'm the only one who is working with you right now, so if I don't immediately get back to you, be patient. Agreed?"

"Absolutely." He grinned.

Jennifer stood, and Michael followed. She reached out her hand, and he grasped it with both of his.

"Now Jennifer." He still held her hand. "I know I will never be able to thank you enough, but here is a small token offer. I am meeting a friend at Lonigan's for beer and pizza. You could go back to the Stanley or wander the tourist shops or join us and allow me to buy you a gourmet pizza and beer in celebration."

Already she was choosing doors. "I do have to leave early in the morning, but a slice would be nice."

"Wonderful."

The sunken room was friendly with a cozy seating near a large oak bar. Michael seemed to know everyone. Two grungy men greeted him at the door, and the one with all the tattoos shook his hand as they passed telling him it was good to see him back in Estes. The waitress hugged him hello with a kiss on the cheek, and the bartender delivered a long neck as they sat in the maroon vinyl chairs on the curved end of the bar.

Jennifer looked at the beer. "I don't suppose they have Perrier?"

Michael raised his bottle. "Name your flavor."

She pointed at the beer. "That will do."

"Another?" The bartender verified.

"Yes, please." She felt herself smile at the bartender sporting a ponytail and beard.

Large hands appeared on Michael's shoulder, and she turned to see a sandy-haired man with a charmingly boyish face laughing as he leaned between them.

"You amaze me." The man had a gentle smile that beamed when he looked at her. "How do you always find these beautiful women?"

Her first thought was *he's cute.*

Michael nodded to Jennifer, smiling, and reached for the beer the bartender was handing him.

"Jennifer." Michael grinned. "This character is my buddy, Jimmy."

Jimmy greeted her with a friendly hand and warm smile.

"Jennifer is a new business associate."

Jimmy nodded. "I see. You must be the lady from this too-good-to-be-true Foundation."

"The Chadwick Foundation," she smiled. "Fortunately for Michael, we are not too good to be true. We specialize in supporting new talents. Michael and I have just agreed he will become our newest client."

"Really? Fantastic!"

"Michael is very talented."

"You know, I have no doubts." Jimmy turned to Jennifer. "You've seen The White Room?"

"Truly amazing images."

"The White Room?" Jimmy pushed on Michael's shoulder. "You show beautiful women, but you won't show me."

"Beautiful women?" Jennifer mocked curious eyes.

Jimmy waved her away. "Don't get me wrong. As far as I know, only three people have been in The White Room, Michael, you, and a friend from this summer. She too was beautiful."

Acknowledging his off-handed compliment, she smiled, realizing it was a door she should not open.

"Tell you what, Jimmy. Jennifer has convinced me it is time to share my work. You can see the gallery anytime you want."

Jimmy reached up rubbing Michael's shoulder. "I'd like that, buddy. I'll be out for breakfast tomorrow." He pulled out the stool on the other side of Michael, and sat up to the bar. "So does this mean you're trading in people for animals?"

Michael raised his glass. "To living the dream."

"Fantastic." Jimmy tilted his beer both looked at Jennifer.

She smiled, lifted her bottle, and all three bottles touched at the neck. It amazed her as she sat with these men. There was comfort in Lonigan's, and she wondered if Alexandria had been here.

Beer seemed to magically appear as did the pizza. It was spicy with thick, bubbling cheese and fluffy crust. While she managed to fill herself with one slice and another beer, Michael ate four pieces and Jimmy devoured five before finishing off the three black olives left on the tray.

The tattooed man waved a pool cue toward them. "Hey Michael, I need a partner."

Michael stood up. "Jennifer, I'm going to leave you in Jimmy's kind hands, only because I know he's a pussy cat."

As Michael stood from his stool, Jennifer reached to him. "I really must go, Michael. Thank you for the pizza and beer."

"Still not quite an even trade, your grant for pizza and beer." His eyes became deeper brown as he looked down at the well used bar. "Have I thanked you yet?"

Jennifer was sincere. "Someday I'll see your images in people's homes, in feature exhibits, and in galleries all over the country. I'll watch people react the way I reacted seeing The White Room. I will be thanked every time someone is touched by your gift."

"Thank you." He felt a bit awkward in the praise. "Let me run you back to the Stanley."

Jimmy interrupted, "I have a better idea."

"I thought you might," Michael laughed.

"I'm parked in back," Jimmy pointed through the bar.

"I'll see you on December first." She ran her hands through a long strand of hair that had fallen over her eyes. "If there's anything you need, any questions call my cell. Remember," she pointed playfully at his nose, "I'm your personal project manager. Only I can make decisions, so the most effective communication is to contact me directly. If we need to talk, I'll give you a call too."

They shook hands, and Jennifer leaned forward. He felt her whisper brush across his skin.

"Next time, Michael, remember that anyone who paid attention in high school biology knows that deer are deer, elk are elk, moose are moose, and bullshit is bullshit."

She could see the embarrassment in his face, turning white then deeper shades of red.

His head fell into his hands fighting embarrassment. "My apologies." Sincerity pressed from his eyes, unable to hide the redness.

"Apology accepted. Consider this your metamorphosis." Her smile relieved him. "Always remember Michael, don't mess with those who sign the check." She teased, squeezing his hand firmly before releasing, laughing the whole while.

As they walked through the, Jimmy laughed, "He really tried to pulled the metamorphosis story on you?"

Jennifer was grinning as she nodded.

Jimmy shrugged. "You'd be surprised at how many people believe it."

From the dimly lit room of the Stanley Hotel, she watched Jimmy's truck roll down the drive and disappear toward town. She checked her watch; after midnight. They had sat downstairs at the Whiskey Bar before the 1909 Rothschild Bar of old west grandeur, talking as she sipped wine, Jimmy sipping Amaretto.

She turned from the window. It was after midnight. She stared at the antique wooden headboard and thought of how warm the bed would feel. For an instant, she thought how much warmer it could have felt, and glanced out the window to make sure his taillights had disappeared.

Her mind wondered what Alexandria had gotten herself into, and how she'd ever walked away? But Jennifer knew what Alexandria must have realized; she was not of them. Alexandria was destined to become the matriarch of Denver society. While she didn't particularly relish the title, she played the role to perfection. She leaned back, slipping deeper into the pillowed chair. *Alex*, Jimmy had called her. During the conversation, it had only slipped out once, but it had hung in the air like the answer to her questions.

Jimmy said she was like a song they'd written. *"Lighting the night, a falling star flashes bright, the mystic blue in your eyes."*

Chapter 21

Al Atwater sat across from William in his Chadwick Building Office.

"Nothing?" William repeated. "I can't believe you found nothing."

The security specialist shrugged. "It's been three months, William." Atwater held up an overstuffed manila envelope. "Our full report's in here. Daily logs, photographs, receipt copies, cell phone records, where she went, when and with whom, everything. Nothing unusual. No contacts out of the ordinary."

William was shaking his head. "I don't know what I was looking for. There was a change. She quit listening to me and started..." William rocked back in his leather chair. "She's like a teenager going through puberty; rebellious, independent, and damn cocky thinking she can do things as she pleases." He shook his head. "You found nothing?"

"Nothing out of the ordinary."

"And you were discreet?"

"Absolute discretion."

William glanced up at Atwater. "No signs of another man?"

"We were on her twenty-four hours a day. Three different investigators for three months." He shrugged helplessly. "Our best people found nothing. It's all in the report."

William nodded, staring down at his desk. "I have no doubt in the quality of your work, Al. I just thought there must be an answer." He pointed at the envelope in Atwater's lap. "I'll look it over."

"I wish I could be of more help, William." Atwater laid the envelope on the desk between them.

William's forehead wrinkled as he looked down at the bulky manila folder. It made no sense.

Chapter 22

Alexandria was listening to Jennifer tell of her holiday plans, Christmas just three days away, when the receptionist knocked on Jennifer's office door.

"UPS just delivered this."

The package was very long, only eighteen inches wide, and thin. Jennifer unwrapped the thick brown paper to expose a box with a card taped to it. She slipped her long fingernails under the envelope.. The hand printed card read *Thank you for your belief in me. I'll be in Jackson much of January, then to Mexico in March for the whale migration. Merry Christmas - Michael.*

Jennifer felt the nervousness when she saw Alexandria's anticipation.

"Why the embarrassment, Jennifer?" Alexandria leaned forward smiling. "A Christmas gift from an admirer?"

"No." Jennifer laid the card on the desk. "A thank you from Michael."

It was hard to detect the slight twist in Alexandria's face before she smiled. "He's doing well?" She asked calmly.

"Yes, quite well." Her eyes diverted. "But I think he's lonely."

"Jennifer, please." Alexandria stood before her. "He's staying on track with the plan you laid out?"

"He's incredibly intense, taking full advantage of his time. He has plans to spend the winter in Jackson, Wyoming photographing Yellowstone and the Tetons. He's thrown himself completely into achieving this dream."

"Good. That's what we want." She waved her hand, gesturing to the box. "I'm sure he appreciates all you're doing." She turned, a delicate statue in her heeled boots, jeans and oversized sweater; and walked from the office waving a reassuring goodbye.

Left alone in her office, a strange excitement swept her. Opening the end with a letter cutter, she pulled the long frame from the cardboard box. Sheets of bubble wrap covered the image, and she unwrapped it quickly.

When it appeared, she covered her mouth to quiet her laughter. The frame contained four pictures and a brass engraved title, each image in an equally matted opening.

The fawn looked shyly beneath a tree limb, the mule deer buck gazed alert with enormous velvet antlers, the same bull elk she had seen with Michael at Thanksgiving held a massive pose, and a moose with intimidating antlers stood on the edge of a clear mountain lake, its reflection in the water. She laughed out loud, reading the title engraved on the brass plate. *Metamorphosis.*

PART 3: Summer
Chapter 23

Alexandria's acceptance of her life brought a sense of tolerance back into their relationship. Somehow, in the two years since Michael, she and William had begun to chat again. Tonight he seemed quite mortal without his gray business suit, wearing tan slacks and the sweater she'd bought him for Christmas.

In his formal way, his interests had broadened to include her and their daughter. He asked about their cross-country ski trip a month before. Surprised by her excited explanation of the cold and snow and the deer herd they had shared a meadow with; he had listened with genuine interest.

When her story ended, he reflected uncharacteristically, "It sounds peaceful."

Cautious as she always was, she gazed at the quiet elegance of the Victorian Inn. William had been granted a private dining room on the second floor of the historical home. In the secluded corner, reflections from the chandelier prisms pranced in the flickering candlelight.

A year ago, following extremely difficult negotiations, the bank merger had been completed after Senator Clayton's renewal of the banking bill. Since then, there had been a subtle change in William, and he had begun taking moments to return to himself.

Though they were just moments, Alexandria found she could like him when those moments came. As if hints of her transition two years before, William seemed to be searching for his own way. So they had pledged Thursday nights to each other, and, to her surprise, William had honored the pledge.

The waiter brought their salads, elegantly prepared Caesars on wide-brimmed crystal plates with gold edgings. He motioned to Alexandria, and she acknowledged with approval setting the plate first before her and then before her husband. The waiter freshened each of their wines, and exited without saying a word. Alexandria allowed the wine to mesmerize her thoughts, appreciating the quality, texture, and uniqueness of the moment.

"I wish I could join you this weekend." His eyes watched her.

Despite the renewed feelings, the mountains had remained hers, while the business world dominated William's life. This mountain adventure was not where she wished their worlds might cross. Tensing, she took a long sip of Chardonnay, masking what he might distinguish as fear.

"You could," she waved, challenging him where he was most vulnerable. "Just forget work for three days and join us."

He chuckled at her absurdity. "Sometimes I envy the way your family is so different than mine. I wish I could ignore work for three days and disappear into the mountains."

Another revelation or was it criticism? Alexandria waited for more, her eyes transfixed by the Chardonnay.

"My family puts on formal attire, walks straight-backed, and lives banking." He was smiling at her now, laughing at his own image. "Your family goes on hikes, shares stories, and roasts marshmallows. I don't know if I've ever shared a story over flaming marshmallows."

She was surprised that he even knew they would flame. "You've made some progress lately," she teased.

William glanced at her near empty glass. "I'll never have the freedom to roast a marshmallow without the fear that something may have slipped. The bank, its holdings, so many details."

"Life is more fun than you know." The words escaped her, softened by the playful wine.

"You don't think my life is fun?" He laughed sarcastically.

She tried not to laugh. "Do you think it's fun?"

"Maybe not as you would define it."

"William." She waved her glass in the air. "Neckties, business meetings, and dinner in the executive dining room are not fun. There's nothing wrong with those things, but that is your life. No variety, no fun, and, most importantly, no true personal connections. Life is not about the deal; it's about the people that are impacted. So please, don't ever confuse the intensity of a business deal with fun."

He listened to her curiously, wanting to be irritated but pushed the anger downward. "How do you define fun?"

"This weekend Josephine and I will be in Estes Park. We'll hike with my parents, spend evenings grilling charbroiled burgers, and eating baked beans and potato salad. We'll laugh for hours without once mentioning the fluctuating exchange rate of the Japanese Yen." She reached her hand under the table, touching William's thigh. "Fun is spontaneity. It's a personal connection. It's suddenly leaving work to have pizza with Josephine and me. It's you and I driving fast up Lookout Mountain, and sitting at Buffalo Bill's grave while watching the lights of Denver spread out in all three directions." She winked, a little laughter in her eyes.

William recoiled a bit. "Fun is negotiating a national banking bill that brings millions of dollars to your business and ultimately the employees and your family." He smiled a slightly arrogant grin. "Now that's fun."

"How about this for fun." She challenged. "One afternoon, in the middle of the week just because you want to," a slight exasperation escaped her, "set business aside, go to Josephine's school, and have lunch with your daughter. She'd cherish such attention."

Her husband leaned forward, smiling in a silly way, looking beyond as if seeing something in the distance. Then he laughed, "It does sound nice."

He turned his eyes to the wine bottle and refilled her glass. "What time are you meeting your parents?"

"Daddy said they'd be in Estes early tomorrow afternoon. I'll pick up Josephine from school, and we'll leave from there."

William spoke with surprising calmness. "She loves the mountains, Josephine, doesn't she?

"Oh yes." Alexandria's thoughts drifted back to their early spring weekend together. Two days of cross-country skiing through pure white wilderness. That morning, Alex had fluttered the snow cover from her tent crawling out to feel the sun warm against her face. The trees stood unmoving as six inches of fresh powder rested softly on each branch. Josie was huddled before the fire, her twelve-year-old crush so obvious as she sat across from their handsome young guide giggling in the frigid morning air. Too quickly, Josie's hormones were beginning to show.

"The outdoors, it's good," he said. "It's a beautiful world out there. I hope she finds her own way."

The slight catch of Chardonnay in her throat caused an unrefined cough. As her lips separated Alexandria's eyes stared, shocked at the confession.

"She doesn't think twice about spending a night in ten degree temperature as a new layer of snow falls. She thrives on putting on her hiking boots and heading off into the backcountry in search of wherever the trail may take her. You should see how fresh she looks, how capable, with a layer of trail dirt covering her face." Alexandria laughed. "Don't be disappointed if she grows to abandon banking in favor of the fight against global warming."

"She loves the outdoors that much?" William's eyes softened. Then he said words she never thought she would hear from a Chadwick. "I want for Josephine whatever Josephine wants. I've had so many strings attached to my life. I hope she'll be string free. Global warming or banking or anything in between, I just want her to be happy."

"So," she looked at him rather mischievously. "She could, say, shorten her name to Josie."

He laughed loudly, both hands flopping on the table. "Don't act innocent, Alexandria." He pointed at her. "You've been calling her Josie for two years. So have her friends. Everybody has but my family and me. In that little game of informality, you've secretly won."

"But will you play?" Her eyes were seductive.

"I'll tell you what. I'll try it on for size, but when we're with my family, let's maintain our formality."

"Chicken?"

"Maybe." Then he grinned sideway and added. "My mother scares me to death."

They both laughed, and Alexandria winked triumphantly.

Chapter 24

"You're positive he won't be there."

Jennifer leaned emphatically on Alexandria's desk. "He's on the west coast doing a series of art shows. He left last Friday on a three-week swing. He will not be there."

"I just couldn't do it again, I just can't see him."

"You won't." Jennifer stood up. "So go home, put on your hiking boots, throw a hat in the car, pick up Josie, and head for Estes. Have a wonderful weekend with your folks."

"Mom?" Josie was resting her stocking feet on the Mercedes dash, "why don't you buy a Jeep?"

Her mind flashed the image of a rugged yellow Jeep. "Why a Jeep, Josie?"

"It'd be fun, and when we drove into the mountains, I wouldn't feel like I'm still in our house."

"This car's kind of like that isn't it?"

"A lot like that." Josie shivered the cold feeling away. "So, why haven't we gone to Estes Park before? I hear there're some amazing hikes."

Alexandria shrugged. "We've gone to a lot of places."

"We have." Josie's toes wiggled. "Are we staying in the cabin Grampy and Grammy used to take you to?"

"The very same."

"Can I sleep on the porch like you used to?"

"I'd like that, Babe."

"Me too."

Josie kept her feet on the dash, her arms wrapped around her legs as the mountains passed. She watched and pointed at the passing scenery, feeling that sense of excitement she got every time her mother took her back into the mountains.

"Remember that waterfall, the first one in Vail?"

"When we were riding the horses?" she clarified. "Of course."

"I always remember that, the way the mist made me feel wet, cool, and warm all at the same time."

Alex's father, Hank, sat on the natural wood chair in front of the cabin watching the clouds drift over Long's Peak. Anne and Josie played with a

Frisbee, Josie trying to teach her Grandmother to use muscles long ago left unused. They all laughed at Grammy's floppy attempts as the Frisbee fluttered wounded to the ground.

"She's a beautiful girl." He gripped his daughter's hand.

"Thanks Dad." Alex rested her fingers on his aged wrinkles. "It's great to be back in Estes. It's been too long."

Hank shrugged, watching the next fluttering Frisbee. "Sometimes life gets in our way. It was a busy time when you were graduating high school. I was finishing my doctorate, you were off to college, and then you got married."

She nodded knowingly. "I've missed Estes."

"Me too."

From the yard of the hillside cabin, she looked over the rooftops. She had no doubt that if he came walking up Elk Horn Drive, if he stepped into the yard and stopped to play Frisbee with Josie, instantly, she would love him again.

She held her father's hand, and she wanted to go. She wanted to be in Mickey's cabin, to sit on his sunny patio after sleeping a secluded night in his arms. She thought of Lonigan's and listen to Jimmy sing, and she wished she could go to his gallery. She wanted to stand before his images and be in love with him as she had been two years before.

Hank slid his hand from beneath hers, patting it tenderly. "I'd like to hike with you and Josie. I can't do Long's Peak, but I'd like to go with you."

"Oh Daddy, there are lots of options." The Frisbee fluttered, and Grammy Anne threw her arms up in frustration. "All the trails around Bear Lake, the Ute Trail down from the Visitor's Center, Cub Lake out at Moraine Park, you pick one, and we'll have a wonderful day together."

After dinner, Alexandria excused herself. She knew there wasn't any beer in the refrigerator, leaving her with no choice but to go buy some. She pulled on a sweater and grabbed her favorite ball cap.

Leaving the cabin with an explanation that she would be back soon, Alex walked southward down Elk Horn Drive. She crossed the highway and strolled down the steeply curving hill into town. Memories floated though her mind, and she chuckled thinking of Rocky Mountain Oysters, which brought the laugh-out-loud vision of Leslie and Daisy. She stopped at the corner, standing at the intersection and scanned the main street east and west.

Even at eight o'clock tourists filled the streets, couples walking hand and hand on a cool summer evening. She blended nicely in wearing her hat, the beat-up Rocky Mountain National Park cap she'd had since her youth hiding her face. Her jeans were her most comfortable as was the cotton shirt she wore only in the mountains. Looking like a wrangler, she waited for the main stoplight to change, and moved inconspicuously with the crowd. Just for a moment, she wanted to feel the joy of being back in Estes.

Comfort overwhelmed her as the sounds of Lonigan's reverberated around her. She stood at the door hearing the familiar melody of the 12-string guitar and the sweet voice of her friend. Listening, she stepped aside as tourists tumbled into the bar, laughter raining back out onto the crowded sidewalk. Mustering up her courage, Alex pulled the ball cap down over her forehead.

A low-hipped waitress with flowing strands of straight brown hair took Alex's beer order and was gone with a smile. Along the railing above the bar she found a pillar by the pool table. Her hat pulled down and her arms wrapped tightly to her chest, she leaned against it and listened.

Soft melodies rang from his sweet voice. Jimmy played with conviction, dedicated to the joy of sharing mountain music. Alex allowed herself to feel the melody, to love the sounds and the wonderful man, and to wish Mickey were not in California.

The waitress returned with a happy smile on her beautiful round face. As she handed Alex the beer, she asked, "If a table opens up, you want me to snatch it for you?"

"No thanks." She sounded sad. "I won't be staying long."

The beer was cold and the bar overflowed with laughter. It was a mixture of working men in torn jeans and tank tops, mountain women in slender, trimmed bodies with long lengths of dreadlocks, and tourists in khakis and pullovers. Three girls, hardly old enough to be in the bar, danced in the aisle between Jimmy and the tables. The songs continued one after another bringing her home.

Four songs later, the waitress brought a second beer without Alex ordering. "You know, you stand out in this bar. If we don't find you a table, these pool morons will start harassing you."

"Harassing me?" Alex glanced back over her shoulder, and a boy with a scraggly beard holding a customized cue nodded with a finger to the bill of his hat. "Oh. Well, I won't be staying much longer. Could you bring me a six pack to go?"

"Sure." The short, happy waitress beamed.

Alex began to hand her three bills for the second beer, but was waved away. "I told you, you stand out in this bar. This one's from the gentleman playing the guitar. Nice guy. His name's Jimmy."

Alex stared at the beer in her hand. Jimmy kept singing, playing to the crowd, his eyes were locked on her. She watched him, their eyes staring at each other from across the room, and, as the phrase of the song ended, he nodded her way.

Instantly, she knew she had stepped back into a place she should never have returned to. The fear rushing though her told her she had pushed too far.

The waitress sat the sack of beer on the railing beside Alex. This time she took the money offered, and Alex placed the half empty beer on the tray.

"Leaving so soon?" she asked cheerfully.

Alex nodded, "I must."

And in the background she heard his bold words, pounding from the powerful speakers.

"Sometimes in life we meet very special people who are a part of our lives for much too short of time. I'd like to dedicate this song for one of those people. It's a love song."

Jimmy was looking directly at her, his hands already beginning to play the music. Alex wanted to look away but was unable to. The music was beautiful, and the crowd quieted, listening as her heart pounded in her chest.

> *Alone in the night, a song about rain*
> *A guitar player's pain fills our hearts*
> *As poems of love in quiet reflection brought the stars*

The chorus came back to her quickly. The words, the memories, the flash of light, how long since she had thought of them.

> *The mystic blue in your eyes*
> *As the sun dips from the sky*
> *Lighting the night a falling star flashes bright*
> *The mystic blue in your eyes*

His eyes locked on her with his stage smile.

> *The mystery of an intimate night*
> *Sweet sounds of a lover's delight*
> *With soprano singing on a mountain night to the breeze*

He played through the chorus again and into a soft and magical instrumental. Trying to hide, she felt her own smile return as if feeling a momentary bright flash of warm light.

> *Where have you been, my beautiful friend*
> *Walking to this moment in time*
> *Where have you been, my amazing friend*

Smiling mystic blue eyes

The rhythm of the pine tree sings
The song of a lover's new chance
Where life and dreams and dance to be touch the sky

From beneath the bill of her protective hat, her hand covered her mouth as she stared across the bar. Fidgeting nervously, she reached for her Kokopelli necklace as the words blended into the music. His gentle brown eyes still watched her as she turned, slipping between the rugged workers playing pool, and moved toward the back door. When he started the last chorus it all came back to her, the emotions, feelings, and memory of his touch all came rushing back.

Mystic blue in your eyes
As the sun dips from the sky
Lighting the night a falling star flashes bright
The mystic blue in your eyes

Lighting the night, a falling star
Lighting the night, a falling star
Lighting the night a falling star flashes bright

The mystic blue in your eyes
As the sun dips from the sky
The mystic blue in your eyes

Turning to flee, she rushed out Lonigan's back door into the parking lot. She walked briskly along the stream to the sidewalk and main street shops where Alex disappeared into the crowd of tourists.

"Hi Honey." Her mother was drying a dinner plate. "Where'd you disappear to?"

Alex imitated a cheerful smile. "Walked into town." She pulled the six-pack from the brown sack. "I thought Daddy might like a beer. In fact, I think I'll have one. Join us?"

"Oh?" Her mother was drying another plate. "You know I'm not much for beer. I didn't even know you liked it."

"It's the mountains, every now and then it feels right." She pulled two cans from the carton, placing the rest in the refrigerator.

In the living room, Josie and her grandfather were watching the Discovery Channel as a mountain lion bounced gracefully across a tree-lined meadow. Through the window, Alex could see the evening light fading as she pulled a moose decorated blanket from the couch and handed her father a beer.

"Care to join me?" Walking past, he patted her father's shoulder.

Hank picked up a hooded sweatshirt and followed her through the screen porch to the wooden lawn chairs. Pulling the tab on the beer can, he sucked lightly on the foam. Alex, wrapped in the blanket, pulled her knees against her chest. Silently, she stared toward the final hints of light outlining Long's Peak.

"I thought it'd be nice," she shrugged innocently. "We haven't had a beer together since that first night in Lonigan's."

"That was a tough one." Chuckling, he took a sip. "Drinking beer with my little girl. A right of passage I was never prepared for." Despite the awkwardness, the beer tasted good. "We're so glad to see you and Josie."

"It's been too long, Daddy."

"Well, we get trapped in our lives and lose time." He smiled a bit. "So when did you start drinking beer?"

Her mind flashed to the moment. "About two years ago here in Estes Park. I spent some time with friends, and we drank beer."

"I can't see William as much of a beer drinker."

"Ah yes, poor William." She laughed a little, doubting her own life. "William's come a long way in the past couple of years, but you're right. He could never be a beer drinker." Suddenly she burst laughing. "Talk about out of your element."

"I imagine so," Hank added. "How are things?"

"What things?"

"Alexandria." Hank turned a bit in his chair. "You're mother and I have been concerned. We know you have a good life, that giant house and those expensive cars, and, of course an amazing daughter, but..." He used the beer to hide his hesitation. Then he asked the question he always asked, "Are you happy?"

His tone caused her to tuck the blanket in around her legs.

Hank whispered, "Tell me honey."

She was surprised at her lack of wavering. "I'm sure you saw it long before I did." Then, after a long hesitation. "In many ways this is the happiest I've been since we married. We're talking. And Josie and I, it's wonderful to be her mother. I've rediscovered nature, and William has allowed me to share that with Josie." She looked to the distant sky. "The Foundation gives me a sense of purpose. Yes, there is much happiness."

Her father's voice was soft. "So who'd you drink beer with?"

"What do you mean?" she asked.

"Maybe I'm off base. If I am, tell me, but I've got this feeling." Her father stared into her eyes. "You rediscovered nature. You drank beer with friends in Estes Park. There's much happiness, but I'm not convinced you're happy. Maybe I'm prying, but shoot, at my age a father has a right to pry." He hesitated. "So, who'd you drink beer with?"

For the longest time, Alex did not speak, staring straight ahead at the stars now filling the sky. Then, she patting her father's arm, unwrapped the blanket, and walked into the house. A moment later Hank heard the door, and Alex stood over him, handing him another beer.

"You sure you want to know the answer?" Alex asked.

"If you want to tell me."

"Will you still love me, Daddy?"

He took the beer. "So, I need at least one more to hear this?"

"I should have bought a twelve pack." Her eyes big, water appeared to pool. "One for each of us."

"I have a feeling, Alexandria." He patted the chair beside him, instructing his daughter to sit. "It's just…well…I think it's something you need to talk about."

Hank popped the beer knowing a father has a choice. He didn't know what was to come, wasn't sure he wanted to, but she needed him, so he would listen. "You should never doubt my love."

"Unconditional, I've always trusted that." Her tears welled up. She sat down, pulling the thick blanket back around her. The night was black now, and they were alone.

Then, after a time she turned quietly, unable to find the right words to start. So she started with her desperate need to reconnect with herself, telling him that the best person she knew herself to be was the person she was in Estes Park. She explained the distance in her relationship with William, and the yelling, directives, and harsh expectations. She reached sideways gripping her father's forearm, thanking him for giving her Estes Park to escape to.

Alex told him of her early morning drive up Fall River Road and of a chance meeting with a photographer. She described a gentle, strong man of warm brown eyes and wavy dark hair, and how that chance meeting turned to an evening of dancing.

As she went on, Hank shuddered at the thought of his little girl rappelling off a mountain cliff. He heard about the waterfall, a description so vivid that he felt the cold waters, but she continued to hold her naked adventure as something private. He smiled about the story of their laughter and being required to eat Rocky Mountain Oyster musketeer style.

Mostly, he was impressed at the depth she went to in describing his photography. It was one thing for his daughter to be enthusiastic but quite another to be passionate. Through her descriptions, he could see the eagle soaring, the deer in the morning mist, and the poppies painted on the morning hillside. She talked about her time in The White Room and how it was a moment that changed her life, and she believed, changed his.

It was the way she called him Mickey, the way he called her Alex that made him understand. He forced his discomfort away as she told of an intense emotion she had never dreamed she would feel. She talked of writing a song and the meaning behind it. Then she told him of hearing Jimmy this evening, of listening to him sing the song and the way it gripped deep to her heart. She told her father that she missed Mickey and Estes Park, but most of all, she missed herself.

Finally, she shifted in the chair, sitting upward. "So now you know."

"So now I know," he squeezed her hand. "And yes, I still love you."

Then she began to cry, big, sobbing tears, her body shuddering as he pulled her to his chest.

After a time, when she began to calm, he whispered, "May I ask you one favor?"

Alexandria nodded, wiping her face with the warm blanket.

Reassuring, he said, "Let's not share this with your mother."

They both burst out laughing as their hands gripped tighter until she fell back against her father's chest. She laid there as he held her, and he reflected on his daughter's confession. He knew her well, had always understood her, and he feared for her. To have done what she had done, there must be something terribly wrong in her life.

They decided on the hike to Cub Lake. A long, flat walk; slightly challenging in the middle, leading to a quiet pond set between a steep hillside and large glacier boulders. Josie led the way, confidently walking into the woods.

When they reached the lake, Josie climbed atop a boulder to eat her sandwich. The beauty of the lilies in bloom filling the lake with yellow blossoms surprised them. It was a quiet moment when they both heard Josie's whisper.

"Mom, Mom…look."

Seeing her daughter pointing, Alex looked across the lake to a dark spot moving among the green woods. Then, just as Hank spotted him, the young bull moose stepped from the shrubs to the edge of the lake. Josie's hand came to her mouth, holding her quiet as the moose meandered into the water.

For the next half hour they watched the moose moving slowly across the lake, his head disappearing underwater only to emerge with water raining down while weeds dangled from its mouth.

The clumsy look and smooth motions of the moose cast a spell over Josie. With each submersion, she held her breath until the moose reemerged, then giggled as the waters streamed from his antlers.

Watching, Josie turned whispering, "My first moose!" Then she turned back to the live nature channel, intrigued until the massive animal finally wandered from the lake, disappearing back into the pines.

When they returned to the cabin, Anne was on the screened-in porch crocheting somebody's Christmas gift. Josie was out of the car quickly, telling her grandmother of the moose, her hands over her head like antlers as she wobbled imitating the entertaining beast. She followed her into the kitchen, still giggling as her grandmother began making Josie another sandwich.

Alex, walking slowly, knew about where it was, a few doors west of Lonigan's in one of the older original buildings remaining in downtown Estes Park. A slightly tilted log building, at the turn of the century it had been the first general store, so said a brass plaque beside the door. She stood before it, her father reading the sign. "Nature's Way. The Photography of Michael Cabelli."

"This is he?" He pointed at the name.

Alex nodded, unmoving as she looked at the large carved sign.

"Should you be here?"

Alex's grin was happy as she turned to her father. "I just want to see it. It's okay. He's out of the state. Nobody knows me here."

As they stepped into the gallery, a voice welcomed them. "Hi. Nice to see you again, and welcome to Nature's Way."

Hank's forehead wrinkled, looking under his eyebrows at Alex.

The fear that shot through her disappeared when she saw the cheerful round face of the waitress from the night before.

Alex reached out her hand. "Well hello. It appears you keep yourself busy."

The girl's familiar smile grew as she grasped Alex's hand. "My name's Carla. I assist Michael here in the gallery."

Alex did not offer an introduction.

"Lonigan's is what I do for fun and to pay the rent." The young woman waved her hand over the gallery. "This is my love. I was an art major, and working with Michael has given me a chance to use that knowledge. Have you ever visited Michael's gallery?"

Alex shook her head, wondering if The White Room still existed. "No, I haven't. Please, tell me about it?"

"Certainly." Carla waited for Hank to rejoin them, having wandered toward a large print of an eagle in flight over a mountain range. "Michael Cabelli is an outstanding young talent, quickly becoming known throughout the world of nature and wildlife photography. Much of his initial work was done here in Rocky Mountain National Park. He now travels North America capturing the images you will see in the gallery. All of the prints are limited editions done in three phases, one hundred prints in each phase. We are at the point now where, due to his growing popularity, the first phase of each limited edition is nearly sold to private art collectors prior to their release to the public."

Hank turned toward the eagle that filled a full section of the gallery wall. "Tell me how it works to purchase this print?"

"Full Flight is one of Michael's first truly dynamic images. This is number 67 of Phase III. As demand increases, so too the value of each image. This is a cibachrome print from a 35mm slide, taken before the digital world took over. The image is 36 x 48 inches, museum quality double matting and glass with dark oak framing. When Phase III is sold out no more prints of this image will be made." The friendly young woman stepped toward the image. "As you can see, only thirty-three more editions of Full Flight will be sold. We expect this image to be retired in the fall."

Carla guided Hank toward the image, and Alex began her quiet passage through the gallery. The images she'd seen were more dramatic in the lighting of the gallery environment. The new images revealed a deeply talented and creative artist.

The photo before her was taken from inside an aging mountain log cabin. Without a roof, the sun shown against the weathered grains of an interior pine wall, and through the window the cabin wall framed the image of dramatic greens on a mountain hillside, a sharp snow covered peak reaching upward to be surrounded by a deep blue sky.

He truly was an artist of unique capabilities. Jennifer had told her things were going well. She had described his unique approach to limited editions, creating a demand and increased value for each print phase. And he had been working.

His latest release was an eagle collection separate from Full Flight taken during an expedition to the Kenai Peninsula and Alaska Chilkat Bald Eagle Preserve. On the back wall was the series of four prints, each drawing the dynamic nature of the bald eagle in its own incomparable solitude. She wandered from print to print imagining the depths he had explored to capture the images.

Hank was standing to the side of the front door, reading a biography of Michael displayed prominently on an easel. Above the framed paragraphs was a picture of Michael Cabelli, standing beside his camera and tripod, a herd of elk grazing lazily in the background.

Alex slipped her arms around her father's. "Impressed?"

"A wonderful talent and handsome young man." He pointed at the words introducing the second paragraph, saying with deep concern, "It appears you have yourself entwined in a complicated soap opera."

Alex read the words. "Michael owes much of his success to the support shown by the Chadwick Foundation of Denver. Grants provided by the Foundation has allowed a commitment to his work, and through this Michael has collected his most dramatic images to share publicly."

Alex took a deep breath. "He has no idea of my connection to the Foundation. My assistant, Jennifer?" Hank nodded, knowing of Jennifer, "She's done all of the work with Mickey. I told you Daddy, I walked away two years ago."

"But you'd love to walk back, wouldn't you?"

Her arms were wrapped tightly around his. "I have William and Josie. I told you, there is much happiness. I have gone on with my life, and I've helped Mickey go on with his."

"I don't believe he has." Hank pointed at the picture to their right.

In it's own private corner, bathed in light, was a framed photograph. Large, nearly life-size and alive, Alex stepped away stunned by the subtle jolt of the vision. She was swept back to the moment when she had first tasted the purity of the mountain water. She had not seen this image or even realized he had taken it.

In the solitude the falls presented, she had walked into it, disappearing in the wall of water. But she hadn't disappeared. While reaching upward, stretching to feel the rain of the falls, the icy massage had created an obscured, sensual vision. He had captured her in that moment, that instant in which she felt the height of her seductive powers.

She was the mystery of the surroundings, the unrecognizable woman in nature's image adding to the credibility of untouched beauty. Glancing downward she read the title, *Mystic Blue.*

"Enchanting, isn't it." Carla appeared beside them, her voice startling Alex. "Unfortunately, this one is not for sale. Michael is a bit of a romantic, and this woman is incredibly special in his life. Part of the mystery is the way the details of her features are hidden by the waterfall. While you can't recognize her, that seems to make her image even more captivating. He has made just three prints of this image. This one is permanently on display here. Another is a part of his traveling show. The third is in his private gallery in his home, The White Room." In a softer voice, Carla acknowledged, "I believe he's searching for her."

Hank put his arm around Alex, smiling at the young woman. "Whoever she is, she's incredibly beautiful."

Chapter 25

"She was here?" Mickey stared at Jimmy in disbelief.

"I don't think she came to see you, Michael." Jimmy pressed his hands against his friend's solid shoulder.

Michael leaned heavily on the gallery counter. "You're positive it was her?"

"Positive Michael." Jimmy lifted his arms and dropped them limp to his side. "Same hat, same striking features, but she didn't stay around. She disappeared as soon as I recognized her."

"Where? When?" His forehead rested heavily in his hand.

Carla's round face looked across the room from dusting the frame of *Full Flight*. "Everything okay?" she asked.

Michael did not respond.

"A week ago Friday at Lonigan's, I was playing when I looked across the bar. I thought it was her standing at the railing by the pool table. It looked just like her, the same stature, long and beautiful and damn hot in that outdoorsy sort of way. I was sure it was her, but her hat was pulled down partially hiding her face, so I sent her a beer and played our song." Jimmy turned his attention to Carla, "You remember. I ordered the beer for her."

"Sure, I remember," Carla glanced from Jimmy to Michael, searching for understanding.

"Are you positive?" Michael turned and stared at the ceiling, his hair hung thick over his shoulders.

Jimmy nodded. "I sang *Mystic Blue*. She stared at me while I sang, and then she was gone. She just left, Michael."

"The pretty blond lady?" Carla said, duster in her hand.

"Yes, the one you took the beer to?" Jimmy said.

"Uh huh," she shrugged. "She came in the next day."

Shock filled their eyes. "In the gallery!" Michael blurted.

"Yeah." Carla pointed at the eagle. "The guy she was with really liked *Full Flight*. I thought he might buy it. They spent time wandering the gallery, really nice people. Then they seemed interested in *Mystic Blue*." She glanced toward the waterfall picture. "I described it to them, the old guy commented on how beautiful the girl in the waterfall was, and then they suddenly left."

Michael turned to Carla as if to say something, looked at *Mystic Blue*, then back to Jimmy. Without saying a word, he walked out the gallery door.

Carla frowned, her eyes following Michael until he disappeared. "What's going on, Jimmy?"

"It was her."

"Her who?"

Jimmy pointed at the photograph.

Carla's voice squeaked an octave higher. "The waterfall lady?"

Jimmy shook his head yes.

"You're kidding me." Carla stared at the image. "She was so beautiful, so nice."

"You said she was with a guy?" Jimmy asked.

"Uh huh." Carla still stared at the lady in the image.

"What was he like?"

"Like?" She wrinkled her eyebrows. "Like a father. It was like he was her father, and they were comfortable together."

"Much older than her?"

Carla was looking at the image again. "Yes, older. Kind looking, gray hair, soft blue eyes, I assumed he was her father."

Jimmy found him behind the MacDonald's Bookstore, sitting by the river. Michael was smiling deep satisfaction, a strange contrast to the disbelief of moments before.

"I'm still important in her life." He was almost joyful. "She wouldn't have come, she wouldn't have been in the gallery if I wasn't still in her life."

"Come on, Michael." Jimmy tried to shake him. "She doesn't want...or she can't have you in her life."

Michael nodded his understanding. "I know. It just feels good to know I'm still important to her."

Chapter 26

"You went to the gallery!" Jennifer glared at her, her voice rising.

"Jennifer, you told me he wouldn't be there. I knew he wouldn't be there. I just wanted to see his work."

"You couldn't look at his website?" Jennifer walked around the desk, red anger rising over her neck. "Instead, you wandered around the gallery."

"He's so talented. The gallery's an amazing place."

Jennifer turned with a harsh glare. "So what'd you think of your picture?" Her voice was sharp, almost demanding.

Alexandria did not respond, diverting her eyes to avoid Jennifer's stare.

"Damn it, Alexandria." Her voice rose. "What'd you think of the damn waterfall picture? It's you, isn't it, in the waterfall."

Alexandria did not answer, lifting her arms to place her elbows on the desk, eyes pressing into the palms of her hands. She could feel the furry growing in the heat from Jennifer's eyes.

"It's your memorial. He's enshrined you in the most prominent place in the gallery." Her voice demanded an answer. "What'd you think?"

"I had no idea. I never thought he'd display it."

Jennifer grew incensed, moving beside Alexandria. Her hand on the back of the chair, she turned her boss around and bent down until eye-to-eye, yelling into her face. "And now you know!"

Alexandria's eyes turned from Jennifer. Sad and shallow, she nodded slowly, unable to look at her angry friend.

"I'm sorry Alexandria. You're my best friend in the world, and you are my boss. But you put me in touch with Michael, and he has become a dear friend. His talent has gone on and grown, but emotionally he's stopped. There's this huge void in his life that he believes can only be filled by that stupid image he has of this woman in the waterfall." With each word her anger heightened. "You may think you loved him, but you damaged him, Alexandria. It hurts him to know you're out there somewhere. And now you pull this stupid stunt. You've got to stay away from him, and he needs to sell that fucking picture and go on with his life."

Alexandria turned away. "I didn't know."

"Well now you do." Jennifer stood before her, resentment penetrating Alexandria. "So leave him the hell alone, and let the poor guy move on."

Jennifer turned and stormed from the office, the door slamming with a wicked crash behind her.

Chapter 27

Leslie's phone call offered the diversion Alexandria needed. The tension at the Foundation had grown over the past weeks, and it would do both Jennifer and her good to take a break.

She telephoned William leaving a message because Valerie insisted his meeting was uninterruptable. Relieved that she didn't have to defend her decision, Alexandria explained that she and Josie were going to Vail with Leslie and Allison for a few days before the school year started.

His secretary happily took the message, leaving Alexandria wondering what there was to be so cheerful about. Was she Mrs. William Chadwick of New York City?

Josie and Allison took their roller blades, spending non-eating hours terrorizing the village. Alexandria was just the opposite. The first two days were spent on the deck wrapped in leggings and a big wool sweater until the mid-day sun brought warmth and the chance for a late summer tan. She read intriguing novels that took her to places away from her life, watched the mountains before her, and tried to untwist the confusion.

Jennifer was right, and she had not anticipated the commitment to Michael. She deeply regretted going to the gallery. Looking into the stillness of the mountains across the valley, the questions kept repeating themselves. Disturbing questions about Jennifer and Mickey. And why was William's secretary so enthusiastic? Her father was right too. She had become entwined in a potentially devastating soap opera.

As the deck door opened, Alexandria turned to see Leslie in a thin chenille robe, a pitcher in her hand. She squatted beside Alexandria, filling her half empty glass with fresh ice tea.

"I've made a whole pitcher. It's time for a warming Jacuzzi."

Leslie walked to the edge of the red wood tub, setting the pitcher within arm's reach. She took off her robe, revealing a dazzling one-piece black swimsuit with gold accents. Alexandria watched her ease into the water, allowing her body to adjust slowly.

"It's wonderful Alexandria." The light wave of her hand was playful. "Join me."

Alexandria placed the bookmark between the pages, setting the paperback beside her chair. She carried her tea and placed it beside the pitcher. Looking around the mountains she thought once again about freedom. Stretching, the sun pressed warm over her face. Reaching up under the length of her sweater, she slipped her fingers under her leggings and slid them down from her thighs. Crossing her arms, in one motion she lifted the sweater over her head revealed first her hips and then her breasts.

"Well," Leslie's face turned red. "I had assumed there was a swim suit under there." She glanced at the distant homes on each side. "All the neighbor men will be running for their binoculars."

"Sometimes, it feels good to be naked in the mountains."

As Alexandria stepped easily into the Jacuzzi, Leslie stood up pulling the straps from her suit down to reveal shapely breasts. With two steps, she pulled the swimsuit from the water holding it dripping overhead. Bending her elbow, the suit flew from her hand landing with a heavy splat on the middle of the open deck.

"Yes," Leslie beamed. "Naked can be good." Then she blushed. "It's just," she glanced around. "I've never done this."

Grinning, she felt like herself. "I've only done it once before."

It was over dinner that Leslie began to pry. "So what's up with the quiet reflection and reading?"

Alexandria looked up from the menu. "Would you like some Rocky Mountain Oysters?"

"Hell no." Her face distorted. "I can't believe you did that."

"So, no oysters?" Alexandria's lips pressed together.

Leslie scanned the left side of the menu. "I believe I'll have the French onion soup and a dinner salad."

Alexandria stared at the menu. "I'm thinking spinach salad."

The waiter arrived with a friendly nod. "Something from the bar?"

Alexandria looked up at the young man with the three loop earrings in his left ear. "Iced tea please."

Leslie agreed and before he disappeared to the bar, they ordered their meals. Alexandria grinned and pointed past Leslie. She turned around to see the girls weaving in and out of the walking people, moving directly toward them.

"Hi." Josie's smile was big.

"You won't believe it," Allison squealed. "We've bladed all the way to Eagle's Nest and back. The bike path is so smooth."

"All the way?" Leslie acted impressed.

"But some boys followed us back." Josie frowned.

Allison nodded, "They kept trying to talk to us."

"So did you talk?" Alexandria asked.

"Sure," Josie giggled. "A little bit anyway."

Allison glanced back over her shoulder. "There they come."

Leslie turned to see three teenage boys rollerblading across the bridge toward the village shops.

Josie's eyes got big. "Gotta go."

And both girls took off, the boys flying right behind them.

"Home before dark," Leslie yelled.

Without looking, Allison waved.

Leslie shook her head. "I knew this was going to happen the moment she started growing boobs."

Laughter spread across Alexandria's face. "Wouldn't it be nice to keep them young forever?"

"Simpler anyway." Leslie looked back up the street but all roller bladders had disappeared. "Changing subjects, what's up with the solitude, and no, I do not want any fried bulls' balls."

Fiddling with her glass, Alexandria knew better than to share too much.

"It's a difficult time for William. It impacts me, so it's a difficult time for us."

Leslie laughed at the phrase. "It impacts you?"

Alexandria tried to figure out what she really meant. William always expected to be in control. He demanded it of himself and those around him. But he was not happy. To the Chadwick family, control meant more money. It was a simple life plan. He'd traded happiness for control, and he was just beginning to understand his loss.

"You know Leslie, without the Foundation, I might go nuts."

Surprised, Leslie stared. "So what's making you nuts?"

"You know what my Dad and Mom do every morning?"

She didn't wait for Leslie to answer.

"Every morning my Dad sits on the couch and reads the Kansas City Star with one arm around my mother. She cuddles up warmly, and he holds the paper in front of them. He reads about the world, the Middle East, Congress, medical research. She reads about local interests like a new program in the high schools, flower clubs, fashion, and advice columns. Dad tries to figure out how to fix the world, and Mom focuses on family values. Every morning they read the Kansas City Star in each other's arms."

Leslie grinned. "You paint a pretty picture."

"That's it Leslie. I want a pretty picture."

The image of Mickey waltzed through her mind.

"Doesn't William want that too?"

"Leslie. You're married to money." Alexandria didn't have to say any more. "I don't know about Ben, but I believe William's scared to death. He's 38 years old and president of one of the country's largest banks. What if he failed?"

Leslie stared in disbelief. "That's absurd. William's as successful as anyone I know."

"Exactly," she added. "It must be terrifying to have such a burden. Look at the instability of the nation's banks, the world economy. The fear of failure must constantly drive him."

"And where does that put you?"

"Basically? Alone." She didn't look at Leslie. "He leaves for the office before I get up, comes home late at night. I'm never sure how he's going to respond, consistently at work, moody at home. But I know he's trying. He's scheduled me in for Thursday nights." Alexandria looked up quickly. "He's trying to open up, to make me a part of his life. On Thursday nights for a couple of hours, I'm his partner. At social events, I'm the adoring wife. The rest of the time we live separate lives. It's a real lousy way to live in a marriage, to be scheduled in on Thursday nights." She stared down at her spinach salad. "I can't remember if we've ever sat on the couch, his arm safely around me, while we read the morning paper together."

It was quiet while they ate their salads, the French onion soup slowly turning cold. Couples passed by holding hands. A young woman welcomed a handsome man with a hug and desperate kiss. It was an active late summer evening in manufactured Vail.

Leslie reached across the table and took Alexandria's hand. "Can I offer a suggestion?"

Alexandria closed her eyes, nodding innocently.

"For about a year, I've been seeing a therapist. She is a wise and wonderful woman. She listens and lets me talk, and it sorts things," Leslie shrugged happily. "Things clear when I'm with her."

Chapter 28

The Foundation receptionist interrupted Alexandria's thoughts.

"Mr. Chadwick is on his way up."

A thousand thoughts went through her head.

"Which Mr. Chadwick?" she asked.

"Your husband Mr. Chadwick," the voice came back.

"William?"

"Yes ma'am."

"He never comes up?" She searched the possibilities. "Did he say what he wanted?"

"No, sorry."

"Okay. Thanks." Thoughts of an afternoon picnic flirted in her mind.

When she'd taken over the Foundation, she'd hoped it might somehow bring them closer; maybe opportunities for lunch now and then. But she had quickly learned he did not allow such things in his schedule. Once he got himself functioning at seven in the morning he was in his bank president mode. He stayed intently in that role until the day ended sometime after eight in the evening.

The lesson had been learned during her second week when she stopped ten floors down at his office. It had seemed strange how seldom she had been in his office when he had turned from the telephone, covering the receiver with his hand, irritated at the invasion. Her smile and offer of lunch had quickly been dismissed with sarcasm at her blindness to the importance of his work, and she left with that common emptiness in her stomach.

As the receptionist buzzed, her office door pushed open and her husband stood stoically in the doorway. His suit was a deep gray complimenting his narrow hips and square shoulders. The strength in his eyes was obvious, off set by his square jaw and distinctive cheekbones. As he walked across the room, he straightened his conservative maroon and navy stripped tie.

Alexandria stood grinning from behind her desk. "William, this is a pleasant surprise." She caught the disapproving glance at her gray denim jeans, and thought it better to stay behind the desk hiding the fashionable cowboy boots.

He moved the leather-cushioned chair to sit down. "Sorry to disappoint you, Alexandria, but this is not a social call."

"Well then," she smiled pleasantly. "What brings you to these heights?"

William crossed his arms firmly. "I was disappointed this noon. Ben and I had a quick lunch together."

Of course, he would have time for lunch with Ben.

"Oh," she put on her best smile. "I haven't seen Ben for so long. How is he?"

"As always Ben is fine, and I'm sure you know Leslie is too."

Alexandria watched William's eyes and felt a scolding coming. "Good. I'm glad he's doing well."

"But apparently I'm not."

Alexandria's forehead wrinkled. "Pardon me?"

"Alexandria, did you tell Leslie I have a fear of failure?"

Her defenses rose quickly up her spine. "What do you mean?"

"I'm sure you know what I mean." Glaring intently, he added. "Leslie told Ben I was burdened with a fear of failure, and that is what was driving me."

"Please William, don't misinterpret what I said. Leslie and I were talking. It was simply two friends sharing some concerns."

She put her hand up to stop his interruption, but he talked right through it.

"You have no right to make blanket statements about my professional life. My job, my responsibilities, and how I approach them is without fear, and you made a complete misinterpretation." Anger rose in his fixed stare.

"I was talking to a friend. I only said your job is demanding, so time consuming." She fought to stand her ground.

"Damn it, Alexandria," he shifted straight in the chair, "of course it's demanding. My family's name is on this bank, and it's my responsibility. Your thinking out loud made me sound weak, and I cannot be perceived as weak." He puffed his chest like a barrel. "My wife cannot be critical or undermine the confidence our shareholders have in me?" His hand rose and the finger came forward, pointing. "You need to learn to keep your mouth shut."

The chastising stabbed at Alexandria. "Oh no, William. I never meant to discredit you. I was talking about us, about you and me. I'm concerned about us, and I'm concerned about you. It's not about criticizing you or undermining your leadership. It's about caring for you, wanting you to be successful and happy."

William's stare turned hard, and Alexandria knew he was no longer listening.

"What will make me happy is if you never again think out loud about me publicly." He stood before her, an imposing figure in a power tie with a sinister glare reminding her of a horror movie haunting her late in the night. "Do not let this happen again."

She watched the charcoal square of his shoulders and back as he walked through the doorway, leaving it open behind him. Her receptionist glanced back, and her eyes met Alexandria's. As William exited the office, the receptionist closed the door to Alexandria's office protecting her boss's privacy.

The emptiness crawled through her. He had come in domineering, left demanding control, and she felt helpless, angry, and dismissed.

Chapter 29

Being in the waiting room created a sense of relief. In the converted house, this room would have been a formal dining area just to the left of the front door. The decor was designed to relax with delicate blues, green plants in front of the split pane windows, and soft chairs that welcomed.

The room was empty with soft music coming from the small speakers hidden behind the greenery. Alexandria found a chair that allowed her to see through the plants into the front yard. She picked up a magazine from the table, smiling to herself. Not one psychology journal among them.

Ten minutes passed before Alexandria heard voices. She looked up to see two ladies standing at the doorway. One, dressed in an ankle length denim skirt and a flowered blouse nodded pleasantries and opened the door saying good-bye to a middle-aged lady. With a sweeping smile of welcome, she turned toward Alexandria sharing a gentle face with rich, deep-set brown eyes.

"Good afternoon," Her tone was soothing. "You must be Alexandria." The denim lady took Alexandria's hand in both of hers. "I'm Dr. Elaine Jesson. Please, call me Jessi."

"It's nice to meet you, Jessi," Alexandria smiled shyly. Then her grin broadened. "I'm Alex."

Alex followed her through the foyer and down a hallway into a quiet room that seemed solitary. Jessi motioned to a soft chair, and the doctor sat in her own comfortable chair.

Nervously, she joked, "No couch?"

Jessi smiled. "I've got a room with a couch. Would you be more comfortable there?"

"No," Alex dropped her head embarrassed. "This is fine."

"So. What brings us together today?"

"Well," Alex's shook the nervousness. "As I said on the phone, my friend Leslie referred me."

Dr. Jesson nodded.

"And," she shrugged, "there's some things in my life that are muddled. I can't really talk about them, but that's exactly what I need…someone to talk to."

"Go on, please."

Jessi fit none of the common misconceptions about shrinks, creating a sense of relief that eased the tension. Alex started slowly, describing her relationship with William, traditional values, arrogance, image, and male dominance.

Alex smiled sadly. "It's like the radical anti-abortion advocates?"

Jessi raised her eyebrows. "I'm afraid you'll have to explain that one."

"They have this weird sense of justice." Alex searched the room. "They're very moral in what they believe, so they do immoral things. Bomb clinics. Shoot doctors. Scare tactics."

"So," Jessi remained calm, "how is this like your marriage."

"It's this weird sense of morality." Alex's frown turned distorted. "Very virginal and conservative; rich, uptight, autocrats. High morals defined by money, yet while professing to be focused on family values, William ignores family in an effort to provide more money to a wife and child who don't know what to do with the money they already have. It's contradictory that he professes family values yet has abandoned me emotionally."

"If this is how you describe your marriage," Jessi gave a look of understanding, "I know why you're here."

Alex laughed, embarrassed, her eyes now diverted as if she was being revealed.

"I'm sorry. Maybe I'm over-dramatic. He's a good man with this weird sense of values. Family is vitally important but just the image. Like the anti-abortionist bomb clinics to stop the killing, William's answer to the perfect family is lack of involvement. He's consumed by fear of misrepresenting his image. That's our marriage. All image, and after that, there's little left to call ours."

That was it, she told Jessi. Their lives had become detached with different focuses, different directions, occasionally crossing paths allowing them to give broad-toothed smiles showing the image of a perfect family.

She explained his effort at their Thursday night commitment, adding that it seldom lead to intimacy. Passion, even tender embraces had disappeared as the detachment had grown. So she lived lonely and found her only salvation in her work at the Foundation, love for the outdoors, and her own desire to be true to herself and to Josie.

Jessi listened, empathetic. "Explain *be true to yourself*."

Alex looked sadly back at Jessi, pulling her blond hair up and away from her face. Her blue eyes shifted to the wall behind Jessi, to Jessi, and back to the wall. She thought of Mickey, of Mickey's life. Sharing laughter, exploring together, friends with passion; that was being true to herself. That was what a lifetime relationship should be, someone to hold her and love her while reading the morning paper.

She turned her eyes back to Jessi, felt the pressure begin in her heart and work upward to encase her temples. To be true to herself, she wanted the strength to be true to herself.

"Another thing that drives me crazy," she added, "the Chadwicks do not get dirty. Their entertainment is purchased. I'm teaching my daughter to love the outdoors. Experiencing nature makes one capable. William's world teaches confidence, but my world teaches us about our capabilities. Years ago," Alex closed her eyes, "without even realizing it, I gave into the money and have lived isolated since." Alex opened her eyes again. "I can't be isolated any more, and I can't let Josie become a victim of the Chadwick attitude. I have to be true to my daughter and myself. I haven't truly been that for many, many years."

Jessi watched Alex's foot bouncing up and down.

Alex looked at the psychiatrist. "I like your dress, casual."

Jessi watched Alex, waiting.

"It's the simple things," she went on. "Remember when you were a little girl, and you would stomp through mud puddles. I want to wear more denim, stomp through puddles, and laugh at being soaked. I'm so sick of the uptight image of perfect."

Jessi nodded, reassuring. She raised her hand, quietly halting. "I'm sorry, Alex, but our time is running short."

Alex glanced at the clock against the opposite wall, surprised that forty-five minutes had disappeared. "I've really been rambling, haven't I?"

"You said you needed to talk, and talk you did. May I ask?" Jessi continued comfortably. "What you would like to gain from our time together?"

Alex slumped, "I want to learn how to be true to myself."

"Good. I'd like that for you." Dr. Jesson scanned her finger down a calendar on the table. "How about this same time, let's say once a week for this month and then we'll see after that."

Alex felt good knowing she would be back. She nodded thankful. "I feel better already." Her chin lifted showing the soft strength of her high cheekbones.

Jessi's finger tapped the calendar. "One thing. You might think about the abortion analogy."

Her forehead wrinkled, and Alex squinted. "A little severe."

"A bit."

Alex nodded. "We have our issues, but William's not a mad bomber."

They both smiled understanding.

Chapter 30

William was long off to the bank when she saw Josie off to school. Alexandria stood on the grand columned terrace in her favorite holey blue jeans and oversized Denver Bronco sweatshirt, waving goodbye. Returning to the kitchen, a breakfast of toast, orange marmalade, fiber-rich cereal, and hot tea awaited. She carried the tray to the sunroom and settled in. The fall sun cast shadows among the hedges creating a maze effect in the garden.

When her breakfast was left with the remains of crust and cooled tea, she walked the colonnade staircase to their master suite. In her absence, the bed had been made. She closed the door and walked to her bathroom. Removing her sweatshirt, she stared in the mirror. Her stomach remained flat, breasts firm. Feeling healthy, she turned on the shower and sensed the warmth.

She left for the office feeling the confident freedom that just the right clothes can give. Her first stop was Jennifer's office and an invitation for lunch. They agreed on a trendy vegetarian bistro just down the street. Quick discussions followed with updates on several projects. The sculpture for the park entrance was on target for the October unveiling, the Art Institute was looking for support to bring a Monet exhibit to Denver, and yes, the symphony was being well attended to.

Exactly at noon, Jennifer appeared in her office. Alexandria was happy to see her, and they chatted from the lobby to the elevator. Outside, the day had brought the coolness of an early fall afternoon. There was a short line at the bistro, so Alexandria and Jennifer sat on a cushioned bench in the entryway.

Alexandria spoke quietly, her hair pulled back behind her ears and held in place under her hat. "I've never asked, and please tell me if it's something I'm better off not knowing."

Jennifer frowned, mildly curious.

"The picture? The waterfall?" Alexandria's eyes widened. "You knew about it?"

Jennifer rubbed her hands as if cold.

"I've never told him about you, our connection. He doesn't know. And I didn't fully understand this secret mission you sent me on until the gallery opened, and there was *Mystic Blue*. You were there in the image, so…How do I say it? So flawless." Her sandy brown hair hung unmoving as she spoke. "For the year before the gallery opened, I worked with Michael. He has so much passion and determination, and he's one of the nicest men I've ever met. Then he opened the gallery, and there you were. That's when I understood. Yes, I've known about the picture for some time."

The hostess called out *Chadwick*, and Alexandria looked up with a wave. They followed her to a small table in the back.

Alexandria spoke as if there had been no interruption. "How did you know it was me?"

Jennifer almost looked melancholy. "I'm sorry, Alexandria, but I asked him about it."

Alexandria just looked at her.

"Michael didn't say much," she shrugged. "He said it was a woman he hoped someday to love again."

Alexandria's eyes lifted up and stared blankly beyond Jennifer.

"I'm sorry, but I felt guilty knowing he never would."

Still staring beyond her friend, Alex eyes were distant.

"He's in love with an image, and it's not healthy. It's not right to be in love with a mirage."

Alexandria's words were soft. "What can I do?"

"I don't know. He just needs to be free of you."

In the quiet, Alexandria reached for her menu, gripping it to stop the shaking in her hands. Her voice was a whisper. "Yes, he does." Alexandria stared quietly at the laminated menu. "He needs to find someone, to go on. That is my hope for him, to go on." Very businesslike, Alexandria looked up giving matter-of-fact instructions. "I need assistance with one last matter." Her face was stern, her eyes distant. "Would you order for me the 36 x 48 inch framed print entitled Full Flight? Please forward it to my father in Lawrence." Then she added, "And if you would, do it all in your name. I'll reimburse you."

Jennifer's stare was blank. Slowly, she nodded agreement.

"Thank you." Alexandria picked up her menu. "It's such a beautiful September day, isn't it?" She looked back at the menu. "What looks good to you?"

That afternoon she kept her second appointment with Jessi. Alexandria told her about Mickey, crying even before she began speaking. She told her that being with him felt true, but she could not be with him. She painted the picture and sang the song, and she held herself so tightly as if in his arms. After forty-five minutes she left Jessi's office, but it was four hours later before she was able to drive home to her daughter and the security of her life provided by an intense man who had lost his own way.

Chapter 31

Usually they went to quiet restaurants on Thursday evenings, but this week Alexandria suggested The Club. William liked the idea and the familiar surroundings. Alexandria surprised him wearing pleated Hollywood cut pants with a matching black satin jacket fitting snugly over a white halter-top vest. He dressed sportily in corduroy slacks, a deep v-neck sweater and blue blazer.

They had cocktails in the lounge, visiting with many of William's friends. The conversations were light and pretentious, drinks of scotch and bourbon being waved about as stories were told. William never left her side. They shared the time as a couple, and she sensed the sincerity of his effort.

After dinner, they sat together on the terrace watching the last few golfers coming in off the course. Alexandria sat elegantly with her legs crossed, her shoulders turned to share the time with her husband. She was surprised when William began rubbing his fingers slowly over her forearm. She could feel the hint of sensation up her arm and into her shoulder.

"I know I've not been very attentive. Actually, for a long time I've not been very attentive." He moved his hand to her forearm. "It's confusing to me, Alexandria. I don't know when to turn off this bank president personality."

She put her hand over the top of his, rubbing.

"Alexandria, tonight could we go home and make love?" He sounded almost apologetic.

Her nod was slight but sure. To be held again, in a way it frightened her.

She wasn't quite sure what to do when he closed the bedroom door. She watched him walk across the white carpeting, slipping his jacket down off his shoulders, and disappear through his bathroom door. She went to her own bathroom, stepping into her closet.

Under the dim light from the bedroom, she found a lacy pearl Carmeuse gown. She placed it back where it hung, and carefully removed her clothing. Taking the sleeping gown from the hanger, she slipped it over her head and tried to think about looking sexy.

When she stepped from her bathroom, the lights were dimmed and William lay naked, his body covered to the chest. He watched her walk across the bedroom, and pulled the satin sheets back. She nuzzled in close to him, and his arm pulled her body closer.

In his whispered voice, he complimented her, "You are an incredibly beautiful woman." Then he kissed her gently over her neck and cheek until their lips met.

He tried to be gentle. It had been so long. He lay on top of her and pressed slowly as they kissed. His motions were slow, and she welcomed his touch. To be held, to feel loved, she breathed deeply, searching for his scent. Each motion was slow and sensitive, and he tried to resist, but he could not wait. He pulled her to him.

It had not lasted long, but it was a beginning. He whispered that he loved her, and she whispered back. She fell asleep that night in his arms with a sense of warmth and safety. She slept soundly through the night, and in the morning, she felt his kiss on her cheek as he left for work.

Chapter 32

"I'm glad to see you back, Alex." Jessi searched her eyes for signs. "How has the week gone?"

"I've accepted things, and there's relief." A life of happiness without being happy, for her family it would be okay.

"If *accepted things* is where you are, we may have some things to talk about it." Jessi leaned forward. "What happened this week?"

"It'd been two years," she said, "since we've been intimate."

"Since you've made love?"

"Last night was the first time in two years."

"And…"

Alexandria shrugged, "It was what I remembered it to be."

"Oh, oh."

Alexandria nodded, "William, in all his distinguished power, is a confused interpretation of power and prude. I'm sure there's some Freudian psychological deeply rooted in his relationship with his mother. He doesn't know how to connect love with making love, and he doesn't know how to enjoy the pleasure of receiving. In fact, he's pretty intimidated by me. His love making skills are, well, as a teenage boy would say, wam-bam-thank-you-ma'am. So, two years ago, I decided to change him."

Jessi nodded for her to go on.

"I've only had orgasms during sex once in my life." She looked disappointed. "When I made love with Mickey, he pleased me first and that made me want to please him." She felt a sensation, pressing her legs against each other, "If I'd stayed I'd have faced a life of gentle lovemaking and orgasms. I traded it in believing I could teach William to be more like Mickey."

"He wasn't a good student?"

Glancing down nervously, Alexandria took a deep breath. "The morning I left, I wanted to make Mickey feel wonderful. I'd never been given the chance to take control, to be the one making love to the other. I was curious, it was part of the adventure, and I wanted to leave Mickey feeling, is *special* the right word?"

Jessi grinned, "*Special* is a good word."

"Anyway, when I got back to Denver I was determined to change our lives. So one night I pulled out all the stops, and I was more me than

William had ever known. But he tried to stop me when I, you know…kissed him there." Alex got a goofy look on her face,. "Mickey liked it," she laughed. "I liked it a lot. I assumed William would too."

Jessi nodded waiting for her to go on.

"When William resisted, I persisted, and it was obvious he enjoyed it. But he couldn't let me lead. He even blurted out something about being like a New York hooker…" Alex paused, the words *New York hooker* repeating in her mind. "And then…" *A New York hooker,* she looked up more shocked then explaining, "And then he stopped me and forced himself on me. I wanted him to let me love him, but instead it turned harsh. It hurt me. After that, we didn't make love again for two years. That's why I think his mother's twisted in there somewhere. Freud would love it."

Jessi turned the pencil in her hand. "Explain?"

The phrase *New York Hooker* repeated itself in her mind. "Sophie's so formal. I'm sure I'm one orgasm up on her."

"One," Jessi repeated.

"The one and only night," she felt her body shudder. "The first and last orgasm was with Mickey." Then she blushed, "Okay, the first and last night of the orgasms, plural, was with Mickey."

"Wow." Her eyes jumped open causing them both to laugh loudly. When the calmness returned, Jessi asked, "And now?"

"How do you understand a guy like him?" Alexandria grinned, laughed again. "Wouldn't you think a man with his standing would think he could do anything? God, he must be afraid."

Jessi's brown eyes were always soft. "And how does a man of power overcome fear."

She shrugged, "With more power."

Jessi's nod was slight.

Alexandria stared disbelieving. "You mean sex with his wife is a control issue."

"Yes."

"I only thought of it as love." Alexandria was slumping in the soft cushion chair. She smiled up at Jessi. "Then I wish he would try and control me like Mickey did. I'm badly in need an orgasm."

Once again the two women broke into laughter.

Chapter 33

With the soothing chimes, Carla looked up as the gallery door opened. Her smile broke wide. "Hey, what brings you up here?" she giggled, scooting to hug Jennifer.

Jennifer embraced her friend. "Good to see you too."

Carla stepped back in admiration. "You look fantastic. So are you here for fun or business?"

"Pleasure. I decided to take the weekend." Jennifer rolled her eyes as if this was some spontaneous escape. "Is Michael around?"

"He was earlier." Carla waved in explanation. "Off somewhere, but he'll be back this afternoon. He'll be so happy to see you."

"Me too." Jennifer glanced around the gallery. *Mystic Blue* still graced the corner. "Some quick business first. I need one of Michael's images."

"Sure."

"We have an associate with our bank we want to give a special gift. He's a huge wildlife fan. He mentioned that someday he wants to go to Alaska just to watch the eagles. I was wondering, are you sold out of Full Flight?"

"Almost, but you're in luck." Carla walked to the eagle print. "This is print number 89 of Phase III. Only eleven are left."

"Wonderful." Jennifer searched her purse for her credit card.

"Oh no, Jennifer." Carla was shaking her hand. "I'm sure Michael will not want to charge you for the print."

"That's why I want to do this now, before he can interfere. Let's charge it, and let me give you the name and address. I'd like you to ship it directly if you would?"

Carla took instructions like any good employee. While Jennifer certainly wasn't the boss, her importance was known.

"I'll ship it this afternoon."

"Perfect." Jennifer took the credit card back. "Tell Michael I'll be at the Stanley. Have him call, okay?"

"He'll be thrilled." Carla waved happily.

Jennifer's afternoon break, a mid-day run, had felt good. The elk had already begun to migrate down from the park into town. Jennifer had seen a small herd wandering through the trees, watching as they curiously looked back at the figure on the road.

Now in the confines of her room she turned the bath water on, stripped clean of the damp clothes, and hung them on the door.

A growing pillow of bubbles rolled to the edge of the tub, and she tested the water with her toes. Perfectly warm, she eased down and allowed the bathwater to surround her.

Alexandria had seemed to make a decision. Yes, Alexandria had said, Michael needed to be free. Over sprouts and greens, she had listen to Alexandria's proclamation that Mickey should be free.

Michael had become a friend, a close friend that she enjoyed a great deal. Escaping to Estes had become an often sought after opportunity, sometimes to hang out with Michael, other times Jimmy, and often with both. They were her mountain buddies.

Jennifer knew she could just show up, knock on either of their doors, and be welcomed immediately. While she had found a unique coziness and endearment that had brought her closer to Jimmy, she had avoided any deeper thoughts of Michael fearing it would complicate her relationship with Alexandria.

The warm water both soothed her muscles and eased her private thoughts. Then her body flinched at the pounding on the door, bubbles splashing outward to the floor. Leaning over the bathtub she looked through the crack in the doorway.

"Who is it?"

"Michael." His voice was strong, even through the door.

"Hi," her voice rose. "I'm in the tub, but come on in."

Michael pushed the guestroom door, and to his surprise the door opened. "I thought hotels had better security than this."

"Old hotel," she yelled back. "Be out in a minute."

"No hurry."

She lay for a moment feeling warm and excited to see him.

Michael spoke from the other room. "How ya been?"

"Good, real good," she called back.

"Are you staying all weekend?"

"'Till Sunday evening." She reached for the towel beside the tub. "Anything special going on?"

"Not really, but we'll hang out. We always seem to find fun?"

She stopped drying herself, smiling into the towel.

Michael looked up at the bathroom door. It opened and Jennifer peeked out, her body wrapped in a deep rose colored towel. She looked much smaller, more petite, without clothes. He winked, grinning, "Nice outfit."

Jennifer stopped, smiled seductively then leaned back into the protective bathroom.

"What's Jimmy up to?"

"Off to Steamboat this weekend," his voice carried into the bathroom. "Playing some music festival over there."

"Too bad," she answered, dry herself. "I was hoping to spend some time with him. So how was the trip to Alaska?"

"Amazing, absolutely amazing." Michael sat on the hotel room bed, leaning back to look upward at the decorative ceiling. "At one point, I sat quietly behind my camera with six Brown Bears less than fifty feet away. It was like a gathering of magnificence and fear all in one small place."

"Wow, incredible."

"Remember that Thomas Mangelson image I showed you before I left?"

From the bathroom, she said, "The one with the salmon jumping into the bear's mouth."

"Yep. I was in the same spot. Brook Falls. The brown bears come to feed during the salmon run, and, well, it's more than amazing."

"Are brown bears grizzlies?"

"Same family but bigger. Fat from the Salmon."

"Good shots?" she called out.

"White Room quality," he answered.

From her bag, she picked a red stretch cotton sweater and sleek white jeans. Viewing them with a discerning eye, she thought once again about her friend, Alexandria. "So, how good has the year been?"

"I just bought the cabin."

Jennifer popped her head around the door. "Really?" Her smile had a new coat of bright red lipstick.

"It's mine, mine and the bank's."

"Fantastic." She disappeared, fluffing her hair for a freer look.

"I've covered my overhead at the gallery and working with a good profit, enough for my down payment. I never expected it, Jennifer, to be this far this quickly. Our ideas, the marketing concept, and your financial support, well, it's have been amazing."

Jennifer looked at her reflection up and down, tiny hips and a stretched sweater. She shook her hair again allowing it to fall where it may, and stepped out into the room, curious to see if Michael approved. Jennifer glanced to see his head lifted from her bed.

Her stride was smooth, gliding across the room. One at a time, she slipped the red heels over her feet, standing three inches taller. She turned with provocative eyes, full and happy lips of red.

"Too much," she asked.

"I love it," he said, pointing up and down her body. "Nobody wears heels in Estes."

Jennifer raised an eyebrow grinning confidently. "I do."

They parked the Jeep just beyond the water wheel at the west end of town. Walking along the storefronts, Michael acted nonchalant. From that moment two years before in the Stanley, he had liked her. She was more than just the money lady. Her business intuition had convinced him to review his entire gallery and marketing plans. She had a sense of style and knew what would sell, and that ability had created a wonderful partnership.

"So was this trip planned for Jimmy?"

"Of course." Her eyes diverted. "I was hoping both of you would be here?"

"Of course."

"What's that mean?" She grinned slyly.

Michael shrugged.

He led her to the Wapiti Restaurant where they were served beers and chips with salsa. In the bar named for elk, they sat on the tall Aspen wood chairs at a table along the back wall.

"I have an attitude," she announced confidently, her eyes rounding wide.

"An attitude?" He bit into a nacho chip.

"Yes, an attitude," she nodded. "A kick-back, coyote-howling-at-the-moon attitude. I want to have some fun tonight. I want to go just a little bit crazy and dance in the moonlight, laughing out loud. I've got a howling-good-time attitude."

Michael looked skeptical. "A howling-good-time attitude?"

"Yep. Coyote moon."

"I'm more of a wolf." He howled softly. "Jimmy's the coyote."

"Well, you may be the alpha male, but tonight you're my partner in crime," she teased. "So let's have some fun howling?"

He laughed, accepting the silliness. "Hey, you should have been here the other day. I saw an elk in metamorphosis. Looked damn near like a moose," he laughed.

"You are so full of it."

He winked a thank you, giving a little howl.

As they stepped into Lonigan's, Jennifer was full of life. Michael grinned when her eyes fluttered. "Bad day at the office?"

Jennifer shrugged, closing her brown eyes. "Tough lunch with my boss. I'm just ready to escape all the drama."

"Fun we can provide." Michael reached over rubbing her back, a moment of affection for his friend, then winked at her soft smile. "Scooter," he called to the bartender, "two shots of tequila."

"Okay," she answered his challenge. "Now we're howlin'."

And howl they did, alternating beers with shots and chasing shots with beers. The bar was full of friends and curious onlookers wondering if

Michael was either breaking out of his celibate past or just proving the rumors untrue. They laughed, and every now and then Michael would tilt his head and howl bringing more attention to the well-known pair that seemed to be acting like a couple.

Michael leaned in whispering. "You know," he confided, "there are rumors I'm gay."

Jennifer leaned away, her eyes to him. "Then they're not paying attention."

Michael teased, "My rugged look give me away?"

"No," she answered flatly. "The girl in the waterfall? *Mystic Blue*. Did you make her howl?"

Michael, giving a sly, sure grin, sat back adjusting his beer in the wet ring on the bar. "What does that have to do with sexual orientation rumors?"

"If you were gay, the waterfall wouldn't be on display?" She shrugged, her eyes dancing a bit. "A gay man would display it as art. You display it like a wanted poster."

Michael howled with a silly laugh. "A wanted poster?"

"You want her," she answered, her eyes not leaving his.

"Mind games Jennifer?" He lifted the mug, emptied it into his mouth, swallowed hard, and waved to Scooter for another round. "How did we jump back in time?"

"That's just it, Michael. The picture may be in the past, but she's still making you whimper."

"Whimper?" He began to laugh, snorting instead. "Whimper? I don't whimper."

"When's the last time someone made you howl, Michael?" Jennifer challenging. "After all, that's why there're gay rumors."

Michael thought to the last time, that time with Alex it had been sensual and consuming. He had felt the energy, her soft skin, and the touch of their lips, but most of all, he remembered the flinching prick of the needle in his heart.

She had just left. That had caused him to stop emotionally, but Jennifer and her Foundation saved him and his return to Estes Park was the pulling up of the bootstrap.

Now, he enjoyed mornings at sunrise in the wilderness with his camera. In the silent, windless morning a moose and her calf would wander into view. From his blind he would wait, watching, focusing. She would move with ease and awkward grace, taking the willow leaves. With leaves still full in her mouth, she would stand alert, her eyes darting, framing the landscape. And once in a great while he would capture an image that was so wonderful it could never be duplicated.

"Right now, I'm captured in my work." He avoided the topic.

"Too bad," she answered. "There are a lot of wanting women in this town."

Michael looked around nodding, and then his eyes landed back on Jennifer. He didn't know if it was the tequila or the howling, but he liked what he saw, something different in her, the ways she smiled toward Scooter with her eyes glancing back to Michael. His smile broadened as Scooter set two more shots before them.

This time Jennifer took the lead, tapping her shot glass on the bar. "Here's to howling-at-the-moon."

Michael grinned, licked the salt from his hand, tossed the tequila burning against the back of his throat, slammed the thick glass on the wooden bar, and sucked hard on a lime. "Damn," he shook the fogginess from his head.

An hour later, on the sidewalk in front of Lonigan's, local kids sat on the bricked shrub planters and wooden benches eating slices of pizza. Music floated from inside, a twangy country song. Jennifer lifted Michael's hand, spinning a half turn to the country beat, and fell against his chest, her hips still moving. With a rhythm matching hers, he moved his hips as he took her in his arms. In the exaggerated pulse of country swing, they danced to the music. Teenagers stopped in mid bite, tourists laughed as they watched, and Michael and Jennifer consumed the walkway enticing each other in hip grinding tempo of country swing. As the music faded, their laughter filled the air and two teenage girls began to cheer.

Happy eyes lit her smile. "Dancing in the moonlight."

"Howling-at-the-moon." He twirled her again into his arms as the crowd joined in applause.

Arm in arm, they swayed down the street laughing like goofy teenagers on their first drunk.

At the Wheel Bar, beerman Brad greeted him with a brew. Michael waved for another, handing Jennifer his. He led her directly to the shuffleboard table and began to explain the rules. She knew how to play, but she didn't know his game. He warned her that the winner would be crowned Champion of the Civilized Universe, and thus entitled, the word *entitled* hanging in the air like a piñata full of treats.

Jennifer picked up some shuffleboard sand, sprinkling it on the wood. "Want to hike tomorrow?"

"Could," he answered, "but I was thinking about heading to the other side of the park. Lots of moose."

"Tell you what." She waved an unsteady finger. "If I win, we hike. If you win, I'll ride to the other side with you."

"So," he laughed, "we're going to the other side."

"We'll see." She flicked a bit of sand at him.

He had assumed an easy victory, but she too had gone to college. A boyfriend had been a shuffleboard addict, and she had never been a good observer. The first game went to him, but she pressed him to within three points irritated that for her fuzzy vision, she would have kicked his ass. The second game she teased him, wiggling her tight backside before each shot. He found his concentration drifting from the intensity of a championship, and before he regained focus, she had won easily.

Brad brought two more beers, his eyes taking in Jennifer and nodding approval to Michael. Michael picked up a blue puck and walked toward Jennifer, backing her against the shuffleboard table. He whispered a dare. The loser would have to stand out front on the sidewalk and howl like a coyote in the night.

She liked the challenge, so she whispered back, "You might as well start howling," and punched him in the shoulder, causing him to stagger sideways. "You're up Mr. Wile E."

The battle was playful and intense. Each puck left near the edge was knocked off by the other's, the wooziness of the drink unseen in the skill of a bar game. Intense points one at a time added up until Michael missed knocking off a three. Jennifer grinned confidence, blocked the puck with a two and lagged a three on her final throw pulling away to win by four. She gave him a congratulatory hug, one hand patting his Levis as she howled.

"Where to now," he swayed before her.

"The sidewalk," she laughed. "Then The Whiskey Bar at the Stanley. We can walk there."

"Okay," he agreed. "I'll howl all the way there."

He turned leading her through the narrow passage along the length of The Wheel bar, howling like a wild coyote. Some of his friends howled back, others just laughed, and Jennifer reached forward taking his hand as she moved behind him, giggling uncontrollably in a drunken navigation through the maze of mountain men and envious women.

The sun struck Jennifer's eyes causing her to wake, blinking in the brightness. For a moment she wondered where she was until the white ceiling of her Stanley Hotel room came into view. The sound of another breathing caused her to startle. Stiffening, she turned her head to see the unmistakably long black waves of Michael Cabelli. She bit her lip pulling the sheet up to her neck, freezing as if asleep, unsure of what she'd done.

Believing she was still asleep, he slid sideways from the bed and eased out. Trying to straighten his rumpled tee shirt, he closed the bathroom door and stared at his stubbled face in the mirror wondering why the hell he'd drank so much tequila.

Picking up her tube of toothpaste, he pressed a glob onto his fingertip rubbing the white cream over his teeth, cupped his hands with water, and sucked it silently in.

When he opened the door, she stood before the window with the bed comforter covering her like a little girl in an oversized prom dress.

"Good morning," he smiled shyly.

"It's a beautiful day, Michael," her voice was unconvincing.

"Sunshine in the mountains," he answered upbeat.

"We're go for a hike today" She walked toward him, looking up into his eyes as if it was yesterday, and she'd just arrived.

Tequila sloshed in his brain. "You ever been to Gem Lake?"

"Nope."

"How about I'm back here in a couple of hours?"

"Great," she tried to answer with enthusiasm, but too many questions were bouncing in her mind.

"It's a date then."

The words hit her like a scared schoolgirl.

As he left, she turned and watched out the window, a sadness sweeping through her feeling as if she had betrayed her friends, Alexandria and especially Jimmy. For a moment, she tried to convince herself that nothing had happened, yet she stood naked under a bed comforter, and she had the worst hangover in years.

The hike to Gem Lake was a steady climb; a short hike, yet like walking a mile and a half up stairs. Still, like all hikes it rewards you when you reach the top. Michael had started out with vigor and determination, but Jennifer had soon taken the lead. Following her three steps behind, he wondered what was bugging her. Uncharacteristically quiet, she seemed to be pounding her feet with each step.

Sweat was beading on her forehead, and she could feel the same down the slight curve of her back. Carcinogens, she thought. Her body was expelling the poison of the night before, the alcohol overdose pressed her body to expel the bad and replace it with good.

But she knew that was likely the easy part. How could she undo the night with Michael? What would make the night go away and allow their friendship to return unscathed? She loved him in so many ways, but in that way, the way it had been in their drunken liaison was not how it should be. What had she been thinking? What if Alex ever found out? Worse, what about Jimmy?

At the peak, they stood before Gem Lake, quietly watching the reflection of the red stone towering above the amphitheater lake.

"I want to go up there." She pointed across the lake to the top of the rock cliff.

Immediately, without a comment Michael was off toward the lower end of the cliff.

Jennifer watched him for a moment wishing she could back up twenty-four hours. Howl at the moon? *You idiot.*

Michael ducked under a Limber pine and began to climb the sloping rock. She followed him to a crevice filled with soft sandstone. He stopped halfway through to reach up and pull, lifting himself up over the side to the rock surface above.

Jennifer looked up, seeing him turn and reach down for her.

"I don't need your help," she yelled.

He stood straight, his head half bitten off. "Okay." Then he disappeared.

For a moment she waited, realizing he was gone. Frustrated, she jumped once for the handhold, missing. Looking at the red rock before her, she leaned her forehead against the sandstone, thought about calling out then shook her head in determination.

Stepping backward, she pressed her hips into the opposite wall. She lunged forward in two quick steps jumping to a fingertip handhold. Hanging full length, she pulled and did a chin up to the rock, swinging her leg over the ledge.

When she rolled over, Michael was sitting a few feet away on a toadstool rock. Lying on her back, she looked up as he stared blankly out over the canyon.

"Sorry," she said from her prone position.

"What's with you?" He asked.

She crawled over to sit beside him.

From the peak above Gem Lake, you could see the newer homes in Devil's Gulch. To the east was Lake Estes and to the south Long's Peak casting a powerful presence over the town.

Jennifer sat looking over at him. "Tequila was a bad idea?"

"Tequila," he laughed, his voice dry. "Jimmy sings a song about tequila." He thought then sang. "*Tequila Makes Her Clothes Fall Off.*"

"Yes," she said, stringing the word out like an ominous warning. "Tequila. A bad idea."

Michael laughed. "Don't worry. A little hair-of-the-dog tonight, and the headache will go away."

"But the complications and the … the guilt."

"What do you have to feel guilty about?"

"You and I had sex." She screamed in a low voice. "I can't sleep with a client. What about our friendship? What about Jimmy and our circle of friendship? God, Michael, what have we done?"

Her anguish was genuine, and the guilt of Alexandria finding out twisted in her tequila wrenching gut. It meant she might lose her best friend just as she had jeopardized her friendship with Michael and Jimmy. What a mess they'd created.

Michael was laughing until her eyes bore down on him.

Then he smiled. "Over the last two years, what we've done together, the work and your guidance, all of our goals have been met and exceeded. Through it all, our friendship has grown into a personal commitment. You are an incredibly important person in my life." He reached, rubbing his hand slowly over her back, leaving it rest on the rock behind her. "I'd do anything for you, but I don't ever want to be without your love and friendship."

"Wow." Breath eased from her. "That may be the most beautiful thing anybody's ever said to me." She looking out over Devil's Gulch. "Thank you for your love and friendship."

"About honesty."

"Yes." She hesitated.

"You seem to think something bad happened last night."

"Michael, we slept together."

"Exactly." He answered. "We finished off more tequila in the lounge, I walked you upstairs, you stumbled through the door and into the bathroom. A minute later, you came out and crawled into bed." He laughed at the memory. "It was like you didn't even know I was there. I couldn't drive home, so I crawled into bed, and we fell asleep."

"But I was naked."

"Yes," he nodded slowly. You walked out of the bathroom naked and crawled into bed.

"And you were naked."

"Nope." His hands opened, explaining as much. "I was fully clothed."

"You were?"

"Love and friendship, Jen."

"But I walked across the room fully naked."

"Yes you did." His eyes grew big.

"And you watched."

He gave her one big nod. "Absolutely." Then he smiled. "Very impressive."

"Oh my God. I was so drunk."

"Howling-at-the-moon."

"I was naked?" She asked again.

"*Tequila makes your clothes fall off.*" He laughed-out-loud.

On the hike back down she was more alive and talking.

"I know some things, Michael."

"Yes," he answered from ahead of her.

"But I need to understand something."

"Okay." He fought against the loose rocks under his boots.

"How did three days with one woman affect you so much?"

He hesitated, asking, "Jimmy been talking?"

"You talked when we first met," she shrugged. "Jimmy verified. And I've watched you and that damn waterfall picture for the past two years. You're obsessed."

His silence took him far away, back to her and that moment he found the note and she was gone. He hadn't been able to get over that because he was sure it wasn't what she wanted. Maybe it was what she had to do, and with that, he'd always felt there must have been a better way. There were too many solutions than just walking away, so when he'd found the note, from that moment on what might have been had haunted him.

"So help me understand *Mystic Blue*. How did three days consume you for two years?"

"What's with you and the waterfall picture?" he asked.

She stared at his back. "What's with me and the waterfall picture?" Irritated, she kicked a rock his way. "Just tell me, Michael. For the sake of our love and friendship, tell me."

He shook his head as if to say *no*. "She was special."

"She was special?" She laughed. Michael, I'm special, and you had the perfect chance, but decided to sleep in your jeans."

"Love and friendship, Jen."

"I'm serious. Tell me. How did she do it in three days?"

"It was," he closed his eyes, "I don't know how else to describe it, but as the best three days of my life."

It hung in the air like an answer without explanation, and Jennifer knew he still wasn't free.

Chapter 34

Michael spent the afternoon in the gallery. He sat back and absorbed each image. He dusted, adjusted, and rearranged until the room felt perfect. Carla offered, but he smiled her away, insisting that he wanted to do these chores.

Occasionally, he would slip from his meditation and visit with a customer. Welcoming them as if a guest in his home, he would share stories about the images. To those who did not know his life, he was the great adventurer out in the wilds among the animals.

He kept looking at Alex's image. He kept feeling her touch and seeing her beauty, so vivid in his memory. He wanted to take the picture away, to place it in storage, or find an appropriate place, an artsy gallery or above a quiet table in a bookstore coffee shop.

Oh, but once that first twinge of pain passed there was a warm memory and it felt good. Maybe the memory had become greater than the reality. Time twists things to the better, but he knew their hearts had connected. Every time he felt that twinge, the slight pain, it was his heart unable to pull away from her.

He left Carla to close the store and walked to Jimmy's house. It was a cool evening, even for an early fall. Unseasonably, Jimmy wore a gray tee shirt and floppy shorts. Michael was happy to see that, and he followed him into the living room. The fireplace was ablaze, and Jimmy picked up his guitar and began strumming chords as they talked. Jimmy loved to play music in front of the fireplace, the warmth helping old songs come to life and new songs grow in the heart.

"Heard a rumor." His friend mentioned casually.

Michael looked at him, sat down on the floor, and leaned his back against the couch.

"Well actually, I heard a rumor about a rumor." He kept strumming, looking down at the guitar bridge.

"It's true," Michael said.

"So," he played a chorus of an old song. "You've proven to the disappointed women of Estes that the gay rumor is no longer their excuse for your indifference."

He smiled despite how he felt. "Apparently."

"Do you think Jennifer was a good person to end your celibacy with?" Jimmy's hands froze.

"Well, it wasn't really ending celibacy. It was more like camping out in middle school except there was lots of tequila involved." Michael started laughing.

"What do you mean?"

"Basically, we drank too much, she passed out, so I crawled in to bed and fell asleep. Didn't even shed my jean, but when she work up and found me there, it scared the shit out of her."

"No sex?" Jimmy strummed a G chord. "Still celibate?"

"Nada," he shrugged. "Jennifer is fantastic. Your song about love and friendship, that's Jennifer and me."

Jimmy played softly *Mystic Blue* on his guitar.

"Sometimes I wish I'd never met Alex. God damn, she messed me up."

The room went silent until Jimmy spoke, his direct words. "She's gone. It's you holding on that's messing you up."

Michael put his head back on the couch closing his eyes. The room was warm with the crackling fire. "Play me a song, Jimmy. Play something sad. I'm feeling sad."

"You're pathetic." He told him the hard truth, as he started the distinctive introduction to *Why Don't We Get Drunk and Screw.*

"Funny," Michael spoke from behind closed eyes

"What the hell were you thinking?"

"It was more about drinking than thinking."

"Played a dangerous game." Jimmy pounded harder on the guitar.

"Jimmy, we both know that's your game to play." Michael's eyes turned toward him. "When are you going to make your move?"

Jimmy didn't answer. Instead, he began playing a song he'd been working on since they'd meet.

Chapter 35

The family was all together, Robert and Sophia, William, Alexandria, and Josephine, all there for Josephine's ballet recital. Alexandria had loved ballet as a child, but she had never known if she were gifted for her teacher was not. Still, she'd loved dancing.

Josephine, too, loved to dance and her talent was rich, but it would always be the joy of the performance that motivated her. This is why Alexandria knew Josie's future in ballet was limited with joy overshadowing drive. Others, trained by Denver's premier ballerina, worked with an intensity driven by even more intense mothers. But Josephine just loved to dance and Alexandria encouraged her daughter when she was dancing.

She wondered if this would be her last recital, already seeing the conflict between treks into the mountains and weekend performances. She knew that the end would bring a huge battle of disappointment from Sophia, her mother-in-law viewing ballet as the most valued of endeavors. Josephine should be a ballerina, debutant, and princess in that order.

But Alexandria already knew that while debutant was a possibility, ballet was quickly giving way to 14,000-foot peaks, rock climbing, and rappelling back down. Sophia would be shocked beyond belief when Josie blazed her own path, one that would likely lead her on a long walk into the woods.

They watched her from the comfort of the third row in the renovated opera house. Josephine shared her talent, dazzling among the five girls who were the feature of the recital. As Josephine danced, without looking, Alexandria reached to where she knew William's hand would be. She felt a sense of family as her fingers interlaced with his firm grasp. It was a beautiful time to be Josie's parents, to watch the joy in learning and growing with every new adventure.

A few weeks earlier, she and Josie had decided on a picnic at Brainard Lake. There had been a windless, blue sky on a departing summer day. The picnic had been prepared as ordered, with rich, thick sandwiches, fruits with breads and chilled soda. They had laughed and talked and been more like friends than mother and daughter. William had even been tempted to come, but in the end, he had kissed them both good bye and returned to his study.

While she sat gazing past the ripples created by the subtlety of the lake,

Alexandria tried to remember the one time William had read poetry to her, years before beside this lake.

In her solitude, Josephine had wandered to the edge of the clear water. There she had danced, the music in her mind, and Alexandria had loved that moment, watching her daughter be a part of the lake and the mountains. No matter where she was, what she did, she seemed more a part of nature.

After the recital, the family met in the lobby where a photographer took group pictures of the girls. William visited with the gentleman coordinating another photo, and after the young ballerinas were all done, he motioned them over. Together, they stood in the grand entryway of the opera house posing for a family portrait. Sophia and Alexandria on opposite sides, William and Robert standing tall behind them, and Josephine posed in perfect posture, beautiful in the center of the family.

PART IV: Spring
Chapter 36

William slept soundly as Alexandria listened to his distinct breathing in the shadows of the suite. Eyes adjusting to the unfamiliar room, she slipped into her swimsuit. Through the large glass doors, she could see the hint of sunrise east of the Hawaiian Islands over the Pacific Ocean.

The burnt orange horizon gave the water the black look of night while one full-mast sailboat drifted toward the colors. Sixteen years before, she smiled at the memory. Years before it had been a magnificent wedding, and now, she was enjoying this anniversary. So many had passed with informality and token gift acknowledgements. This one, William had surprised her. It would be spent together, just the two of them in Hawaii.

Still, morning time was hers, the time before the people awoke and began to take away the quiet. Because she would be swimming, she had chosen the one-piece suit, but she looked forward to the afternoon and the beach. Being vain or daring, she wasn't sure which, but she had bought a bikini for this trip, starved away five pounds, and felt wonderful in it.

Running each hand alternately over her head to ensure tightness, she pulled it back into one strand and looped the tie around the thick blond ponytail. Quietly, she slipped her worn football sweatshirt over the suit and took a towel from the bathroom, the only things she needed. William's breathing was the only sound in the room as she left him in the king bed, closed the door, and walked briskly toward the elevator.

The white beige of the beach had been smoothed as if a hand on the sheets had evenly pressed each wrinkle away. Her footprints were the first hint that people would soon cover the sand with big colored towels and cabana umbrellas. She set the hotel towel and her Bronco's shirt on the ground and edged to the darker damp sand. There she stood waiting and watching as the waves broke one by one, rushing closer to leave bubbling traces of air near her toes. Yards out into the ocean, she could see the waves growing, and knew that soon they would reach her, pressing a chill around her ankles.

With sudden daring, she rushed forward into the breaking waves. Coolness splashed over her thighs, a drop of salt dampening her lips. She pressed hard, and leaned forward, lunging. Slicing into the curl, she met its power with her own determination. When she surfaced she was swimming into the current, and with each stroke she felt the power of the ocean.

The buoy was a quarter mile out, but she knew if she fought to it, she could ride the tide in a comforting recovery back to the beach. It was important, this early swim, to evaporate the tension she woke with every morning. It made it easier to appreciate William and the efforts he sometimes made. Mornings swimming in the ocean, the waves breaking over her made it acceptable.

As she swam, she only thought of the next stroke, glancing now and then to find the buoy. She put her head down determined, the ache making her arms heavy and larger than they actually were. With one last glance from the water, she circled the buoy and began her recovery back.

Emerging from the ocean, it was amazing how quickly the tropical sun had warmed the air. She dabbed the towel over her suit, absorbing the water away. Pressing her hair, she drained the water from her ponytail and pulled the tie away shaking her hair free to dry in the sun. With the perfect morning she walked for a while along the beach in the sun and morning breeze.

Standing where the hotel grass ended, separating the natural sand beach, she slipped her jersey down over the slight dampness of her suit. Searching the hotel terrace, her eyes scanned the two rows of umbrella tables. She selected one along the white stone buffer. There her morning felt complete as she sat politely, sipping orange juice, and savoring bites of fresh island fruit.

For two days they had enjoyed the resort, William uncharacteristically sleeping lazily in the morning while she slipped away to the beach treasuring her solitude. During that time, William would call the office, then return to bed and sleep well into the morning. Somehow, he had accepted he could not change the market and was actually enjoying some semblance of vacation.

The steam was rolling from the open bathroom door, and she quickly moved to join him. His grin was unexpected as she stepped into the spray, pulling the foggy door closed.

"Good swim?" He asked, kissing her dry forehead.

She tilted her hair back, allowing the warm water to roll behind her ears and down her shoulders. She reached to him, rubbing her hands over the slight graying in his chest hair.

"Can we do something different today?"

"How different?"

"Fun different," she rubbed her body against his. "A guy on the terrace told me about the road to Hana. Have you heard of it?"

He massaged some shampoo into his hair, scrubbing. "Hana? Vaguely. Maybe? I'm not sure."

"Can we go there today, the north side of the island?"

"To Hana? You mean rent a car? Why not just stay here and be served cocktails on the beach?"

Her smile was fresh. "It's been done. Let's rent a Jeep."

His frown irritated her, and she felt the tension.

"A luxury car would make for more comfortable riding."

She patted his chest in disbelief. "My dear. This is not a cruise to The Club. This is an adventure. A Jeep is more appropriate."

He opened the door, reaching for a towel, and stepped out. "If it will please you, I'll call the desk and have them arrange it." He closed the steam gray shower door.

She wished he would have stayed and covered her back with rich suds, a cleansing massage. She wanted the feeling of a touch against her hips. Now, once every three or four months they had relations. Somehow it seemed he missed her when he had been gone, particularly his business trips to New York.

After returning from New York, he would begin with a subtle nuzzle that would quickly turn more aggressive until he would climb on top and take her. As her mind thought of those few times, she pulled against the shower door, and swung it open.

He turned startled to see her standing wet and angry in the water.

"Doesn't this arouse you?" Alexandria threw her arms into a seductive Playboy Bunny pose.

He stared at her dumbfounded. "Arouse?" he asked. "Alexandria, you're in the shower. It's not like we were in bed together." He reached forward, chuckling at her silliness, and pushed the shower door closed.

She yelled through the closed door. "William, it's our anniversary trip, and we haven't made love."

Muffled slightly through the steam, she heard his calm directive. "Finish your shower, dear."

"Finish it with me," she shouted back.

His mind flashed to his favorite friend in New York. They always took a shower before she left, her pressing him against the wall. In those brief moments, he would relinquish his dominance and be completely at ease. She would rub him, the warmth of the water arousing, and then she would slide down, and he would concede all control.

"I'll call and check on a car."

"A Jeep," she shouted through the steam.

"A Jeep," he relinquished.

She rubbed the small bar of soap over her stomach, soft at first, then harsher to clean the salt-water residue from her skin.

The open air of the red Jeep rushed the salty warm breeze freely over her face. Alexandria sat with her hands gripped the roll bar of the open top. Her hair was pulled back, gathering through the opening in the back of a sky blue cap, dancing in the winds.

"This is it, William. This is what Josie and I love. There's freedom being outdoors, going someplace different." She reached over, tousling his hair, breaking the tension. He laughed, running his fingers over his head to bring the hair back into place.

"Want to have some fun?" she asked.

He watched the road knowing that her fun usually made him uncomfortable. "What do you have in mind?"

Alexandria's head dropped down, only her eyes watching him from under the bill of the ball cap. "I won't know till it happens."

His laugh was nervous, a chuckle of disapproval.

The blacktop narrowed with a steady climb into deep lush forests of bamboo and fruit trees. They both wondered where they were headed with the changing of the foliage and the roughage of the road. The black top had become a trail of cracked pavement with the edges fading into the earth. Trees hung tall and looping over the road creating tunnels between the openings of scattered one-lane bridges.

Even before she motioned to him, William had slowed the Jeep. Falling from the hilltop south of the road, yards back from the bridge was a winding vista sharing three waterfalls, the first a rolling cascade from the distant one falling tall and wide with a powerful roar. Between them was a pleasant falls with a large, inviting pool next to the towering remains of a wooden mine shaft.

They watched from the bridge for a moment until William felt Alexandria's hand on his arm. "Let's hike back there."

"Back there?" he said. "There's no trail, thick ferns, and steep hills. No, I don't think so."

"William, lighten up. Let's have some fun."

He pointed ahead to the side of the bridge. Alexandria read the yellow, bent, and rusted *No Trespassing* sign as the Jeep rolled past and onward, up the road to Hana.

"William," she hung her feet out the Jeep window, wiggling her toes in the wind, "you know, you can truly be boring."

"Maybe," he shrugged, laughing at her. "But I don't call not breaking the law boring."

"Next great waterfall, we're going in."

He grinned unconvinced. "You've already decided that?"

"This is the road to Hana." She waved her hand in the air. "We're in Hawaii, and there are waterfalls inviting us to play."

William stared at the road, telling himself to relax. It's Hawaii. Enjoy it. You're on vacation with your not-conservative-enough wife. Loosen up a bit. Still, her playfulness made him nervous.

"There," she reached over pushing foot toward the break.

The waterfall was next to the road, an amphitheater with a large pool; a soft, narrow beach divided the road from the water. William stopped the Jeep behind two other cars parked on the edge of the road. There were three kids playing on the beach and others swimming in the pool. William could see their legs kick to keep them afloat, and he knew the water was deeper than it appeared. The amphitheater walls climbed upward to the height of the waterfall maybe fifty feet above the pool. Two teenagers stood above the falls on a rock jetting out from the lush green growth.

Alexandria pointed at them. "That's what we're going to do."

"Climb to the top?"

"Do you know what their doing, William?"

He raised is eyebrows, clueless. Wearing a golf shirt and matching shorts, his sandals were the only diversion from an afternoon on the course at The Club, drinking cocktails, and hitting white balls in the general direction he wanted them to go.

Alexandria smiled at her contrast in a well-worn ball cap, cap sleeved-oversized t-shirt, frayed jean shorts, and Margaritaville flip-flops. Sensing a feeling of freedom, she had worn her bikini underneath planning to expose her sensuality to her prudish husband.

He was still looking at the boys on top of the falls. "What do you mean? You want us to climb up there like they did?"

"And I want us to come down like they will." A big, beautiful smile of full lips dared him.

As she turned to watch the boys, the first one let out a yell. William looked to see him push from the rock, and felt himself startled, seeing the boy tumbling arms waving and legs kicking toward the pool below. The boy stiffened as he reached the water, and his body plunged into the pool, waves and water splashing upward. Just as quickly, his head broke the surface letting out the same yell as when he'd jumped. The second boy returned the yell, and lunged freely into the air. His body rotated, his feet moving upward and his head turning as he reached toward the water. With much less splash, he dove through the water near where his friend swam.

"Are you nuts, Alexandria?"

"Oh, quit it." She pulled her tank top over her head revealing the orchid print bikini. "Let's go cliff diving."

She was out of the Jeep when he realized she was serious. She ran her fingers under the bikini brief, pulling it into place, and jogged across the small beach.

With a slight panic, he reached behind the seat into the beach bag, pulling out his seldom-used swimsuit. Looking around, he realized there was no bathhouse to change in. Looking back again, he pulled an oversized towel from the bag and laid it open across his lap. Working his hands under the towel, he kicked his shorts down his legs, lifted them from the floor, and laid them neatly with their crease in place on the back seat.

When he lifted the towel, William was embarrassed to see that the blue pattern in his suit did not match the green striped golf shirt. He pulled the shirt over his head, bumped his elbow, and recoiled at the instant blare of the horn. All within hearing distance turned their eyes, and he looked at the shirt in his hand as if exposed. Reaching into the back seat, he folded it neatly, and placed it next to his shorts.

His walk was fast around the Jeep, trying to catch his adventurous wife. "Wait Alexandria?"

Her smile broadened when she turned to see him.

"I'll hike up, but I'm not going to jump off."

He looked toward the top as she climbed the first few feet of hillside. From the steep angle, the falls looked much taller than from the Jeep.

"Yes you will." She stood on the hillside fifteen feet above him. "I'll shame you into it when I jump." Laughing, she climbed on.

He was only halfway up when Alexandria waved to him from the rock the boys had stood on. He was shocked at how young she looked, the sun passing through her shoulder length hair as she dancing playfully in the slight breeze.

Strong, long slender legs with narrow hips were revealed by the high cut of her bikini. Seeing hints of her ribs, sculptured below her breasts, he appreciated Alexandria's beauty as she stood with the waterfalls in the background.

Her voice teased, calling, "Come on, slowpoke."

He winced, his feet tender on the hard rock and roots that covered the half grown trail. Despite the pain, he too was soon on the rock, looking down, and wondering why he had followed her.

"It's a long way down," he said, tipping his head over the edge.

Playfully, she put her hand on his hip as if to push, and he quickly backed away from the edge.

"So this is what you and Josie do for fun." He was standing behind her now. "Take stupid risks?"

Her hands moved with determination onto her hips. "This is much less a risk than you take everyday in your job. Probably thousands of people have jumped off here and never been hurt. Look," she pointed down at the clear water to the rocky depth. She took his hand gently. "Come on, we'll jump together."

He stiffened, "I don't think so."

"Just relax your body, and I'll pull you with me."

"Alexandria, this is dangerous." His body became rigid.

She stepped to him, her eyes on his, her breath sharp against his lips. "No William, not living life is dangerous."

She dropped her grip from his hand, grinning. With one sudden motion she turned, stepped, and lunged. Fear dropped into his gut as she disappeared from the rock. Edging forward, he could see her falling below the rock. Becoming smaller with distance, he saw the water splash outward before he heard the sound.

Alexandria bobbed up from the ripples, waving with a scream. "It's great," she yelled up to him.

And he knew she was right. She had shamed him into it.

He looked up at the blue sky standing with both feet on the edge, his toes gripping the rock. Below him, Alexandria drifted backward, away from where he would land. He swung his arms twice, then stood up, shuddering slightly. Bending his knees he looked at the beach where several children and the teenage boys stood watching him. Again, his arms swung, and he lunged forward with all of his might, jumping away from safety.

The fall took much longer than expected, and he felt his body drifting backwards as the rocks, bamboo, and ferns passed like a slide show flipping images. He looked down as the water closed in, preparing for the slap of impact. Among the sounds, he heard Alexandria screaming delight.

The water rushed closer, coming fast. He braced and hit with a bearable force, but his feet pushed forward with the impact, and his hips hit the water hard. As the pool surrounded him, he felt the stabbing rush of water into his body like a colonoscopy tube causing him to recoil in a protective ball. Warm water bathed him as the pain released to a dull ache. He burst from the water with his own excited yell.

Alexandria was still laughing five miles up the road to Hana. "Don't tell me your butt hurts. Just admit it was fun."

"Okay, okay. Yes. It was a rush." He pounded the steering wheel. "I just wish my rear hadn't taken the impact. Damn," he shifted in the seat, the pain still penetrating.

She gave him a pouty look of pity, then burst out laughing again. "Poor tooshie."

With a silly look, he said, "I just got a waterfall enema, and you're laughing like it was a pat on the butt."

"Listen William, flying through the air, you looked scared to death. You're eyes were bulging and your mouth opened screaming like a little girl on her first rollercoaster." His wife was laughing loudly. "So, yes, your waterfall enema was hilarious. I only wish Josie could have seen it."

"Would she have jumped?"

Alexandria grinned, "Without a moment's hesitation."

"She's that daring," he asked.

"Not so much," she answered. "She just knows her capabilities."

She saw the twinkle in his eye. Bouncing on, William chuckled to himself, shifting for comfort in his seat. When he did, Alexandria chuckled back, and he gave her a teasing grin.

The Seven Sacred Pools were terraced from the top, each pool lead downward to the next. It was a vision of long flowing waters from clear, pure pools with narrow waterfalls filling one from the other until the seventh drained to the ocean hundreds of feet below the first.

Alexandria decided to swim, one pool after another, to the ocean. William wished her well and sat down on the black rock under a Banyan tree. From there he could see all seven pools as he ate pineapple and watched people playing in the waters.

Alexandria was in her element. He had forgotten her playful beauty, and the uniqueness she could bring to life. In that moment, he watched and appreciated. She stood in profile, her body against the waterfall. They were both magnificent.

So seldom had he enjoyed this, this time to sit and relax without thought. Here he could not control what was there, and no one had predetermined expectations of him, so he sat quietly in the shade and enjoyed the sweetness of a fresh pineapple. Solitude was uncharacteristically his, secluded as he watched her radiate the Seven Sacred Pools.

Alexandria was surprised at the warming from one pool to the next. Each a little closer to the ocean; each a little more exposed to the sun. It was a fun way to explore the pools. She had stood the twenty feet above the first pool, watching the narrow plume of waterfall to the pool below and dove. Swimming the length of the second pool. There she sat on the edge feeling the cool waters swell around her before they fell to the warmer pool below.

The view was serenity, and she was a part. How long since she had felt such absolution? This was the distinctiveness of her life, to swim freely in the pool of a waterfall. She stood feeling aroused and dove into the next.

Surrounded by the gentle, caressing of the moisture, she thought of a cooler waterfall and a different time.

Chapter 37

She awoke with a sense of sadness for her husband. He had been working two hours before in the darkness of the pre-dawn light, and now he slept again. When he woke the remainder of their last day in Hawaii would be a delightfully shared, congenial day.

She skipped her morning swim, deciding instead to take the long walk along the beach into the village. As she walked, she gazed out toward Lanai, watching for the whales that spent their winter in the warm, shallow channel between the islands.

The village was peaceful, not yet invaded by tourists in the early morning hours. She strolled along watching aged Hawaiian women setting up their enterprise of weaved palm frond hats.

She was surprised, pleasantly, to find that many of the Wharf Shops had already opened. Strolling into each, she gazed about at authentic island souvenirs and t-shirts in several before moving on disinterested. It was the art shops that most attracted her, and she spent time appreciating the work of many the local artists.

On the second floor of the Wharf's shopping maze she found the most intriguing shop. The walls were lined with magnificent photography dedicated to the whales and surrounding island scenes. Drawn to the images, she caught herself glancing at the signatures curious that their lives might somehow cross again.

It had been some time since she allowed a pleasant memory from years past. Every now and then, she would read his name somewhere. In the Denver Post there was an article a few months ago about the successes he was experiencing, and his contributions as an Artist in Residence at Rocky Mountain National Park. She knew he had come here once. Jennifer had mentioned his trip to Maui to photograph the whales. But in the photographs of giant tails dominate above the water's surface or a whale full-force lunging upward and caught in the stillness of the camera, none bore the name Cabelli.

Alexandria wandered from the shop to a storefront cafe, finding a seat to watch the ocean from the second level. Her espresso and muffin arrived as she felt a moment of peacefulness. She had enjoyed the vacation, the time with William, but she found it strange that most of all she liked her morning time, that quiet without him when it was just her and the beginning of a new day.

Alexandria had booked the whale-watching cruise recommended by the hotel concierge. It was a little more luxurious than the others with captain's chairs on the upper deck and young Hawaiian girls serving Mai Tais and purple Hawaiian chips. This was fun for William, sitting back in a comfortable chair, sipping cocktails, and waiting for whales to burst from the water. It was his version of the great outdoor adventure.

With William comfortable, she wandered the boat, exploring while he sat. For a while, she watched the waters looking back to see William sitting in the sun. He lifted his umbrellaed glass in a playful salute, and she waved back to him. She had rarely joined him on his trips, mostly business travel, and certainly not since he had started his trips to New York. As she looked back to the waters a wave of sadness rush through her.

The whale spotter's voice interrupted her thoughts, and Alexandria leaned on the railing next to a young couple. Through the gray of the water, she could see a disturbance seventy-five yards from the boat. The craft seemed to adjust to run parallel to the mammals, and Alexandria jogged back along the boat to the deck ladder, climbing to join William; the entire time watching the slight grayish humps emerge through the ocean's surface.

He too was out of his seat, leaning against the railing. William pointed toward the whales as a large hump rose followed by a massive tail lifting upward well above the surface. William was laughing, and Alexandria turned distracted when she heard him. He was watching intrigued, amused and amazed as the group of whales emerged above the surface. She had forgotten the sound of his laughter, and how wonderful it could be.

"Look." His arm thrust forward.

A whale shot upward, like the photograph she had admired that morning, towering above the water before falling sideways, crashing back into the blue. William stepped to the viewing scope attached to the railing. He adjusted the scope, words of wonder rambling from his mouth. The whales continued to rise up, an eye large in the direction of the boat, and fall back to the safety of the channel. Others would surface and disappear, their giant fantail above the waters before returning to the ocean's depths.

"Here, look," he stepped backwards.

Alexandria stepped to the scope. Magnification brought the whales into full view. Their size was frightening, yet several swam in a mellow rhythm. She wanted to swim with them and play with the babies. She wanted to feel their freedom and power.

Alexandria stepped away from the scope, and William leaned around her to get another look. Against the railing she watched them like a herd of elk slowly moving across the mountain meadow. The movement was not hurried but constant. Easily they glided along, their backs raising a gigantic ripple above the surface.

For the third time that day, her thoughts connected with him. He had been here. Day after day patiently paralleling the whales, waiting for the perfect moment to capture the image. She thought of the difference if Mickey were beside her, if she were helping him. Carrying camera bags and retrieving lenses at his request, committed to sharing his adventures. She would have organized the trip arrangements, been his photographer's assistant, managed the galleries.

They settled back into the captain's chairs as the boat turned and the whales disappeared deep into the channel. William wouldn't stop talking about them, repeating his description of the gray and sleek backs, massive in the incredible ocean. Then William looked at her, his eyes almost laughing.

"I understand," he said. "You should keep teaching her this. The whales are incredible. If this is the world you're teaching Josephine about, she should know this."

Somehow, as the boat drifted slowly back to port, William continued talking, his excitement for the whales a rare joy. He wished they had another day, he wished he had time to rent a private boat and be among the whales. The excitement kept him rambling on, talking as he seldom did. When he quieted, they watched the port growing closer, and there was a sense of contentment.

As they pulled near the dock, he interrupted the quiet. "What do you think at moments like that?" her husband asked.

Startled, she gave him a goofy smile. "What do you mean?"

He shrugged. "Back there on the boat, watching the whales. There are times, usually when we're outdoors, when you disappear, when you drift away."

Her smile had not changed. "Oh, don't be silly?"

"I'm not." He tilted his head. "When we're driving in Denver, you'll look at the mountains and for a moment it's as if you disappear. Once, when we went to Vail together, the whole drive you stared out the window, and it was as if you felt such pleasure, but when you came back, when you reappeared, you seemed sad. I've seen it other times. When I come home in the summer and find you sitting on our bedroom balcony staring off toward the mountains, I just wondered where your mind takes you when you do that. You did it back there watching the whales. Where do you go?"

She turned quickly back to the ocean scanning over the waters behind them to the distant coast of Lanai. The scattered afternoon clouds were clearing to a hazy halo over the pineapple island. She did not answer him.

"Damn." His voice echoed in Alexandria's mind. "I didn't realize," he said with a slight crackle, "I didn't realize my question would be intruding."

The back of her neck turned red.

"It's that private?" he quieted. William stood silent, waiting for the answer that did not come. He stared intently, but she gave him nothing. "Where is it you go, Alexandria?"

"William, don't be silly." She waved him away without looking.

"I'm being honest? I need the answer?"

The tone of his voice left her no choice. She did not turn to him, trying to gather the thoughts in her mind.

He put his fingers to her shoulders, guiding her to face him. "For a long time, several years ago, I thought you were having an affair."

It took all of her strength not to look away. She stared into his eyes seeing his control and was unable to answer.

He looked away, disturbed. "In time, I dismissed that. But I know there's something in your life different than me, separate from me. I don't know what or who it is, but you go places in your mind, and I'm not there. I wish I were. I wish I could go there with you, but I know you always go alone."

His hand moved gently from her chin to rub her shoulder, and the confrontation seemed to be drifting away without anger.

"Our life, Alexandria, it's not what I planned it to be." He scanned the ocean one more time. "There should have been more vacations, more time together. I should have gone to the mountains with you and Josephine. I should have found a balance between the bank and made us more of a family." He took her hands in his, and his confession shocked her.

Without looking, she whispered, "And you shouldn't have gone to New York so much."

"I know." He hoped she did not sense his guilt. "I'm not very attentive, and maybe that's caused you to find solace in the mountains. Maybe that's why you go places without me, and that scares me. It scares me because as a husband I have often failed. As a provider, I have been quite successful. The only problem is from the very beginning you've wanted a husband, a partner, and despite that missing from your life, you've stayed with me, supported me, and, I believe, loved me."

Alexandria nodded, summoning her pride. "Yes, I love you."

He clinched her hands tighter. "I know, but you stayed with me at great cost, and now we have this volatility in our relationship. Even when we're together we bounce from each other's worlds. I turn the hotel suite into an office four hours a day, and you lead me up the waterfalls to jump off, and neither feels right for the other. I wish it weren't like that, but what scares me most is when you go to that private place in your mind."

The first tear broke away from the pool in her eyelid falling down her sun-red cheek.

"Since I'm being honest." His nervousness surprised her. "What I'm saying is I know you go on trips in your mind, and I hope you're happy there. I hope your life is good because you deserve a wonderful life." He closed his eyes. "I'm sorry I haven't been able to give you whatever your private place gives you."

When he opened his eyes he was staring beyond her.

"You are a good person, Alexandria, a wonderful mother and a extremely patient daughter-in-law." They both chuckled, still not looking at each other. "I wish our lives weren't so separate, but that's the way it is. You've made great sacrifices, and my sacrifice is that I know you live a life in your thoughts and in your wilderness adventures, and I'm not a part. That's my great sacrifice."

She stood strong before him, finally looking at her husband. "It's only now a sacrifice, William. Until maybe this vacation, you hadn't taken the time to notice what you might be missing."

His look was as confident as she knew. "That's true. Sadly, that's the way things have been."

Neither was aware of the person who appeared beside them. "Did you enjoy the cruise?"

William turned to the girlish whale spotter who had left her post at the boat's bow to greet guests before docking. Her sun bleached hair and bright smile bubbled enthusiasm. "You had a rare opportunity, following the large number of whales we did for such a time. On a scale of one to ten, the cruise was about a nine."

"Only an nine?" William seemed surprised. "I was amazed. I've never seen a sight so spectacular, such a combination of serenity and power. I can't imagine a ten."

The young woman's grin widened. "I've only been on one ten cruise. I was on the bow, and a huge whale lunged upward right off the starboard. People standing right here were looking up seeing that whale as if they were in the city looking up at a skyscraper. I felt like I could reach out and touch her. She was that close."

His enthusiasm was back. "Incredible. How far off was she?"

"Fifteen feet at the most." She reached out over the railing.

"Incredible." He looked past her hand. "It must have been amazing."

That evening they dressed for dinner, dining in the elegance of the hotel's five star restaurant. They had lobster for two, and looked the dashing couple of exquisite taste and sophistication. He sipped his favorite brandy and she, the same champagne his assistant Valarie imported especially for her each Valentine's Day.

She teased him as he signaled for the waiter, billed their room, and laid the paperwork aside. "Did you ever notice how people watch us?"

"How do you mean?" he asked.

"You're probably used to it, growing up with it, but I've always found it amusing."

He noticed the way her hair was pulled back in tight strands, complimenting the sleekness of her cheeks and the full smile of drawing, generous red lips. As silly as it may sound, her eyes truly were the ocean's blue. She was that beautiful.

"You mean people just watch us. As we sit here, people watch us?" His eyes moved in mock disbelief.

"It's your image," she laughed. "They see this dashing man of affluence. They don't see the up-tight husband we know so well." She returned his light smile. "They only see the dynamic image."

For the second time that day, his laughter was free. "Who do you think you're kidding? I may have an image, but you're real. Men envy me because I'm with a woman so intriguing. Your looks can be intimidating."

"I've never intimidated you."

"I'm very lucky to have you on my arm." He answered.

"So, we're the image people watch."

He reached for her hand. "I live this basic life with starch in my shirts and wide stripes in my ties. I do the same thing everyday, and I do it damn well, incredibly well at times, and that effort produces an image few own." William sipped his brandy with square-jawed dignity.

She was doing it to him, her eyes sparkling, contrasting the diamonds around her delicate neck. He loved the directness in her eyes, the way she could make you desire her while controlling with her confidence. She placed the linen napkin next to her fluted champagne glass.

"It all sounds so elitist, William, this image we present." Her smile held despite her words.

"I understand, Alexandria, but I won't apologize for my success."

"Nor should you," she acknowledged.

Alexandria liked him much more now then she had before the vacation. Their anniversary had been a success if only in the sense they had shared time and intimate thoughts. But sadly, he was right. They were the image people desired. That, she knew, was why they protected the truth so. If people truly knew, few would desire to be them.

Together they stood from the table, tall and slender with squared shoulders, his strong, hers alluring. She moved away, a well-practiced celebrity stride. He followed adjusting his sport jacket she walked before him through the dining room.

He watched the eyes of the men focus on her, envy as they passed. Standing taller, he motioned for the maître d' to escort them to the foyer. As he had so many times before, William left the room conveying magnetism as Alexandria strode captivating a half step before him.

Chapter 38

Alexandria heard the front entryway door open and stiffened with recognition. Setting the crystal vase of freshly cut white hyacinths, lavender squall, and sun bright daffodils on the gold lamé runner; she turned toward the doorway.

Sophia stood staunchly with all of the sophistication of a cubby Cruella de Vil.

Alexandria looked at the arrangement, smiling satisfied "Was Josie a good girl this past week?"

"An angel," her mother-in-law's eyes widened. "Always an angel."

"Mom." Josie appeared from behind her grandmother and danced across the marble entryway. She wrapped her arms in a hug around Alexandria's shoulders, kissing her cheek.

Alexandria held her tightly, the only thing she had missed.

"Good trip?" Her daughter stepped back nearly eye-to-eye.

"Wonderful. Hawaii is so exotic." She brushed a black strand of hair from over Josie's eyes.

Josie's eyebrow raised, a teasing smile. "Exotic and romantic? Fun on the beach?"

"Really, please." Her mother-in-law's disgust was chronic.

Alexandria winked mundanely.

Josie hugged her mother again. "I'm so glad you're home, but I need to call Allison. Important stuff." Her eyes rolled without her grandmother seeing. "I'll be in my room."

Her daughter's energy lifted her up the staircase two steps at a time. Alexandria wondered when life had become such a race, these days always in a hurry forgetting pleasant manners.

Sophia was standing in the middle of the marble entryway being a domineering she-devil. She was wearing that look of ultimatum she had mastered so many years prior.

"We must talk!" Such demands were common.

"We must?" Alexandria cut her sentence short knowing mockery would enflame whatever was on fire.

"Josephine tells me she is going to public school next fall." Her face turned from indignant to unacceptable, twisting animosity in her crooked ruby mouth. "This cannot be. I will not allow it!"

"Oh Sophia, don't get so excited about such a little thing." Alexandria waved dismissing.

Sophia stood direct, clasping her hands to her tired breasts, indignant again. "A little thing? Alexandria, do not dismiss the quality of your daughter's scholarly upbringing as *a little thing*."

"Sophia, you know very well that my father taught for many years in the public schools and then at the University of Kansas. I am well aware of the need for a quality education."

Sophia scowled, "Public institutions, all."

Alexandria clinched her jaw. She walked to the intercom beside the main entrance and pushed a button. "Josie."

"Why must you insist on calling her an improper name?" Sophia rebuked sharply.

Alexandria closed her eyes, releasing a deep breath. "Josephine."

"Yes Mother."

"Would you please come down and join your grandmother and me for a visit?"

"But Mom, I'm on the phone?"

"No options, Sweetie."

William appeared from the other side of the entryway. Despite working in his study, he was wearing clothes of comfort. Golf slacks, soft blue oxford dress shirt, and v-neck wool sweater with tan tassels on his loafers matching the color of his slacks. He held a glass with fresh ice and still sparkling spring water in his left hand.

Sophia moved toward him. "Your wife and daughter are conspiring to dissolve a family tradition and decimate your daughter's future."

"Well good afternoon, Mother. Our trip was quite nice, thank you." He stepped to meet her, kissing her lightly on the cheek. "And how was your Sunday brunch at The Club?"

"Horrifying, just horrifying." She did dismay so well. "Josephine announced to my entire guild that she was transferring to public school in the fall. Imagine the shock and horror."

"Now Mother, don't over react." William gave a subtle, reassuring wink to his wife.

Alexandria was watching William wondering what in the world he was doing. Sophia had the same look with her eyes. William's restrained admonishment angered her.

Animation flowed as Sophia said, "I am not overreacting, and this cannot be allowed. What in the world are you two thinking?"

Alexandria waited for his reaction. While she and Josie had discussed it, they had not shared these thoughts with William, waiting for the right time to plead their case. William glanced past Alexandria and all eyes turned to see Josephine standing in the middle of the staircase.

"Come join us, dear." Her father drew her toward them with a gentle wave.

She walked to him giving a faint hug, a quick kiss to the cheek. "Welcome home, Daddy."

"I missed you." Uncharacteristically, he leaned forward, a firm, tender kiss to his daughter's forehead. "Apparently, you've been up to some shenanigans."

Her eyes dropped to his chest.

William led them all back to his study, and reluctantly Sophia joined around the carved sleigh edging of the European tea table.

"I'm sorry, William." Alexandria shared the couch with Josie. "Josephine brought the idea to me, and we have discussed it."

His calmness astonished them all. Usually he directed, seldom listened. He sat back, attentively, as Alexandria explained that Josephine had come to her prior to their trip. She had outlined her reasoning, and Alexandria stated that there were several pros that she had not previously considered.

He nodded, encouraging. "I'm sure there are."

Josie and her mother's lips separated slightly with the same surprise. He watched them calmly, his hand waving to continue.

Sophia could contain herself no longer, her hands slapping the arm of the stiff backed chair she sat in. "This is outrageous."

William reached from his chair to his mothers, grasping his hand over hers. His lips pierced to quiet her.

Her eyes narrowed, darts flying. "Don't shush me, son."

The calm remained as he squeezed her hand firmly. "Let's listen before we judge."

Sophia started her protest, but William ignored her.

"Well, Josephine. It appears you've been manipulating things, so let's confront this issue. I want to hear your rationale."

Even Sophia was surprised at the depth of Josephine's reasoning. While it might have been a teenager's whim, it had turned into a well thought out, plausible explanation.

She stated that in the Academy she was secluded in a world of pretty girls all dressed in the same uniform, trained to talk the same, walk the same, and act the same. She balanced this against quality academics citing rising test scores and graduation success of public school with the social interaction, the importance of knowing not just wealthy white girls, but boys and girls of Hispanic, African-American, and Asian decent. She moved well beyond Sophia's sophisticated isolation by discussing the global marketplace and connecting to the world through technology.

Sophia was unbending, offended that Josephine questioned the Academy's proper breeding.

William looked at all three, his eyes stopping on Josephine's. "You seriously want to consider this." The corners were closing in, the room warming around Josephine. William gave her one of those deep eyebrow fatherly looks of *you created this with your bold announcement at brunch, now get yourself out of it.*

"Yes Father."

"Have you visited the school?"

Josie and Alexandria leaned forward while Sophia fell back against the stiff chair.

"Alexandria, please arrange a visit for you and Josephine. And if you would, have the school principal call me at work. I have several questions for him. After we've all had a chance to learn more, we'll consider this together." His tone was almost soothing.

Sophia was aghast, Josie leapt across the table to hug her father, and Alexandria smiled, unable to look at her mother-in-law for fear that her own pleasure would outrage the family matriarch.

That evening, Alexandria found William in the recreation room watching CNN on the 70" flat screen television. She sat down smiling at the thought that CNN was as close as she would ever come to reading the morning paper in each other's arms.

"You can be so good, William." Her smile was sincere.

He glanced from the television, grinning to himself. "I do have my moments. But please, Alexandria, do not place me in such a situation again. I didn't appreciate being blind-sided."

"You know Josie and I never intended that. I'm sorry," she shrugged, surrendering. "It appears your daughter has learned a bit of her grandmother's manipulative skills."

He nodded acceptance, rolling his eyes at dealing with a teenager.

"Can I ask you a question without offending you?" she asked.

William leaned back. "I've gotten better at listening."

"So you won't be offended?" she asked.

He picked up the remote and muted the CNN newscaster, his concentrations focused on his wife.

"Why can't you be that person you were with your mother, why can't you be him all the time?" Her arms folded before her, holding herself tightly.

"That is me," he frowned, glancing at the T.V. screen. "My work persona. The majority of my day I listen to proposals, analyze the pros and cons, and if they have merit, move forward for a closer look." Her legs crossed next to him. "My personality tends to turn harsh when I release the stress from work. Unfortunately, when it explodes, it's here at home, and you've taken the brunt of that. I know it's unfair. I also know its part of the reason I've lost you." His hand stopped on her thigh. "But I have become more tolerable, haven't I?"

"You're not so bad, William."

He fiddled with the remote, flipping it in his agile hand. "It's sad to see our marriage become so much like my parents. We each have our separate roles, and we play them well. But it's separate, and I'm sure there's some great void somewhere that you've hidden so well." William began laughing, and then shrugged the laugh away. "At least you haven't become my mother. I'm glad you've held on to your values, and I'm glad you're passing them on to Josephine." His eyes turned sad. "And I'm glad you've stayed with me."

He couldn't tell what she was thinking, her face turned down, hidden in the flow of her hair. "I have to ask you a question." He waited for her to look his way, but she did not. "It's important to me. Will you allow me?" he asked.

Despite her fears, she gave a slight nod.

He did not hesitate. "Do you think you'll ever leave?"

Her eyes turned further away.

"I just want you to know." His voice was quiet, leaning closer to her, and he could tell she would not answer. The sadness of their reality flowed through him. "If you left," he said, barely a whisper, "I'd miss you."

He leaned back into the sofa, his hand reaching to rub her shoulder. Alexandria felt her own surrender. Leaning to him, she allowed her face to press into his shoulder. For the longest time, they sat together, his hand stroking her hair.

CNN remained muted.

Chapter 39

Dr. Jesson sat it the chair opposite Alexandria. Alexandria sat with her legs crossed, traditionally dressed in a business suit and attractive matching heels. Her hands rested in her lap while she searched the room. Her eyes went beyond Jessi to the wall, down the corner to the mauve carpeting, and back to Jessi's feet. She lifted her eyes to meet Jessi's and shrugged helplessly.

"I thought things were going well," Jessi asked.

"They are," she answered. "It's just that this human side of him comes bursting out, and it scares me to death."

"Human side?"

"Okay," Alex shook it away. "He's human. I know he's human. He's a good man, but he's basically ignored the people closest to him. I've learned to coexist within his life but without him. We do occasionally talk. It seems like we've even grown to like each other again. But he is a task-oriented machine focusing on the processes of banking and money.

So lately, he throws in this human stuff, this understanding person who cares about family, and it really scares me because I don't know how to react. I'm used to the machine, and I don't know how to handle this pleasant person that appears at a whim."

"So how do you react?" Jessi asked.

Alex shrugged. "I sit there dumbly and feel all emotional. I don't know why. I like him more than maybe I ever have, at least when he's a good person, but the love is gone, the passion-love that is. I mean you don't just stop loving a person you've committed your life to. In some ways I do love him.

You see the confusion. It's like we've become business associates. We talk pleasantly, we enjoy time together, but that's it. I dress up and he dresses up, we go about the business of being the image of a perfect bank president's family, and when the whistle blows to end the day, we pass each other at home. Next day, alarm goes off and it's back to the job of image."

Jessi sat quietly.

"I know, I know. We've been through this before."

"So, my dear Alex. What's different now?"

Perplexed, she searched skyward. "At least I like him now. It's like a boss you've hated who's had a life changing experience. After all these years it's hard to trust the changes. There was a time, right before and after Mickey, when I didn't like him. He was slowly squeezing the life out of me. God, I resented him for that. But now, I like him again. I'm just not happy."

Alex crossed her legs, then crossed them again, the opposite one on top. She looked proper in her attire, manicured hands with a large diamond on one.

"He said he'd miss me if I left, and I'd miss him too. But the freedom would be amazing, the chance to find passion with love again. So many good things in our lives, yet it seems like a change is inevitable. I miss being happy, and," her head swayed sadly, "the loneliness is exhausting."

Jessi sat calmly, her eyes fixed. "So where does that leave you?"

Alex grinned in frustration. "I wish just once you'd have an answer instead of a question?"

The therapist only smiled.

"I guess I'll do the same thing I've done for sixteen years. Be the semi-satisfied, adventure-seeking, Mickey-fantasizing wife of a wealthy man whose only turn-on is the power of money."

"Okay, Alex," Dr. Jesson leaned forward looking at her patient, "Did you just hear yourself?"

Shrugging surrender, she did not see the glimpse of sadness in Dr. Jesson's eyes.

Chapter 40

Jennifer unlocked the three locks on the door of her security-building apartment. It always irritated her that even in Denver the need for security seemed so obvious. Closing the door behind her, she kicked off her heels wiggling her toes at the freedom. Setting her purse on the desk, she slipped her cell phone out and looked quizzically at the phone icon. Checking the switch, she realized she'd had it on vibrate since her one o'clock meeting. She sat it down, activated the voice mail, and hit the speaker button.

Lady, lady, lady, you chastise me about not answering my phone? So, if you don't want me calling your office, answer your cell? Never mind, it's just one of your silly quirks of not mixing business with business. I'm back from Seattle, and I need to visit with you. Big plans coming together. Can you come to Estes this weekend? If you can, Jimmy and I will be at Lonigan's. I'll order a double pepperoni with green olives served at eight Friday evening. Dress is casual. Jimmy says to bring your dancing shoes. It'll be great to see you.

Her mind raced through her calendar, nothing on the weekend, Friday evening only tentative, easy plans to change. Even if she stopped home after work, she could easily be eating pizza at eight.

Four days had passed since Michael left the message, and now as Jennifer drove her Jetta convertible up Highway 36 from Boulder she felt the feeling Alexandria had so often described. Each time Alexandria went to the mountains, three days before she was giddy, like a five year old on the days before Christmas. And each time she returned it would take another three days for her to work through the disappointment that she wasn't there any more.

Jennifer had always thought Alexandria to be a bit dramatic until she discovered Estes. It had been six years since she had first met Michael at the Stanley, and Michael, Jimmy, and Estes had become a part of her life. With their friendship and the great outdoors, she'd grown to understand Alexandria even better.

She had begun spending most of her weekends in Estes. They would hang out together sometimes joining Michael on his sunrise photography adventures or going to one of Jimmy's high school students' concerts. They were her family.

In summer and fall, they would share short hikes with picnics, Jimmy bringing his guitar. Always, she and Michael were discussing plans for his growing business, reviewing his photographs and narrowing selections to those worthy as limited editions. Even with Michael's travels, she found herself in Lonigan's on Saturday nights listening to Jimmy, engaged in the spirit of his music. Next to Alexandria, it was the best relationship she'd ever had, her friendship with these two good, talented men.

The European style streetlights were shining brightly on the people mingling among the shops of Estes Park. The joke was people always knew when Jennifer drove her recognizable Jetta into town because she always got a parking place right in front of Lonigan's. It was one of life's laughable quirks that in a town where nobody could find a parking place, she always found the best one. And again, right across the street, two open spaces waited for her to choose.

At 7:55 on a cold mountain evening, the bouncer was setting up his cash box to take the cover charge, and he waved her by with a smile. Jennifer stepped into the pizza kitchen, picking up paper plates, plastic forks, and oversized generic napkins.

"Michael's pizza ready?"

The high school boy turned and opened the pizza oven, glancing over his shoulder to her. "A couple of minutes yet."

Jennifer smiled a thank you and turned into the restaurant. Michael's leather jacket was hanging over a chair at his favorite table. She could hear Jimmy tuning his guitar, setting up for an evening of fun. Michael was at the pool table staring intently down his cue at the eight ball. She put the pile of plates, napkins, and plastic forks on the table and hung her fleece jacket over her chair.

When she turned to Jimmy, he was smiling at her, still tuning his guitar. She stepped the two stairs up to his makeshift stage, and he leaned over his guitar to return the kiss she gave to his cheek.

"Where you been?" he asked, chords coming from the guitar. "It's been a couple of weeks and texting just isn't as much fun."

"Busy, busy, busy; always too busy." She knew she turned younger when she was here with them. She could hear it in her voice, almost teenage like from the excitement of being back.

"Listen," Jimmy leaned his ear close to the strings, adjusting the tension for the perfect sound, "even when I'm not playing you should come up and see me. I'll take you to exciting places. You know, adolescent band concerts, a high school rendition of *Bye, Bye, Birdie*, some mediocre basketball games. It's an exciting world teaching here in Estes Park."

"I should," she smiled, reaching up to touch his cheek. From the kitchen, she heard a timer chime, and playfully her eyes grew big, cheeks lifting with her peppy smile. "Pizza's ready!"

She already had the pizza slices on three plates when Michael joined her and Jimmy. He leaned over the table to hug her, and she held the sauce covered knife and fork away to protect his shirt.

"Right on time, I see." He always looked so optimistic with his dark skin and fluid movements.

"Of course," chasing a string of cheese from her mouth to the slice. "So, what're the big plans? What's going on?"

Michael laughed, nibbling a stray olive from the side. "Always on task, aren't you?"

Jimmy shrugged.

Jennifer did the same. "Michael, my dear. I have come tonight for fun and dancing. Let's get the business out of the way, so my dancing hips can enjoy Jimmy's acoustic magic."

Jimmy leaned toward her. "I like your *dancing hips*."

"Dancing hips," she nudged her shoulder into his. "So what's the news?"

"Big news and bigger news." Michael stopped eating. "An acquaintance in Seattle, a collector who appreciates my work has offered to invest the start-up funding in a partnership for a series of galleries. I'm expanding outside of Colorado and Wyoming, seven stores over the next two years along the west coast. Two in Washington and two in Oregon open within the next six months. With all the coastal tourist towns, three more will be opened in northern California by next summer."

Her hands clasped together, and she reached across taking his face between her fingers. "That's fantastic. Seven galleries, eleven with those we've opened in Colorado and Jackson. It's amazing how successful you've become."

"Yes," he clapped his hands twice. "That's the big news."

She sat back, her eyes glancing from Jimmy to Michael. "There's bigger news than this?"

"Yep." He took a bite of pizza, teasing her as she waited for him to finish. Wiping the napkin across his mouth, he placed it back over his thigh. "Remember when we opened the first gallery, the way we talked through every detail. And then we made sure the ones in Steamboat and Winter Park were even better. Each detail you coordinated, they were all centered on creating an intrigue that gave the customer the feeling each image was special to them.

Then we decided to take on Jackson Hole, and you convinced me to turn it over to Carla to manage. Remember how hesitant I was to go there and take on the local talent. You took the details and refined them to perfection, and Carla created an enthusiasm that has caused Jackson to excel."

Jennifer's hands moved animated. "They're good galleries, Michael. But we can still make them better, even more successful, and the coast will need some subtle differences from the mountain galleries. People have a different eye for nature, different surroundings that they love including the ocean."

Jimmy was laughing at the way Michael was looking at him. "I know," Jimmy raised his hand. "You told me. I know." They were both laughing now.

She shook her head. "Boys, boys, share the joke."

Sitting straighter in the chair, he ran his hands through his long hair, pulling it back off his forehead. "No joke, Jennifer. I just told Jimmy that you are so creative you would immediately know what we needed to do to move these galleries in the right direction. If there's a joke, it's only that we both know how good you are, and that leads me to the bigger news."

"Okay, bigger news." She clapped her hands together. Michael winked. "Being a nature photographer means nothing if you cannot share your images, and the vehicle I've chosen is limited editions sold through my galleries." He shifted his hands slightly. "But to be successful, I must also be in the field creating new images. You see this whole thing is getting too big. There are two distinct sides that rely on each other, the artistic side and the business side. I cannot do both well anymore, so I need the skills, talents, and knowledge that has made the mountain galleries the success they are." He opened his hands. "Jennifer," his eyes were sincere, staring confidently. "I want you. No, I need you to come to work for me as my Director of Galleries."

Startled, she stared back. She had no idea this was coming and her eyes grew huge, unable to comprehend what he truly meant.

Michael reached his arm across the table. "I know you, I know your talents, and I know your business sense has helped create all of this. I also know your commitment to the Foundation, so this is what I would like to offer. I want you to take this position, but I want it to be right for you. So," he was loving this, his chance to offer this opportunity to one of his most trusted friends, to one he owed so much, and one he knew would do an amazing job, "the agreement with my investor is to let you name your price and make your home here in Estes. I've told him you are the key, and he wants you as much as I do."

"Michael," she was stunned, "I don't know what to say. It is big news, news I wasn't expecting, haven't considered."

"I know." He put his hands up again, his brown eyes smiling. "Let's have fun this weekend. No more pressure from me. I want this to be right for you. Ask any questions you want whenever you want. Then on Sunday afternoon, we'll sit down and discuss the details. Fair enough?"

Jennifer's mind was already racing, developing and promoting Michael's galleries; traveling to different cities, hosting showings, and working with the national wildlife organizations. The impact they could create together had her mind flying high.

Michael pulled his hand back. "Of course, the salary will be excellent, but more to your liking, a profit-sharing program. I know what you've done for me, and this is more like a partnership. If the first four galleries are any indication, we will both find ourselves financially well off a few years from now."

"Oh, Michael. You know if money were the issue, I'd stay with the Foundation. Al…" her eyes did not leave Michael's. "All the Chadwick family can be quite generous." She took a deep breath, expelling it slowly. "Sunday afternoon we'll talk more."

She was direct, in control, and smiling like a child, her eyes catching Jimmy's as they each reached for their pizza.

She lay staring at the ceiling of Michael's spare bedroom, wondering if he had heard her come in or had heard Jimmy drive away. The kiss good night had been a pleasant surprise. Surprised at the tenderness in the way his lips would not leave hers, surprised that she had not expected it. A grin grew across her face, surprised at how much she'd liked it.

And now Sunday, decision day. She was already fairly sure which way to go; yet she had grown secure in her work at the Foundation and relationship with Alexandria. She also knew that of all the work she did at the Foundation, it was working with Michael that she loved most.

When she reached the kitchen, Michael moved deliberately with his back to her.

"No French Toast today?" she muttered in her morning voice.

He smiled good morning, turning the omelet maker on the stove. "Thought omelets and hash browns might be a little sturdier. Besides, I want you to remember the quality of these breakfasts. After all, Jimmy only serves bran, flavor-resistant muffins, and Total cereal."

Jennifer blushed. "Very cute."

"He's nuts about you, you know."

She pulled the terry cloth robe closed over her chest. "Actually, I didn't know. We've always been such good friends."

He took a large red mug from the cupboard and poured it full of hot water. Placing it on a saucer, he sat it before her with a tea bag resting on its side.

"So where'd you and Jimmy disappear to?"

She dipped the tea bag in the water three times, smiling to herself. "After we left Lonigan's, he took me to Mary's Lake Lodge. A beautiful, rustic lodge, and the atmosphere was so friendly."

"You like the giant Lodge Pole pines framing the structure. It's a romantic, turn of the century mountain retreat. Not many left."

Jennifer thought of how magnificent the idyllic balcony was as they gazed over the valley and Mary's Lake, breathing in the fresh air of the hillside.

"Sat on the balcony nibbling on a buffalo steak hors d'oeuvre, then went into the lodge saloon. Talk about historic, like slipping back into the old west. He introduced me to Dick Orleans."

Michael glanced back over his shoulder. "The gentle man," he described Dick. "Great guitar player. He and Jimmy play charity events together. They're a favorite draw."

Jennifer smiled, thinking back at Jimmy joining Dick on stage. "They played together in the ambiance of the old lodge, framed by logs and wood and rustic. It was a perfect backdrop for acoustic music." Then she smiled into her mug. "It was a magical evening."

"Wow," he grinned. "Can I tell him that?"

"Not if you want to live." She smiled, blowing on her hot tea.

He didn't look back, just finished filling her plate with the sausage and mushroom omelet, hash browns, and whole wheat toast lightly buttered.

When they'd finished eating, he sat the plates in the sink, and motioned for her to follow him. At the top of the stairs, he stopped before The White Room door.

"If you take this job, your first major promotion will be a bear series. I've picked four shoots, one of each North American bear species. Well, three species and one subspecies. I want you to see them."

He opened the door and as she had many times, stepped into his private gallery. The white still shocked her with its pure compliment to the vibrant colors of nature. Four images hung side by side, two up and two down in a grouping on the wall. In the upper left a black bear lounged on her back, her paws holding a sprig of berries while her yearling cubs lay nursing on her belly. To the right, a grizzly, humped back with frosted face and shoulders, meandered at a riverbank. The phosphorous gray-blue of the soil surrounded the rippling reflection in the river, the pristine waters complimenting the clarity reflecting the reddish fur.

Michael pointed to the next one, to the left below the Black Bear and cubs. "Alaskan brown bear, same family as the grizzly. I took this one last spring, before my first trip to Seattle. It's at Brooks Falls. The Sockeye Salmon were swimming up stream to spawn, and in the process offer a feast for the winter hungry bears. I got several good shots, but this one is different, special. There was only one bear that caught fish this way."

Jennifer stared at the image, the giant bear bursting up from the river, the falls rushing over him from behind. The bear seemed to be exploding, streams of water rushing down away from his fur as he reached his head skyward, the large salmon still struggling in the bear's fanged death grip.

The final image was a sharp softness contrasting the viciousness of the

Kodiak. The white of the polar bears was against the arctic pure background of Hudson Bay. The bear sat curiously as he rocked backward in play, its front paws lifting its back paws into the air, balancing on his hips like a child.

As always, all images were matted in double frost white with white wooden frames against the stark walls of The White Room. Each picture challenged a different emotion in response. There was the tender mother, the solitary wanderer, the vicious hunter, and the cuddly softness of a bear at play. It was these moments that made Jennifer feel special, to share this privacy with Michael's talent.

Michael's hand rested softly against her back. He pointed at each image deliberately. "I want to release them as a group. It encourages the true naturalist to purchase all images maintaining the series integrity."

Michael left her then, as he had many times before, left her to determine for herself her impressions of the images he was considering. Each image was impressive in its own right, but she had not anticipated the contrast, the impact they would have together. He had chosen the images not only for the individual quality, but also for the impact each had upon the other. Each photograph stated something special about the personality of the bear. Michael had combined amazing talent with marketing genius.

Twenty minutes later, as she reached for the door handle, she stopped, looking once more at the grouping. Magnificent, she thought. And then she glanced back over the other shoulder, knowing she would still be on the opposite wall, standing waist deep in the pool before the falls. Easily recognizable, Alex's hands caressed the waters around her. This was the secret image, the one that revealed who the woman in the waterfall was. The magic of her mystical image still dominated the privacy of The White Room.

That afternoon, as he carried her bag to the Jetta, she challenged him. "How long is she going to grace the wall of The White Room?"

He lifted the bag into the back, closing the lid. "It is kind of weird, isn't it? But it's different now. Couple of years ago she was still a vision. Let's just call the picture a memorial now. A remembrance of a time past, an appreciation for a moment and a woman in my life."

"You given up on her?"

His shoulders lifted up. "There's a time to move on, to leave the past." He opened her door for her, and she kissed his cheek as she always did before she slipped behind the wheel. "How about you, Jenny? Is it time to move on to new challenges, Miss Director of Galleries?"

She winked back with her cheery smile as confident and assured as always. "I'll call you soon."

Chapter 41

When William arrived at the Esquire Hotel, his regular driver retrieved his bags from the trunk of the limousine. The driver turned to William, a noncommittal look. "Will I be escorting your friend back to the hotel this evening?"

William's mind drifted to that moment when they were standing on the boat watching the whales with Alexandria beside him. He remembered the distant look in her eyes just before the whale emerged, that far away look that so often over took her. He felt that distance as well, the lack of them he was suppose to feel as a loving, married man.

Smiling at the question, she was beautiful, voluptuous and a bit tawdry. She spoke with a dark, New York accent and wore too much lipstick and heels a bit too high. When she arrived he always felt a hint of guilt, yet she would pull him by the tie, lead him to the bed, and take control like no one controlled him. He relished those moments when he lost control, when he gave it up completely and allowed her to work her magic. Why he was so drawn to that, he didn't understand, but he knew it was a private, secret moment he would not give up.

"Yes," he answered. "Bring her by at ten."

"As you wish." The driver nodded with a tip of his hat.

Three days later, Alexandria knew William's flight was to leave at six in the evening. It was at six that she dialed the hotel.

"Esquire Hotel," the young male voice answered. "How may I be of service?"

"This is Mrs. William Chadwick." She hoped he couldn't distinguish her nervousness.

"Yes, Mrs. Chadwick."

"When I left today, I'm afraid I might have forgotten a yellow scarf in our room. I was wondering if you could check for me."

"One moment please."

Alexandria paced the bedroom back and forth, afraid of the answer. She needed to understand his life in New York.

She heard a click as the desk clerk returned. "I'm sorry Mrs. Chadwick, but housekeeping did not find anything in the room. Perhaps you left it in the limousine."

She took a long, deep breath. "Yes, the limousine. I'm afraid William made all of the arrangements. Can you remember the name of the service?" Then she added, "I'd like to call and check. The scarf was an important gift from a friend."

"I believe you use Executive Town Car Services, at least that is who we usually call for you."

"Of course, Executive Town Car Services." She could barely hold the phone in her hand. "Thank you."

Chapter 42

It was a rainy, dreary spring day, the wind causing a coolness that was unusual for the season. Alexandria stepped from the elevator feeling vulnerable. Her receptionist greeted her with a cup of coffee, her messages, and word that Jennifer needed to see her.

Alexandria settled in reviewing her calendar, making notes for the day, and returned one important telephone call to the Arts Council. When she hung up, she tapped the intercom button and pressed Jennifer's extension.

"Yes."

"Good morning."

"Good morning, Alexandria."

"Can you believe this weather? What happened to spring?"

"It's hiding from us. Anyway," her voice was breathy. "Are you free?"

Alexandria sensed something in Jennifer's tone. She hesitated before answering, "Come right in."

In a moment the door opened, and Jennifer stood face to face with her good friend. The two successful businesswomen looking the perfect part for greater success in similar business suits, hair pulled back conservatively, and make-up flawlessly applied. They both smiled, Alexandria coming around her desk with cheerful chat to sit in the chair beside Jennifer.

As she chatted, the hesitation in Jennifer's eyes told her that, yes, she had heard something in her voice. "Everything okay, Jen?"

"Yes, yes. In fact, everything is quite good, but I need to do something and it's quite difficult for me."

Alexandria began to speak, but Jennifer's blunt smile stopped her.

"Alexandria, you have been a wonderful friend, an amazing boss, and have truly impacted my life. We've shared much more than many sisters share."

"My God," blankness overtook Alexandria's stare, "you're leaving."

Jennifer nodded, and her eyes began to fill with tears.

Alexandria felt like the unexpected break up with a boyfriend you adored. Without anticipation, without knowing your world was about to tip sideways, he would announce that he *just wanted to be friends*. She already missed her and wanted to beg her to stay.

"But why, Jennifer?" Her face maintained professional optimism, though it was all a façade. "Is there something wrong?"

There was warmth in her face as Jennifer smiled. "Alexandria, things are wonderful here, but I've been offered an amazing opportunity. It's something that creatively and professionally I cannot turn down, so I've decided to make this change. I've been very happy here, and you've been more than generous. Maybe more importantly, your friendship is something I value greatly. I can't thank you enough, but I've made the decision, and I will be leaving at the end of the month."

Alexandria sat back dismayed. She trusted her impeccably, her judgment and her friendship. She had assumed things would not change, but she felt obligated to support her. She wanted good things to come her friend's way.

"Well, this must be a wonderful opportunity." She put on her best smile, feigning enthusiasm. "What's enticed you away?"

Jennifer had somehow hoped this question would never be asked, somehow hoped she could just walk away without sharing. Her eyes diverted from Alexandria's as she began to talk.

"Alexandria. It's Michael." She felt the catch in her voice. "Michael Cabelli is expanding his galleries from four to eleven, and he has asked me to serve as his Director of Galleries."

She didn't mean to look stone-faced. "I see." Her mind was spinning, her words empty. "What a wonderful opportunity."

Alexandria's voice was curt, and she couldn't hide the shock in her eyes. Standing quickly, she offered a congratulatory handshake. Jennifer stepped past the handshake to hug her friend. She held her tenderly, and felt Alexandria's body lean heavily against her, her arms limp. Jennifer wished there had been a way of never mentioning his name.

Alexandria was in her car driving away from the Chadwick Building. She punched Jessi's number into the cell phone, and listened to the distant rings.

"Good morning. This is Dr. Jesson."

"Jessi. It's Alex."

"Yes dear," she hesitated. "You sound distressed."

"I need to see you."

"I'm free until one o'clock. Can you come over now?"

"I'm already on my way."

The doorbell rang, and Dr. Jesson glanced at her turquoise watch, surprised at the little time that had passed. When she opened the door, Alex stood before her tall and proper with make-up darkening the tears that flowed over her reddened cheeks. Jessi reached out her hand, taking Alex's and led her through the corridor to her session room.

Slumping into the gliding rocker, her jacket hung open to reveal a tear stained ivory camisole. Her head hung with drooping shoulders. Her lap now captured the tears that escaped between her fingers where her hands covered her face.

Alex struggled to control her uncontrollable tears as Jessi tried to soothe her. But each time there was some semblance of recovery, Alex broke again, sniffling back sobs that wouldn't stop.

Jessi knew to wait. Strong Alex, confident Alex, she knew she would recover soon. Then she would share. And she knew this was not simple; she knew what it must be about. Death did not bring this type of anguish. This was deeply personal, and she wondered how Mickey must have crossed through her life again.

Slowly, Alex's sobs subsided to tears. For some time, she sat crying as if she were alone. Years of misery were finally coming to some reconciliation. Finally, Alex looked up, laughing a bit through her tears before her face again distorted into hurt. She pounded her leg, angry and resistant, her fingernails digging divots into the palms of her hands.

"I'm sorry." She reached for a tissue from the table and looked up with an angry smile. Her voice was defiant. "It should have been me. I should have been her." Angry sobs filled the room.

Jessi nodded as if she understood, patiently waiting for Alex to share more.

"She's going off to live my life." Her shoulders heaved upward. "Somehow, I always thought it would be me. Somehow, I believed this fantasy would become true. He's so good, and I wanted to give him more. I wanted to be his partner, to share his life, his successes." Alex looked up, wiping the black from beneath her eyes. "I wanted to drink wine sitting in his arms by the fireplace, making love on a llama wool rug. I wanted the complete freedom to love him and celebrate his talent. I wanted to be a part of it." She turned away. "All these years, that's what I've thought about. It kept me going believing that someday I would go there." Her eyes turned back to Jessi. "Somehow, I thought it would happen. I thought we'd be together, and we'd always want to be together. If we didn't make love, we'd be best friends. If we had a fight, we'd be excited to make-up. Somehow, I thought Mickey would come join me in bed on Sunday morning, and we'd make love, and he'd hold me in his arms afterward, and…" She laughed, looking away from Jessi. "This probably sounds stupid, but somehow I thought we'd sit on the couch, he'd hold me in his arms, and we'd read the Sunday morning paper together."

When Alex's eyes finally lifted, Jessi took her hand resting it in hers. "My dear, what happened this morning?"

Alex shook her head, strands of hair falling disarrayed from the tightly held bun. "Always, in my fantasy, we would go to his gallery and greet customers, and they would compliment us on the amazing work displayed. My contribution to our lives was the artistic coordination, the presentation of images in the gallery. He created the images, and I managed the gallery. That was our partnership."

"So," Jessi tried to sound compassionate, "Today, reality struck right at the heart of the dream."

Alex nodded sadly. "Jennifer quit the Foundation. Mickey is expanding his galleries and opening several more, and Jennifer is going to be his Director of Galleries." Pain twisted in her face again. "It hurts, Jessi. It should have been me. That's my job, that's my life. It's like my dream was stripped away, and he's gone forever. And it hurts, Jessi. It should have been me."

Jessi allowed her to cry. This was her time. When Alex tried to speak, Jessi comforted. She saw that Alex knew her life was changing by remaining the same. Alex slipped into ramblings of her days with Mickey and her thoughts since then. She described vividly his home, the smell of his body, and the softness of his hair. She cried about telling her father, and wondered if she would ever be happy. And she talked about wanting to be angry with Jennifer, and how unfair such anger was.

"But I am angry, damn it." Alex stood defiant, turning, looking for something to smash. "What does she think she's doing? She knows how I feel." She turned hard to Jessi. "It should be me. This is all messed up. Doesn't she see it?" Anguish seethed from her mouth. "I should have done it years ago. God damn it, when he first started going to New York, I should have left then."

"New York?" Jessi asked.

Alexandria waved her away. "William and all his trips to New York. I should have just left."

She glared out the window, off toward the mountains. Quieting, her forehead slumped, a thud against the glass window.

"It feels like hope is gone, and it hurts."

Jessi leaned forward to hear the whisper.

"It could have been so wonderful."

Jessi spoke calmly. "I'm going to say something, Alex, and I want you to listen. You always give me a bad time about only asking questions." Alex laughed, wiping a tear from her check, turning back toward her friend. "This may sound harsh, Alex, but it needs to be said. You've spent the past years fantasizing about a life you have no idea could have ever happened."

Alex stared glassy eyed.

"Mickey was a few days in your life, and he became an image that you expanded into a fantasy and the basis for all of your happiness. The reality is you have no idea what life with Mickey would have been like. And more importantly, you have no idea if there would have been a life with Mickey. You give your life quality, and you limit the quality by measuring it against an unknown, an improbable fantasy. A guy in the mountains."

Alex stared straight into Jessi, unsure how to react.

"Quit depressing yourself and limiting your relationships because one guy you hardly knew gave you an orgasm."

Alex responded with anger. "Is that what you think this is about? An orgasm?" Her eyes raged through Jessi.

"Please Alex." Dr. Jesson's said in a calming tone. "Don't misinterpret this. I don't mean to belittle your relationship with Mickey, but you made a choice to never see him again. Yet you won't release the memory of this guy who took you to the top of the mountain and made you scream with pleasure. You know life is more than that. You lived a three-day fantasy that few of us ever experience." Jessi leaned forward, quieting her voice. "Congratulations Alex. But it's wrong that you've let three days become you definition of happiness. He's gone, Alex. He's been gone since the moment you decided to stay with William. So let him go. Let him go take pictures, and let Jennifer work for him. But stop," she gripped Alex's knee, pressing forward, straight at the problem. "Stop defining happiness based on an image you've created. Release yourself or you'll never be happy."

There were no sobs, just tears, harsh, continuous tears. "But I don't want to let him go."

"You must." Jessi's voice was quiet. "As he has, you must move on."

"No, no. Not without him."

Jessi nodded. "With his memory, a pleasant memory. That's what you move on with, a memory of a good man and a wonderful moment. That's it. Appreciate the memory, knowing that your life is better because of it, but move on."

But grief came first, and Alex was grieving. Loss brings pain, and after that, healing. With healing, Alex would finally step forward and live again.

The morning had long passed turning to afternoon when Jessi walked Alex to the door. She felt comfortable seeing the strength begin to return.

"May I make one more suggestion," Jessi asked.

Alex took a deep breath, easing the tension. Her nod was simple.

"As we move forward, you should not do it alone. It's time for some joint counseling, you and William. If your marriage is to truly work, you must begin to heal together."

Alexandria's memory flashed to the phone call, *You use Executive Town Car Service*. "We may be beyond healing."

Jessi watched her patient sadly. "We won't know until we try."

Panic froze in her blue eyes. "We can't talk about Mickey!"

Jessi's soft smile reassured her. "Absolutely not. What you have shared with me is strictly between us, but there are still deep problems in your relationship. You can't address those alone, Alex. If you're to heal your relationship, you and William must do it together."

Chapter 43

For the longest time, she didn't want to go home. People were there and so was her life. She drove to the Red Rocks and walked up on a tall ledge sitting on the damp rock, sometimes allowing the tears to creep back into her eyes.

Staring west into the Colorado Rockies, snow still covered the peaks as gray waves of mist blew across the Front Range like a thin warn out blanket. She laughed at the way she looked in her business suit and run-filled nylons, sitting with the red dust staining the fabric, her satin heels on the rocks beside her. She had already decided, for whatever irrational reason, she would throw the suit away when she got home.

She waited long into the afternoon; until the sun's angle took away the warmth, until she knew Josie would be home. She waited as long as she could until finally she had to go.

In the Mercedes, she looked in the lighted vanity mirror, laughing at the horror she saw. Using a wet-wipe, she gained a hint of clean feeling. Her hair was allowed to fall loosely down over her shoulder, and the brush gave it some resemblance of order. She applied a new covering of make-up to camouflage the smears and swollen eyes. She was determined to arrive home intact.

When she entered the estate, she parked the car where the help would clean and garage it. Slipping in the side door, avoiding both the front entryway and the kitchen, she took the back stairway to the second floor, moved down the hallway undetected, and into her bedroom. Closing the door behind her, she pressed the intercom for Josie's room.

"Hi honey. You there?"

The music from Josie's room quieted to a lower decibel. "Hey Mom. You just get home?"

"Yes dear. How was your day?"

"Great."

"Josie," she felt so tired. "I'm going to take a bath right now and clean up before dinner. You're joining me this evening?"

"Yep," her daughter giggled. "Nothing more exciting tonight than Algebra, Shakespeare's *Julius Caesar*, and Mom."

Alexandria laughed too. "All three classics. I'll see you downstairs in an hour."

"It's a date," she giggled again.

Alexandria heard the music rise to deafening as she turned on her own soft music to fill the quietness.

The water's steady swell seemed to flow smoothly with the soft music. She slipped off her jacket, laying it on the counter. The silk camisole was ruined with runny circles of mascara spotted on the front. Reaching behind to unzip her skirt, she let it fall to the floor. She pulled the fabric into a ball and stuffed it down into the wastebasket. Lifting the plastic liner, she tied the ends tightly to hide the balled up clothes and set the trash by the door.

With a fingertip test of the bath water, she reached for the bottle of oil beads. A little pampering, she thought to herself. Settling slowly into the warm water, she allowed it to surround her until she lay back in the comfort of the large tub.

She would not turn on the air jets today. No harsh bubbles. She wanted quiet, solitude, and peacefulness. If she were to move on through the evening and into tomorrow, this day of turmoil demanded peacefulness.

Still in her towel, she intercomed the kitchen requesting that dinner be served in the sunroom. It always felt like being outdoors. She looked in her closet at all of the wonderful clothes, then saw her warn and faded Broncos sweatshirt. She remained free without a bra and dropped the jersey down over her shoulders. Slipping on holey jeans, she picked a pair of her most comfortable flip-flops.

Josie was waiting in the sunroom and removed her ear buds when she saw her mother. One of the rules Alexandria insisted upon. The headphones were for private time, not time to ignore others. She rubbed her hand over Josie's dark hair, kissing her lovingly on the top of her head.

"Cool outfit, Mom."

Josie's grin was mischievous. "Not many mom's get away with going braless."

Alexandria flipped her hand playfully at Josie.

Dinner was salmon and fresh broccoli. Josie had passed her disagreeable stage and was back to appreciating broccoli. Though she did her usual complaining about the Academy, Alexandria had to remind her that she could stop politicking. The decision had been made weeks before. She could go to the public high school in the fall.

"I've been thinking," Josie announced.

"That's good, dear," her mother teased.

"Are you going to take me seriously?" Josie placed a bit of broccoli deliberately in her mouth, teasing her mother back.

"I always take you seriously."

Josie moved the salmon on her plate. "So, I've decided what I want to do for my sixteenth birthday."

"Josie, your fifteenth birthday is this summer. Aren't we getting a little ahead of ourselves?"

"Nope, because this is special."

Alexandria raised her eyebrows in suspicion. "Bike across Europe maybe?"

"Nope," Josie's eyes got wide with imagination, "but that's a great idea."

"Let's stick with your plan, which is...?"

"I'd like to do what you did on your sixteenth birthday."

For a moment Alexandria had to scramble her brain to remember.

"I want you and me to hike Long's Peak together."

Alexandria suddenly looked sad.

"I'm sorry," Josie stared at the strange distortion in her mother's face. "I thought you'd be excited."

Alexandria gathered herself. "Yes, of course. I'm sorry dear. Yes, it's a wonderful idea. It's just that everything seems to be focusing on Estes Park today. Jennifer resigned this morning. She's going to work for a photographer in Estes Park, be the director of several galleries he has throughout the western states."

"Oh Mom, what are you going to do without her?"

Still stuck within the day's turmoil, Alexandria wasn't sure. Bucking up, she told Josie, "Well, we'll survive. I'm sure we'll miss her, but this is a wonderful opportunity for her." She was surprised at her composure. "Hiking Long's Peak? That would be quite a challenge. Maybe your father could join us. A family event."

Josie was laughing now. "Mom, you know Daddy would die halfway up. He'd start out strong, thinking he was bold and manly and could handle it. But he's not conditioned for the mountains. He'd fade fast. It'd be pathetic, leaving my father gasping for air on a mountainside while we danced on to the top. *Teenager Hikes Father to Death on 16th Birthday.*" Josie was laughing as she finished. "Nasty headlines."

Alexandria could only grin. "I bet your father could make it."

"Well, maybe he could, but I know we could do it together."

Alexandria smiled despite where her mind took her. The mountains stood fully in view, teasing her of a life they might have offered while the people she loved moved on without her. Resentment rushed through her, pounding into her heart, and she felt guilty at her uncharitable thoughts. She had no desire to return to Estes Park, at least not now.

"We'll see dear," she finally said.

"I thought you'd be excited, Mom."

Her mother nodded, "I am. It's just, well with Jennifer leaving and everything, I've got a lot on my mind." She put on her best mother's face. "It sounds like a wonderful plan."

When Josie was ready for bed, she found her mother in the master suite posed on the floor before the fireplace. Her back against the love seat with her legs tight against her chest, it was dark except for the small fire adding heat to the warmth left from the afternoon sun. Josie sat down beside her, resting her head on her mother's shoulder.

They sat quietly in the dark watching the fire, slight waves of flame dancing from the ash logs. They had done this before. Camping in the mountains, chilled by the night air, comforted together before the fire. For Josie it was warmth and safety. Her friends envied that she and her mother would do such things, backpacking, rafting, or cross country skiing; always they were off on great adventures.

Her mother had guided her away from the prissiness of her girlfriends. They had never been in the wilderness, therefore, never fully understood. They had never been face to face with a bull moose lying in the fresh snow; his antlers, nose, and back covered in whiteness. They had never faced the rage of a June river and held the paddle to fight for control, tossed about in the white water. Her Academy friends had never looked up a mountain wondering how anybody could get up there, and then hours later, breathing labored with sore feet and tired legs, looked down from the mountain top at the sprawling valley from which they came.

Alex was staring straight into the fire, a slight reflection of the flames in her blue eyes. Watching her, Josie wondered what had happened, why all the sadness in her eyes.

"Mom, is everything okay?" She wrapped her arms around her mother, hugging. "You're a wet puppy?"

A stray tear began to form. "A wet puppy?"

"So sad," Josie's smile turned sad. "Wet puppy sad."

She tipped her head to rest on Josie's, comforted by her smile. "Oh Honey, just business. Everything is fine."

"I don't like it when you're sad, Mom."

"It's just been a tough day, dear." She patted her daughter's arm where it wrapped warmly around hers. "Lots of change."

"Mom, can I ask you a question." The softness of her voice made Josie sound much younger than she was. "I don't know if I should ask this, but, well, it's been bugging me, and you always say I can ask you anything."

"And you can," Alexandria shifted to mother mode.

"Okay," Josie took a deep breath. "Don't be mad at me asking, but do you think you and Daddy will ever get a divorce?"

The question came bluntly, shocking. Alexandria glared into the fire, her eyebrows wrinkled in pain. "Why in the world would you think that?"

Josie leaned fully against her mother. "You and Daddy, well, you kind of live different lives. He does his business stuff, and you and I do our outdoors stuff. You're happy when we're out in the wilderness, but you're not happy when we get back home. Dad's always off in New York or traveling for the bank and tonight he's working late like always, and you're sitting here all alone and sad. I know you and Daddy like each other, but you aren't together much. And then you get sad." She nestled in tightly to her mother. "So I was just wondering, it's not unusual, divorce, so do you think you and Dad will ever?"

Alexandria watched the fire. Too smart for her own good, too worldly, she had raised Josie well to see, understand, and ask. She should have known, she should have realized teenage perceptiveness would see the truth. Alexandria wondered how long that question had been nagging in her daughter's mind. What insecurities had it created?

"Your father is a wonderful man."

"I know that, Mom." Josie looked over her full dark eyebrows. "I love Daddy. I can't believe he gave in to leaving the academy." Her voice deepened to formal Chadwick. "A public institution for heaven's sake."

Alexandria pulled her closer. "I hope you know how much he loves you. He wants you to make your own way in the world. From birth, his future was decided, but he's very generous when it comes to his little girl. He wants you to choose your own course. You're very lucky to have such a father."

"I know, but how about you, Mom. What's your course?" Josie and Alexandria both stared into the slight flames of the evening fire. "I want you to be happy too."

Alexandria lifted her hand over her daughter's head, stroking the deep satin hair that hung beyond the middle of her daughter's back.

Alex knew why she'd stayed, and it felt wonderful to have her daughter nestled close to her. Josie was she and she was Josie, confident, adventurous, and full of excitement. Her daughter was growing to be all that Alexandria wished she had the courage to be. Alexandria knew she had made the right decision six years ago. Staying had been the right decision.

PART V: Fall
Chapter 44

He looked through the side window of the limousine staring down the freeway at a long lane of bumpers one against the other. He knew he had to fire two vice presidents. His patience had already been costly, and the pettiness and unpredictability of the recent days had retching his gut sideways.

Knowing action was necessary, he also knew their lives would be undone. In a strange twist, he asked himself, *If this were the Foundation, what would Alexandria do?*

He reached for his cell phone, scrolled his contacts, and hit the number he searched for. Two rings and the receptionist answered.

"William Chadwick calling for David Brice please," he stated.

"Yes sir, Mr. Chadwick." William appreciated the recognition in her voice.

"William." Enthusiasm rose in the CEO's voice. "So good to hear from you."

"You too David. Did your golf handicap survive the fall?"

"Fall would be the key word. My driver failed me."

William grinned, knowing his pain. "Sorry to hear that." Unusual for William, he took a deep breath. "David, I'm reaching out for some help today."

The CEO's voice remained enthusiastic.

William's driver slowed with the traffic. "I've got a gentleman who's worked for me for years. He's our Human Resources Vice-President. Tremendous skills in searching out and finding talent, an amazing recruiter, and two years ago we promoted him. Unfortunately, his skills seemed to have been limited in their transferability." William hesitated in thought. "May I speak confidentially, David?"

"Of course."

"I've got to make a change, and you know it won't work to keep this man within the organization. His credibility has been shot, and unfortunately, many people won't recognize the wealth of skills that moved him to the level he's currently at. They'll only see the problems he had as head of Human Resources."

The voice on the other end turned intent. "William, do you believe this gentleman could train recruiters?"

"Absolutely." William saw the first sign for his exit. "If he can teach without the stresses of daily management decisions, but he has difficulty making tough decisions like the one's his current responsibilities require." William looked out the window. "Give him a specific responsibility, the freedom to coordinate his schedule, and encourage his self respect, and David, this is a good, hardworking person who has been quite successful in the right situation. Unfortunately, we moved him out of that situation. That was a mistake I made, and now, we've got to make a change."

"Beyond the management responsibilities, you recommend him unequivocally."

William glanced sideways feeling the movement to the inside lane as the exit approached. "If you have a position for a trainer, I believe it would be an ideal match of talent, motivation, and responsibilities. He's a good man who will work hard for you."

"It would involve a lot of travel both nationally and abroad."

William smiled at what was happening. "He traveled previously for us. Besides, his options are limited."

"Understood." Encouragement returned in the voice on the other end of the line. "We'll take a look. Have him call me, and we'll see what we think."

"I'll do that." William smiled thinking that Alexandria would be proud of him. "Give him a few days to adjust. I'm sure he'll call within the week."

The next call was to the legal department directing them to produce the necessary termination papers. Thinking again of Alexandria, he added a more than generous severance package for the Human Resource V.P.

The end came quickly. For the Human Resources Vice President, the severance pay and recommendation were lost with the shock that he had just been dismissed. He had driven to the same building each workday for nineteen years, and he would not drive there any longer. His second thought was his mortgage, then his daughter's tuition to the expensive private eastern college he had insisted she attend.

The Trust V.P. was different. Brought in six years ago to replace William when he took over as CEO, he had slowly and methodically dismantled the caliber of excellence William had so staunchly demanded. William found his arrogance and insistence on transferring blame quite distasteful. He dismissed him with survival severance and encouragement to do some serious self-analysis, advice William was sure would be ignored.

By 8:30 a.m., William was meeting with the remaining management team, and by lunchtime, to the relief of his division leaders, both dismissed employees had vacated their offices under the supervision of the bank's head of security.

As they so often did, William and his assistant took lunch in his office. They ordered in tuna fish, potato salad, and fruit from the Executive Dining Room. William always laughed at how amazing his chef could make tuna salad taste. Valerie too appreciated it.

Mid-thirties, with a mind that could read his, the irony often occurred to William that he enjoyed lunches with his assistant. He still smiled that over lunch she would sit on the opposite end of the couch from him, her high heels left on the floor, and her nude legs resting on the coffee table. No other employee would dare such a cavalier presence, nor would she demonstrate such unprofessionalism outside the lunch break behind closed doors. He wondered how this corner of privacy had ever come to exist.

He bit into the tuna salad, lifting a napkin. She took a sip of diet cola.

"It was good of you to set up that interview."

William dabbed the corner of his mouth. "Do you think he understood what I was saying?"

"If not now, tomorrow. He'll appreciate it when he meets with Mr. Brice."

Her eyebrows lifted as if to say *what's done is done,* and he realized she had changed. A touch older since she joined the organization seven years previously, she was more confident, more at ease with him. Despite her role as administrative assistant, she had grown much more valued in the organization for her insight and ability to maneuver issues to resolution.

The two women in his life were his wife and his most trusted associate, different people that he somehow treated similarly, another of life's inequities.

"Anyway," she said, "it was nice of you."

Chapter 45

Josie danced through the kitchen, her hair skimming to and fro across her shoulder and her smile beaming with her morning make-up finely in place. She stopped at the sunroom to see her mother smiling up at her. Dressed in a red long-john thermal tee shirt covered with a matching flannel print shirt, a frayed hole opened at the knee of her blue jeans. Her father would have a fit knowing what she got away with at the public school.

"You hate this as much as I do, don't you." Her eyes took on a playfully evil grin.

Alexandria laughed a little. "Whatever do you mean?"

"Every time we get home from a trip, you do this." Josie moved to kiss her mother's cheek. "I get ready for school, but you, you just don't want to admit you're not in the mountains anymore, so you sit out here and stare at them."

Alexandria reached, rubbing her daughter's arm. "Don't worry about me. Besides, aren't those hiking clothes you're wearing?"

"Cool, huh!" Josie's eyebrows were animated, her arms raised for admiration of her outfit. "We could just move there, you know; get a cabin in the mountains and live there forever."

Alexandria's laughter was a youthful soprano as she waved her daughter away with a loving dismissal. "You go to school, tell your friends of the elk and the afternoon rain. It's time for me to get ready to go to the Foundation."

Josie yelled back. "It's about time your mind came back home," and she disappeared laughing through the kitchen.

She knew it was silly, but she found it irritating when she came into their bedroom and the bed had been made. She wondered if she had dreamed it. When she had gone to sleep, she had assumed the car she heard had been his. When she awoke, she assumed he had spent the night beside her, leaving early for the bank. But now that the bed had been made, she could not be sure.

Alexandria stared at the bed's colors and matching pillows. She shuddered a bit. Jessi was right. They hadn't gotten counseling and things had grown more distant, falling back into the routine of separate lives. Damn him. He never talked. Was there anything left between them besides the legal obligation of marriage?

In a black mood, she put on black jeans and a matching corset turtleneck. Her black belt was accented with a large silver buckle and leather half boots with silver tips. She didn't know how warm it was, so she grabbed her black Wilson bomber jacket. She stopped to look into the full-length mirror. Black. Determined power, she thought, projecting non-compliant feminism.

Without going to her office, she took the elevator in the Chadwick Building straight to William's floor. The door opened to the receptionist, and she waved a hello. Valerie was at her desk, standing guard.

"Is he in?" She had always liked Valerie. Wondered about her, but she liked her just the same.

"Oh, I like the black look, Mrs. Chadwick." Her smile was familiar. "Let me see if he's available."

Valerie pressed a button on the intercom, speaking into the receiver. Her smile was again pleasant.

"Go right in." Valerie hung-up the phone as she passed.

William stood formally from behind his mahogany desk, straightening his silk tie. "Welcome back from the wilds."

He moved around the desk, and Alexandria reacted, reaching for his arm as she turned her cheek to welcome his automatic kiss.

In his monotone voice, he stated, "I only have a moment."

Alexandria's smile turned tense. "Hopefully, this will only take a minute."

He motioned for her to sit in the chair while he moved back behind the desk.

"Where were you last night?" Her eyes and smile seemed pleasant enough.

He stiffened, unprepared. "Well, Ben and I went to the Bronco's game then to The Club for a drink. I came back to the office to clear my desk, and I got home about 9:30. You were upstairs, so I watched ESPN highlights, replays of the game and scores. I finished a brandy and came to bed about 11:30. Why?"

Alexandria sat before his desk, all in black, her legs crossed. "I just wanted you to describe what our life is like. You go one way, I go another, and darn it, William, I didn't even know if we'd slept together last night. Isn't that pathetic? Don't you think there's something wrong with that picture?"

It didn't surprise him, this gentle outburst. He didn't look at her though he knew she was locked in on him. He loved her eyes, but knew the blue could turn determined. That someone so beautiful had such a range of expressions always startled him.

"I want you to go to marriage counseling with me."

Now he looked up at her and saw she was serious.

"You can't propose that we share this with someone else."

Her hands flipped in the air. "Just take a break, William. This is not about image. This is about you and me and our marriage. Counseling's also confidential, so chill out, my dear. I want this for our sake."

He lifted his hands, palms to her. "Okay Alexandria. If you want to get serious, let's get serious about this. When is the last time we made love?"

"Hawaii."

His look was almost indignant. "Do you love me?"

The blow sat her back limp into the chair. Her eyes looked painful. "Do you love me?" she asked back.

He cleared his throat, glancing to the photographs on the bookcase. Alexandria and William, the governor and his wife. There were pictures of the family at Josie's ballet recital with Alexandria and his mother on opposite sides. The three of them at Josie's Academy eighth grade graduation, Josie's blue eyes matching Alexandria's.

"Alexandria, you haven't wanted to touch me for months, and the sad thing is, and I have to admit this. I've been okay with that." He shook his head sadly. "I love and respect you, but do you really think counseling will make a difference?"

Alexandria stared in disbelief, subdued. "Have you given up, William?"

"No," he responded quickly. "Of course I haven't. But sometimes I believe you have."

She stared at the deep shine in her black boots. "I want to keep trying." Her eyes moved up connecting directly with his. "We've got so much invested in this, William, and we're both good people. I don't know how this has happened…" she hesitated. "Yes I do. Time has passed, and we've allowed it to. You've become more entrenched in high finance, and I've escaped with Josie."

"You're right, Alexandria." He shook his head. "Set it up, any afternoon next week. It doesn't matter when. I'll have to reschedule something anyway. Just set it up, and I'll be there. I'll do this if it is what you believe will get us back on the right track."

She still stared at him. "This is for us, William."

"I know." His dismissal was more blunt than he intended, and he added a quick smile. "Please, set it up, but not a word to Valerie. I'll put it in my phone with a reminder."

In the elevator, she leaned against the hardwood wall. Sometimes, even when you know it is coming, you're not prepared. Her breath escaped but did not return. *Do you really think counseling will make a difference?* She gasped, her hand to her chest wondering when it had happened, when he had made the decision to move on without her.

Chapter 46

She wore black again, knowing defiance would not make this any easier. She and Jessi were sitting facing each other, Alexandria's legs crossed with the familiar movement of her foot nervously up and down. He was late, more than a few minutes late when the creaking of the door caused them both to look.

The perfection of William's image always amazed Alexandria, how he could look fresh and confident any place no matter what the situation. William reached out his hand as Dr. Jesson stood.

"Dr. Jesson," he spoke boldly, "I'm William. William Chadwick. It's very nice to meet you. I apologize if I'm late."

Alexandria stared at him looking for clues.

Jessi nodded calmly. "May I call you William?"

"Please," he nodded, taking the seat beside Alexandria.

"William," Jessi settled back into her chair, "I'd like to share a thought or two, basic understandings to facilitate things along."

William nodded, catching Alexandria's agreement from the corner of his eye.

"I've encouraged Alex and you to come."

William's hand lifted between them. "Alex?" He looked from his wife to the shrink.

Jessi waved back to him. "I'm sorry. Sometimes I'm a bit informal." She went on. "Alexandria and I have been visiting for some time. She's expressed a desire to work through a few things in your marriage. As she's shard, there are some unresolved issues." Dr. Jesson smiled as if singing a hymn. "Let me assure you that there are unresolved issues in all marriages, and even in the most healthy relationships."

William glanced at his watch.

"Now, I want us to be willing to speak freely, but we must do so agreeing that number one, we do it in an effort to build a stronger relationship, two, it is shared in the confidence that is your marriage, just between the two of you, and three, it is done with respect of each other's feelings."

"Dr. Jesson," he tugged at the button of his suit jacket.

"Jessi, please."

"I want to assure you that I want this to work too, so please, let's move beyond the formalities." His smile looked forced, his voice controlling.

"Alexandria and I don't talk much, but we can. There's not dislike here as much as different focuses in our lives. Let's move on with things, please."

Alexandria resisted the desire to be completely irritated, the brash way he took control without listening, without allowing any vulnerability. As her ire rose, so did her willingness to release until she decided *to hell with it*, and got irritated anyway.

"Good then," Jessi smiled at each of them. "We have to begin somewhere, so Alex." She corrected herself. "Alexandria, would you like to begin?"

William watched her eye-to-eye as she spoke. He listened to the fact that they never made love, that he never had time for her, that they had to schedule Thursday nights or they'd never talk, and that he loved his job more than her. Surprised at the obvious depth of her frustrations, he was shocked at how easily the anger flowed from her. She had always repressed this, but in the safety of Dr. Jesson's office bitterness prevailed. She rambled on with a distasteful attitude; defiant and determined that he'd heard her.

When she stopped he continued to stare. Without breaking eye contact, her flame red glare matched his livid contempt. Feeling ambushed, his own blood began to boil. "You're absolutely right on all counts. And do you wonder why that is?"

"It's because of that stupid competition your mind has with your father's success," Alexandria countered. "It's because of your own fear of failure, and because you'd rather be at work then home."

His anger rose so easily, but he masked it with an unruffled business response. "True or not, Alexandria, I have to ask you. When did you stop living our life and separate from me into your own private life?"

This wasn't Dr. Jesson's role to interrupt, but she did anyway. "You know," she said. "I'm sure there is plenty of blame to go around. But we are not here to blame. Blame doesn't heal, and we are here to heal." She turned her shoulders toward William, her hands held together before him. "William, what would you like from Alexandria to make your marriage stronger?"

He nodded, and began to speak.

"No William. Not to me." With a slight motion of her finger, she moved his eyes to Alexandria's. "Please. Talk to your wife."

When William looked at her, his anger faded, replaced by sorrow for the pain he saw, her anger having turned watery.

Dryness suddenly gripped his throat. "I'm sorry." His eyes moved to Dr. Jesson, then back to Alexandria. "There was a time when you looked at me as if there was no other man in the world. I was so confident that you loved me. I trusted that you loved me. That seems so long ago, so distant from today, and it began when you started living a separate life."

She fought not to look away.

Dr. Jesson watched her. "And Alexandria? What do you think about that?"

Their eyes still watched each other. "I just want to believe that I'm as important to you as your bank."

Dr. Jesson allowed the quiet for a moment. When Alexandria's eyes finally turned to her, Jessi spoke, "This is what marriage counseling is all about. Now you each have something to build on, something you've shared with each other. Alexandria, would you tell William again what you want?"

Alexandria looked at her husband. "I want to believe I'm as important to you as the bank."

"And William?"

William nodded too. "I want to trust that our life together is as important to you as your life apart."

Chapter 47

Michael stood knee deep in the icy flow. Nearly noon, and the sun was just breaking above him. He looked straight up the hundred and fifty feet to the top of The Narrows. He could see the sun moving down the wall of the slot canyon. Up ahead was a curve in the canyon, a curve that would be lighted for a few brief minutes when the sun peaked straight above.

This is why he had hiked nine of the sixteen miles through The Narrows, leaving his rented Blazer behind at Zion Lodge in Amy's hands. Amy, the lodge manager, had become a friend during Michael's other trips to Zion National Park. She always found him a good room and shared the best and only Mexican food in Springdale. He looked forward to coming here.

He was lucky to have a sunny day to hike The Narrows. Sixteen miles of sunless canyon, the Virgin River runs wall-to-wall creating a beauty mysteriously hidden. He was seeking that spot where the sun would contrast the darkness on the curve of the towering stone wall and the rush of the water through the narrow divide.

Autumn was the only time to hike The Narrows. Then the water level was down, making the current manageable; replacing the ravage of snow run off and spring rains blasting through the sometimes five-foot-wide canyon. It was a good day for taking pictures. Afterward, he would hike the remaining seven miles through the river to the opposite end of the canyon.

Michael set his pack securely on a small ledge just above the river. His boots heavy from four hours in the current, he waded back to the middle of the ankle deep waters. Taking the tripod from its pack, he released the locks extending each leg one section.

As suspected, the current's pressure on the legs created too much movement. Any picture would be a blur. He looked back over his shoulder along the slightly curving canyon. A dry spot, maybe three feet by three feet covered with small, rounded pebbles was his only option. He lifted the tripod from the water and worked his boots through the stream to the dry ledge.

Extending the tripod, Michael set the legs and looked. The bend in the canyon wall allowed the opening before him and the large curve beyond to stand in full view. He scanned up the walls to the spot where the sunlight was inching downward.

Wading back to his protected pack, he took his Canon body and 24 mm lens from the bag. Still safely in their waterproof bags, he carried them back across the river. There he set the lens and mounted the camera on the tripod's quick release. Flipping his Rockies hat backward, he looked through the viewfinder.

He had never been to The Narrows and had only heard tales of the hike. He looked up over the camera. Magnificent. While here the canyon was only about twenty feet wide, the walls scaled ten times that high narrowing at the tops to provide a glimpse of sunlight at mid-day.

Scanning the wall, he saw in the shadows the geological curves carved out by the rush of flash floods between the tenuous ledges. With the sun at mid-day, the lines would brighten the swirling canyon walls and create a spectacular blending of color and sunlight. His eyes turned upward. He glanced at his watch, a few minutes until the sun illuminated the canyon wall.

On the manual setting, he adjusted the camera to a longer, one-minute exposure. The belief was that with the sunlight, the camera would drink in the golden exposure while blurring the flow of water to soft lines. With the limited time, he hoped in five minutes he would get five shots and one spectacular image.

Michael watched the sun move down the wall, waiting for it to peak the canyon rim and strike the river before him. He checked the viewfinder, adjusting the image a millimeter.

In his hand he held the cable release. The exposure was set, ready, and he waited. Then a speck of light reflected the base of the canyon at the river. He looked up over his head and saw the first blazing ray.

Standing unmoving, knowing the shutter eye was open, he waited for the click of closure. Motionless as the light moved across the river bottom, the current rushed past him inches from his feet. He balanced his hand against the canyon wall. Five minutes and five shots later, he was done.

Already the far wall had begun to lose the sharpness of its details, the golden reflection fading to slight rays of light. So quickly, the opportunity had passed. He could still get pictures, but the perfect moment for art had lasted only minutes.

Concerned, he reviewed the photos on the camera's digital screen seeing the golden glow accentuating the canyon walls and the green and white streams of the river's flow. The tiny images looked amazing, and that gave him hope.

Michael waded into the middle of the river, the cold pressing over his boots and edging up his jeans. He tipped his head back, balancing to watch the slight opening of blue sky straight above. The smile broke across his face, and laughter came as it so often did. He raised his hands to the sun, stretching upward as the black waves of his hair flowed in the canyon breeze.

As he loved to do, he released the emotion of the moment. From the exhilaration of the sun, water, and breeze, his yell was strong and full as his joy echoed through the narrow canyon.

At four o'clock he emerged from the north end of The Narrows, and the brightness shocked his eyes. Hours before, his feet had turned numb in the cold. Amy waved from the ledge above him, and he grimaced from the nettling pain in his feet, glad that he would soon be free of his saturated boots.

He handed Amy his tripod bag and slipped the pack from his shoulders, rubbing the cramp that had become a part of his neck hours before. Amy opened the back of the Blazer, and Michael laid his pack on the carpet. He sat on the bumper and took his flip-flops from inside the truck.

"Good day?" Amy asked, her reddish hair hanging in long waves.

"Amazing." Michael's voice was hoarse, weary.

"Did you get the shot?"

Michael took his boots off, pouring water onto the ground. His soaked socks clung to his skin, and when he pulled them away, his feet were deep, blotchy red. He began rubbing one foot as Amy rubbed the other, pressing warmth back into the fading blotches.

"You never can be absolutely sure until they're enlarged, but I believe so. Even in that small digital image, the sun looked like a gold miner's heaven," he shrugged, still rubbing. "I was there at the right moment. Could be something special."

"Hard hike, isn't it?" Amy was staring at him, grinning, as she continued to rub his feet for warmth.

By the time they reached Springdale, his feet were an even pale pink, his stomach churned for food, and his mind craved a beer. Amy pulled into the Bit & Spur Saloon.

"Keep moving those feet," she pointed at his flip-flops. "Keep the circulation moving."

She had to help him from the truck, and each step up the wood plank stairs was delicate. He didn't say a word, but she could see the pain. She'd seen it before from every person who hiked The Narrows. At the doorway, she grinned at her friend greeting guests.

"A table by a heater. We've got a case of The Narrow's feet."

The pleasant young girl, a casual acquaintance, picked up two menus, and she motioned the way. "Frozen feet, Michael?"

Michael only managed a smile and a nod.

The table was next to a baseboard heater, and Michael put his bare feet on the wobbly wooden chair between the table and the heater. The waitress brought a cup of coffee with a double shot of Amaretto to warm and relax him. "On the house," she told them.

For a time, Amy sat smiling a mixture of appreciation and sympathy. Michael felt worn and chilled, beaten by the elements, but the hike had made him strong, more capable. He raised a shot of Amaretto. Amy appreciated the self-satisfaction of his grin, and Michael thought it was nice to have her company.

At his lodge room, Amy left him with a hug and a kiss on the cheek. Michael sat on the bed; his body limp. He stared at the T.V. watching the late night news, his feet tucked under the blanket. What time was it in Seattle, he thought to himself. An hour earlier? Yes, an hour earlier. He reached for the phone.

Three rings and she answered.

"Gaud, you sound awful," she said.

"Feel awful," he answered.

"So what's up? And where were you? I've tried to reach you all day."

Jennifer's business mind could not conceive that cell phone reception in the wilds of a deep, narrow canyon was not an automatic.

"I hiked The Narrows."

"What's The Narrows, and why do they call it The Narrows?"

"They call it The Narrows because it's narrow. I'm in Zion National Park."

"Cool, but why didn't you carry your cell phone."

He was looking at the ceiling. "Just what I need. Alone in the wilds, the quiet only disturbed by the breeze, the mellow rain of the river flow, and the ringtone of a cell phone. Besides," he laughed, "it was The Narrows. I had my phone, but no reception."

"Awe, yes. The Narrows," she was still laughing. "Okay, think satellite phone for safety. Until then, stay out of canyons when I need to reach you."

"I love your logic."

She turned business serious. "So here is the problem. I have four showings set for six weeks from now. Over a two-week period we'll unveil the bear series including short presentations by you, social events to sell a limited edition by auction while we make the rest of your collection available. We'll get T.V. and press coverage and attract the wealthier market. One here, one in Portland, one in Napa hosted by the Jarvis Winery in their magnificent cave ballroom. The other is in Aspen with lots of movie types and corporate money. Trouble is, the one in Aspen is hitting roadblocks. With no gallery of yours in town, the local art association is protesting that there isn't enough support for local artists, so why would the Chamber bring in someone else. They want their own showing. Stingy bit of self ego."

Michael shifted crossing his feet under the edge of the blanket. "Maybe they're right. Let's offer a joint showing."

"But that defeats our purpose." The pitch in Jennifer's voice rose. Michael knew she was pacing, her voice filling the room. "If we share time and space, we share publicity."

Michael chided her, "Stingy bit of self ego."

"Or appropriate public relations management."

He shrugged. "Okay. How pissed are the locals?"

"Not so much pissed as demanding. As inflexible as an evangelist with his own television show."

Michael shifted on the bed, his back cracking away the stiffness. "We have the showing set, all the details in place?"

"We just need the final okay," she said. "But the Chamber is afraid to give it and offend the locals."

"Call them back tomorrow." Michael's mind was coordinating. "We'll headline it, but have the Chamber coordinate four other artists, each from a different medium. Tell them we want their best, but let the Chamber choose the artists. We'll coordinate the showing, and do all the work. We'll be the center focus, but the four other artists will each have a featured presence with display space and opportunity to sell their work. They simply have to do what we do and help us with the local advertising. What percentage are we donating?"

"No percentage," Jennifer answered. "Just the auction of the initial print offering. We donate the auction receipts. Any sales beyond that go to us."

"Great, so we auction one set of the bear series, and everything else being shown is sale profit."

"Correct," she was firm.

Michael liked this idea. "Okay. The only other thing the local artists must do is provide one top quality item, minimum retail of $1,000, preferably more. We'll auction one item from each of the four artists and our bear prints, enhance the donation to the local charity, then their profits will come from the showing sale too. Let's bring this all together and support the local artists as well. There's plenty of wealth in Aspen to go around."

"Michael," she was thinking it through. "I'm not sure we should share publicity and exposure."

"It could enhance our relationships when we try to move permanently into that market," he added. "Will we lose money?"

"No, I'm sure we'll do quite well."

"Actually then," he was now sitting up in the bed. "When we open our gallery in Aspen, we'll do it as friends."

"Okay," she softened. "I just wanted a big kick-off in Colorado. This seems to dilute it."

"Jennifer." Firmly, he held the phone. "You have done a wonderful job in setting these up. The bear series gets big publicity. The rich people spend a little money to attend, and they buy our art. Charity wins, we win, and the rich people get to own some great limited edition images. It works for everybody. We'll make this adjustment and move on without enemies."

Listening, her optimism returned. "I know you're right. I just felt Colorado was the place where we could count on a big initial showing to give us momentum." She released a deep sigh. "But this is still good. I'll take care of it first thing tomorrow."

"Good work, Jenny."

"Thanks Michael." They both listened to each other breath for a moment. "So, when will you be back in Estes?"

"Three days," he answered. "Taking the rental back to Las Vegas tomorrow. Going to spend a couple of days in the desert by the pool drinking sun-warmed beer and sharing some money with the black jack tables. My flight gets into Denver mid-morning, so I'll call you late afternoon when I get back home."

"Good, that gives me time."

"Time for what?"

"Time to get all these showings finalized," she said. "Next time I talk to you, these should all be a done deal. Big events beginning in six weeks."

"It's exciting, Jennifer. You've got us moving in leaps and bounds, leaps and bounds."

"I do, don't I?" Her laughter was confident.

The knock on the door interrupted is laughter. "Hey," he said reaching for the doorknob. "I've got to go."

"Company?" She asked, teasing.

Amy stepped into the room, her hand on his forearm, her lips leaning in to kiss his.

Jennifer gasped. "Was that a smack I heard?"

Amy whispered, "How are your feet?" Kissing his cheek.

"There's a woman in your room?"

"Got to go, Jenny." He stepped back and Amy moved into the room, the outdoorsy flow of her walk, enticing. "Great work on the showings."

"Michael, do you have a girlfriend." Jennifer was giggling.

Amy winked, "Yes Michael." Hearing the words from the phone. "Do you have a girlfriend?" Her hands came to her chest as she laughed.

"I'll call you tomorrow."

"Who is she? That park lady?"

Laughing, he ended the call.

Chapter 48

"Mr. Chadwick. It's your wife on line one."

William looked at the telephone. "Thanks Valarie." He glanced at his appointment book, the clock. Their session wasn't for hours. Impatient, he picked up the receiver. "Hi. What's up?"

Despite the interruption, there was always something about her voice that he liked, the fun, cheerful softness that he had somehow been reminded of during counseling.

"I thought since we were only a few floors apart, and we're both going to Dr. Jesson's, I thought we might ride together. You know, one car for the two of us."

He tried not to sound irritated, looking at the clock again. "We could, Alexandria, but I can't fool around." He listened to himself, and tried to choose his words carefully. "Honestly, I'm not trying to put you off, but I have an important appointment later this afternoon. I need to get right back after the session."

"God forbid you spend a few moments with your wife instead of romancing the bank." She hated the sarcasm in her voice.

"Be fair, please." He was as sharp as she was. "I have every intention of being at our session, and yes, we can ride together. I just wanted you to understand I have an important meeting later. I'm trying to hire two vice presidents, and it's not something I can ignore or simply reschedule. You can understand that, can't you?"

"Yes, of course William." Her voice shortened the words. "I'll meet you in the parking garage at 1:40. The appointment will begin promptly at 2:00. We'll be back here by 3:20. Does that work?" She tried to sound upbeat.

He forced a smile, a pleasant tone to his voice. "I'll see you in the parking garage."

"One-forty," she said.

"One-forty."

As the black Lexus pulled onto the downtown street, Alexandria looked at her husband. "See, isn't this nice."

William looked sideways to see the way her eyes stared up at him. He had to smile. "Yes, this is nice."

When they arrived at the appointment, the edge had worn off. Replaced by a semblance of comfort, they almost seemed happy with each other. William was much less direct, Alexandria much less impatient, Dr. Jesson much less involved as the two talked. She observed their mood, listened to their words, and was pleased at the difference from the previous session.

Alexandria explained to William their lives were so separate they'd forgotten they liked each other. The tension of no communication was all they felt. Marriage, she reminded him, is something they had to work at. An unprofound statement, but in truth, it was the only thing in their lives they failed to work on.

William listened attentively. He allowed her to talk. He practiced patience, but was tired of being the target. She was placing blame, so he looked her straight in the eyes, and he told her the truth about herself. He described their conversation on the whaleboat in Hawaii. He reminded her he had asked where she sometimes went, where she disappeared to deep in the corner of her mind, and he reminded her he had never received an answer.

Alexandria could not help but look away. She watched the wallpaper, saw her foot bouncing, and stared at Jessi's hands folded neatly in the lap of her denim skirt. She could not look at William's eyes when he explained that it hurt him to be with her and know that in her heart she must be somewhere else.

"Yet here's the surprising part," he told them. "I know you're not having an affair. Several years ago, when you seemed to be changing…I know this is going to make you angry," he explained, but no longer cared. "Several years ago I had you followed. Periodically, for years since then, whenever something seems amiss, I'd have our security firm check. I needed an answer only to find there were no answers."

Shocked at his admission, the harshness welled up in her eyes and the blue became hard.

"I'm sorry, Alexandria." His matter-of-fact attitude angered her. "I tell you this because I know I was wrong. But all the signs were there. You'd changed. You changed your style of dress, turned indifferent toward me, started running off to the mountains, and Josephine became Josie. So much changed, and I had to know why. But I never found out, and you sure as hell wouldn't tell me. Something changed, and I'm still mystified."

Jessi watched Alexandria stare at the floor. She knew this had to be Alexandria's decision, and was shocked when the emotions did not flow. She had expected a blow up or a break down, something other than control. Instead, Alex stared straight down, gathering composure. Silence passed with no words.

William and Jessi stared at Alexandria, and Alex stared at the floor, but William would not give in. He waited in silence, only hesitating glances toward the clock beside Jessi.

"This is part of our problem," her voice cracked the silence. "You cannot accept me as an individual. Yes, I changed, and I like me better, yet you never accepted it. The only times you have truly been comfortable with is when I've stood dutifully by your side, playing the role of the perfect woman supporting her super human, financier husband. Our problem is not that I changed, but that you struggled to allow it, and when you determined you couldn't control it, you sic a fucking investigator on me?"

With the return of silence, Jessi waited for thoughts to clear before she stepped back in, but Alex couldn't give it time.

"If you don't give a shit about my life, William, stay out of it."

The ride back to the bank was deadly silent.

When William stopped the Lexus in the parking stall, he turned to Alexandria.

When he did, her finger pointed harsh and unmoving except for the quiver, "Don't you ever."

"It was a few years ago." His hand came up between them. "You changed, and I didn't know why. You don't want me to do these things, then tell me what's going on."

"Never," her eyes burned raging blue. "I'm your wife, not some sleazy woman who needs a slink-around spy."

"Then quit hiding things from me."

"I can't believe you." Her eyes flared daggers. "Quit hiding things? Well," she reached for the door handle, her hand freezing on it unable to move or stop the words. "Maybe it's time you took another trip to New York. Apparently, they know Mrs. Chadwick well at the Esquire Hotel."

Her firm pull on the door lifted the handle and her back moved away from him until she slammed the car door. Walking as he stared in disbelief, she did not see him slump into the driver's seat. When she was alone behind the closed elevator doors, in shame her head dropped into her hands overwhelmed with guilt.

Chapter 49

The landing was one of the smoothest Michael had ever experienced, and as he exited, he smiled mightily to the captain offering his congratulations.

He strode down the walkway, his suede camera backpack slung over his shoulder. Dressed comfortably for the cool fall weather, he tugged on the taupe tapestry vest he had bought at a trendy men's shop in Caesar's Palace the night before. Fitting neatly over his natural gray tee shirt and under the sharp sand-tone sports jacket, all went well with his ever-present faded blue jeans and ruff-out logger boots.

While in the air he had been thinking about Jennifer, sure that she now had the showings in place, everything in order. He was confident that the Aspen Chamber had been pleased with the compromise. Her disappointment must have faded, and she was well into the enthusiasm of moving forward with their plans.

Cameras secured, he cinched the pack tighter over his left shoulder and stepped into a newsstand along the terminal walkway. A gentleman standing before the nation's newspapers had the Denver Post folded inside out, awkwardly holding it in one hand as he ate a bagel from a terminal deli. Michael glanced at the headline below the picture. A new bank vice president had been named, pictured in a formal, posed handshake with President and Bank CEO William Chadwick.

Sometimes ideas came to Michael like that. A single motivation and immediately he knew the idea was good. Smiling broadly, he adjusted the leather pack and grabbed a copy of the Denver Post.

The energy in his walk was more vigorous than in the The Narrows. For the first time in days his legs bounced beyond the rubbery feeling of weary recovery. Ideas brought enthusiasm, and a new idea was quickly molding itself in his mind.

The possibilities were of creating the grand production that Jennifer envisioned, an unveiling of the bear series with huge publicity potential. This idea was good, he thought. Yes, this was a terrific idea. Jennifer would be ecstatic. His mind searched the long term parking area for the location where the Jeep had been left a week before.

The parking attendant gave him the directions he asked for, and Michael sped down the airport thoroughfare and onto the freeway. The Jeep flew along, and it felt good to be in the familiar bouncing machine, racing past smooth flowing luxury automobiles that offered comfort yet absolutely no challenge to experience the world. This was a good day. His body recovered and his spirit stronger, he moved forward quickly. Jennifer would be surprised, surprised and pleased.

He swung into the parking garage under the blinking *parking available* sign. The elevator directory guided him, and he followed the numbers to fourteen, pushing the button to brighten a yellow light. The feeling in the elevator was a slight stir, the only movement detected was the swaying of his digital pad hanging from his right hand until the tone announced the door's opening.

Stepping out, Michael stood before the large wooden doors emblazed with *The Chadwick Foundation*. He pressed his hands through his hair, pulling the length of his dark waves into place. He walked the few feet forward, opening the thick wooden door.

A sweet young girl sat at a desk in traditionally designed extravagance of an old money office. Before she could look up from her keyboard, Michael was introducing himself. She smiled back politely listening to his story. He was a former client who would like to visit with someone about a business proposal that would benefit the Foundation. Her pleasant smile remained unmoved as she listened. When he stopped, she gave a simple nod and looked down at the appointment book on her desk.

Looking back to Michael with the same smile, she responded, "I'm sorry, Mr. Cabelli. Mrs. Chadwick is not available today, nor is her associate. They have previous commitments out-of-the-office. May I schedule an appointment for you next week?"

"Not available?" he thought out loud. "Won't be in at all?"

She shook her head. "I'm sorry sir." She glanced at the appointment book, turning the page. "I have some time with Mrs. Chadwick's associate tomorrow, Friday afternoon, or several openings with Mrs. Chadwick early next week." She watched him, thinking how attractive his vest fit his chest. "You say you were a previous client of the Foundation?"

"Yes." His face showed optimism. "Nature and wildlife photography. Listen, I'm not sure of my schedule next week. Can I call tomorrow and set something for Monday or Tuesday?"

Without looking at the appointment schedule, she answered, "I'm sure that will work fine."

Michael reached into the inside pocket of his jacket, handing her a business card showing a silhouette of two elk with the image of magnificent racks perched for the evening on the barren tundra. *Nature's Way. The Photography of Michael Cabelli* the card read.

When the elevator doors opened at the fourteenth floor, he stared into the empty elevator disappointed that his idea would have to wait. He took two steps inside, and turned to the buttons, staring at the directory.

Corporate Offices...4th captured his brown eyes. He pushed the button. It was worth a try.

On the fourth floor the elevator opened to the reception area indicating the entire floor was the corporate office. Michael introduced himself to the grinning, middle-aged woman who alternated between people and the telephone with a button panel of extension options.

"William Chadwick, please."

Smiling well-trained politeness, she asked, "Do you have an appointment?"

Michael returned an identical smile. "Unfortunately, I do not. You see, I am only in town this morning, and I am a client of the Foundation. It's important that I have just a moment."

The receptionist's smile remained, but her eyes questioned.

Michael thought of an end run. "Maybe if I could visit with his secretary, I might be able to set an appointment."

Her eyes soften as she said, "Follow me, please."

The walkway was half a block long through workstations and middle management men and women in daily action on computers and telephone headsets, frantically on task. When the glass door closed, a calm seemed to surround the quiet of the CEO's office.

A pretty lady, sharply dressed in a wool suit, greeted them.

Michael returned his best grin. "Good morning." He offered his hand, and she stood, accepting his greeting. "My name is Michael Cabelli. I'm a nature and wildlife photographer, and I have been a recipient of the generosity shared through Mr. Chadwick's Foundation. I'm only in town for a few hours, and I wanted to thank him for the success his Foundation has supported. Would it be possible to get just a couple of minutes to offer my thanks?"

"Actually," Valerie reluctantly released her hand from his. "The Foundation is located on the fourteen floor, and..."

Michael moved his eyes, agreeing.

Valerie appreciated the smile in his lips, the intensity in his kind stare. She was sure she was being charmed.

"I was just on the fourteen floor, and no one is available today. As I said, I'm only in town today, and I only need a moment."

She knew she was softening. Normally, she would intercom Mr. Chadwick, but his expectation for confidentiality encouraged her to check with him directly. "Excuse me a moment."

Michael watched her walk to the private office door several feet behind her. She knocked softly three times, and then entered.

William held his hand up quieting her as he continued speaking into the telephone. When he finished, he set the receiver aside.

"Yes," he looked up patiently, smiling to see her.

Valerie gave a similar smile, motioned back toward the door. "There is a nice gentleman who would like a moment of your time. He is a former Foundation client, a nature photographer, and he wants to offer his thanks for the help the Foundation has provided." Then she added, "I think he's sincere."

In one sweeping glance, William checked his appointment schedule and the time. "Shouldn't he be visiting with Alexandria?"

"She's out, and he's only in town for a few hours." Valerie stood more formally. "He's a nice guy, William. Maybe a minute or two for the Foundation?"

"You've already determined he's nice?" He teased her.

Valerie turned a hint of red. "Charming and handsome. To me that equals nice."

"Woman's intuition or professional judgment?"

"A bit of both. His name's Michael Cabelli.""

Accepting her judgment, he clarified, "Just for a moment?"

"Yes sir." She turned quickly to the door.

When Michael entered the office, the man moved around the desk to welcome him in a warm, professional greeting. They stood at similar heights, with the CEO being a hint taller, the formality of his body was disguised under the perfect fit of the tailored shirt and gray of the tapered Italian suit. His handshake was firm.

"Mr. Cabelli," William motioned for him to take a seat as he moved back around his desk. "I understand you've been a beneficiary of our Foundation."

Both men sat.

"Yes sir." Michael adjusted the fit of his vest at the waist. "A few years ago, your Foundation provided me with funding to begin my career as a nature and wildlife photographer. Not only did you give me a jump-start in developing a collection of unique images, but I was able to open my first gallery in Estes Park. I say with both enthusiasm and thanks that today I have nine galleries in four states, and we will be expanding into California soon."

William listened politely, nodding his congratulations.

"In fact, you may know my Director of Galleries, Jennifer Wilson."

William leaned his head back in recognition. "Oh yes, now it's coming together. You see, Mr. Cabelli, my wife is the Foundation Director, and I rely heavily on her to manage that aspect of our family charitable trust." William glanced at the single-family picture facing him from the corner of his desk. "In actuality, I have little to do with the Foundation, although I am a bit surprised we had a project outside of the Denver metropolitan area. Nevertheless, the Foundation has been quite successful under her direction. The greatest tragedy in the many years that she has run the

Foundation has been the loss of Jennifer." William's grin widened. "So you are the culprit that grappled her away from us."

"Guilty." Michael raised his hands in playful apology.

"I understand she's quite talented."

Michael agreed, seeing the pleasantness in the CEO's smile.

"I must apologize, Mr. Cabelli, but I only have a few moments."

"Of course." Michael realized he must be brief yet convincing. "Jennifer is why I'm here. We are about to launch a new limited edition series in an effort to promote the expansion of our galleries. I must tell you, Mr. Chadwick, this new series is an amazing grouping of extraordinary North American bear images."

William listened patiently, yet Michael knew time was short.

"Jennifer has done a marvelous job of establishing four showings in three states to make the initial four limited edition series available. As I visited with her recently, she was searching for one opportunity to initiate the showings, a kick-off if you will. Let me offer a proposal as my small effort to thank the Foundation, allowing us both to benefit."

William's eyes motioned for the younger man to go on. He was a nice person, William could see that, and he appreciated his approach to the discussion. Business firm, concise, and specific, the man who looked like a modern day cross between Buffalo Bill Cody and Ansel Adams spoke with clarity. Communicating through gestures of his strong hands and intent dark eyes, his words were articulate with a charismatic flair.

"We would like to co-host with the Foundation a showing and auction of our number one, limited edition series North American Bear prints. This would be an event in which my images would be presented to the social community of Denver, the proceeds from the auction going to the Foundation, and I would donate an additional fifty percent of the net sales to the Foundation."

William listened, watching the concentration and confidence of this man, curious as much about the art as the individual. "Tell me more, please." He waved his hand in a smaller circular motion.

"I would exhibit my limited edition collection for the guests to appreciate over a glass of wine. The collection includes some incredible images of North American landscape and animals." Michael laid his digital pad on Mr. Chadwick's desk showing the first image of the brown bear bursting from the waters of Brook Falls with a giant Salmon clenched in his jaws.

William slowly flipped through the photos, impressed with each image, astonished at the vivid details of the animals in their natural habitat. Most striking to him was a new image of two bald eagles in playful mating flight, one upside down, it's talons clenching the others as they fell in a lithe tumble through the air.

As William scanned the images, Michael continued. "We have done similar showings many times over the past four years. This showing would go much beyond these. It would be the unveiling and national release of the bear series." Michael adjusted the shape of his vest, flattening it smoothly against his chest. William tugged to straighten the shirt cuffs showing from beneath his suit jacket. "I want this showing in Denver to bring national attention to the Foundation as well as the bear series release."

Intrigued, William nodded. "How would this look?"

"Following the social time of introductions and review of the exhibition, I would give a brief twenty minute presentation sharing the excitement and challenges of stalking each of the four North American bears to achieve the unique images. I can guarantee, Mr. Chadwick each story will provide a vivid, entertaining dialogue of adventure in capturing each bear image.

Following the presentation, we will auction the number one set of the limited edition series. I would estimate the biding to reach well into the tens of thousands of dollars. Following the auction, guests would have an opportunity to purchase any of the images on exhibit."

Impressed, William stared at the picture of a lone wolf curled and covered in a fresh layer of snow, it's frosty coat barely visible and it's soft eyes deceiving.

"I see the potential, Mr. Cabelli." William patted his hand on the image indicating his appreciation. "You're an exceptional photographer, and I see how this would be an excellent publicity opportunity and a significant donation to the Foundation."

"I agree," Michael watched Mr. Chadwick's eyes. "And it is something I would appreciate the opportunity to do, giving back to the Chadwick Foundation for what you have done for my career."

"Mr. Cabelli?" His hands rested before him. "My assistant tells me you will be in town for just a few hours. Is it possible?" He scanned his appointment book and glanced to the clock on the mantel. "Could you meet me back here at noon? I'd like to buy you lunch in our Executive Dining Room."

At noon, Michael reported to the Executive Dining Room on the twenty-first floor. He was politely ushered to a prominent table near a row of windows overlooking the center of downtown Denver, the Rockies looming majestically in the background. Moments later, William Chadwick, accompanied by the kind assistant Valerie, walked in procession through the dining room to the table where Michael stood to greet them.

Lunch was preordered in an assumption that Michael would appreciate the chef's talents. As they sat, Michael felt like a schoolboy, a visitor in Mr.

Chadwick's school. He had been quite impressed with the portfolio, and had asked Valerie to research Mr. Cabelli's credentials.

Mr. Chadwick complimented Michael on his fine reputation earned at the national level both with the Sierra Club and the North American Nature Photographer Organization. The Estes Park Chamber of Commerce Director and the manager of the Chadwick's bank in Estes spoke quite highly of him. He apparently was a respected contributor not only to the art environment but also the community of Estes Park. The Bank Manager had commented on his astuteness as a businessperson. Finally, Nature's Way website provided an impressive overview of his work, galleries, and mission as a photographer.

Mr. Chadwick paused, making it clear that this was only an initial discussion and everything would have to be cleared with Mrs. Chadwick and the Foundation prior to final approval.

Valerie then explained that she had taken the liberty of securing the ballroom and banquet facilities at Mr. Chadwick's club, the finest and most exclusive in Denver, for four weeks from now, the last Saturday in October. Would that date be acceptable?

A week before the other scheduled showing began, he hesitated as he reviewed his mental calendar. Knowing of no conflicts, he acknowledged the date.

As their entree arrived, Mr. Chadwick looked pleased with his decision.

"Mr. Cabelli, I am a man of action, and when I make decisions usually they are final. I like you, and I believe from the portfolio you've shared and the reports of your work you are a talented artist. So I've made a decision to step forward in this joint venture, but please understand, my wife is the director of the Foundation. In respect of her, she'll make the final decision. I'll have her contact with you and finalizing the details."

Michael was thrilled. This was beyond the event Jennifer had been hoping for in Aspen. While he sat formally in control on the outside, his enthusiasm was bouncing on the inside, and he couldn't wait to give Jennifer the news.

Chapter 50

William was not comfortable with Alexandria's choice for dinner, but he wisely kept his mouth shut. They had followed Clear Creek up Interstate 70 to Georgetown and sat at the table in the bay window overlooking the quaint streets of the rebuilt mining town. On the past two Thursdays she had dragged him out of the city into the mountains where he dressed in khaki pants and v-neck sweaters he thought were too colorful.

How she knew about these quiet restaurants of mountain character, he did not know, but this is where she wanted to spend their evening, so he did so without protest. Over an artichoke appetizer and mildly acceptable wine, he shared his day.

"I did something today, and I hope you approve."

She was happy to feel them smiling with each other again. Both had over compensated for their guilt, and things had calmed.

"A gentleman came to my office today." As he set his fork aside, she smiled at the sporty feel of her sleek sweater. "Actually, he went to your office first, and not finding you, he persistently came to mine. Apparently, he's been a client of the Foundation, and he wanted to propose a joint project." William pulled at a corner of the warmed handmade bread loaf sitting on the cutting board. "I liked him, and I was impressed with his portfolio, so I made some decisions."

Alexandria had tried to dress in a nice compromise between William's formality and her own need for the outdoorsy look. While her sweater and jacket were stylish with natural colors, her hair was pulled tightly around her face into the small ponytail that the shoulder length cut would allow. Her make-up was slightly fuller than typical, but showed the preciseness of William's business world. He thought it perfectly accentuated, and appreciated that she wore the diamond pendent necklace, a gift William had Valerie pick out on their anniversary.

Alexandria reached over, touching her hand to his. "It's good to see you're interested in the Foundation." She pressed her fork into a bite of artichoke, placing it on her tongue.

"This young man, Michael Cabelli," he said, "is quite the artist."

The artichoke leaf dried in her throat as Alex sat frozen, unable to move.

"Do you remember him? A nature and wildlife photographer the Foundation did some work with?"

Her eyes looked though William. She reached for a glass of water, subtly gulping to force the artichoke down her throat. Alexandria swallowed and tried to breath but for an instant even that was not possible, so she only nodded.

"I thought you might. Jennifer works for him now." William smiled, speaking matter-of-factly. "His talent would be hard to forget. I saw his portfolio. Amazing," he said, impressed. "Anyway, he proposed a charity auction and showing of his newest images, North American Bears. I reserved The Club for the last Saturday in October. I know this would have to come together quickly, but I liked him. Besides, between you and Jennifer, I'm sure things could fall into place quite nicely."

The artichoke sat in the middle of her stomach now fighting the butterflies that flew in a frantic plethora of nerves and panic.

William ate some more bread. "Valerie has all the details. Talk to her tomorrow, and let me know what you think. I made it very clear that the final decision was yours." He smiled pleasantly. "But I hope it works out. Good guy with a great talent."

She ignored the rest of the artichoke and excused herself.

The lady's room had a lounge with two sitting chairs and a large reconditioned claw foot sofa. She passed quickly through it into the single bathroom, closed the door and locked it. Her hands rested on the sink holding her body upright. Shock flashed images of Michael and William shaking hands, smiling, agreeing. *I liked him,* William had said. *A talented young man.* The artichoke regurgitated, and she fought against it, swallowing with the acid harshly distasteful in her throat.

Leaning backwards away from the mirror, Alexandria's back was against the cold cast iron of the radiator long ago relegated to a decoration. Shivers shuddered through her, and she could feel her legs wobbling beneath her.

He stood beside his camera in the mist of the waterfall, he squatted before her holding the repelling harness, and he sat across from her on the rocky ledge overlooking the vast mountain valley. His eyes were the deepest brown as he held her in his arms, dancing to Jimmy's songs. She looked down on him from above, both naked, the hair of his chest full as she ran her fingers over his powerful build.

Then, the most frightening image of all appeared. Mickey was smiling at William, reaching out a hand of partnership as they sealed the deal.

Chapter 51

Anxious as she rushed into the Foundation office, a message had already been left by Jennifer to call immediately. Alexandria closed her office door and turned on soft classical music to rise from the speakers and drown out any words that might accidentally be overheard by her receptionist. She fiddled with the 24 ct. gold loop earring from her lobe as she dialed the number Jennifer had left.

She answered on the second ring.

"Jen..."

"Oh shit. Do you know?" Jennifer was short of breath.

"William told me last night. At dinner in Georgetown for God's sake." Alexandria was up pacing, the phone pressed over her ear as she traced her pattern back and forth. "What in the world are they thinking?"

Jennifer stopped for a moment. "They both think they're doing us a favor. Michael was thrilled that he had arranged the type of showing I wanted to kick off his new series. He thought I'd be ecstatic, even surprised I hadn't thought of a kick-off event this big." Her voice raised a pitch higher. "I suppose William thought he was helping you, supporting Michael's brainchild disaster."

"Jennifer," her voice trembled. "They shook hands, had lunch together. William told me how much he liked this guy, was even bragging about the information he'd found out. He told me about Mickey's Sierra Club publications. It was like William was Mickey's publicist or something. Thank God, it was dark in the car."

"So how do we stop this?" Jennifer words were firm.

The intercom buzzed, and Alexandria glared irritated at the telephone.

"Hold tight, Jennifer." She pressed *hold* and hit the intercom button. "Yes."

"Your husband is on line two."

"Thanks." Now what does he want? "Yes William."

His voice was unusually cheerful. "Hey, take a minute and come down here."

"I'm sorry. I don't have a minute right now." She was sharp.

"You do for this. It's great. Come right down." He hung up.

She hit line one. "Jennifer, it's William and something's up. He never calls me unless something's up. I've got to go. I'll call you back in a few. In the meantime, let's think about stopping this."

"It's seven a.m. here in Seattle. I'm leaving for the gallery in a few minutes but call as soon as you can."

"Half an hour?" Alexandria asked.

"Half an hour," Jennifer answered.

Alexandria tapped her foot all the way down on the elevator. She walked past the receptionist, and when Valerie saw her coming, she buzzed William. The two women exchanged cursory hellos as Alexandria opened the outer glass door. William stepped out of his office to greet her.

"You'll love this," he said, holding the door open as she walked into his office.

She stopped dead cold, staring as her husband stepped beside her. Hanging on the wall where his stuffed marlin had once hung was a huge photograph of her waterfall. Streaks of the falls rushing to the pond, reflected smooth waters at the edges showing the mirror of colors from the Aspen and evergreens and the hillside of brilliant wildflowers. Contrasted on the opposite side by an undisturbed opening of soft sand; clouds drifted in the reflecting lake and the blue sky above. Matted in white with an identical stark white wooden frame, it brought life to the dreary intensity of the traditional executive office. The only thing missing was the translucent image of her naked body.

"It's from Michael Cabelli," he grinned proudly. "The photographer. He overnighted it as a thank-you for the showing."

Frightened and distraught, she bit into her lip.

"What an incredible image." William said, his hand lifting to the waterfall. "I'd never thought of such a picture here, but it's perfect. Valerie thinks it warms the room. Calming." He turned to his wife, adding, "I like this guy."

A hidden mixture of anger and fear filled her stomach. Not knowing what else to say, the words stumbled out. "Yes, it is good, and it really brightens your office, but I never thought of you as a waterfall guy." Faking a smile, Alexandria crossed her arms before her holding on to control. "I'd really love to chat, but I must run. I've got several things going, and a telephone call that must be returned." Stepping forward, she kissed him on the cheek. "I'll see you tonight." Then she turned and strode back out of his office.

Out of the elevator and past her own receptionist, she turned the office music louder and dialed Jennifer's cell number.

"Good. You're there. Does Michael know about me? Who I am, and who William is?" Alexandria demanded.

"No. I don't think so. I haven't seen anything that might make me believe that."

"Oh, I bet he does. He just had the waterfall picture delivered to William as a gift."

"The picture of you," Jennifer blurted.

"No, thank God." Her head and hands were shaking. "His limited edition print of the waterfall. A gigantic three foot by four foot picture of my waterfall is hanging in my husband's office!"

"Relax Alexandria," she tried to calm her. "He doesn't know. It's just a very cruel coincidence. I guarantee you, if Michael knew I'd know he knew. He doesn't. This is still in our control."

Alexandria took a deep breath, her chest rising. She could feel the pinch of her new heels pressing against the back of her right foot. Too many times up and down the elevator.

"Okay, Jennifer. Let's stop this thing before the train goes flying off the tracks." She turned and began pacing. "You work on your end with Michael. I'll work with William. Let's get it stopped."

That day at the Chamber Business Association Luncheon, the train picked up steam. William was the guest speaker, reviewing his assessment of the impact of current government loan rates to the Denver and national economy. He casually mentioned to his friend, the Chamber Director, that the Foundation's next project would be a charity event featuring Nature and Wildlife Photographer Michael Cabelli. The enthusiasm of the Chamber Director was motivated by his own visits to Estes Park and his familiarity with Nature's Way Gallery. He shared this enthusiasm during his introduction of William to Denver's business community and the reporters present. The good work of the Chadwick Foundation was bringing Michael Cabelli to Denver.

In Jennifer's telephone call to Michael, he found it irritating that she could give no clear rationale for canceling the Denver showing. He laughed at her, reassuring that in no way would this be spreading them too thin. The Denver showing would be an excellent kick-off, and it would open up a wealthy Denver market they had yet to tap. Jennifer's persistence was unexplainable, and he found himself perturbed at the way he had to cut her off.

William's telephone call to Nature's Way in Estes Park and his thank you to Michael for the magnificent photograph sealed their fate. Both agreed that this would be an exciting event. Something different for the Foundation and the first time an artist had returned to reinvest back into the Foundation. A good trend to begin, they agreed.

Several thank yous and niceties followed until William finally broke the string offering to kick off their plans through a telephone call to the press, already alerted during his afternoon speech.

It was only after he had Valerie contact the Denver Post that he called upstairs. Alexandria was at her desk where she had already spent most of the day tapping her fingers as she mentally maneuvered the possibilities for stopping this disaster.

Just when she had convinced herself she'd figured it out, the phone rang. William's enthusiastic announcement informed her he had talked to Michael and everything was a go. He felt strongly he could ensure support and column coverage from the Post. This would be so good for the Foundation and family.

Almost simultaneously, Michael called Seattle to reassure Jennifer that everything was on track, and there was nothing to worry about. He described his telephone conversation with William, the press coverage, and instructed her to forward a press release and promotional kit to the Arts Director of the Denver Post as well as the Foundation. Jennifer sat at her desk paralyzed by the speed in which this catastrophe had unfolded.

At the same time, through Alexandria's fears, hints of titillation had begun to filter themselves. After all, she would see Mickey again. Somehow she tried convincing herself it would all work out. But the risks were great. An innocent slip, not realizing as William talked about his wife, Alexandria, the Foundation Director. Did Mickey ever talk about Alex? William was already suspicious of her. Would he sic his Chief of Security on Michael and discover what he had suspected years before? Despite flirtatious thoughts of seeing Mickey again, her anxiety quickly turned to terror as she thought about the moment they would all come face to face.

That evening at home, she sat alone on the down comforter of her king-sized bed. Too many thoughts aggravated her mind. Despite the complexities of the web, she began to believe it might be all right. What had it been? Six years? This would be like two old friends meeting by chance on a street corner.

She knew she was lying to herself, yet it might be like that. Years softened the emotions, and the reward for her discretion would be seeing Michael Cabelli again. Mickey would step back into her life as the successful man and artist he had become. It would be a relief, and there was such joy at the thought of seeing him.

The faint, familiar knock on the bedroom door brought a brighter smile to her eyes. The door opened slightly, and Josie leaned in.

"Hi Honey," Alexandria waved her into the bedroom. "Ready for bed?"

Josie danced across the room wearing a knee length sweatshirt without a collar, joining her mom on the bed. "You must have had a good day."

"A good day?" her mother laughed.

"Well yes," Josie pulled at Alexandria's Bronco's sweatshirt. "This old happy shirt and your silly smile."

"Yes Baby," her mother pulled her closer, closing her eyes tightly. "In some ways it was a perfect day."

Chapter 52

In the week that had passed, like a ping-pong ball between horror and excitement, the showing had been in Alex's constant thoughts. One moment she would see deep, dark eyes watching her from across the room. The next, she was with William moving from guest to guest. Her two worlds were about to collide.

"Are you alright, Mom?"

Alexandria turned her eyes to Josie, looked at her own hand, and realized she was still holding her breakfast toast.

"Never, never land," Josie rolled her eyes. "Where'd you go?"

"Just day dreaming, dear." Alexandria smoothed orange marmalade with the sterling knife.

"Yea, well, you've been a space queen lately." Josie paid her little attention as she spoke, finishing her own breakfast. "Float back down to earth, Mom."

Alexandria thought again about the preparations. "What nights are your volleyball games?"

"Don't you have them in your calendar?" Josie glanced at her.

In the glance, the confidence in her daughter's sapphire eyes startled Alexandria. Accentuated by long lashes, the natural waves in her hair hung over one shoulder. The transformation from innocence to power was compelling. Alexandria made a mental note about her parenting approach and the slight adjustment needed. Josie was growing into an independent, beautiful woman way too fast.

Alexandria sighed, smiling. "When did you get so grown up?"

Josie laughed. "It happened Tuesday." She brushed the toast crumbs from her fingertips, teasing her mother. "Metro tournament is next week. Thursday through Saturday. Districts the following Tuesday and Friday."

"And Wednesday?" She allowed her hand to fall away, and Josie stood from the table revealing long legs. She had that glow of energy and a figure that made Alexandria realize too many boys were calling recently.

"Nothing on my social calendar," Josie said.

"Let's plan on an evening of shopping." Alexandria sat back admiring her maturity. "The Foundation has a big event in three weeks. I'd like you to attend, and we both need new dresses."

"Sure." The glance was back over her shoulder as she moved toward the door, optimism in her bright eyes.

At mid-morning she began to anticipate Jennifer's arrival. Three times she straightened the office. The chairs were adjusted at exact matching angles. A book was straightened on the shelf once and again. Alexandria stopped to stare out the window seduced by the distant mountains.

The sound of the intercom peaked her anxiety. She checked the mirror, stood tall, and strode to the office door. Jennifer, even in the months since they were last together, had grown more mature and assuredly professional. Alexandria moved to her, and their arms spread open to an awkward hug.

Alexandria stepped back discounting the uneasiness, and with a motherly look, gave Jennifer her approval. She wore a pinstriped shirt with a fitted accent. Conforming to the long, notch collar, her heather gray jacket, black leggings, and boots shared the confidence of her role.

Jennifer tried to ease the tension. "Well, Ollie, this is a fine mess you've gotten us into."

Alexandria laughed nervously. "A fine mess. Yes." She tried not to emphasize *fine*. "This isn't something I planned."

Jennifer gave Alexandria a glance like a mother gives her daughter when, despite what she says she means the opposite.

"You know I didn't plan this." Alexandria repeated.

"I know," Jennifer stared at her former boss. "But things are working out nicely for you."

Alexandria looked confused. "That remains to be seen. It could also be the disaster of my life."

With a deep sigh, Jennifer said, "So let's figure it out."

Alexandria reviewed of the details. The Club was reserved, the publicity set, invitations printed and mailed. They went over the guest list, and Jennifer made several suggestions, her mind reacting to years of organizing events.

Alexandria took notes, agreeing with Jennifer's suggestions. They proofed the agenda. A viewing of Michael's work from seven to eight o'clock, wine and finger foods would be served by The Club's staff. Jennifer and Michael would work the room, adding intrigue with descriptions of the images.

As they spoke, the concern became obvious until Alexandria couldn't contain herself.

"All these details, Jenny, we've done this together a thousand times, but..." The event had turned into a soap opera drama Agnes Nixon couldn't have written. "We can't spring this on Michael at the event."

"So how do we break the news?" Jennifer looked distressed. "Hey Mickey, meet Alex, the long lost love of your life, and her husband William. You know, your telephone buddy, and the guy who paid for your first gallery without a clue he was doing it."

"Sarcasm won't serve us well."

"Honesty will, Alexandria, but do you truly understand how this will hit him?"

They discussed the options from a dramatic meeting with Alexandria sashaying into The Club to the other end of the spectrum, a heart-to-heart over pizza and beer in Lonigan's.

Though Jennifer might be the best to break the news, Alex insisted she have time with Mickey. She owed him a chance to understand before they met at the event, so they agreed on a compromise. It would be simple, sensible, and compassionate with timing to allow emotional control for both of them.

A couple of days before the showing, over pizza and beer in Lonigan's, she'd break the news to Michael. She'd confess her role and the past sharing all the details he needed to understand. She didn't tell Alexandria, but she knew she would have Jimmy by her side. His compassion and friendship would help Michael through.

On Saturday, Michael and his assistants would be setting up at The Club, and Alexandria would arrange for a private meeting in one of the Club's executive rooms.

They agreed. It was sensible to give Mickey time to come face-to-face with who Alex was and what she had done for him. Maybe only a few hours before the event, but it would be enough time to regain any composure that might be lost.

"So," Acknowledging the plan, "we're back at the showing. At eight o'clock, Michael will be introduced."

They both stared at each other. As Foundation Director, Alexandria often did the honors as Master of Ceremony.

"I'll have William do it." The words rushed from her.

"Will he wonder?"

Alexandria shook her head. "He thinks Michael Cabelli is his great discovery and new found friend."

Jennifer frowned, "He'll buy that?"

"You should see the waterfall image in his office. He's so proud."

"Alexandria, you'll be amazed." Jennifer's hands clapped together. "In his presentation, he sets things up with projected images and explanations about the heart of photography. It's poetic and soothing and fascinating all at the same time. And just when you get totally amazed, he steps into the world of the North American Bears. Four images. A Black, Grizzly, Kodiak, and Polar. Each image is a story, moving from cute to intriguing to ferocious and remarkable. Believe me, he will capture the imagination of even the wealthiest of our audience. Dainty old women will want to buy this bear series." Jennifer asked. "Would you like me to conduct the auction?"

Alexandria had not thought of this.

"I will be doing it at our other showings," she added.

"Then please do as you've planned."

The evening would end following the auction with all Cabelli collection images available for purchase. Jennifer and Michael would work the floor. Most would be sold, and Jennifer would be in charge of taking orders for those limited edition prints available through the galleries.

Alexandria felt the rush. "This is going to be good, isn't it?"

"Alexandria, the showing will be wonderful." Jennifer brightened. "I never thought pictures of bear and elk and aspen turned to gold could have such an impact. Michael's a true artist, and he is a part of the art. Part of the magic is owning a Cabelli. We will not be the only women in the audience in love with him, I'll guarantee you that."

Alex dropped her eyes into her lap.

Jennifer's voice was soft. "I'm sorry, Alexandria. I didn't mean...I didn't intend."

Alexandria's hand reached toward Jennifer, her fingers extended slender, sleek, and halting. She smiled appreciation. "Yes, we both love him. I am thrilled that he has found success." Her hands were clasped at her narrow hips. "This is not a rekindling, Jennifer. It's been a long time. I would cherish his friendship, but it has been a long time."

"This will be a shock to him, finding out about you and the Foundation."

"I want you to know whatever is between the two of you..."

Jennifer interrupted with a shy smile, "I'm with Jimmy."

"With Jimmy?" Alexandria eyes questioned.

"I mean I travel so much to the west coast, I don't seem to have a home, but when I am home in Estes, Jimmy and I..."

Alexandria's eyes widened, her mouth in full smile. "Jimmy?"

"He's writing love songs about me."

"Really?" Alexandria moved to her, and they embraced. The barrier of time crumbled away, and they pulled each other closer.

Alexandria stepped back. "I always thought."

"You thought I was doing Michael is what you thought."

"Weren't you?" Her eyes dared for the truth.

"For a time, I thought about it, but no," she shrugged. "No. Jimmy and I, well, we're in love."

"Okay," Alexandria grabbed her friend by the shoulders. "Jimmy? Congratulations. He is a wonderful person. Such heart and goodness."

Jennifer's eyes batted, "Yes and an amazing lover."

Alexandria laughed taking a deep breath, the whirlwind of emotions and understanding battling it out in her head.

"It's scary," she admitted.

"I'm sure it is," Jennifer said. "But we're all adults, and we know how things work."

"Yes we do," Alex reassured her. "That has to be clear. It is what it is, not what it was for a brief couple of days so long ago."

Her friend looked with a penetrating stare. "That, my dear, is up to you."

"Yes it is, and I know what it must be," Alexandria answered. "I'll do my best to keep from causing any more pain. I've caused so much damage." Her words faded. "No more damage."

Chapter 53

"So the girls are meeting us?" Leslie glanced her attention away from driving.

Alexandria acknowledged, "Allison is picking up Josie after school." She watched the freeway ahead of them. "What's it like having Allison driving?"

"Usually it's fine." Leslie thought in a mother's terms. "It's at night, when you're not sure where she is when you worry most."

"I'm thinking about getting Josie a Jeep this summer for her birthday." Her voice was hesitant.

Leslie laughed. "A Jeep. Isn't that just like you two? Allison could care less about a Jeep. She'd look at me and ask why? You have to shift it, and it doesn't have leather seats. But Josie would think it's the perfect car."

"Truck."

"What's that?" Leslie asked.

"The perfect truck. A Jeep's a truck."

The girls were waiting by the entrance to the boutique mall. Josie was a bit taller and leaner with a quicker developing chest then Allison who was still girlish and giggling. She wondered what Leslie must be thinking, Allison in her Academy uniform and Josie in her public school boots, jeans, and a black suede western shirt.

The girls welcomed them with kisses and silliness then disappeared for the nearest boutique changing room. Allison had brought other clothes, and while she would be changing several times trying on different dresses, she could not bear to wear her academy uniform any longer than required.

"So," Leslie asked, slipping her arm around her friends, "why this urgency to get a new dress for a Foundation event?"

"I'm due."

Leslie eyed her. "Yes, you're due," she repeated, "It's also something in the bounce of your walk, my dear. What's up?"

The girls caught them from behind, still laughing about a sales clerk with no humor, perturbed about Allison using their dressing room.

Josie danced before her mother as they walked along the shops. "Can I get a condom dress?"

Alexandria's frowned. "What in the world is a condom dress?"

Allison giggled, glancing at her mother. "It's a dress that fits like a condom."

"And how would you know how a condom fits?" There was urgency in Leslie's voice.

"Don't ask me," Allison motioned toward Josie. "She's the one going to public school."

Josie raised her hands, walking backward in front of her mother. "Don't go crazy Mom. It's health class. They demonstrate it in health class."

Alexandria's mouth dropped open.

"On fingers, Mom." Josie held up two fingers. "They teach us by using our fingers."

"And how well have you learned the lesson?" Alexandria wished she hadn't asked.

Josie stopped, and they all stood silent. "Well enough that if ever in my innocent teenage life I should consider using one, I'll know how. Always prepared, Mom. It's like CPR. I probably won't use it for years and years, but I'm Boy Scout prepared."

Leslie cleared her throat, and Allison quickly spoke. "Don't worry, Mom. Josie can teach me."

The girls turned quickly, giggles as they laughed on ahead.

"I could have done without that." Leslie said wide-eyed.

"Sign of the times." Alexandria shrugged dismayed, and reminded herself to have a serious one-to-one sit-down with her too rapidly maturing daughter.

Alexandria took them to her three favorite shops. In each, the shopkeeper welcomed them by name and gave all four her individual attention. Alexandria vetoed all of the condom dresses, excuses about this and that, covering the belief that they made her daughter look way too mature and shockingly seductive. With each of Josie's looks of frustration, her mother would smile patiently and hand her a less tempting dress.

Finally, several dresses aside, the compromise was achieved. A slightly revealing deep rose georgette dress coming to mid thigh. Backless, with slim crisscrossing tie straps; the bodice of the flared skirt gave her a grown-up look. Simply elegant, Alexandria knew her father would be impressed and just a little set back at how developed it made his daughter look. Not nearly as shocked as Josie's grandmother would be, but both Josie and Alexandria knew that would be part of the fun.

Allison found a cute body sliming dress in powder pink stretch lace. Leslie, less enthusiastic, was sure if she didn't find a dress for herself, she certainly had something appropriate at home. Alexandria took three dresses into the changing room, never sure what look they would create until they were off the hanger and neatly on her body.

Hanging them over the dresses Josie had left, she tried on the first two. The first, she didn't like the poufy look, and the second was nice but not designed to firmly fit her hips. She looked in the mirror, turning her hips to see. Behind her she saw the red, poly-spandex condom dress Josie had looked so tantalizing in. She smiled and stepped from the dressing area out into the boutique.

Josie's head was shaking immediately. "It's floppy in the hips."

"Which is exactly why I hate dress shopping with you." Leslie smiled at her friend.

Alexandria nodded and returned to the dressing room.

The third dress was a classic little black dress, sheer mesh sleeves and neckline with a velvet collar and open back. This might be it; she liked the sensual conservativeness. Lifting the dress from the hook, it revealed the scarlet condom dress. Alexandria stared at the red, thinking as a mother compared to its youthful appearance. She looked at the black velvet and back to the red spandex. She lifted the red dress, placing the black on the hook.

Standing naked before the mirror save her bikini briefs, she looked up and down. A smile came to her, and she took the red dress from the hanger. Slipping it above her head, she stretched the spandex, wondering how in the world young girls fit into such dresses. Pulling it down over her body, she felt the material contract to her as she pulled and tugged to slide the dress firmly into place. Once there she took a deep breath, shaking her hair, and looked in the mirror.

She knew immediately this was the dress she should not wear. In her lifetime, she had never looked so sensuous, so able to seduce. It felt so good, looking in the mirror, turning backwards, sideways and around again. She was the lady in red, though the red didn't cover much. With a deep, revealing cleavage and leg magnificent high skirt, it formed a slinky skin-tight fit that spoke very clearly. If Mickey were her date, she would wear the condom dress, driving him wild. She smiled, believing she still could, but Josie would have a fit, dear Sophia would pass out in shock, and a very wrong message would be sent. Yes, the red dress was the perfect dress not to wear.

Alexandria pulled the spandex dress back away from her body, lifting it off. She took the little black dress from its hanger, slipping it back over her head.

When she stepped from the dressing room, Josie gave a slight gasp. "Mom. That's so excellent."

The black velvet created a flowing compliment to her figure with the intriguing arousal of the mesh front and sleeves.

"Stunning," Leslie nodded. "Whatever this is about, that dress will have an impact."

Josie looked puzzled at Leslie while Leslie watched the glare from Alexandria's eyes. "Josie, is your mother still working out?"

Her rich blue eyes glancing from Leslie to her mother and back. "Lately she's an aerobic maniac."

With words spitting toward Leslie, Alex said, "Nothing wrong with a little exercise."

"The dress is gorgeous, Mrs. Chadwick." Allison proclaimed.

Stepping back into the dressing room, Alexandria stared at the red dress, then back to herself in the mirror. Sadly, she left the red spandex on the hook, leaving it in the dressing room as she carried the classic black dress to the shopkeeper.

They had dinner together at a little cafe nestled among the shops. When the girls disappeared, Leslie sat smiling at Alexandria.

Alexandria's perturbed frown returned. "What's with you?"

"Taint me, my dear. What's up with you?"

"Nothing's up with me."

"An affair?" Leslie pushed.

Alexandria fell back. "Leslie, no. Nothing is going on."

"Who's going to be at this little event?" A sly look stared at Alexandria. "I know you didn't buy that dress for William."

Irritated, Alexandria glared at her friend. "An old friend is going to be there. It's nothing. I met him once, and we had dinner. Rocky Mountain Oysters, for God's sake. It's nothing, trust me."

"My God," Leslie's mouth fell open, her eyes wide. She stared deeply into Alexandria's blue eyes. "He's your mountain man. The photographer's the mountain man."

Panic rushed into her thighs, her legs contracting under the table while her face showed no signs of reaction.

Leslie drummed her fingernails on the glass top table. "I knew your description was too vivid."

Alexandria dismissed her. "Quit babbling."

"In Vail. After you tricked Daisy and I into eating those bull's balls. It must have been five, six years ago. That's it." Her fingers clicked like irritating cymbals. "I'll never forget your description of the ideal man, a mountain man. This is him, isn't it? This Michael photographer whatever his name is."

Alexandria waved nervously as her daughter walked toward the table. She stood quickly, pointing down the mall walkway, and led all three from the chic café. As they walked, Alexandria slowed allowing distance between them and the girls.

When there was enough separation, she grabbed her friend's arm. "Once I shared something with you, something about William. You told Ben, and William was furious when he found out. Leslie," she stopped, blue darts peering directly into Leslie's hazel eyes. "You think you know something, but you don't. You're wrong, Leslie, so please, don't say anything that could create a painful rumor."

"How wrong am I?"

"You're wrong."

"I promise, I will not say anything. It's our secret." Leslie sounded reassuring, "but how wrong am I? Would you eat Rocky Mountain Oysters if William asked you too?"

Alexandria's eyelids dropped, mouth tense. "Leslie, please. Just accept that you're imagination is running wild."

Leslie's eyes understood. "Yes," she said, "wild."

Chapter 54

Alexandria was not surprised at the interruption. They had been talking much the past few days.

"Jennifer," she was cheerful, "are the skies blue in Estes."

"Not really." Bluntly, the mood quickly changed. "He's planning on displaying the picture."

"The picture?"

Alexandria listened to the long breath released on the other end of the line.

"It's his thing, this habit. He's always done it, but I thought maybe I'd convinced him to let you go." Distress echoed thru the receiver. "Your picture. The picture," her voice grew exaggerated. "The waterfall. The picture William has in his office, well not exactly the picture. The one Michael displays is of the waterfall plus a stunningly translucent blond standing in the mirror of falling water. Unrecognizable and naked, we both know it's you."

"Oh," the telephone went silent. Alexandria stared at a blank spot on her office wall thinking back to that moment in Mickey's gallery, standing with her father as he eyed the translucent woman and knew his daughter had not shared the whole story.

Jennifer interrupted her thoughts. "I expected you might have more to say."

Alexandria was glad they were on the telephone, and Jennifer could not see the fear in her eyes.

"I'm not recognizable," she asked, knowing the answer.

There was silence.

"He told me he would never reveal my identity."

"And he doesn't, but" Jennifer's voice broke. "We're talking about your husband seeing the picture. William will recognize you."

Alexandria laughed loudly.

"I don't know what the hell is wrong with you, Alexandria. This is your life and you're acting like it's some game you're going to win. William will recognize you." She was blunt. "Then what?"

William would never recognize her. He didn't think sensually, didn't think of her in such a way. He might want to know the price, or how much it would increase in value over time. He might even think it was a striking image. Probably, he'd find it distasteful in his uptight manner, never letting his arousal show. But no, William would never consider the image to be her.

Alexandria could hear the rhythm of Jennifer's deep breathing over the line. She knew her friend was as concerned about Mickey as anything.

Her mind had spent exhausting hours over the past weeks preparing. Anxiety had long passed away, replaced by anticipation. Her focus was different. Had he become serious with time, less laughter consumed with a drive for success? Was his passion still intense, still innocent, still both? When they saw each other would his brown eyes be soft or, as she feared, hard?

"Listen," Jennifer's words were harsh, "are you aware that your husband called your lover this week?"

Alexandria straightened in her chair, standing. The toe of her satin pump tapped muffled on the carpet. "Let's get rid of the sarcasm, Jennifer. Michael is not my lover."

"No he's not. Mickey is." The sarcasm turned brash.

"Okay," Alexandria paused, "stop a minute." She responded. "Why are you suddenly so angry?" Alexandria waited through her friend's silence.

"I'm angry because you've got me in the middle. I don't want him hurt, and I don't want your family caught in this mess. You're playing with fire, with lives, and this is gasoline, and you don't seem to get it. It won't be all hugs and laughter from an old friend. Mickey will be devastated, and, if William finds out?" Jennifer's anger swelled. "I've seen the wrath of William Chadwick. If he finds out, you're screwed."

"I'm not playing Jennifer. I didn't ask for this...this showing. But it's happening, and I'm trying to protect everybody. Am I excited about seeing Mickey again? Yes, of course I am. But I'm not playing games. I have no delusions. Mickey's different, and I'm different. We can get through this without some grand romantic catastrophe."

"You can," she said. "It's Michael I'm worried about. Did you know William invited him to play golf Saturday?"

"He can't." The flash of panic was the picture in Alexandria's mind. William and Mickey standing side by side, leaning on golf clubs and chit-chatting as another in the foursome tees off.

"He's not. I've convinced him there's not time when we have so much to set up. But doesn't that mean your husband will be at The Club during your grand reunion."

Alexandria thought before speaking. "That'd be too risky. I need quiet time with Mickey. Time to explain, time for him to understand." Ideas raced in her mind. "Ferril Lake at the City Park, south of the zoo, can you get him there?"

"It'd help if your husband would stop calling him."

"I'll admonish William for disrupting the set-up plans." Her tone rose. "Can you get him there?"

"By the paddle boat dock at one o'clock."

"Good." She wanted to say more. "And Jennifer. Don't worry. We both care for Michael. I won't be stupid. I'll douse the flames, and we'll go on without serious burns. We'll get through this."

"Good. He doesn't deserve anymore of your pain."

Her shoulder's slumped with the words. She was right.

Jennifer's goodbye was slight, and the phone went dead.

Anxious, Jennifer directed two high school boys to do the heavy lifting. Hard working boys who listened carefully to her directions. Michael stopped her once, laughing awkwardly. Chill out was his directive, though he knew it had nothing to do with the showing. Everything was going fine.

The boys and Michael kept working while Jennifer fretted over details she would not normally fret over. Finally, Michael sent her in to oversee The Club staff in the wine area while he instructed the stage and microphone set-up. The presentation, digital images, lighting, and the screen all had to be perfect to have the impact he was striving for. It kept her busy while he and the boys set up the display panels, lights, and began to carry in the framed stock.

Just past noon, Jennifer reappeared all freshened up and acting as if the trials of the morning had not distressed her. Michael was standing back, guiding the boys in placement of the images, some grouped by animal, some scenics placed strategically for impact. His tee shirt hung loose from his tattered jeans, and a hint of sweat pressed his hair against his forehead under his ball cap.

Together, he and Jennifer silently toured the display area. It was a smaller room than the Grand Ballroom where the unveiling of the Bear Series would take place. Providing a quiet and quaint area large enough for artistic reflection and personal appreciation, the direct lighting of the displays emphasized the dramatic colors. By evening, with the lack of sunlight reflecting through the windows, the impact would be enhanced.

In the ballroom, Michael tested the projection and microphone. Everything seemed to be going too smoothly.

"What about this picture?" The boy's voice echoed across the ballroom.

Jennifer had decided to quit manipulating and allow this to run its course, whatever the course might be. She looked at Michael without commenting, but their eyes projected the tension.

"Okay," Michael scanned the room. "Let's put it on the left side of the archway opposite the promotional display. The waterfall image on one side and the written bio on the other."

From the stage they silently watched the boys set the two-framed images on the easels. Both teenagers stepped back to admire the waterfall image, their young minds defining the translucent image of the naked woman.

"A little dramatic, don't you think." Jennifer could not help it.

Michael shrugged, "It's been with me since the beginning." His smile was stern. "It's important," he spoke softly. "I'm keeping my promise. You can't recognize her, Jennifer, and it's always a draw for the audience."

"William will be the audience." Her words were curt.

"And he'll view an unrecognizable image." He looked directly at his friend.

She accepted it reluctantly knowing that two hundred people who knew Alexandria would pass that picture in a few hours. Somebody would surely wonder with some hint of recognition why the water-embraced image was familiar.

With a shrug, she surrendered turning to Michael. "I'm sorry about all of this." She felt bad about the hostility between them.

Michael shrugged back, his own eyes downcast. "Sooner or later, it was bound to happen. I'm just surprised, knowing what I know now, that it didn't happen sooner."

She had told him three nights prior as he'd munched on pepperoni pizza and sipped a beer. Not butterflies, but bees had buzzed about her stomach, stinging pain, as she knew what was to come. To her relief, Jimmy had initiated the conversation, reminding him of that time and Alex. He talked casually about her mysterious ways and how she had been gone for six years. Michael had responded as if it were a history lesson remembered but no longer significant in his life. That is until Jimmy's eyes had stared at him with intent compassion.

Michael had frowned, "What's with you guys? You both look scared, especially you." He laughed, pointing at Jennifer.

Jennifer looked away, staring at the floor when she said, "We are scared, Michael," her voice barely audible. "We have to share something with you, something that is going to be painful, something I've kept from you since we met, and I'm so sorry, so terribly sorry." Her eyes lifted to meet Michael's. "I'm sorry that I kept it from you, and while Jimmy's here to help, he just found out. I'm the one responsible."

Mickey watched her wondering what the hell she was talking about. "Jenny, nothing's that bad. I've trusted you for six years, and nothing can be so bad that you should be frightened."

"It's Alex," Jimmy had blurted while his voice remained calm. "Last night Jenny told me about Alex," he confessed.

Mickey's expression went blank, his eyes staring in disbelief as if waking from a long, relentless nightmare.

Jimmy took Jenny's hand. "The truth is Alex is actually Alexandria Chadwick, wife of William Chadwick, and she is the Executive Director of the Chadwick Foundation."

His initial glare had frozen Jennifer, eyes cast upon her friend as she offered more words of apology, her own eyes watering.

Michael, with a twisted expression, his eyes searching, left the apology hanging in the air as he turned to Jimmy.

"How long have you known?"

Jimmy leaned toward his friend. "I found out, Michael."

"I told him last night," Jennifer spoke softly as tears of guilt slid down her face.

"You mean," he shook his head trying to understand. "William's wife is Alexandria Chadwick who is Alex." His eyes moved between his two friends, pain and confusion intertwined.

"When we first met," Jennifer said, her own eyes frightened, "She sent me here to help you. She cared deeply, but she couldn't do it, Michael. She couldn't leave her daughter, so she went back to being Mrs. Chadwick and running the foundation."

"She left me, then paid to get this all started." His eyes turned directly toward Jennifer. "You knew all along, you know Alex, and you were part of the deception."

She apologized again, apologized profusely, but he would have nothing of it. Deception kept echoing in his mind.

It wasn't until the next night when Jimmy pulled him out of the gallery and back to Lonigan's that the cloud began to clear. As pissed as Michael was, Jimmy had the patience and perception to see the whole picture.

"I don't know what her reasons were," Jimmy had explained. "Or how Alex ended up here for those three days, but she tried to make it right." They drank beers, many, many beers until Michael seemed to mellow. "She only had one way to try and make it right and that was money. She gave you money, Michael, and you made it all good. You're a success, and now it's time to thank her."

Michael rolled his eyes back staring at the bar's ceiling. "Shit, I met her husband. Rich, successful, powerful, and I liked the guy."

"Step up, Michael," Jimmy encouraged. "Step up and be both the man and the professional you are. Then, after the showing, walk away with her admiration and move on with your life."

"What if it were Jennifer?"

"It's not," Jimmy was emphatic. "It's a history that for a couple of days years ago was Mickey and Alex. Today, it's nationally recognized Photographer Michael Cabelli and philanthropic Foundation Director

Alexandria Chadwick. You can't make yesterday different and you can't change today except to be the good, kind, and professional person you are. Be you, Michael because Mickey no longer exists."

"And Jennifer?"

Jimmy had reached across, slapping his friend on the shoulder. "Jennifer's a victim too. She was only doing her job. Six years ago she had no idea what she was stepping into, no idea she'd become your partner, and no idea she'd fall in love with some guitar playing guy in the mountains."

Michael had nodded, still unable to relent to the ache the deception had caused.

With the details of the showing completed, Jennifer and Michael send the boys back to the hotel with the truck, and they left in the Jeep. She insisted on driving, and directed the Jeep to the interstate and on toward downtown Denver. At Colfax Avenue, they exited, and soon she motioned toward a parking area in the City Park.

Coming to a stop, she pointed toward the sidewalk. "Right through there is a wonderful little lake and by the dock is a great food stand with outstanding hot dogs." Jennifer motioned for him to get out. "I'll park the Jeep and meet you there."

"No," Michael directed her. "You go back to the hotel and get some rest. This is my time, and I'll be fine. I'll have Alex drop me off, or, if things go a different direction, I'll catch a cab." His final words dismissed her. "I'll see you in a couple of hours."

The landscaped walkway led through a tunnel of fading foliage and colors of the fall. Michael saw the food stand right away, a big rainbow umbrella drawing him to it. The sun warmed the cool day enough to draw people to share the outdoors. A small group of boys played with electronically operated boats, little numbers on each sail as they raced through the water. Runners circled the boardwalk along the lake's edge following the path in steady jogs.

He stopped near the stand eyeing the hot dogs and Polish sausage, the peppers and onions, relish and cheese overflowing the bread. He wanted a Polish dog but knew the lesser hot dog would be healthier. He laughed to himself, thinking of hotdogs as healthier. Life had its ironic moments.

Glancing around, people walked by enjoying the unseasonably warm day. He looked back to see if there was any sign of her. In the distance at the edge of the lake, she was walking toward him, something familiar in her stride, the waves of blond in the slightest of breeze. He shook the thought away. His memory had played tricks on him before. She was not more beautiful now. Impossible.

Sometimes in life, he looked once more at the hotdogs, you think you see things, see people, yet you know better, and you turn away. Stunned with doubt, Michael looked again.

She stared directly at him, this woman with the familiar style. This time he did not turn away. The intentness of her path was clear, and she appeared vivid in his frazzled memory. He started to move yet hesitated. She was familiar but not the same. He was mistaken, of course, and he glanced away once again with the disappointment he had felt so many times before when some unknown woman shared something vaguely familiar.

Michael noticed the hotdog vender watching her; he too intrigued. Looking again, she bore closer in fitted denim and a jacket complimenting a slim, healthy figure. The bounce of her hair and the sway of her hips were embedded in his memory, and the twinge of pain struck deeply. Watching her as she watched him, his mind was still diverted by the image, and when she smiled, he was sure as a twinge of excitement warmed him.

"It is you?" he whispered, stepping forward with the most formal of hugs.

Her cheek pressed to his nodding. His arms strong, she remembered his touch immediately.

"Walk with me," she whispered and began pulling him to follow. She stepped sideways moving past him with her head down. Needing to remain invisible, her eyes searched around them shielded from any familiar faces that might hide among the people.

He followed her quickly, questions racing through his mind, and he felt a need to stop, a need to ask the questions.

He started to talk, and Alex pressed a finger to her lips. "In a moment. Just follow me."

His face questioned, "Why so mysterious?"

"I must be," she said, glancing around once more. "People know me, so follow me for a moment."

She kept walking, and a laugh escaped him, reminded of a time she had taken her turn leading up the mountain trail past Mills Lake toward their waterfall.

Past Ferril Lake, she turned from the concrete path through a small grove of shedding elms, down a short embankment to a secluded grassy area with a lone picnic table, green flakes of paint pealing from the tabletop. He stopped and watched her as she circled around the table to face him. Confident and kind, he remembered her smile. Full lips, crimson full, mature and provocative, she still drew his thoughts with an amazing smile of unexpected seduction.

"Why didn't you tell me?" he pleaded.

"Please Mickey," softness overtook her eyes. "Please sit and let me explain."

He stepped over the bench sitting across from her, his eyes into the sun.

"Mickey," she took his strong hands into hers, "I know this is a surprise, but will you please listen? Will you please not talk, not ask too many questions? Please, give me a chance to explain?"

He pulled his hands away. "Okay, explain."

Alex turned away. "I'm sorry," she said.

Despite her determination to be strong, she suddenly felt ashamed. The breeze moved the yellow and red leaves of an elm tree, and one fell, fluttering to the ground. Alex watched it land, took a deep breath, and turned back to Mickey.

Her eyes locked on his. Immediately, he wanted to trust her, but more, he wanted answers. The sun pressed hot against his face, warmth running over his shoulders despite the fall breeze.

"Okay," his eyes were searching hers. "Explain. What the hell happened six years ago?"

"Yes…you deserve an explanation." Alex tried to ease the moment. "In fact, you deserve much more than that." Careful words would shape his understanding. "My full name is," she looked to his hands, his beautiful hands, "Alexandria," courageously, she watched his eyes, "Chadwick," she added. "As Jennifer's explained, I'm Mrs. William Chadwick."

"Yes." The slight separation of his lips was the only hint she detected. "I know. You're the money lady."

She nodded again. "A long time ago, I met you, a man I believed to be the most wonderful person I'd ever met." She reached to the blond strands blowing across her face, laying them gently behind her ear. Her hands dropped to her lap, and she forced herself to once again look into his eyes. "The only problem, Mickey…I was married, and I had a beautiful daughter, and what everybody thought was a perfect life. So I left this most wonderful person and went back to my beautiful daughter and the man who is my husband."

Mickey's head shook, his brow tensed. "But…"

Again she clinched his hands. She asked for his patience, knowing after all this time patience might be asking too much.

Alex told him of her confusion six years before, feeling trapped and unhappy. Those years of confused thoughts now had some organization in her mind. Would he please allow her to explain, to share her thoughts?

He battled for patience. He wanted it all now, every word of explanation that would help him understand years of not understanding. She had just disappeared. "But you just left?"

"I'm sorry, Mickey. It wasn't a good time for me, then you came along, and as much as I wanted to stay, I knew I had to leave. I didn't know how else to do it."

Mickey listened, fighting for tolerance. His eyes squinted, wrinkling his tanned face. He allowed her to go on, listened to her quiet words. For an hour the words flowed from Alex in a random explanation from her heart. With Mickey listening, her explanation was kind, apologetic, rational, and remorseful. She explained the deceptions to help him, the complexities of her own commitments, and her own pain that led him through a maze of emotions. Then, with soft eyes that refused to leave his, told him he had never left her mind or her heart. When her eyes dropped, she added that despite those deep feelings, she had a family commitment as a mother she could not disregard.

When he truly realized she had cared for him, his relief helped him control his anger. All these years she had been so close. Why had she allowed Jennifer to play with him so? In some ways, he felt betrayed? No, the word was not right, for betrayal meant treachery, and she had never been treacherous. Still, she had inflected pain while also trying to give him so much. His mind battled, fighting for an understanding, an ability to forgive.

"Why didn't you just tell me?" He pressed his hands into the table. "I would have understood. There was no need for deception."

"That's just it, Mickey." The explanation was true. "I know you would have understood, but you meant too much to me. I couldn't know you or have any sort of personal relationship with you without violating my relationship with William. I could have damaged Josie. You meant too much. I had to disappear from your life, otherwise, I wouldn't have had the strength not be with you."

Her life had been obligated, she explained. She had been wrong to involve him because she knew she had to put her family first. She could not betray them; she could not devastate her daughter. She had been careless and selfish, and now she could only ask for forgiveness, undeserved as it might be.

She told him about her life since then. Constant conflict only found some sense of balance by returning to the mountains. She called her daughter Josie now. She had given her daughter a life she herself wanted. Together they had discovered adventures in Mickey's world. He had changed her, and she had opened his world for her daughter. That balance was the only hint of happiness in her life. Alex leaned forward, her lips pressing against the back of his hand with gentle cool moisture. He could feel the breath escape from her.

"And now our lives have crossed again," she looked off through the trees. "Jennifer is furious with me, you know. She's trying hard not to show it, but she's furious that I might hurt you."

His strong eyes looked back at her. "If I'd known, it wouldn't have happened." Turning more serious. "You could have stopped it. If you'd told me, I would have stopped it. So," he asked, "why didn't you stop it?"

Alexandria's grin turned guilty. "Pure selfishness, Mickey. All of this has been about my selfishness. I wanted to see you. It's my weakness, and I must apologize for what I've done."

He drummed his fingers over the table. "So what's changed between now and six years ago when you just walked away."

"Time," her voice was a whisper. "Time and maturity. I guess I hoped we might become friends."

His eyes bore down on her. "You don't ask for much, do you Alex?"

"I know. It's terribly unfair to ask. If you want to be angry, be angry at me." She stood from the picnic table and walked to the edge of the trees. Lifting a leaf from the ground, she dropped it, watching it flutter back into place. "It's terribly selfish of me to ask for your friendship. If you can't give it, I'll understand. But please, I've made such a mess of things, and Josie and William...they're innocent in all of this. Can we find a way to get through this without causing any more pain than I already have?" The slump in her shoulders spoke of surrender, standing away from him. "The day you came to William and suggested this showing...I've been terrified and excited ever since. I've wanted to see you, but not at their cost or yours. I don't want my selfishness to hurt you my family now any more."

His eyes watched hers, turning back to a secret of the past, the good man in him only wanted to help.

"You're friendship would mean a great deal to me, Mickey." Her blue eyes pleaded. "I betrayed you and my family. I'm sorry. Please forgive me and just be my friend. And please keep our secret and not cause pain to William or Josie."

"Or to you if they found out." He added bluntly.

"Or to me," she acknowledged.

He was surprised at the quiet in a park filled with people only separated by the fall trees. Despite the heartfelt confusion, he wanted to hold her, not be her friend. Here she was, having once again come out of nowhere, and she was asking so much.

When his voice broke the quiet, his words were diminished. "You've never told him?"

Her eyes moved slightly.

"I have to tell you, Alex, that despite all my mental preparation, seeing you is a shock." She sat silent before him. "Do you understand you've had years to prepare for this? I've only had a couple of days. I don't know how to respond." He hesitated, his eyes turning hard. "I know this, Alex. I've never felt love like ours. All these years, I've assumed I wasn't alone in that." He waited for her tears to begin, but she stood firm. "I would never hurt you, but I can't talk about friendship now, and I can't imagine letting you walk away again. But yes, I can promise not to hurt your family. I will get through tonight without causing your family pain, but at this moment, it's my turn to walk away. I need time. I need to think, to fully understand this. I thought I was ready," he shook his head, "but right now, well, I know I wasn't."

"I'm sorry." Her words were barely heard.

His voice was stronger. "You see the confusion here. You've stepped back into my life to tell me you can't be a part of my life. That means we'll pull ourselves together and have a successful showing tonight." He closed his eyes seeking calm. "Tomorrow...I don't know beyond today. Tomorrow will come after tonight. But for the moment, I have to walk away because friendship is not what I feel."

A rush of emotions engulfed her as she watched him stand, turn quickly, and begin walking away. She had misjudged his depth with her own selfish romanticism. As he walked strongly, square-shouldered across the grass, she knew he was right. Friendship was a naïve expectation, and it was not what they were about.

Dynamic in his stride, she allowed Mickey the dignity to walk away.

Chapter 55

Driving to The Club, Josie kept asking about this Cabelli guy. Where's he traveled? What animals has he photographed? Maybe he needs a photographer's assistant? She'd go to Alaska or Africa or someplace cool like that and be his assistant. Wouldn't that be cool? William tried to answer as many questions as he could. He didn't know Michael enough to answer them all, and Alexandria was no help. Instead, she stared quietly out the window ignoring the absurdity of her daughter's naïve ramblings.

William stopped his new Lexus along the curb at The Club entrance. Alexandria hesitated, tilting the visor down, and the vanity light brightened the car. She checked her eyes for recovery from the late afternoon puffiness, dabbing at the corners.

The valet opened the door for Josie, then for Alexandria, and the two women stood in front of The Club they so often visited. Alexandria straightened the velvety front of her black dress down to the mid-thigh length. As she did, William strode around the car, tall and debonair to join them. Handing the young man in the cropped red jacket the Lexus keys, he smiled to the familiar image of his perfect family.

"You both look incredibly beautiful. And you, young lady," his grin teased his daughter. "You've become a debutant too quickly."

Josie did not reveal the blushing teenager he expected. Instead, she shone the bright eyes of poised woman. "Thank you Daddy."

Standing as tall and soft as her mother with a leanness that fit her figure perfectly, the rose in her dress was a brilliant color that accentuated the silky black waves of her long hair and contrasting eyes. William both appreciated and feared her charm. Inwardly, he smiled to himself unsure if he was ready for the beautiful woman she was becoming.

The doorman welcomed them by name, and William offered a pleasant evening. Standing in the atrium, Alexandria was not ready for the evening to begin. With the guests just beginning to trickle in, she took her daughter's hand.

Nodding for William to go ahead, Alex led Josie to the ladies room knowing she wanted her entrance to be subtle, not the grand arrival William was used to. The entrance would be Mickey's first look at the true Alexandria. While she secretly hoped she would captivate him, she tried to banish the unfair thoughts.

In the foyer of the powder room, both women stared into mirrors seeking perfection. Alexandria stepped back, her vision in the full-length mirror. This was Alexandria, she thought, feeling the disappointment in the mixture of black velvet and three inch heels. Josie stepped behind her, her arms wrapped around her mother.

"I don't know what's up Mom, but you look amazing." Josie gave her mother a secretive smile, rolling her eyes playfully.

Alexandria laughed. "Nothing's up. I'm just excited to see this photography. I've heard he's very good."

"Didn't you work with him through the Foundation?"

Alexandria corrected her. "The Foundation funded his early work, but Jennifer worked with him. That's how she became his Director of Galleries. My knowledge of his work, well, it's limited."

Josie straightened her dress, checking her lipstick. "We're like the night and day," she looking into the mirror. "I'll be dark intrigue, you be radiant sunshine." Her eyes watched her mother's smile. "It's cool, being dressed up with you, Mom."

In the mirror Alex saw the image of two faces, her daughter's narrow chin resting on her own shoulder. "Two worlds together," she said. "With this nature and wildlife theme, we should have worn our hiking boots and khakis."

Josie raised her eyebrow, naturally joyful. "You'd be beautiful either way."

This was Alexandria Chadwick. This was the image William had always demanded, the image she had used to make so many entrances on William's arm. Her life was illusionary. She lived a facade, acceptable as it was. Breathing deeply, she drew strength from her daughter's anticipation.

"It's time," she said, turning to Josie. "You are such a special young lady. I love you."

Josie gave her mother a questioning look, then answered with a slight laugh. "I love you too, Mom."

"Next summer. Let's hike Long's Peak."

Josie's eyes danced a mountain sky day. "You and I, Mom, peaking 14,000?"

"You and me."

Her mother's image soared before her.

"I'd love it. For my sixteenth just like you and Grampy."

"Yes, just like me and Grampy, but now my dear, it is time to perform." She rolled her eyes playfully. "A little Chadwick charm. Are you ready to turn it on and be the hostesses we must?"

Josie wiggled tall in the natural sway of the chic dress lifting her chest slightly. "Definitely."

When the ladies room door opened, the crowd was arriving dressed from relaxed style to enticing cocktail dresses with the men in casual sporty jackets with khakis. Three couples halted, marveling at the Chadwick women entrance. Alexandria greeted them as did Josie.

Both Alexandria and Josie were charming in their welcome of the guests, hands extended, eyes genuine, and smiles charming. The guests offered pleasant greetings, complimenting Josie on how elegant she was as their husbands nodded politely, smiles offered to Alexandria and her daughter as they passed before them.

Appreciative of his benefactor's kind introductions, Michael felt a twinge of guilt at William's infatuation with the waterfall portrait. Standing next to it, they welcomed guests entering through the archway to view the display of images. Michael's deeply pleated gabardine slacks seemed perfectly casual with the indigo cotton shirt, dobby print vest, and brush suede blazer. Michael looked down and saw William's black Italian leather next to his own Timberland hikers. They were men of contrast.

When he looked up, he was stunned at their radiance as Alex and a beautiful young woman walked toward them. He was shocked. With velvet stunning elegance, she captured the room in the glistening flow of her walk with a smile that must have captivated the thoughts of every man.

Such rare beauty, Mickey smiled to himself knowing he had captured it as no one else had or ever would in the deep richness of a hidden mountain waterfall. As he grinned, her rich blue eyes penetrated his, and he fought the thoughts engulfing him.

"Ah, yes," William's hand touched the back of Michael's suede blazer. "My wife and daughter. Let me introduce you." The banker turned to face his wife. "Michael Cabelli, this is my wife, Alexandria."

Mickey reached his hand for Alex's, her touch gentle and damp against his palm. "Alexandria, finally a face to go with the Foundation name. It is so nice to meet you after so many telephone communications with your office. As you must know, I owe my career to your belief in my work and the generosity of the Chadwick Foundation. I hope you appreciate this evening as my small gesture of thanks."

"I so appreciate your work, Mr. Cabelli." Poised, her lips moved in a fluid motion. "As you have shared with us in your correspondence, may I call you Mickey."

His eyes diverted downward in a slight laugh. "As only my closest friends do," he offered. Slowly, he released her grip, his eyes rising to the necklace laid over the sheer nylon neckline. "A most unique necklace. My compliments."

A slight blush rose in her smile. "Thank you, Mickey."

She moved her hand to touch the silver and turquoise Kokopelli figure.

"I haven't worn it in a long time. For some reason it felt appropriate this evening." Laughing a touch, she reached for her daughter's hand.

"Please, I'd like you to meet our daughter. Mickey, this is Josie."

He took her hand, soft with long fingers. So much like her mother's. With her blue eyes exotic against the richness of William's dark features, her smile charmed him. "It's very nice to meet you Josie." She held his hand confidently. "And what is Josie short for?"

William's voice interrupted formally. "Josephine is her given name," he announced with a playful sideways glance at his wife.

"A wonderful name." Mickey complimented her father. He turned back to the young woman. "Your father tells me you're a wildlife enthusiast."

"Yes sir." Their hands released. "My mom and I, we do a bit of outdoor exploring."

"I'd love to hear about your adventures," he acknowledged.

"Oh," Josie was confident as they talked, "I'm sure they're nothing like your stories. I am so excited to learn about your North American bear series."

In his playful way, he challenged her. "It's good to hear we have a common interest. Would you do me a favor, Josie?"

"Of course, Mr. Cabelli." Infatuated as young girls will be, her composure suddenly became youthful.

"Two favors then. First, please call me Mickey. Second, I'm always interested in the impressions of young adventurers. If I'm to grow as a successful photographer, I must know what the next young outdoorsmen are drawn to. As you view the images, I'd like to know your impressions, particularly if one image strikes you specifically. Would you tell me which one is your favorite?"

Josie bubbled agreement, as Michael's hand directed her toward the exhibit.

Leslie, Ben, and Allison stopped to greet the Chadwicks and meet the honored guest. They passed quickly, moving with the flow of the crowd and only Alexandria noticed Leslie's secret wink of approval.

A middle-aged woman, striking and intent watched from further down the line as the guests were greeted at the archway. Jessi had brought her husband as camouflage to her observations of the evening. There was much more hidden in the evening than the guests could know.

Passing though the archway, Josie stopped to view the prominent image. For a moment she stood, romanticizing the waterfall knowing that this ruggedly handsome photographer had shared it with the translucent woman. As she examined the details, the flowers and swirling white waters at the base of the falls, she felt someone beside her, turning to see Jennifer.

"My, how you've grown," Jennifer squeezed each of her arms.

"Jennifer," Josie's voice rose surprised then lowered quickly as they shared a hug. Josie pointed over her shoulder at Jennifer's boss. "He's gorgeous."

Jennifer smiled silently, her eyes dreading the possibilities of the evening. They chatted about lost time, Jennifer's new life, and Josie's jealousy at all of her travels to the northwest. With another hug, Jennifer encouraged her to enjoy the exhibit.

Viewing each image, Josie wanted to find each scene in real life. She wanted to watch the elk nurse her young. Wobbly legs and frightened by the world, her mother was the calf's only security. Like Josie's father, the image of the eagle flew high and powerful above the rest, looking down upon the world below him. A captivating image, the reds and taupes of a swirling canyon, a beam of sunlight streaming to illuminate the circle of sand. This was something she had never seen, and she was amazed by the art of nature, standing drawn to the focal points.

Next was and image called *The Narrows*. The blurred rush of clear waters surged between the golden walls in the narrow canyon. Light defined the impact of water on the sandstone during the rush of canyon-captured rains. Places she had never seen, places she had never been, places where, at that moment she determined she must one day stand.

While the wait staff began circulating, encouraging the guests from the exhibit to find their place in the Grand Ballroom, it was not until the very last moment that Josie left the exhibit. Moving quickly among the people, she overheard them describing the images, each seeing them a bit differently. Mickey was seizing their imaginations.

She broke from the crowd to find her way to the front of the room where the tables stretched from each side of the podium. Seeing them waiting impatient as always, she shuffled past her mother and Jennifer to greet her grandparents.

"Darling!" She knew the exaggerated look of her grandmother. "You are the most beautiful girl here. Isn't she Robert?" She tapped his forearm. "Isn't she the most beautiful girl here?"

Robert stepped to kiss his granddaughter's cheek. "Of course you look quite lovely."

"Have you seen the exhibit?" Josie glowed. "Michael's amazing. He's soooooo good," she exaggerated the *so*, "and soooooo nice."

"Such silliness." Sophia waved her hand toward the archway. "The Foundation is meant to support true art. How we ever got involved with this, I will never know." She glanced at Robert, and then turned to Josephine. "Well, of course I know. Your mother's lack of sophistication. Pictures of animals; my word. Thankfully, William has maintained a focus, and we haven't abandoned the symphony, and of course, the Monet exhibit was quite an artistic success."

Josie had grown used to and weary of her grandmother's harshness, growing stronger with what must be snobbish senility. "Have you ever, Grandmother," Josie winked at her grandfather, "have you ever been walking at 10,000 feet where the air is thin and the scent of pines fills the breeze? Have you ever stopped at a hint of motion, a color slightly out of place; and seen the eyes and full rack of a bull moose glaring severely at your intrusion, it's guttural breath the only sound? Have you ever stepped away from the path, back into the thickness of the pines, to allow the massive creature to stride past unintimidated by your meager presence? It is the symphony of the Rockies, Grandmother, and Mr. Cabelli's photographs are the Monet's of wildlife."

Taken back by the vision, Sophia grunted moose-like. "Your mother has corrupted your mind with such bizarre thoughts."

Unseen from behind her Grandmother, Robert raised his hand to quiet Josie. "Are you sitting with us?" he asked.

Josie laughed, her eyebrows surrendering. She glanced along the table at the name cards, moving to switch hers. "Now I am," she grinned happily like the good granddaughter she was.

William stepped to the microphone, urging all to take their seats, as the guest's table talk focused on this new artistic discovery whose images enthralled the social powers of Denver.

Michael was sitting at the table between the guts and heart of the Chadwick Foundation, Robert, Sophia, Josephine, Michael, William, Alexandria, and Jennifer.

Alexandria watched the crowd mingling as they took their seats. That's when she saw Leslie. Before the image of the waterfall, her friend stood stone still. Her hand resting on her chest, Leslie's eyes did not leave the image of a rare woman mysteriously captured in the abstract waves of the waterfall. When she turned, her eyes bore directly into Alexandria, mouth agape. From across the room, Alex knew and Leslie knew, and Leslie was astonished.

Michael was the only man in the room looking as if he belonged to the mountains with his rugged good looks and leather. It was something Sophia obstinately pointed out to her granddaughter, a fact Josie found even more enchanting.

William motioned toward the archway, now empty of people. "That's the same waterfall as the photograph you sent for my office?"

"The very same," he said with a tone of disinterest.

William pointed again, this time with his sterling fork. "We stood looking at that one the entire time we greeted the guests. I see why you display it separately, so mysterious and a bit risqué. How much do you sell a print like that for?"

Jennifer, leaning toward Alexandria, pressed her shoulder into her friend as she glared directly at her boss. Michael nodded toward William, looking to see Alex's pleading eyes.

"As Director of Galleries, Jennifer does much of the pricing." Again he tried to deflect the discussion.

William challenged him, "I'm just curious at how your business works, how much the value of these images increase. Let's say I invested in that image, what could I expect in return ten years."

Michael was quick to respond. "Well, fortunately William, that particular image isn't for sale." He presented his business persona with directness. "It's a unique image and has personal significance, therefore, I made the decision years ago to only make three prints and not include it in my limited edition series. Besides," he turned back to Alex, his eyes looking to Jennifer and his voice portray light-heartedness, "With your beautiful wife," he nodded, "you don't need a mysterious image like I do."

"Of course, you're correct. Besides," William smiled then looked again toward the waterfall, "the waterfall image in my office, that is a particularly wonderful image especially without the nudity. I do greatly appreciate the gift."

Alexandria stared at her husband realizing with a degree of disappointment how well she knew him and his bland perception.

With the guests seated, Jennifer motioned for the lights to be dimmed and a spotlight beaming on the podium. Behind them, in a slow humming motion, a giant white screen appeared from the ceiling. William folded his napkin, stood and stepped back to the podium. He waited for the hum of the screen and the murmur about the room to quiet.

With sophistication, William quoted the introduction that Jennifer had written as if it were his own words. As applause rose to fill the room, Mickey felt the eyes of Alex following him as he stood taking the welcoming handshake of the Master of Ceremony..

"There are unique moments in life," he paused for the quietness to grow complete. "There are unique moments in each of our lives, moments that shape and guide us. Six years ago, I began my career with a passion for nature and wildlife photography. Tonight, I have the special opportunity to thank the person who has given me this moment. She is an incredible individual, heart and soul. In the little time I have had the opportunity to share with her, I have seen great passion that enriches lives, and while I have benefitted to the point of standing here before you today, I know that many others have been the benefactors of the Chadwick Foundation. For the opportunities she has brought to my life, I want to offer a heartfelt thank you to the Director of the Chadwick Foundation. Alex..." He turned to the woman whose eyes had not left him. "Would you please stand, Alexandria?" Michael put his hands together. "Ladies and gentlemen, Chadwick Foundation Director Alexandria Chadwick."

Standing, she hid her emotions, revealing dignity and grace while acknowledging the kind words. As the Chadwick Foundation Director, she was dynamic and enthusiastic with skills that mesmerized those she touched. As a mother, she lived a sense of adventure feeling the freedom of a mountain morning. Standing, she was not sure which one she was at that moment.

Jennifer stared blankly at the table hoping that Michael would stop with the simple introduction of gratitude. She wanted to trust him but feared his emotions. This could be so bad, so bad. She looked past Alexandria to William, staring up from his seat and joining the applause from the guests for his wife as he gave her that publicly adoring look so well practiced.

Innocence in his eyes, it was the first time she had seen the power and control unaware of his own naivety. What he was watching was something he could not imagine, something he did not realized he was seeing in the translucency of the waterfall.

"This amazing individual," the power of the microphone filled the Grand Ballroom. Michael reached his arm in recognition of Mrs. Chadwick. "Mrs. Alexandria Chadwick and the Foundation supported by William Chadwick." He reached his hand stepping to William, shaking it again as William stood to be recognized. "And Mr. and Mrs. Robert Chadwick," the poised young man with long locks of hair acknowledged Robert and Sophia Chadwick as Robert assisted Sophia to stand, "and of course, Josephine Chadwick." Josie stood, embarrassed at the unexpected recognition, but just as elegant and poised as her mother.

"The Chadwick Family and the Chadwick Foundation, without the courage of Alexandria Chadwick to embrace my work," a breath of hesitation escaped Michael, "without such an endorsement, today I would be taking baby pictures, senior portraits, and wedding photos in a little studio in downtown Bismarck, North Dakota." Hearing the laughter from the audience, he reached past William, taking her hand, and smiled generously staring into her eyes. "Thank you Mrs. Chadwick, for taking me away from the windswept prairies where crying babies, teenage egos, and demanding mother's of the bride were dominating my life. You, and the Chadwick Foundation, brought me back to my dream, a dream that I hope to give a hint of today as we unveil our North American Bear Series."

Alex's lips whispered a subtle thank you.

Michael turned back to the microphone. "Before we move into the presentation, there is one more person I must thank. She is the Director of Galleries for Nature's Way, Inc., and a former employee of the Chadwick Foundation." His head bowed slightly. "I guess I owe the Chadwick's another debt of gratitude. I stole Jennifer Wilson from the Foundation where she had been a most valued employee for many years." Again, laughter rose from the crowd as his voice gained power. "The facilitator of tonight's events, Jennifer is a talented, perceptive, and dedicated individual who has demonstrated an amazing commitment to friendship and the success of Nature's Way. I owe her much, and I ask you to appreciate her impact on the success of not only tonight's event but of Nature's Way, Inc. Ladies and gentlemen, please join me in a huge thank you to our Director of Galleries and my friend Jennifer Wilson."

As Jennifer stood, she and Michael watched each other, and laughed at the way he had just forgiven her. She waved momentarily toward the applause before stepping forward to embrace her good friend Alexandria. As both squeezed tightly, Jennifer whispered, "He's an amazing person."

Poised, Alexandria mouthed, "A man you can never doubt."

A few rows back in the center of the ballroom Jessi applauded in admiration as Leslie, mouth agape, watched the beautiful man with the long, dark hair, rugged good looks, and adorable smile.

Michael went on to capture the guest's imagination. As charming and daring as his introduction, each intense description of the projected digital image was followed with a winning smile, broad and playful, sincerely capturing the intrigue of men who lived behind desks while at the same time melting the hearts of the pampered women.

He took the guests on a seasonal journey through his world. The winter brought them a snowmobile adventure into the heart of Yellowstone. Bison were chest deep in powder white snow that dusted their harsh brown coats. In contrast, a herd of fully mature elk with a maze of magnificent antlers moved shrouded by the steaming geyser mist in early morning.

Michael's words were compassionate as he shared the spring migration of the Sandhill Cranes to the shallow waters of the Nebraska Platte River. Then fields of color were slowly brought into dramatic focus. First the desert flowers of Arizona followed by the massive poppy fields in southern California. Spring, he explained, could not be complete without inception. The elk and her calf, nursing; a baby bighorn standing boldly on a rocky ledge in the shadow of the ram he hoped to become; the frosted gray fur of wolf pups nipping playfully at each other's ears; and the white tail fawn, curled protected and still among the green and purple clover, white spots and frail chestnut eyes with delicate feminine lashes.

The summer was powerful and Josie immediately nudged her grandmother at the sight of the massive animal, the moose rising dominant from the depths of the lake as water rained from the captive antlers. The massive tail fin of the gray whale silhouetted in fiery Hawaiian hues with red to waves of golden heat at sunset. A massive valley of caribou wandered the brown-red tones of summer in Denali National Park, Mount McKinley a contrasting mass of white on the distant horizon.

From there, the treasures of fall reemerged with the thick tan coat and giant antlers of the bugling elk, the migration of the snow geese guided by the Missouri River, and the giant spruce decorated with a dusting of snow and the majestic ornamentation of bald eagles rising supreme above each branch.

He delighted the audience with his tales of adventure. In the Badlands he'd captured the birth of a buffalo calf in early May. Describing how he laid still, silent on the cold, damp earth waiting for the birth, as a herd of bison meandered by, grunting and snorting their displeasure at his presence while life was being created a few feet away. In an instant his eye caught movement near the dew-covered grass tickling his chin; and he froze. Six inches from the camera, eight from his face, a diamond back rattle snake slithered by unaware of the impending birth or the photographer's prone presence.

He captivated the crowd with his story of camping at Alaska's Brook's Falls to wake at the thunderous pounding of tenacious paws against the earth, the scraping of the giant claws as he looked through the tent wall into the morning light to see the silhouette of a male Kodiak saunter by an arms reach from where he slept.

An image filled the screen, and to William's pleasure he saw the waterfall that graced his office wall. Michael stepped away from the microphone, joining the audience in appreciating the image. He watched Alex's soft smile as her mind drifted to another time, and he caught the warning in Jennifer's eyes.

"This image is so similar to the one that you may have appreciated as you entered the exhibit." Michael explained. "Seldom do I believe people enhance nature. So often we invade a people-free world. There was one exception in my life to this belief. You must appreciate that a woman from my past, an incredible woman actually, changed her life in the moments between this image and the one displayed at the archway. She is a woman much like many of you, yet one day she dared to follow me into the wilds on the great adventure of discovering this waterfall. What she did not know was that to get to this waterfall, we had to rappel down an eighty foot cliff."

A slight murmur rose in the audience. "Now ladies, imagine this," he paused. "And gentlemen imagine your wife, the beautiful woman seated next to you in the graceful dress and delicate high heels confronted with this situation. It was as if she were standing atop an eight-story building with manicured hands in front of her gripping a rope, the other hand behind her gripping the same rope." Michael's hands moved naturally, demonstrating the rappelling stance, the grip of the rope. "To get to the boutique below to purchase that outfit that you know will change your life, you must jump backward off the building with only the control of the rope between looking fabulous in that outfit or become a splattered stain on the concrete sidewalk."

Laughter rose from the men as women gasped, leaning to each other with whispers of impossibility. A huge, playful smile spread across his face.

"This, ladies and gentlemen, is what my friend faced one morning years ago. The only difference is the building she was to rappel down was a jagged rock cliff hidden in the depths of the Rocky Mountains." He paused, glancing up and down the table as an excuse to share Alex's eyes. "This woman, beautiful and perfectly manicured, was so unaccustomed with the rugged demands of nature, yet she stood at the top of the cliff, gathered all of her courage, even more than she realized, and she jumped backwards off an eighty-foot cliff." Michael's hand rose, a dramatic imitation of the fall of a body down a cliff.

"When we take steps beyond the safety of our secure worlds, when we expand our lives to meet challenges never before considered, we gain strength and our lives change forever." He scanned the room. "I must describe to you the difference between the two images." One hand gestured to the screen, the other to the archway at the opposite side of the room.

"Successfully navigating the cliff, once we reached the waterfall, I stood in a spot away from my friend, the exact spot to capture the light of sunrise breaking over the eastern peaks against the raining falls. As I snapped this image," he gestured to the screen, "I knew that I had captured something special. And then it happened. There appeared the image of flowing grace, of the sleek and subtle musculature that is the image of desire. In times long ago, she might have been Eve first stepping into her garden; Lady Godiva, a mane of blond flowing the length of her body; Dudley Moore's perfect 10 running in full strides on the beach in the magic image of the cinema." Sparks of laughter rose from the room. "Or, ladies and gentlemen, she might have been more."

"In the sunlight breaking across the lake, she walked into the icy chill of the mountain waters. Her hands caressed the ripples as water waved from her body. Each step was a cleansing, each a reawaking in the icy cold of nearly freezing waters." There was a slight pause as a few shuddering in the cold. "What amazed me is this woman seemed completely unaffected by the cold. At that moment of her life she was experiencing the joy of accomplishment and reawaking, and I was honored to capture her transformation." He stopped to settle the soft murmurs rising in his own stomach. "Despite the impact her heart was having on my life, I am a photographer. It was instinct that gave me the presence of mind to take the picture." Slight laughter joined his. "As she emerged from the lake, stepping gracefully into the translucent shower of the falls, I snapped the image displayed in the archway." The faces of the crowd glanced from the projected image to the framed photo on the easel at the archway, eyes straining for a closer look. "In my lifetime, she is the only human I have known to enhance the beauty of nature."

He gripped the sides of the podium for restraint.

"So many have asked to purchase her image, as I have had offers this evening. But, you see, a few days after we created this image, she left. This woman in the waterfall, she has remained a mystery in my life since she disappeared two days later. So in my own selfish desire to hold her close to me forever, I shall never sell her image for it is priceless."

A hush fell over the room. Josie sat startled, feeling the tears falling from her eyes at the unexpected emotion of the story. Leslie stared at Alex, her hand covering her mouth. Further back in the audience, Jessi knew the question that had agonized her patient had finally been answered. Mickey still loved Alex.

As the professional he was, Michael allowed a moment for impact then quickly moved into the unveiling. He had lingered long enough. This was the intended moment of the evening, the moment the bear series was presented to the public and the Denver press.

As instructed four waiters had moved to stand beside each easel with the image covered in soft velvet. Michael briefly described the unique and powerful capabilities of the bear, the history of the disappearing habitat, and the strength of their recovery as man realized the mistakes of the past. He explained in short, vivid words the differences between the four North American bears, and with dramatic effect, described the value of owning the Phase I, Number One edition of all four prints in the series.

With Michael's nod the first waiter stepped to the easel. At the same instant the cloth was lifted, an identical image was flashed in mammoth proportions on the screen behind Michael. At first there was a hush, and then faint breaths of appreciation. It was fun, this giant image of the Black Bear, details of each strand of black fur as the sow pawed the red berry sprig, her vulnerable cub nursing vigorously at her breast. Michael stood away, quiet and without comment, allowing the image to make its own statement.

With the photograph firmly captured in the minds of the invited guests, he nodded to the second waiter. The image of the grizzly took full attention with intensity of power. Even in the afternoon stroll along the riverbank, the icy reflection of the blue river contrasted a softer image of the silver-tipped fur opposed to the grizzly's fierce intimidation. The third image bought gasps of astonishment at the giant Alaskan brown bear exploding from the waters below Brook's Falls, the large sockeye salmon arched in the death grip of the crushing jaws. In contrast, the final image returned the audience to the joy of nature. White polar bears against the white arctic background set in the trademark Cabelli white double matting and stark white frame. Two young bears in play sat as if in conversation. One in laughter, its front paws lifting its back is if playful children in the joy of their toy room.

At Michael's command, the waiters lifted the four images and moved to each table, stopping about the room as the guests viewed, nodding in appreciation. With the audience's focus on the four-framed images, Jennifer stood and moved to the microphone. Michael returned to his seat among the Chadwicks, William greeting him with a congratulatory handshake.

Jennifer masterfully worked the crowd to bids beyond their imagination. Even she had underestimated the charismatic power of Michael. It was a huge charitable success with the rich fighting for position to outbid the richer until the boldest paid back the Foundation twofold, its investment in Michael.

When the bidding was completed, the resounding applause concluded, and the obligatory bowing of the highest bidder nodded in appreciation, potential clients hastened to the exhibit, each hoping to lay claim to their choice of Michael Cabelli images.

Michael stayed behind, autographing the back of the Phase I, Number One prints for the generous new owner, a ski resort land developer who planned to display them in his mountain retreat near Steamboat. From the resonance in his voice and the generosity of his bid, Michael was sure it was a multi-million dollar cottage. As he finished signing, he felt her presence beside him.

Alex leaned close to his cheek, his scent so strong, she breathed deeply, whispering, "Nothing but amazement beyond my expectations. That is what you have brought to my life. Without you, there is only affluence. You have soothed my heart and delighted me once again."

He turned, his lips a breath from her. "Be Alex," he held her, "for Alex is unique and incredible."

Then, his name uttered in disruption of the moment, he turned to another benefactor wanting to shake the hand of the artists whose photography was about to adorn the wall of his home. People continued to approach him, and he visited politely, enthusiastically giving. Among the congratulatory handshakes and thank yous, he saw her standing with another young girl before the *The Narrows* image.

Working his way through the crowd to stand beside her, he asked, "Is this your favorite?"

Josie turned delighted. "Hi. I loved your presentation. Your life's so exciting."

He laughed a bit. "And who is your friend?"

Allison rocked forward onto the toes of her awkwardly stiff new high heels. "I'm Allison."

"Well Allison," he said, "Do you like the slot canyon image?"

"It's beautiful with the wall's waves and colors."

"Thank you. I value your opinion." His smile turned to Josie. "It was taken in Zion National Park. Tell me why you like it?"

Josie looked back to the image as he stepped beside her. "Do you see the light reflecting on the canyon wall and on the floor leading into the glowing tunnel? It's as if it's taking you to a secret place, a beautiful secret place of gold and mystery."

Grinning broadly, he lightly patted his hand over her back. "A perfect description." Michael stepped forward and lifted the white-framed Narrows image from the carpeted display panel. "You are a perceptive young lady, Josie, and I owe much to your family. I will have my assistants wrap this for you. It's my gift to you."

Her teenage mouth fell open astonished. "Really?" She bounced a bit, her eyes taken back. Then, regained her practiced Chadwick composure, she said, "No Mickey, it's too much."

"A simple gesture, really," he charmed her. "And considering all the Foundation has done for me, it is nothing. I want you to have it."

Michael held the gift to his side as Josie's arms lifted to wrap around his neck, a warm, sincere thank you. It was a familiar feeling, one he had missed for so many years, and over her shoulder he could see Alex through the crowd. Far away smiling at the moment, she watched as her daughter connected with Mickey. She was grateful they might, just a bit, know each other.

PART VI: Summer
Chapter 56

The words shot harshly from the bedroom with the sarcasm Alexandria
had learned to expect. She knew she was a part of it, the distance they'd
felt in the months since Mickey. It was more her than William, yet his
patience had dissipated, responding with bitterness. Thankfully, he didn't
know his anger was valid.

Her husband appeared in the doorway. "What do you mean you've
made plans for Josie's birthday?" William's white cotton oxford was
opened at the collar, a maroon and navy striped tie waiting to be cinched.
"Damn it, Alexandria. Sometimes I wonder who the hell you think you
are."

Meticulous words shot back. "I think I'm Josie's mother, and if you'd
pay attention to her like a father should…" Alexandria regretted the anger,
pausing with her head down trying to regain some sensitivity. "Josie wants
this. It's her request."

William fought with the tie, anger twisting in his face. "I know exactly
what she wants. It's her sixteenth birthday. It's her coming out party, and
it's a family tradition that's important to my mother. This is Josephine's
Debutante Ball. My mother has planned and prepared for this for sixteen
years, and instead you want to climb some fucking rock."

Alexandria turned facing him head on, standing in blue jeans and a
white lace bra; her hair was half curled. "Where in the world did you get
the idea you could talk to me that way?"

"I got the idea when you quit listening to anything I said. Alexandria,
when did you separate so much from our family that things like our
daughter's sixteenth birthday became only important to you?" His eyes
stayed locked on hers. "Get this straight, Alexandria. There will be a
Sixteenth Debutante Ball hosted by my mother. You will be there, and
Josephine will have a wonderful time. Got it?"

Anger burst with the screams, "With no consideration from you or
your mother for Josie's feelings."

The crimson in her face turned to ugly blotches of white. Alexandria
knew she was being unreasonable, but ever since the showing, her
tolerance had disappeared. The life she lived was one she had lost
indulgence for, and every time William pushed her, she wanted to scream,
and now she was screaming.

William responded with the same anger. "Listen, I could care less if you want to go hike somewhere. Do it the day before. Do it the day after. But on Josephine's sixteenth birthday we will celebrate as the Chadwick's are expected to celebrate."

Her burst interrupted him, "For God sake, wake up. Josie has *been out* for years. Maybe if you'd been around more, you'd have noticed. But you weren't, and now you want to make her *coming out* official because you've been too busy to notice your daughter's been a young woman for some time. The fact that you haven't noticed is pathetic." She turned back to the mirror, her hands on the granite countertop, "and the arrogance of your mother anointing her a debutante has nothing to do with her maturity."

Redness overtook his face as his finger jabbed into the air. "This is tradition, and this is what is expected of our family. This is not debatable. I will tell my mother to go ahead with the plans. You will be there, and Josie will be there. Nothing else is acceptable, so don't defy me with your sophomoric games."

William turned, yanked his suit jacket from the bed and step toward the door. His last glance, a dagger at her forehead was finalized as the door slammed shut.

Later that morning, still unable to shake the anger, she wasn't sure if it was at William or the way she had acted. This was unlike her, and so unfair. Of course, he was right. They could work around the birthday party. Birthdays are family events. Josie would understand and it would be fine, but why had she turned it into a confrontation?

As Alexandria sat working through a series of grant applications, her fingernails made a clicking noise on the desk.

"Mrs. Chadwick."

She looked at the telephone. "Yes?"

"There's a gentleman here to see you."

"A gentleman? Who's he with?" She fought to take the edge from her voice.

Alexandria heard the receptionist repeat the question.

"He told me to ask you if you'd sat on a mountain top and written any good songs lately."

Puzzled, she wrinkled her chin, still staring at the intercom. Then her smile broke free, she pushed away from her desk, rushed to open the door, and step into the past.

Like flying back in time, his hair still hung musician length framing his charming smile. Alexandria walked right to him, and they embraced in a long, lost friend hug.

"Jimmy, so good to see you."

"Hello Alex." He stepped back grinning.

She led him into her office with instructions not to be disturbed. Instantly, they talked as old friends, times remembered yet much to catch up on. He was in town to pick up Jennifer at the airport, arriving from San Francisco where she had just opened the Napa Valley gallery. After listening to stories for the months since the showing, he had left early to stop and see the real Alexandria Chadwick. He'd always imagined she was living lost somewhere in Middle America. He never imagined she was the queen of the ball.

"Sometimes crowns are an obligation, not a choice. Besides," she did not look at him, "it's all bells and whistles. So," she looked up happily, "Jennifer tells me life is good between you two."

Jimmy laughed to himself. "You know she's a driven and determined woman. Sometimes I laugh at her, tell her to slow down and appreciate all she has. But there's a time when it's just us, and it's wonderful. Thank you for that Alex."

Alexandria sat back, her hand against her chest. "Thank me?"

"You're the connection. Jennifer and I, well, there's no one I'd rather laugh with. She's my best buddy, my most cherished friend, and an amazing lover. She even eats Rocky Mountain Oysters with me," he laughed, pointing at her old friend. "I've never felt like this. She's amazing."

"I couldn't be happier."

"I write songs about her when she's off opening a new gallery. When she gets back, I sing her one or two. It's mushy romance, but the results are incredible," he winked. "Without you, we never would have met."

Alexandria liked that. "I'm glad."

"Can I ask you a question?" His tone quickly changed. "The night in Lonigan's when you appeared then disappeared? I sang our song. Why'd you leave?"

For a moment, she looked toward the family pictures on the office shelf and felt the guilt of the morning's argument. "It's all been about protection, Jimmy, years of protection. I made a mistake years ago, yet that mistake was the most cherished three days of my life. I had to let those three days go. I guess I was still trying to protect myself and my daughter, yet I wanted to touch the past, touch that time just for a moment." She shrugged sadly. "When you recognized me, I knew I'd stepped back into something I shouldn't have. I've created quite a mess, haven't I?"

"Don't be too hard on yourself." His eyes were gentle.

His visit made the past all seem genuine; an old friend stopping to catch up on lost times. She told him of how Alexandria had left for a few days and returned as Alex and of how Josephine had become Josie. She showed him pictures of Josie recovering from the hike up to Amphitheater Lake sitting in the sun on a speckled volcanic rock atop the Tetons. She laughed, telling him she was the family outlaw with outrageous behavior like sending her daughter to public school and taking her on outdoor adventures.

Jimmy shared that he was still teaching, but there was good news. His life was about to change. With the return of acoustic music and the popularity of country, he'd sold some songs. The royalties far surpassed his teaching income, and a song broker in Nashville wanted him to sign him. Some of the best crossover talents would be singing his songs. He shared his excitement, thoughts of money disappearing as an issue, allowing him to write and play music full time.

"But I've never thought of you as a country singer."

"Taint," he faked a twang. "My songs give country singers the crossover edge, popular acoustic and folksy love songs that draw the chic country crowd and the top 40 young buyers. They put my songs on their country label and more people without cowboy hats and big buckles buy the albums."

"Make's sense," she agreed. "Whose the guy in Nashville?"

Jimmy spurted out a name and a label, then shrugged. "Over forty, and my teenage dream's finally coming true."

"You're music touches lives, Jimmy." She reached for his hand.

They talked more of how she'd like to come back to Lonigan's. Now that Mickey knew and Jennifer wasn't bound by some secret commitment, maybe she'd call one day, drive up, and they'd drink beer while Jimmy sang some songs. It all sounded so easy.

And yes, Michael was doing well. What had happened, it seemed healthy despite the turmoil. Part of it, Jimmy guessed, was Michael's desire to make sure she was happy. Jimmy smiled at his own memory of a girl he'd been in love with in high school. What had he called her? Francie, he laughed. He'd called her Francie. Years later, he'd returned home for her wedding. After much turmoil in her life, the wedding brought closure and a sense of happiness knowing she was okay. For Michael, there was closure knowing she was safe.

When Jimmy left, his hug was warm, and she felt cheated that she had missed his friendship for so many years. She returned to her desk and punched some keys into the computer. She found the name of the music agent that had been so helpful in promoting the fund raising concert for the Denver Symphony. She dialed his L.A. number. Put through by his receptionist, he was delighted to hear from her. Yes, he was familiar with the gentleman, president of the fastest rising country label in Nashville.

An hour later the music agent called back. "I talked to the man directly. Your boy's good and so is his contract. Got a good man working for him, an agent of high integrity. I hope I didn't over step my bounds, but I called Jimmy's agent too and shared a couple of ideas. They're pretty far along in negotiations, and if they take my advice, which I think they will, it might get him a few thousand more up front and additional security in the length of the contract. Everything appears to be on the up and up. Sounds like you've discovered a winner."

"He's a great guy. I really want this to work for him."

"It's songwriters that make the money, you know. The singers get the glory while the big checks go to the songwriters. Shouldn't be long before your friend finds himself financially well off."

She smiled into the receiver, amazed at the power of the wealthy to get results. "I owe you."

"Naw," the confident man spoke back. "This was probably a done deal. I offered some ideas. They like him, and said his music's good. It's up to the attorney's now. Just details. Glad I could help."

It was six o'clock she arrived at the downtown office, just five blocks from her own. They had agreed on a time when fewer people would be present, the receptionists and legal aids gone for the day. Alexandria kept her head down, her eyes hidden by her hands as she crossed the shining terrazzo lobby floor. As promised, Brandon didn't make her wait long.

When he appeared, she was relieved to see the strength in his stature as she remembered. A youthful look with the security of mature gray hair replacing the dense black, his handshake was warm and kind. He led her down a long hardwood hallway into his corner office of windows, tall plants, and framed crayon drawings created by his young daughters. His wall of credentials read Brandon David Anders, Attorney at Law.

He gestured for her to sit in the comfort of the leather sofa, while he sat in the sofa chair, the oak coffee table between them. Brandon reached for the large Looney Tunes embossed pitcher in the middle of the table, and Alex laughed at the row of mugs on each side. The face of a different cartoon character was featured on each as if the mug were their heads. Brandon picked up Yosemite Sam and filled the mug with ice tea.

"Please," he motioned toward the table, "pick a mug."

Instantly, Alexandria felt at ease. She looked specifically at each caricature. This must be some sort of perverse attorney humor, guess the personality of the potential client by the mug they choose. Despite that, Alex could not help but pick the one she felt like. Daffy Duck. Brandon grinned at her choice and filled the duck, bill and all, with iced tea.

A huge step, he explained, with many more ramifications than she might have imagined. He painted a gloomy picture describing the efforts of William's vast legal resources. Power and control would be a major issue, not necessarily of the actual divorce but of the process. William would demand that he was in control of the proceedings, and to please their CEO, his legal councils would become vicious. Brandon nodded emphasizing vicious. If necessary, he too could be vicious. The analogy drew an uncomfortable laugh from them both.

He did not talk details, but rather laid the general scenario out before her. He explained the law, the procedures, and the impact she could expect it to have on her life. Then he took a moment to discuss alternatives.

Was there a potential they might be able to resolve their differences? Had they been through counseling? Had they discussed this with their pastor? And what about the impact on Josephine? He advised her to go slowly in making this decision, to take time and consider all of the implications. Yes, he would represent her, but only if this was the last option.

At eight o'clock, William found her in the garden, a quiet walk to appreciate the flowers and the warm setting sun. When she felt him beside her, she masked her surprise, bending to cup her hands beneath the petals of a yellow rose. She breathed the scent realizing how skilled she had become at pretending.

"It's beautiful," she said.

To her surprise, he bent beside her.

"I'm sorry things have been so ugly between us," he spoke kindly. "We've both been angry. Can we call a truce, so both you and my mother can be happy about this sixteenth birthday?"

"You've forgotten the most important person," she said, walking on through the garden.

"I'll talk to Josie." He reassured her.

Alexandria approved. "She'll be very considerate of your mother's wishes."

"I don't want this to end." William surprised her.

"Is that why you're here?" She stopped at the edge of the garden, the pool between them and the house. Josie and a friend sat across the pool on lounge chairs sipping soda and listening with ear-buds that shared a digital player.

From behind, William wrapped his arms sensitively around her. Despite the desire to break away, she stood still watching Josie. The familiar breath and cool scent, the slight roughness of his cheek against hers made her realize he had never meant to be cruel. Demanding, yes, impatient, well, she had helped encourage that. It felt nice to have his kindness, but there was nothing else, so slowly she slipped from his arms.

He did not follow her, but stood silently as she walked back through the garden, her head down, arms limp at side moving toward the pool and mansion behind it. Swallowing hard, he felt the despair inside, the heaving in his gut when he realizing his absence had been too severe.

Chapter 57

"What kind of car?" William glanced sideways from the driver's seat at his wife, unsure of what he'd just heard.

Alexandria laughed that he would be surprised. "If you want her to be happy that she got a car, give her a BMW. If you want her to be ecstatic, buy her a Jeep Wrangler." Her shoulders lifted at the obvious. "It's what she wants."

"A Jeep?" he repeated.

"A Jeep." She accentuated the obvious as William's own luxury car pulled to a stop.

Jessi was ready for them when they arrived, and she complimented William on coming. There was a slight rebuke for not seeing them together for so many weeks, but she took today as a good sign.

Feeling his own desperation, William had suggested coming, despite the fact that he had grown to see these sessions as tedious. It was time spent without results, ineffectual. But Alexandria found them valuable.

"Well," Jessi over emphasized her pleasantness, "what shall we talk about today?"

Alexandria patted William's knee. "How about who we are?"

His irritated glance caught her eye. "I know who I am. A bank president, father, and husband. You're the one who seems to be questioning who you are."

"I'm sorry." She dropped her head. Then she looked up staring her husband in the eyes. "Do you really know who you are or do you know who you think you should be?"

"Alexandria," his face annoyed, "I've always been the same person. The day you met me I was in law school and preparing to some day take over the bank. You knew who I was, and I thought I knew who you were."

Alexandria's shoulders collapsed, her eyes turning away. "I thought I did too."

"But you weren't in Kansas anymore."

"I loved Kansas," she said.

He lifted his hands in apology. "I'm sorry. Your parents are wonderful, and I know you had a wonderful home. The point I'm trying to make is I know who I am. I've always been the same person. Eighteen years ago, you were ecstatic about that person. Now, we politely communicate and tolerate each other. While you're challenging who I am, I'm telling you I've always been the same person. You're the one who's changed."

Jessi had seen this before, the theme of whose terms life would be lived on. They couldn't blend their lives, so they argued about it. She'd decided long ago that this was a marriage destined to fail, yet they held on through polite communication and tolerance. She listened and tried to guide them to the fact they needed to be honest with each other.

"I'm sorry, William," Alexandria spoke in a whisper. "I apologize for finding your life pretentious. Yes, I do like the freedom of your money. I do like dressing up and going out. I like the fact that you have given me much. But all of the money, all of the gowns, the cars, the mansions, and the status, I just find them all so arrogant. You work to make money, so much money you're not even sure how much you have. You have power and acquaintances, but there is no one in your life, no one in your mother or father's lives who any of you can truly call a friend."

His annoyance peaking, voice raised. "That's absurd."

"Absurd," she glared directly at him. "If you went flat broke today. If you were dying of some dreaded disease, who'd stop their lives to commit to you. Name one person."

"I'm sure there are many people who owe us such a commitment," disturbed that Valerie was the only person who entered his mind.

"I'm not talking about owing, William. I'm talking about giving. William, there's only one person who would give you such a commitment." She looked at Jessi then she turned back to William. "Me," she stated. "For eighteen years I've given up my life for yours. Besides my commitment to you, there are no other genuine, unconditional friends in your life."

William turned away, looking toward the doorway and the polyester carpeting in the hallway. It was a cheap shot. Yes, he had power, but with power came friendship. There were people all over the world that owed him, and if he ever needed them, he was sure they would come through.

"Only with collateral, William."

He turned surprised. "What?"

Jessi raised her hand to soften them.

"They'd only help you, these friends of yours, to gain collateral. You've got to be able to pay them back. Otherwise, William, it's like you and your bank do daily to hundreds of thousands of people. No collateral and with a smile, the door is held for you on your way out. That's not friendship." Her body began to shake, and she was shocked at the level of anger and her determination to go on. "You see; there's no depth, William. Your relationships exist purely on a business level. When the business is gone, so is the friendship. I'm sorry for that, that you don't understand there is no depth in your relationships, William."

He sat back quietly not speaking. He wondered why the anger didn't rise up and take control of this absurdity. A bead of sweat appeared on his brow. While he felt it trickling down his forehead, he did not feel the need to wipe it away. When he finally spoke, his words were harsh.

"You think you have all of the answers, don't you Alexandria."

"Some, but…"

He ignored her words. "Let's put your life in perspective. You want to run off and wander around in the mountains. You have a job that I've provided, a home that I've provided. In fact, your whole life is what I have provided. But for some reason, you can't appreciate it. You know what you remind me of?" His head shook disgusted. "A spoiled child. I wish I could be irresponsible, but we've both known from the beginning, I'm not. So you live a spoiled child's life. I work to support you in an unbelievable lifestyle, and it's still not enough. So spoiled, you can't even appreciate what I give you. Without me, you'd be nothing."

He looked at Jessi, his eyes hard until a calm seemed to come over him, a slight upward turn in the corner of his mouth. He thought about the image in his mind, still so clearly vivid.

"You remember that wildlife photographer?" William asked Jessi. "You were at the showing at The Club?"

Jessi acknowledged, no hint beyond that.

"Michael Cabelli," he said.

Jessi did not look at Alex. "Yes, I remember."

"He had a picture. I stood for a long time looking at it. My first thought was to be offended. It was a bit perverse, a picture of a naked woman in a waterfall. Not a detail picture, but an image of a figure, the details of the woman hidden in the waterfall. Do you remember the image?"

Jessi nodded a slow, deliberate yes.

"The more I looked at that picture the better I thought I understood. I think that is the type of person Alexandria wants to be." He turned and looked at his wife, her eyes turned away from him. "It was inappropriate to have that picture at our showing, some tawdry woman naked in the world." He raised his hand, nodding. "I'm sorry, but that's the belief system I've grown up with. But seeing that picture, it helped me understand Alexandria and her crazy need to go off on outdoor adventures I pay for. Anyway," he wiped the second trickle of sweat from his brow, "I looked at that picture, and I understood that if she had a choice of walking naked into a mountain waterfall or walking into The Club on my arm in a priceless dress with a string of perfect diamonds around her neck, she'd pick the waterfall. I can't for the life of me understand it, but that's what she thinks. She tells me every time she takes Josie to the mountains. She doesn't want to be with me. Like a spoiled child who has everything, she throws all of that aside and runs away paying for it all on my debit card."

Alexandria was crying. Her face turned from his hidden in her hands with sad, sobbing tears escaping her. In a moment she had come undone, and Jessi reached a comforting hand to her knee.

"See what I mean?" William pointed his wife. "A spoiled child."

Jessi's hand rested on her leg, feeling the sobs shaking Alex.

William threw his hands up in despair. "So what do we do, me without friends and you without whatever the hell you want."

Alexandria heard the challenge, and when her mind came to realize her own husband had admitted what she for so long had fought against, that is when composure began to return. She allowed the silence to be hers as her strength returned. When she finally felt the emotional control, when she had gained the composure to face him, she did.

"Then for the first time in our lives," she stared at him dead on, "let's be completely honest. You're doing a pretty damn good job of it right now, so let's keep it going." Alexandria looked up surprising William with a smile. Delicately, she wiped the smeared make up from under her eyes. "I've been so angry for so long, I've accepted it in my life. The problem is you can't accept the truth."

William's eyes dared her. "Try me."

Jessi sat deep in her chair, panic racing through her mind. "Alex, are you sure?"

As Alex nodded, the fear vanished from her. "I knew you'd never see through the water." There were no more tears. "It's the narrowness of your vision, William. You can't see what's right in front of your face." She glanced down as she took a deep breath. Her eyes rose again to meet his. "It was me," she said, "in the waterfall. Michael Cabelli took that picture of me seven years ago."

William was fading from her mind, and she felt a rush of refreshing freedom. She reached over as if to touch him.

He tensed, withdrawing. "What are you saying?"

"I'm sorry, but you wanted honesty," she said. "It was me in the waterfall. I've loved that Mountain Man all my life."

The clearness of her blue eyes terrified him.

Alex stood and reached for Jessi's hand. As Jessi took it she felt a firm squeeze of thank you. Confidence filled her client's smile, and Jessi sensed Alex was happy. William sat stunned staring at her, his shirt slightly ruffled at the waist. Before he could speak, Alexandria walked poised to the door and turned to face him.

"I may be spoiled, William, but I have sacrificed much." Her eyes had become clear. "Ever since I repelled eighty feet backward down that cliff to that waterfall, everyday since then and long before then, I have sacrificed. Spoiled yes, but with it has come great sacrifice. That is something we both need to understand."

Before he could speak, he heard the sounds of her heels growing muffled on the polyester carpet. Then there were the clicks as she crossed the foyer, and from the distant room he heard the closing of the front door with a hollow echo.

Chapter 58

He sat in the darkening den of his multi-million dollar home and wondered if this is what life had become. In America you work hard, build a business that provides for thousands, and one day you wonder what happened. He stared at the leather planner on the leather blotter on the eighteenth century Victorian desk authenticated to have been owned by 18th century English royalty.

The soft glow of the iron Cambridge lamp transformed the room from the fading daylight to an eerie glare in the darkness. His mind rationalized. He had been pensive, unresponsive to her needs because of life's demands. And now, he was being punished.

He looked at the demands of the planner. The next day was fully booked, and his list of priorities beyond the hours in the day. If he disregarded tomorrow to try and save his marriage, it might cost him thousands.

He was responsible, fully responsible. It all rested on his shoulders. When things didn't work, he had to respond yet she still demanded more. If she didn't get the time she demanded, there was no loyalty, and she ended up with some Mountain Man. It was impossible to be all that everybody demanded him to be yet she demanded that he give more.

Twelve to fifteen hour days for eighteen years, and what had he accomplished? He was a name in the banking world. He ate a chef's meal every day, dressed immaculately, drove the finest of cars, and could simply make any personal choices without a thought about finances. Money drove his life, but did not control him. Power controlled him. She was right. Life was a financial relationship. If he had to involve others, his power allowed him to involve them on his terms. Alexandria knew that. She knew if he lost power, lost his financial empire, then he was lost.

So that was his life now. Power, disquiet, and aloneness filled the room of expensive leather and noble antiques. A massive library with books never touched maintained the image. Family photos he could hardly see were in the darkness, placed there years ago by Alexandria and dusted daily by the help. They were the image of what he wanted to be but seldom felt. He hadn't noticed the pictures in years, even wondered if they'd been changed since Alexandria had first arranged them. Squinting to see, he realized that one showed him and Josephine laughing, but he could not remember when or where it was taken.

Once again, he filled the tumbler half full of twenty-year-old Scotch. He set the decanter beside the Cambridge lamp. The glow against the Scotch pissed him off. In one sweep the planner flew from the desk, fluttering angrily into a collision with the bookcases. It fell with a thud on the floor, and he stared unmoved, still pissed.

Once, a long time ago, he had been excited to give her this life. He had imagined the thrill in her eyes each day when she realized he had given her wealth. It was their domain to control, and she would never want; only desire and then have.

He took a deep, hard swallow of the drastic Scotch. And what had she desired? A guy with long hair and hiking boots, muscles bigger than his, a youthful confidence William had lost years ago. One day while he had worked to give her everything, to provide them the exaggeration of the American dream, she had walked naked into a mountain waterfall while another man watched. While he fought for them, she slept with him. That was probably it.

She was a woman expecting more. What was sex to her; cuddling, coddling, sweet whispers and soft skin? Yes, he had tried that. Probably not enough because there wasn't enough time for such foolishness, but he had tried. Still, he wasn't some ridiculous John Wayne of the mountains, always the massive image of a woman's fantasy. He could give so much, but never enough to satisfy a spoiled child.

He gulped the last burning drop and filled the glass half full again. Seven years she had been unfaithful, and then the son-of-a-bitch had walked into his office and played his buddy. What kind of a jerk would send him that waterfall picture? And what was this bullshit of calling her Alex. He should have known something was up. Nobody called her Alex. Jesus. He banged both fists ricocheting off the antique oak desk.

That son-of-a-bitch had used Chadwick money to fund his business. They had both used him; used his success to fund her boyfriend's hobby. It was some sort of adulterated, plot of deceit. Then they had flaunted it in his face, in the face of his friends at The Club. God damn, his lawyers would rip them apart. He had the power, and his power could take away everything. She'd find out how much she missed him once she was penniless.

He heard the slight echo of the side door closing from the kitchen atrium. He could barely read the Arabic numerals on the tambour desk clock. He squinted. Eleven seventeen. Her heals clicked across the marble foyer, and he wondered if she had the guts to face him. He sat staunchly in the straight back chair, the tumbler of Scotch hanging from the grip of his fingers. His snide glare turned to nausea when he saw her shadowy image in the doorway.

His words were meant to hurt. "What the fuck do you want?"

She reached to her right and flipped the switch to the overhead light. Reflexive, he covered his eyes against the brightness. She walked across the room, a sway in her stride as she glanced sideways at the planner resting in disarray on the floor. Alex picked up a glass, and when he reached for the Scotch, she pulled it away and poured herself a shot. Sitting down in the chair, the lamp light between them, she gulped in one swallow.

She licked her lips, distasteful. "I could never understand how you drink this stuff."

His eyes were hateful. "Because I can."

She could never remember his eyes being hateful; determined, controlling, angry, even resentful, but never hateful. Turning the glass in her hand, she asked genuinely, "May I explain?"

With venom in his eyes, he shot back. "Why should I listen to anything you'd say?"

She ran her fingers up over her forehead and through her hair, strands of blond falling back over her shoulders away from her face. "I can only give you one reason." She kept her eyes locked on his. "I'm asking you to."

He sneered, his eyes turning away. "That's all the better you can do?"

Her glare caught his glance. "That's all the better I should have to do."

He waved his glass at her, Scotch splashing against his hands, through his fingers and onto the antique desk finish.

"I'm sorry I walked out of Jessi's office." Guilt rushed through her. "I…"

A finger rose from his glass pointing at her. "You've got a hell of a lot more to be sorry about than that."

"William, I asked if I could explain?" Staunchly, her eyes begged his patience.

In a clear, unaffected voice, she spoke and he listened, his mind fading in and out between the Scotch and his own intense anger. Though clear in her own memory, she gave sketchy details of what was private in her own life. She talked of her own need to break from the confines of her life, and of three days in Estes Park seven years ago. It was intended as an innocent escape, a few days in a town where no one knew her. She and her father used to hike there. It was familiar and necessary in her heart to feel the comfort. Then something happened. She didn't mean for it. It was innocent in the beginning. It wasn't Michael's fault.

William glared taking a last swallow of Scotch. Alex pushed the near empty bottle toward him. William dumped the remaining liquid into his glass, shaking the last drops from the bottle lip.

"Listen William," her tone was a gentle rebuke. "You want to blame Michael for this, but this had nothing to do with him. The problem was right here. The problem was and still is with you and me. If that problem hadn't existed, I never would have been in Estes." She sat watching him, her legs crossed and foot bouncing. "I know your ego wants to divert the blame to Michael. You want to transfer your guilt thinking he has taken something from you, but understand this, William. You have to have something before it can be taken away. You and I are the problem."

Suddenly lurching forward, he screamed at her, standing with both hands slamming down on the desk. "You are my wife. He had no right."

She froze at his sudden outburst, closing her eyes, waiting silently for him to calm. In their lives together, she had never felt him to be out of control. Her eyes held tightly shut until she finally heard him sitting again. When she spoke, she remained strong. "Blame me, blame us, but Michael didn't know."

Looking down, she was devastated by her own guilt.

"I know it was wrong, supporting him with Foundation money. I just wanted to help him." Shame showed in the distraught sagging of her face. "Until Michael walked into your office, we hadn't had any contact in over six years. Michael had no idea that the Alex he met had any connection to you or the Foundation."

William shook his head in revulsion. His voice was low and groveling. "You expect me to believe this line of shit."

"Oh, William," she shook her head in her own loathing. "You've been drinking so everything's shit."

"Our marriage is shit." His eyes drove into hers.

She remained calm. "Yes, that's the sad truth."

"I've tried to make this work," he said.

There was no reasoning with him. Still, she talked, "Yes, we both tried, but you gave up years before I did."

"Maybe you think that," he dropped the empty tumbler on the leather blotter. "But I didn't go out and fuck somebody."

Her eyes flared, glaring down on her husband. "How long are you going to live that lie, William? How long are you going to blame me and claim innocence? And how many times have I called your hotel in New York and claimed to be the woman staying with you, the woman who just checked out or forgot her scarf? The clerk was always so nice, telling me how much they appreciated having Mr. and Mrs. Chadwick stay at their grand hotel."

She flinched as his arm flexed as if to grab the tumbler. He did not look at her, his head turned away, and they both knew.

"Please just listen." The quiet in her voice disarmed him. "I loved you and I still love you. You have given me much, but I'm tired of being lonely. I'm tired of feeling like I live by myself. I'm tired of waiting for you to get home from work at some ridiculously late hour or return from another business trip to New York so I can play a small part in your life that some other woman has been playing. I don't know if you'll ever understand how lonely I've been."

There was a long, quiet moment with unforgiving daggers in his eyes.

"I hope you can find some understanding and forgiveness in your anger." She lifted the tumbler in her hand to place the glass on the desk. "I'm going to bed now, William." She stood before him, her clothes wrinkled after the long day. "You can sleep with me or in the guest room. It will not matter. With you or without you, I've always slept alone."

Anger rose with the last parting shot. He watched her walk from the room, and his Scotch filled mind raged. Anger burst from him that she would turn and walk away, and he began to shake, overwhelmed. In a swipe, he grabbed the neck of the Scotch bottle, hurling it toward the door. End over end, it hurtled crashing into shattered pieces, sliding over the marble foyer.

On the staircase, Alex froze. She looked down over the railing as the glass sparkled in the dim light, sliding to a halt on the mirror finished floor. Fear wrenching pain shredded the confidence in her. She doubled over, clenching her stomach with both arms. Lunging forward, she ran up the circular staircase, down the wide hallway, and through the French doors. Instinctively, as she slammed the door, she turned the dead bolt and fell helplessly against the white wood frame, shuddering in fear.

Chapter 59

She liked the fact that whenever they visited, Brandon never sat behind his desk. They would sit at the sofa, Brandon in the chair with pen and legal pad copiously taking notes. She hated the whole ordeal, but somehow felt comfortable meeting with Brandon.

"I heard from William's attorney today," he said. "Actually, I believe he's got three lawyers working on this."

Alex shrugged, "It's a business deal."

"Despite that, he's stalling."

"Stalling?"

Brandon took a sip of coffee from his Yosemite Sam mug. "He wants to discuss reconciliation."

Alex's Bugs Bunny mug dropped away from her lips. "What?"

"My guess is it's a stall tactic." Brandon set Yosemite on the table. "We're talking about a great deal of assets here. They're stalling to make sure they know where everything is, so they can hide as much as possible."

Alex shook her head. "It's been weird. Things seem not that much different at home. We don't talk, but we never really did. We're back to coexistence, only now it's with a sneer. We haven't told Josie, and William is sleeping in one of the guest rooms. But otherwise," she shook her head again, "we share space. I like him a lot more when I don't think of him as my husband. He's a great roommate. Never around and pays all the bills on time."

Brandon smiled. He always saw this in divorce cases. At some point, some level of separation begins to soften the anger. Optimistic people easily forget the anger, but once back together it doesn't take long to raise its ugly head.

He watched her for a moment. In his life, he had known many beautiful women, yet most had been tainted by arrogance or an incredible ability to manipulate. Here was a genuine person. Yes, incredibly beautiful, but she honestly was trying to do the right thing. After many years of sacrifice only she could understand, it was down-home, middle American values that were showing through. In a family driven by money, she had remained because of a marriage vow and her commitment to family.

With his personal touch, he refilled her Bugs Bunny mug. "Okay, so let me tell you how it is." He set his pad on the table. "Within your husband and father-in-law's corporation, there are many other corporations." He searched for an illustration.

She nodded understanding.

He lifted his pen and began drawing circles, connecting lines as his elbows rested on the edge of the coffee table. "Corporations work like this. All these circles, they represent separate businesses. And when you want to reach one, you go the shortest route available to get there. But if you want to take the scenic route." He traced a path through several dots. "Another time, this way, or this way through many other corporations." He traced again. "Many routes, but some very hard to follow or find a connection."

She nodded understanding.

Brandon pressed on. "Think of your husband's enterprises like this. The bank is the major host, but he has a web of affiliates, and it is often difficult to connect one corporation to the other. Your husband's family is worth much, but much of that worth is tied up in other business affiliates or held by your father-in-law. Not only is it attached to a variety of businesses and corporations, your father-in-law still controls much of this. Let's say William's actual personal liquid assets are spread through these corporations. His lawyers have hidden a million here, ten million there, twenty-five million hidden down a complicated trail in another distant corporation.

"The length of your marriage entitles you to much wealth. In order to determine what is rightfully yours, we must first piece the corporation puzzle together and identify the assets directly tied to William. His lawyers will fight this because the family does not want to reveal either the complexity of their corporations or the true value of their net worth."

Alex was grinning. "Okay Brandon, now let me tell you how it is." She tapped her finger against the paper. "This is the mechanics of it, but in reality we are talking two issues; power and image. William cannot stand the thought that he has lost control of me. Image is part of the power. I will guarantee you his mother, as much as she might like it to happen, will not allow a divorce. The Chadwick family is above such scandal. She hates me but more then that, she hates that a divorce will eliminate the image of perfection. They will keep me from their money, yes, because they don't want to give me any, but primarily because they want to maintain the control they have over me that maintains the image of perfection."

Brandon agreed, "Whatever the reason, his lawyers will be vicious in keeping any funds from you."

She laughed, despite the sarcasm. "And all the while, trying to control me with efforts at reconciliation which will allow the image to remain in tact." She shook her head, staring at Brandon. "Too many games being played."

"So what do you want, Alex? I can push this as far as you want. Eventually, we can discover the vast majority of his assets and go after them. That, I'm afraid, will take a great deal of time and money. So, what do you want?"

She sat back on the couch with Bugs Bunny resting in the lap of her favorite faded jeans, a slight hole in the knee. Her eyes searched beyond Brandon and out the window to the building across the street. The gray gloom of the city stared back at her.

"I want Josie. Josie has always been the issue, and damn William if he tries to make her a pawn in this. Money?" she shrugged, "I don't want to escape with the family jewels, but I have committed to this family for many years. To some level, I have earned some assets." She looked once again at the kind-faced attorney. "I want to live comfortably in the mountains. I don't want his mansion, and I don't want half his assets. I grew up on a teacher's income, and I had a wonderful childhood. Adulthood hasn't been quite as wonderful, and today there are literally millions for my taking but that's not what this is about. I want some security and the freedom to be with Josie without restrictions."

"You could get much, much more than that." Brandon watched her from behind his rich salt and pepper eyebrows. "Are you sure you want to sacrifice millions?"

Her laughter burst from his question; playful, happy laughter.

"Oh Brandon, I've sacrificed much more than money. Despite it all, I've lived a lonely life. William has never known the happiness my father knows, and I have never known the happiness my mother knows." She laughed again, a broad, full-lipped smile breaking across her face. "Early in the morning, my father and mother sit and read the newspaper together. Her head is on his shoulder, and his arm around her while he holds the newspaper in front of them. That is what marriage should be. They begin their day sharing their lives. What I want?" she smiled honestly. "Money could never buy that."

Brandon saw the suddenness at which her eyes turned sad.

"I knew a man once who would have given me that." She quieted, blinking. "I don't know if I'll ever have that chance again. But I do know if I stay in this marriage, I'll never share my life with my husband. I want the chance, the possibility of love in a life shared." Her eyes stared directly at Brandon. "I've earned the right to be financially comfortable. If he'd give me that, and of course, not make Josie an issue; I'd have a chance to find happiness again."

"I think we can get you that chance. With all his money, all you're asking for is a fair settlement to live comfortably. His bank account won't even notice that. Unfortunately, corporate lawyers don't think that way. As with many in our profession, they tend to go for the jugular, and..." his eyebrows lifted, "even if they will settle, do you realize you're sacrificing an amazing fortune, Alex."

"A small price to pay to be happy." She was laughing as the words left her lips. "But you're thinking like an attorney, Brandon. It's a sweet financial deal for William, which his business sense will like. Remember, power and image is what this is about. Without power and image, the money has no value. A low settlement relinquishes control, and I'll go quietly. He'll pay the money. Still it will be difficult for him to surrender the image of perfection."

Alex stared down at her mug, thinking if she should. "Okay, Brandon. You want to be in control?"

"Always." He answered.

"William has a lady friend in New York. I know how to track her through his hotel and car service. I suspect she's either a kept woman or an hourly employee." Alex cast a sad look downward. "He'll be terrified of a public scandal. I don't want to use it, but if he knows we can, he'll surrender much more quickly."

"Leverage." Brandon acknowledged.

"Your investigator should check the Esquire Hotel and Executive Town Car Services in Manhattan."

Chapter 60

Her mother had been gone for half an hour when her father appeared on the veranda.

"Daddy?" Josie said, surprised to see him. "What are you still doing home?"

He was dressed in his double-breasted olive suit, white shirt, and silk tie with gold accents. "I wanted a minute with you."

"Oh," she said, then smiled her mother's smile. "Nice tie."

"Thank you." She was so special. He sat down across from her.

Josie watched her father, her head tilted slightly so her hair hung full over her shoulder. "Is this about you and Mom?"

He looked startled.

"I'm not blind, Daddy." She nonchalantly took a bite of toast. "It's a pretty cold house we live in."

"That obvious?" he asked.

She nodded, still chewing toast. "Don't worry about me, Daddy. I love you and mom. Most of my friends' parents are divorced. It's the norm. If that's what's happening, I'm sad for you both, but I also know you guys haven't been really close for a long time. If this is what's best for you, know that I'll survive." Despite her boldness, her eyes filled with water.

William was shocked at the pronouncement, and he wondered when she'd become so honestly confident.

"Josephine, it may be too early to label this a divorce, but there are some issues we're trying to work through. I'd like to work them out if your mother would."

"Daddy, I don't want to get into the details," as if waving the whole mess away, "but mom hasn't been happy for years, and you spend all of your time at work. That's the way you guys are. You kind of live separate lives." It startled him that she saw their lives as separate. Had tears not been flowing over her checks, he'd have thought she too was disconnected. "I've seen my friends choose sides, get caught in the middle," she told him. "It really won't change my life that much cause I'm older now and in high school and, well, in a couple of years I'll be off to college, so I only ask, Daddy, just let me love you both. Don't put me in the middle or make me choose sides." Then she added, "And respect that I can handle it. I love you both too much to not handle it."

William watched as his daughter turned her attention to her breakfast, tears rolling down her cheeks, and he realized her words hid the emotions. At that moment, he hated what they had become and that it would cause his daughter such pain.

Reaching across, he touched her chin. Dampness covered his fingertips. "I love you, Josephine."

She did not look at him, but he could see her tender smile and then nodded as she cried harder. He reached forward, his arm around his daughter's neck in reassurance.

They sat in silence, and William knew Alexandria had been right. He should have spent more time with Josephine, been in her life more. At that moment, he hated that he had not, and promised himself that he would.

"So," he sat back, "you and your mother are leaving for Estes this afternoon. Long's Peak, how high is that?"

She looked up, wiping the tears from her cheek. "14,259 feet."

"Damn high," he said.

"Damn high," she laughed. "Into the clouds."

"You'll be careful?"

She laughed again, "Oh Daddy, you're a flatlander. You think it's all wilderness with bears waiting around each tree for a human treat." They laughed together, and she wiped her young eyes once more. "I'll bet we see a hundred people during the hike. It's a trail. You know, like a steep dirt sidewalk. It's a test of endurance with some challenges near the top. The skill is to keep going."

He gave a slight nod. "I'm confident you will both do that."

"Keep going?" she gave him a look at the absurd thought. "Of course we'll keep going."

"And you'll be back for your grandmother's Debutante Ball, your little birthday party." He looked very seriously, a father's look she'd seldom seen.

"Grandmother and I picked out a dress last week," she said. "It's beautiful."

"Great. This means a lot to your grandmother."

"I know, Daddy." She raised her eyebrows mocking excitement.

He stood and walked around the table, kissing his daughter on the top of the head. He held his lips to her hair, his precious daughter, realizing he should have kissed her every morning.

"Baby," he promised her, "I will do all I can to work this out."

"Thanks, Daddy."

As he stood she looked up at him. "You're an amazing young woman."

She winked at her Dad, "I'll text you a picture from the top of Longs Peak."

"14,000 feet," he winked back.

"14,259," she corrected.

At the knock on the Foundation office door, Alexandria looked up from her desk. It opened a crack and William's head appeared, unannounced.

"May I come in?"

Shocked at his sudden appearance, she stood looking at him. "I guess. Yes, of course," her voice cracked slightly.

Sitting down before her, polite and calm, he began talking softly and slowly, expressing thoughts he had never expressed. He talked about his fear his family was disintegrating before his eyes. He wanted it to remain intact. They were both good people, and he talked about Josephine. He would not let her go. If it was a fight she wanted, that she would have. He would not simply let Alexandria make a decision, and then walk away with his daughter.

Just when she thought William was on the edge, was setting the boundaries, he backed away again. He wanted to believe that Michael Cabelli had been a one-time thing, a blip in their relationship, and she nodded reassurance, not looking in his eyes. But now, Alexandria and Josephine were going to Estes Park. Was that it? Would they spend time with Michael Cabelli? He would not allow her to corrupt his daughter and separate her from him. He would not allow Michael Cabelli to move in and take his family.

He looked away from his wife. "What I've always wanted was a family. I know I was never very good at it, but that's what I wanted. If you see Michael Cabelli again, that will be the end of any chance we have to reconcile or end amicably."

She didn't know if it was a threat or fear. His voice showed fear, his eyes anger, so she answered to both.

"I've told you, this is not about Michael. Going to Estes is Josie's wish. I climbed Long's Peak with my father on my sixteenth birthday, now she is doing it with me. We'll be with my parents, and Josie and I will hike Long's Peak together. Nobody else. I have no plans to see Michael, but if I do, that is my business. Tell your chief of security or private investigator or whomever the hell you've hired to keep his ass away from Estes. You want to know what I do while I'm there? I've told you my plans; and when I get back, if things turn out differently, I'll let you know. Besides, your security guy couldn't make it up Long's Peak if he wanted to. Josie and I will leave him in our dust."

The need to control urged him forward. "I want you to know, if you see Michael Cabelli it will turn this into a fight."

That, she knew, was a threat. She bit her tongue as the words *New York* sat ready to be released. "So how is that different from now? You've already made this a battle."

Shaking his head, his eyes glared. "I expect you to be home on Saturday afternoon. My mother is counting on you. We'll go together, as a family to my parents' house. I know my mother's overdoing this thing, but it's her way. She wants to present her granddaughter to society. Pretentious, yes, but Alexandria, it is an important tradition to our family."

She allowed the edge to fade away. "As always, William; I will come through for you. I will be there on your arm, the image of commitment and adoration. Josie will be incredibly beautiful, looking much more mature than sixteen and so much more confident. You see, when you feel like you've stood on top of the world, self-assurance is no longer an issue. Long's Peak will give her that. Is there anything else?"

He shot an irritated glance. Who was she to dismiss him? "Don't pollute our lives anymore with Cabelli."

"You may leave now," she stated. "We will be there Saturday with perfect smiles. No one will know that we are having conversations such as this one."

He dropped his head, standing quietly. "Alexandria, I'm sorry. I'm trying to be civil about this, but it's hard. You're my wife. Yes, I took that for granted, but I never imagined."

She stood firm. "You should have been paying attention."

He agreed, a sense of loss sweeping through him. "Yes, I should have been," he acknowledged. "I'll see you Saturday?"

Alexandria stared at her husband. "It will be a wonderful birthday celebration."

"Be safe." he added sincerely, fighting against explosive anger.

"We'll be home Saturday." She answered flatly.

"You've been warned," he reverted, unable to let it go.

"William," irritation appeared on her face, "I recognize this as a threat. I'm sorry you feel the need, but threats will not bring us back together nor settle things amicably."

"We'll see," were his final words, for she would not dismiss him.

The drive up Highway 36 into the mountains was comforting. Josie liked to ride barefoot with her toes resting on the dash. They talked and watched the passing of tall, thick pines and winding canyons walls. A sense of relief and anticipation fermented throughout Alex. It was Acoustic Tuesday.

The rented cottage came into view with her mother and father waiting to greet them from the generous front yard. She was excited to see them, yet a pang of sadness crept into her each time she visited her parents. Her father's effort at enthusiasm was just a bit strained, and her mother had lost a touch of weight without needing to, her back slightly rounded. They alternated happy hugs of warmth; Alexandria and her father, Josie and her grandmother, and switching to greet the other.

Her mother told her five times how good it was to see them, three times kissing Josie's cheek. They moved about the house, delivering luggage from the car. Alex stopped in the bedroom, giving them both another hug. Her father stepped away, looking into her eyes, touching her cheek tenderly. Her mother led them into the kitchen sure dinner had passed them by. Alex and Josie laughed a secret laugh having intentionally skipped dinner, knowing it would be waiting for them.

Hank's enthusiasm grew as they talked, laughing as each finished their sandwiches and homemade potato salad. Opening the thirty-year-old door of the white Philco refrigerator, he pulled away the perforated tab, opening a six-pack of Miller Lite.

"Come on." He waved the beer as bait, walking past her, through the living room, and out the front porch. Alex followed leaving her mother and Josie talking over the last few bites.

She sat beside him, both in their own wooden lounge chair.

He handed her the dew wet beer can. "Been here before, haven't we."

"Many times, Daddy."

They both popped the tabs, sucking a bit of foam away.

"I'm sensing something." He set his beer on the wooden armrest. "What's going on?"

She looked at him with serious eyes. "I don't want to go into detail, Daddy. Let's just say I'm trying to get my life back, and whenever things change there's some pain."

"How can I help?" he reached for her hand.

It was so amazing that with a father's touch, a woman's hand could still feel just like his little girl's.

"We sat out here one night, and I told you about Michael Cabelli."

"Yes," he looked up cautiously. "The photographer."

She looked off toward Long's Peak, the evening's sun bright over the northern face. "That night you told me you wanted me to be happy. I told you there was much happiness, and you explained there was a difference between happiness and being happy." She took a deep swallow. "Well, damn if you weren't right. So," she shrugged, "now the happiness is gone too. Without that, life is pretty bleak. It's time for me to be happy."

She looked at the beer in one hand, squeezed her father's hand in her other, and chugged half the can. Alex pulled the aluminum from her lips and shook her head, a shiver running through her body. She winked to her father. "I've got to make a phone call."

Alex heard her friends voice over the phone. "Great! You're in town."

"With my parents and Josie."

"Josie's sixteenth birthday?" Jennifer asked. "What day you doing

Long's?"

"Thursday," Alex answered. "What's going on tonight?"

"Jimmy's playing. I haven't talked to Michael, but he's usually there. You sure you want to meet us."

"What time?"

"Eight."

"What's his cell number?"

Jennifer hesitated, her eyes rolling toward Jimmy who stood over a skillet filled with steaming vegetables. She recited the number.

As soon as she hung up Alex was dialing, her breath escaping her with each number. She waited patiently through four rings then heard his voice. Excitement escaped her with the disappointment of voicemail. She listened to his optimistic tone, taking deep breaths in preparation.

The beep.

"I know I shouldn't be doing this, but I am. I also know you may want to tell me to go to hell, and I understand if you do, but if you aren't doing anything tonight, I'd love one dance at Acoustic Tuesday. It'd be good to see you again."

When he stepped from the shower, he toweled quickly drying the dampness that covered his body. Rubbing vigorously, the towel absorbed the water from wet to damp.

Turning, he saw the slight glow of the phone resting on the dresser. Pressing the button, he waited for the voicemail.

The voice froze him as he stood listening. When the message ended, he realized he was staring at himself in the mirror. Mechanically, he reached for the towel and wiped the dampness still covering his chest.

For so long she had dreamed of returning. To walk once again into Lonigan's like a place of old friends. There's a comfort in a bar that feels like yours with friendly greetings all about. It was a place of welcome where the only expectation is a smile; the only obligation, a beer bought for a friend who'd bought one for you a few days before.

Jennifer was at the table front and center to the stage where Jimmy was setting up, speakers and microphone in place. Jennifer stood, smiling to her friend, and they hugged. As they separated, Jennifer was glad to see that Alex was not sending a message.

Her clothes were subtle and mountain appropriate. Black jeans and matching half boots, she wore a white stretch tank top covered by a black and white thin striped denim shirt unbuttoned to the waist, the sleeves rolled once at the cuff. Most telling, her hair was pulled back through the opening of her cap, no big, wavy, full-flowing curls that every girl knows is seductive.

Jennifer had seen her in similar dress during their years together in Denver. Maybe it was the bright smile, the glow in her blue eyes, maybe it was the confidence in her walk that made her seemed to fit nicely in Lonigan's Saloon.

Alex glanced back over her shoulder to see Jimmy, ear close to the guitar bridge. She moved up the steps, avoiding cords and the microphone. She loved Jimmy's smile, that smile that was always comforting and happy. He lifted the guitar over his head, freeing himself from the strap. With his hug, she kissed his cheek.

"So," he whispered, "are you back?"

"Just a visit," she answered softly. "But, it's great to be able to visit. I've missed your music so much."

"Well, that's silly," he laughed, reached sideways, and handed her a C.D. With a broad smile he told her, "It's brand new, just off the presses. You never have to miss me again."

She held the C.D., staring at the clouds and sunset and smiling eyes of Jimmy on the cover. "This is fantastic. I'll play this in the car every time I head into the mountains. Jimmy, it's perfect."

He put his hand over the C.D., his fingers holding hers. "You're sure you won't sue me."

"Sue you," she laughed. "Why in the world would I sue you?"

"Jennifer promised you wouldn't, so if you're angry, sue her."

He turned the C.D. over in her hands, and Alex read down the list of songs, all written and performed by Jimmy until she got toward the bottom. *Mystic Blue,* it read. Acknowledging the music by Jimmy but the words by two others, *A. Chadwick and M. Cabelli.*

Her eyes radiated with laughter. "I got song writing credit on a C.D. Oh my God, that's so cool." She reacted like a teenager.

"You're not angry?" he asked.

"Angry?" her eyes brightened, elated. "I'm thrilled and honored." She pressed the CD against her chest.

"I hoped you would be," and they hugged again.

The bar was quickly filling as it had seven years before. Tourists in fresh bought mountain garb were eating pizza and sipping imported beers. Locals just off work were wearing dirty work clothes and t-shirts. They all welcomed each other and never bought their own first beer. A Fat Tire or Coors always seemed to appear.

At the end of the bar, two raggedy looking men in bad need of haircuts and a beard trim sat heads together, deep in conversation with the only interruption, a burst of laughter from one or the other. A warm memory rose within Alex. When the waitress passed, she handed her a bill to buy the two men a beer.

A few minutes later, the bartender set the beers before the men, motioning toward her table. The two men tipped their bottles to her, and she tipped hers back. One man, the man covered in tattoos stared at her for the longest time. Finally, with a pat on the back of his boisterous friend, he stood and walked to Alex. Sitting down in a chair, he winking at Jennifer, leaning sideways to look down her body Alex's body.

"Woman, you still got a way of getting to my groin," his voice was gravelly, his eyes taunting.

"It's been a long time, Ralph," she grinned. She lifted her beer, and the long necks clanked together. "Got any new tattoos?"

"Shit. I'm running out of room." His toothy grin was still the same. "How 'bout you?"

"None on me," she said. "But I've thought about a tiny, little fawn curled and sleeping, maybe right here." She pointed at her pelvis, just below her black leather belt. "What do you think?"

Astonished, Jennifer's stare caused her to lean away. She looked at her friend, shocked that she seemed so serious. Alexandria with a tattoo, it sounded too absurd.

"I know just the guy who could do it, a damn fine artist. Has a shop over on Riverside Drive." Ralph winked. "Just let me know when, and I'll hook you up. I'll even hold your hand."

With daring eyes, she answered. "I'll think about it, Ralph."

He stood and nodded to her, saluted his beer to Jennifer. "Damn, my groin's got a good memory. You let me know if I can help with that tattoo." Then he winked. "Good to see you again."

His laughter filled the bar as he walked back to his friend. Slapping him heartily on the back, dust rose from the man's flannel work shirt.

Michael knew Jimmy had been playing for a good hour when he pulled his Jeep into a parking space behind Lonigan's. He had thought about not going, though he knew seriously he could never stay away. If this was some sort of personal torture he was allowing her to inflict upon him, he was a stupid man. But he had to trust she wasn't just doing this for fun. He sat in the Jeep watching the waters of Fall River. Rushing too high and too hard from the extraordinary amount of snow still melting from above tree line, he wondered if he was about to be swept away himself.

He strode in the back door and down the long hallway to the bar, stepping between people and greeted the pool players with a nod. Down two steps to the bar and the waitress station, he waved at Scooter. The bartender waved back, a moment later setting a beer in front of Michael.

Michael watched them watching Jimmy, her style recognizable next to Jennifer, and his mind smiled at the way her hair was pulled back with the ponytail slipped through the back of her ball cap. The hat shaped her face giving it slenderness, her smile, a freedom that he found himself attracted to. Taking a deep breath, he tried to steady his heart, the nervousness and enticement.

He waved at his musical friend who smiled a playful hello without breaking the rhythm of the song; something about an old, drooling dog and the man he loved. The beer at home had not provided enough courage, so he drank this one quickly and waved for another.

As Jimmy started the next ballad, Michael slapped hands with two guys still wearing the days' work dirt on their faces. He passed behind Jennifer setting his beer on the table between the two women. Without breaking motion, he moved on behind the stunning blond as the entire bar watched him take her hand and lift her from her seat. Surprised for a moment, an alluring smile broke radiant from her as she followed him, her hand clinching his. He turned, she cascaded into his arms, and they began to dance face-to-face eyes.

Somehow Jimmy flowed the transition into a lead for a new song, not allowing the dancing to stop. Mickey smiled first, tilting her head toward Jimmy. She closed her eyes and leaned in closer, her cheek against his. Soothing sounds of masterful music from a calming voice were the perfect words.

> *Where have you been, my beautiful friend*
> *Walking to this moment in time*
> *Where have you been, my amazing friend*
> *Smiling mystic blue eyes*
>
> *The rhythm of the pine tree sings*
> *The song of a lover's new chance*
> *Where life and dreams and dance to be touch the sky*
>
> *And the Mystic blue in your eyes*

Scooter shook his head to dissuade two tourist couples that stood to join the dancing, but Mickey and Alex seemed not to notice. They danced on, eyes closed to the special soft sounds of their musical friend.

As the music quieted, Michael opened his eyes to see Alex. It was the smile he had never forgotten. It was the smile that drew his desire, and the smile he always wanted to create. He took her hand and led her from the dance floor, a wave of thank you to Jimmy as they moved up the steps away from the bar.

Out the front doors, the night was now dark on the tourists vacated streets. He turned left, away from the group of high schoolers hanging out and down the street to the next wooden bench. There he stopped and guided her with his hand to sit. He found a spot on the edge of the brick decorative planter, his feet between them on the edge of the wood.

"So," he said, his dark eyes serious. "What's up?"

She looked just as confident. "Do you want to hate me sometimes?"

His eyebrows rose, giving a slight shrug. "Sometimes."

"I've not been good to you, have I?" Her blue-eyed sadness looked at Mickey.

"In a business sense, yes, you've been very good to me. Emotionally? No, you haven't," he agreed. "You leave me with turmoil. So is this more turmoil?"

"I'm here with Josie," she explained. "For her sixteenth birthday, we're going to hike Long's. We're doing it Thursday. And yes, my life's in turmoil too, a turmoil I hope to gain some control over soon. I just know that I've missed you since the day I left, even more since the showing. I'm sorry, Mickey, for any pain I've caused. But you are right. I need to be Alex, and I can't be Alex without your friendship."

He looked two doors down the street at the sign. *Nature's Way, The Nature and Wildlife Photography of Michael Cabelli.* He pointed at the sign then looked off down the long main street of Estes knowing he had no choice. "I've missed you terribly. So," he said, "is that where we are now, friends?"

"I don't want to promise more than I can give." She reached out and took his hand. "For the time being, can you accept that?"

"That's a tough one," Mickey told her, "but I've thought a lot about it since Denver. I don't know what else to do but appreciate what you've done and offer my friendship. If that's the limit, then that's what I'll take."

"I'm sorry, Mickey, but right now that's all I can give."

"Then that's what I'll take." He squeezed her hand, pulling her upward as he did. "Come on buddy, let's drink some beer."

Her hand still warm in his, he guided her, and she followed him back into the saloon where a cold beer waited them both. From the end of the bar, Ralph gave them a long neck salute.

It was an evening of freedom. For the first time in seven years, she was Alex. As the night went on, she drank too much beer, but avoided the tequila shots knowing Long's was only a day away. She danced with Mickey, he danced with Jennifer, and Alex danced a wild dance with Ralph. Jennifer and Mickey introduced her to the locals as Jennifer's former boss, and Alex laughed at how wonderful it must be to live in Estes Park.

One construction worker laughed back, explaining with his arms spread out. "Just stay. We all did."

Yes, she thought, an easy decision, but a hard move.

As the evening ended, she danced a slow dance in Mickey's arms. She listened to the music and warm, steady beat of his heart.

"Will I see you again?" he asked.

"Yes." She gave him a tender kiss just below his ear on his cheek. "But

I don't know when. I'm here for the hike with Josie. Then I have to go back to Denver Saturday. But I promise to call, and we'll talk."

"What time Saturday?" He asked.

"Before noon."

His breath was warm against her skin. "Saturday morning at 6:30, just before sunrise be at my cabin. Fall River Road opens Saturday, and I'll be the first one up. Remember the grazing bull elk. Ride to the top with me, and we'll drive back down Trail Ridge Road. You'll be home by ten o'clock at the latest."

She hesitated, "I don't know Mickey."

"Yes you do," he laughed.

The music faded, and she looked into his eyes surrendering with a promise to meet him on Saturday. With a hug to Jennifer, she reached for the stage giving a fingertip slap to Jimmy's hand, and Alex turned and left Lonigan's, so glad to have been back.

Chapter 61

In the dark, Hank drove the strip of Highway Seven winding up the mountain south of Estes toward the trailhead. Alex sat quietly, barely awake while Josie chattered from the back seat, excited for the climb. As they passed Long's Peak Inn, Hank reminded Josie of the legend of Enos Mills, a man who had hiked Long's over two hundred and fifty times, and pointed out his small cabin, still part of the family land.

This, Hank told her, was a man who truly committed to the quality of nature. Living in a one-room log cabin, he built Long's Peak Inn and later became responsible for the designation of Rocky Mountain National Park as a national park. Enos, he was sure, would be glad to know Josie was celebrating her sixteenth birthday in such a way.

Sharing the parking lot at the trailhead, a few quiet groups prepared for the climb. Still three a.m., daylight would not fully join them until they had nearly completed the first five miles of the nine-mile hike up. Once at the top, it was important to begin the descent before the afternoon rains struck with the threat of lightening bolts spraying the massive peak. Nine miles up and a 6,000-foot climb to reach the 14,259-foot summit was their challenge. Hank handed his daughter and granddaughter their daypacks from the trunk of the car.

"Enough food and water?"

"Yep." Alex swung the pack onto her back.

"Got your ponchos?"

"Check," Josie teased, clipping her waist pack on.

Hank pointed seriously at his granddaughter. "An even pace if you plan to avoid nausea. Always look to see where you're stepping. If you want to talk, stop. It's a 6,000 foot fall if you don't pay attention." He laughed at his own exaggeration.

"Twenty-two years ago," Alex said. "I bet you could still make it, Dad."

He chuckled knowing, "I could give it a hell of a try, but this is for you and Josie. I'll be back by two o'clock. Good luck."

Josie danced on calling back, "I'll wave at you from the top."

The trail was well worn through the lodge pole pines. Alex knew the hike to the Boulder Field would not be the challenge. Six miles and 2,500 feet was a typical hike for her and Josie, but once they reached the top of the tree line and started across the Boulder Field, oxygen would be sparse like the absence of trees. The last three miles and 3,200 feet was rock surface, a sharply increased steepness, and open to the wickedly cold wind.

Three hours later, clearing the tree line they stopped with the Boulder Field in sight, massive rocks rolled one on top of the other. The sun was just peaking over the eastern mountaintops. Flanked by three mountains, each peaking beyond 13,000 feet, the 1,000-foot face of Long's Peak towered above them. As Alex felt a slight trepidation for what they were about to do, Josie pointed at a pika scurrying in and out amongst the rocks. She squatted to watch, only to stand with the sound of voices behind them.

As they watched, four athletic boys, their college proudly proclaimed on their t-shirts and hats, acknowledged them with smiles and faint oxygen deprived hellos. They passed quickly, each of them taking long looks at the women, one staring deeply into Josie's eyes. The women watched them continue on at their rapid pace, almost jumping from rock to rock.

Alex winked at her daughter. "They'll never keep that pace up. We'll pass them before the keyhole."

Josie watched the pika. "Maybe they won't be so cocky then."

"I suppose not." Alex stated, following the brash boys.

Her daughter stepped in line behind her. "How high are we?"

"Over 11,000 feet," her mother called back.

Josie admired the hints of trees still surviving around her. Maybe a hundred years old and not even four feet tall, they were narrow and twisted from the roots fighting for a grip among the rocks. Not far before them was the Boulder Field. The sun rising to the east glowed deep golden reds over the rounded rocks. For a moment they stopped to watch the sunrise.

One thousand feet and an hour later, the college boys were still well ahead of them. There was the faint vision of hikers far down the trail, and Josie picked up a handful of crystallized snow, and tossed it into the clear stream.

"Cold?"

"It's snow, mom." Then she thought, adding, "For my seventeenth birthday, I want to go scuba diving in Jamaica and taste the salt water that was once snow in our mountains."

"Scuba diving?" Alex sucked a breath deep into her lungs.

Josie stepped over a boulder. "My next thing."

Her mother laughed, catching her breath between chuckles. The romance of youth, so wonderful, she thought.

As they crossed the Boulder Field the moraine was a hop-scotch from boulder to massive rock, one after another that had broken from the front cliff of the giant mountain rumbling downward to rest eternally where they walked. Each teetering step was a fall waiting to happen, yet their hiking boots lived up to expectations, gripping nicely when a rock teetered beneath them.

Alex slowed the pace, and they stopped more often now. The stops settled the oxygen in their lungs as the view motivated their determination to continue upward. While they looked down on mammoth valleys and pinnacles, each time they turned to go on, Long's Peak towered immensely above them.

Twenty minutes later, they passed the first of the lingering college boys. Sitting down hill from the Keyhole just below the Agnes Vaille stone hut, the boy so intent on catching Josie's attention sat doubled over on a large pink granite rock, his arms holding his stomach with moans pouring from his mouth.

Josie stopped and knelt, her hand resting on his shoulder. "You okay?"

His face was a slight green.

"Did you puke?" she asked.

His body lurched with an internal convulsion.

"Oh," she stepped away, her hand still resting on his back. "You should slow down, pace yourself." Josie began to move on. "You'll need to give yourself recovery time before you go on. It's the altitude. Let your body adjust, and hydrate." Then she added what experience told her. "Let your body work at the rate it needs oxygen. You can still make it, but you'll need to recover and drink plenty of water before going on."

She left him to his moans, and when the women stopped again, their pace was half the speed it had been below tree line. They were surprised to look back and see they had gone only two hundred yards beyond the nauseated college boy. The altitude now demanded a rest every few minutes for oxygen recovery.

Josie panted, pointed toward the boy. "He thought he was invincible...silly." She raised her eyebrows. "He probably feels bad...a girl telling him...to rest."

"He'll survive..." Alex's grin was hard to distinguish.

Passing through the Keyhole, a giant elliptic of overhanging rock that guided hikers from the north face to the backside of Long's, they found that the mountain had transitioned from elephant-sized boulders to a towering wall rising nearly as far into the sky as it did to a death fall below.

Alex stood for a moment, shoulder to shoulder with Josie, and looked down upon mountains and valleys not seen except from this spot. It reminded her of Sky Pond and the pinnacle of peaks on the untamed side of Rocky Mountain National Park. She felt the rush that pushes hikers onward, and she felt the sense of freedom above it all.

A few hundred feet beyond was a slender ledged stretch of the trail. Two of the college boys stood panting, looking at the narrow passage and the potential of a deathly fall from it. A vertical cliff was on each side of the narrow path, one going straight up, and the other straight down. It would challenge a mountain goat. Alex stood looking, but Josie marched on, smiling at the boys. Her mother quickly followed walking the balance beam with a cautious stride. Their boots gripped and their hiking experience reinforced as they crossed the stretch without incident.

Alex hands rested on her thighs as she turned back to look at the path in the middle of the wall. Standing, she gazed out over the miles of mountains to the south. Since jumping backward off that damn, life-changing cliff years ago, she had ventured on bringing Josie along with her. The last seven years had been a long climb, but she was almost to the top.

"You ready Mom?" Josie's voice was not as breathy.

Alex nodded, looked up, and pulled air into her lungs, "One...last challenge," she said.

Josie did not speak, smiling downward to where the boys stood at the base of the incredibly steep, rock-solid trail that offered three options; an unclimbable wall up, an unsurvivable fall down, and a narrow gauge trail across. Waving, she motioned them upward, grinning. "Come on boys, you can make it."

"Be nice," Alex chastised her daughter.

"Just encouraging," Josie laughed a one-breath laugh.

Cautious, both women slowly traversing the trail along the rocky ledge, winding downward through The Trough, and advancing over The Narrows to the last push, a three hundred foot climb up sheer rock and over patches of glacial ice. Steadily, hand over hand, each foothold tested as they climbed the rock face.

Each arm reach upward pulling them with distinct determination until at 9:12 a.m. they reached the summit standing on top of Long's Peak. Side by side, their hands on their knees, waiting, hoping their breath would balance against the altitude. Slowly, it came to them, and they were able to stand tall and walked without light-headed weaving.

Josie was surprised at the size of the flat top summit. A football field plateau, she wandered for a moment stepping among and over the rocks and uneven surface, her eyes lifting to the blue sky of which she had become a part. Turning slowly in a 360-degree pivot, she saw the world as far as she could see in every direction. Her arms reached outward spanning their full length. She was a slow moving pinwheel on top of the world.

Alex watched her. For this moment, she closed her eyes thanking her father and Mickey. They both had brought her to these mountains.

Josie wandered across the massive plateau working her way to the east wall where she sat a few feet back from the edge, her feet reaching out to the atmosphere. Alex joined her, opened her backpack, and handed Josie an energy bar. They ate in silence, watching the sun brighten Estes Park and the peaks of the Never Summer Range to the west.

Still short of breath, Alex waved her hand toward Estes. "They're watching us... Grandma and...Grandpa."

"Eating breakfast...Like us." Josie gnawed the thick bar.

They looked over the edge down the sheer 2,000-foot cliff to Chasm Lake. In the directness of the early morning sun, the lake was a deep gray, protected most of the day by the shadow of the mountain and still partially frozen.

"This is magnificent, Mom." Josie pointed at an eagle circling far above. "A perfect birthday."

"It was perfect for me with my dad so many years ago. The impression never left me."

Josie grinned, "How could it?" She pointed toward Horseshoe Park and the faint path of Fall River Road. "Someday, this is how I want to live, a part of this." Fluffy clouds drifted by at eye level.

"Yes," Alex thought to her self, "someday."

They stayed on top for an hour eating, hydrating, and recovering. When Alex stood to leave, a young couple, the only others standing above Chasm Lake, offered to take their picture. Alex handed her the phone, and the young man told them to smile. There they stood, the Chadwick women arm and arm. Below were the rolling mountains drifting off to the eastern plains and into Nebraska while behind them, the smattering of white clouds drifted by like pillows in the morning light. The phone clicked the picture with the sky a backdrop, and Alex gave Josie a hug, closing her eyes to feel the moment.

As the couple disappeared, beginning their descent, Josie asked her mother to go on. She would be along soon, she said.

When Alex took the first few steps down from the top, she turned to see her daughter alone on the summit of Long's Peak. Against the blue, Josie's smile broke to laughter, and she raised her arms in triumph jumping in place with her legs pumping up and down. Exhilarated, she reached into the sky and screamed her joy. Alex too smiled, turned, and continued on, leaving her daughter for a few brief moments alone on top of the world.

She waited for Josie at the top of the narrow ridge, patient in the time her daughter needed. Visiting with the college boys who had gained the strength to go on, she told them of the challenge ahead, estimating the time, and offered advice and encouragement. Finally, she explained they would pass Josie as she descended, and to be cautious the last three hundred feet to the summit.

The descent was cautious with easier breathing. Stopping now and then, they looked closely at the small gatherings of flowers growing from shallow clumps of sand among the rocks. Just before they reached the timberline, they saw a lone columbine, perfect blue petals with the purple hues of summer.

The trailhead was a welcome sight 2:20 p.m. Eleven hours and twenty minutes they had hiked. In his aging gait, Hank rushed to greet them, his excitement showing. "You made it."

Josie fell into his arms, giving him a welcome hug. "It was spectacular, Grampy."

On the ride back into town, feet freed from their boots and the socks that had molded to their form, Josie quickly fell asleep. Alex told her father of the climb, and he reminisced about their ascent together so many years ago. At the cottage, Alex and Anne guided their baby to her bed on the porch, then Alex wandered to her bedroom. After a rinsing shower that barely kept her awake, she too found her bed and soon the cottage was quiet.

When Josie woke, she was surprised to see the sun still shining. She rolled sideways with slight discomfort in her legs. The digital clock said seven-twelve. From the porch she could see her grandpa asleep in the recliner, her grandmother the same on the sofa. She eased to stand, allowing her tender feet to adjust. In the hallway bathroom, she took a cleansing shower and washed the grit away. She decided to let her hair dry naturally free, and applied a light layer of make-up, a strong red to her lips.

She put on her favorite necklace, a buckskin leather cord with one full fresh-water pearl and added matching earrings. As always, she admired the anklet of brightly beaded stones and carved peace signs, one her mother had bought her in Steamboat two years before. The white-cupped halter-top and denim A-line skirt accentuated her dark skin with sandaled heels that stretched her legs another three inches. She looked in the mirror, smiling. Her father would go nuts if he saw her in this outfit, perfectly rugged and totally outdoor sensual.

Josie scribbled a note on the post-it beside the telephone. *Went downtown. Back by 11:00. Love.*

Walking the few blocks to downtown Estes, on her phone she searched *Cabelli Estes Park*. A list came up with four in Colorado. One was *Nature's Way Gallery* and another listed an address on Fish Hatchery Road. Her thumbs searched for a map and found Fish Hatchery Road, a short stretch of drive along Fall River Road, just below #57 on the map, Fawn Valley Inn.

At the main downtown intersection, she stood by the trolley stop, waiting and watched the taffy turn in one long glob on the machine in the candy store window.

When the red and green open-air trolley pulled in, she hopped on, surprised there was any spring in her legs. She sat quietly feeling the cool, evening air and wondered if she should have worn something a little warmer. In the trolley turn-around at Fawn Valley Inn, she stepped from the car and walked between the condos. Across Fall River she saw a finely kept log cabin with several cars with a group of people laughing together on a stone patio. She glanced right then left, and saw a small walking bridge just down the hill.

When she reached the front door of the cottage, she pressed the bell waiting nervously. No one came. She wondered if this was his home. If not, surely he was a neighbor, and they could point the way. Listening, she heard people laughing from the riverside patio. She pressed the bell again. This time the door opened, and she stood face to face with Jennifer.

"Josie." Jennifer was surprised. "What're you doing here?"

Startled, she answered. "Mom and I hiked Long's today. It's my sixteenth birthday. Everybody else, Mom and my grandparents, are resting, so I came to say hello to Michael."

Jennifer stepped forward giving a welcome embrace. "Well then, it's good to see you. I'm sure Michael would love to say hello, though he is entertaining."

Josie suddenly felt out of place. "I didn't mean to intrude."

Beyond Jennifer, through the people in the living room, she saw Michael enter from the patio. He closed the sliding glass door behind him, laughing with a sandy-haired man.

He was just as Josie had remembered. The rebel length of too-long hair waved to frame the rugged dark features of his handsome face. Even with the collarless, white gauze shirt, you could see the bulge in his arms and strength of his chest. He was so beautiful. Jeans and leather flip-flops fit his casual, hearty nature.

He looked beyond Jennifer to see who his new guest was, stopping surprised. Realizing he should not be too surprised, his smile grew relaxed as he waved to his young visitor. Walking to the front door, he greeted her with warmth. Gently placing his hand on the small of Josie's back, he guided her through the crowd to the kitchen. There he pulled another beer from the refrigerator, glanced playfully at Josie, and handed her a diet pop. She thanked him feeling even more out-of-place.

"Come on." The sound of his voice comforted her.

Josie followed him, smiling shyly to the friends Michael introduced her too as they passed through the kitchen. He opened the sliding door, following her through and led her to a small table. He was the perfect romantic, she thought, strong and confident.

The sandy-haired man sat at the table, playfully strumming a guitar while the flames of an open fire pit warmed the entire patio. She sat in the chair between Michael and the guitar man, and the confidence of her outfit returned as she crossed her legs before the warmth of the flame.

Michael patted Josie's shoulder, grinning at the other man. "Guess who this is?"

Jimmy still strummed the guitar, looking at the striking features of the young temptress. The eyes were unmistakable. He strummed a few cords, singing. "*The mystic blue in her eyes.*"

Michael smiled.

Jimmy reached his hand from the guitar, Josie gripping it in a cheerful introduction. "For some reason I expected you to be a little girl."

"A young woman," Michael told him. "Aren't you celebrating your sixteenth birthday?"

Blushing a touch, she turned to Jimmy. "Why would you expect me to be a little girl?"

Jimmy struck a few chords, looking helplessly at the fingers working the guitar.

Michael provided cover. "I introduced Jimmy and your mother the other night. I believe it was Tuesday when I ran into her downtown. She mentioned she was here with her *little girl.*" He looked, and Jimmy glanced to his friend nodding agreement. "Jimmy plays in a bar downtown, and your mother and Jennifer stopped in. Actually, they stopped in so Alex could hear Jimmy play. He and Jennifer are madly in love with each other."

"Cool," Josie eyes widened. "Jennifer's great."

"That she is," Jimmy agreed.

Quick to move on, Michael asked her about the hike, and he was thrilled to hear they had reached the summit. He was also amazed to see her out walking around after a day up and down Long's Peak. He asked her about other travels, things she had seen and done. Her descriptions of wilderness adventured caused Michael to remember trips he had taken. Their talk turned casually fun with stories of special moments in the backcountry.

Jimmy kept fiddling with his guitar as they talked, background music to the stories. Josie told Michael she had decided as soon as she finished high school she would begin living a life outdoors. Maybe she would go to college in Boulder or Fort Collins and commute from Estes. She could work summers for the Park Service or become a white water rafting guide. She shared her dreams with the rugged sounds of Fall River raining down from the tundra and past the cabin.

"Keep one eye on the dream and a commitment in your heart," he told her. "That's the achievement of dreams, to continue to believe in yourself and know that one day it will be accomplished. Time is the factor, not if but when."

Michael shared that Jimmy had just resigned from his high school teaching position. After fourteen years, he had signed a songwriter contract with a major Nashville song broker. His songs would soon be on the airways. Sung by the stars, Jimmy was now living on his terms. Michael slapped his buddy's shoulder proudly. His dream had been realized and rewarded.

Josie shook his hand again, congratulating, and felt like she was among the stars. Here she sat with them treating her like a friend. It was exciting and fun, and she couldn't wait to get back and tell Allison. It was the perfect sixteenth birthday, to climb a mountain with her mom, stand on top of the world, and end the day at a party with Michael and a soon-to-be famous friend, warmed by the patio fire and the sound of the rushing mountain stream.

It was still two hours before she said she'd be home, so Josie immediately decided she would stay as long as she could. Michael excused himself for a moment, seeing another guest arriving, and Josie set her pop on the wooden patio table while asking directions to the ladies room. Jimmy, still strumming, directed her through the living room and up the stairs.

Michael returned with two beers and a pop, setting one beer before Jimmy. "Where's Josie?"

"Bathroom," Jimmy said. "She sure has her mother's eyes."

"Yes she does," Michael agreed. "Quite a sixteen-year-old. Intelligent, beautiful, and mature, I think Alex has her hands full."

Jennifer eased through the people onto the patio, her hands rubbing firmly on Jimmy's shoulders. She looked at Michael. "Be careful," she warned him. "I think Josie's got a crush on you."

"She does," nodding at what he already knew. "Don't worry. She's a sweet girl, but I'll create no illusion."

"Where is she?" Jennifer looked around.

Jimmy pointed toward the cabin. "Bathroom," he said.

Jennifer glanced through the patio doors toward the stairway.

"Oh shit," her eyes flared at Michael. "Don't you guys ever think?"

They both looked confused.

Anxious, Jennifer blurted as she turned rushing back into the house, "The White Room."

Josie found the bathroom, funny that it was in Michael's bedroom. She wondered about for a moment, curious. She liked the western motif, the boots sitting beside the closet door. She fiddled with a necklace that lay on his dresser and a sterling silver twisted rope bracelet. He was everywhere in this room, the exact image she had of him and his life. Hearing noise on the stairway, quickly she set the bracelet back in place. Another guest appeared, surprised to see her, and he excused himself into the bathroom.

Three steps down the hallway on the left was a closed door. A guest room, she supposed. Turning the handle, she opened the door a crack. Dark, she reached her fingers for the light and flipped the switch. Brighter than she had expected, Josie flinched with the guilt at intruding. Then she saw the images. The pictures revealed nature all in white. She stepped curiously through the door closing it quietly behind her.

To the left was a large print of three elk striding over the alpine tundra into the sunrise. Bold and beautiful, the velvet of their antlers glowed in the backlight. She turned putting her hands upon a rocking chair she had not realized was there. This image on the opposite wall was one she had seen. The woman she had envied, standing fully naked in the waterfall, the colors of summer and the stillness of the lake. For a moment she imagined being her, the purity of the water rushing chills of excitement over her. She glanced to her left at the image sharing the wall.

Frozen in impossible thought, she stepped closer to the picture. She turned back again to the translucent woman, naked in the falls. Her hand came to her chest as her gaze returned to the final clear image. In the same pool before the falls, standing serene, the woman had wandered waist deep into the frigid water. The naked illusion was of her legs and hips below the surface, her hands tracing the rippling circles of water as they moved away. There was the stark beauty of tranquility in her eyes as her breasts rested just above the surface. Taken back, she had never seen her mother look so beautiful.

Stepping closer, she felt the shock of recognition and confusion in her emotions, yet there was also an envy at the mystery before her. She stared at the image, her mother the woman in the falls? She remembered the story. What were his words, *The only person that has enhanced nature? I shall never sell her image? It is priceless?* She leaned back against the rocking chair, staring at her mother. She had been naked with Michael? When? How could she?

Bewilderment rushed through her. "I want to be naked with Michael," she said out loud.

She looked from her mother back to the translucent image in the falls. Her mother had known Michael before? What had he said? *My friend's life had changed forever.* Those were his words. Stepping away, she gripped her chest, shocked at the realization. Her mother had rappelled off an eighty-foot cliff.

She thought of the cliff they had walked along today, the motherly warnings of not to get too close. Her mother had hiked with Michael, she had jumped off a cliff, and she had been photographed naked in a waterfall. She slumped against the chair.

She had always thought her mother to be beautiful, even daring at times. But this was not right, jumping off cliffs and naked while another man took her picture. Did her father have any idea? Shouldn't her father have recognized her in the picture? Shouldn't he have seen the familiar lines of her body? What was she doing naked with Michael?

She steadied herself and stepped closer to look at her mother's eyes.

They were filled with peace. It was a look she had never seen except in the mountains. Michael had been correct. She was different in this picture. Something had changed her. If Michael asked her mother to hike with him, she would. If he asked her to trust him and rappel from a cliff, she would. But it would be her idea to walk naked into the waters.

Confused, she lowered herself into the rocker seeking balance. She rested her head, and there was a slight sway in her motion. Had her mother's life changed that day, and had she seduced Michael? Had she waded into the pool and become Michael's lover? This was wrong, her mother and Michael. Mothers don't get naked with other men. What had she been doing? She looked again at the naked image. Why did she look so serene? Why had she never seen her mother look so peaceful before?

Startled, the door jarred, pushing open, and her eyes showed the guilt and shock of being caught. Michael stood, his eyes in fear; Jennifer and Jimmy behind him, sorrow over taking their expressions. He stood calmly, motioning his friends, and they backed into the hallway. Michael closed the door between them, and Josie sat back limp in the chair, staring at Michael in disbelief.

He stood looking sideways at the picture on The White Room wall. Michael took two steps and stopped. Bending his knees deeply, he lowered to look up at Josie.

"Can I explain?" he asked.

She bit her lip, looking at the concern in his brown eyes. Afraid and unsure what to do, she simply nodded.

Holding on to the chair arm, he continued looking up at her, this girl he knew to be the most precious thing in Alex's life. This could not be a bad thing in her life. Somehow, he had to take the badness away.

"Angry?" His voice was soft.

She shrugged, unable to look at him.

"I don't know what to say, Josie, but to tell you the truth."

He stood, stepping in front of her, and lowered to the floor, his legs crossed before him. Sitting with his back against the wall, the waterfall image of her mother was above him. Josie's gaze was confused and sad. He chose his words carefully. First, he acknowledged her anger. Then he asked her just to listen, to give him a chance to help her understand.

"I've been through your emotions, Josie, and I know they're happening all at once." His head tilted, looking directly into her eyes. "Life hasn't always been what your mother had planned, but you are the most important thing in her life. You know that?"

Josie almost looked indignant. "Of course I know that, but what's it have to do with these?" Flippantly, her hand gestured toward the wall, anger and confusion intertwined.

His explanation was cautious, deliberate. Her mother had been searching for something, a loss many adults feel. It's natural to go through this, so seven years ago her mother had taken a three-day break in her life. Not to do anything outrageous, that was not her intention. She just wanted a break free of expectations. There were no bad intentions, simply a timeout. It was meant to be a three-day vacation of rest and quiet time. Then their paths had crossed while he photographed elk on Fall River Road. In a reaction, Michael explained, he asked her to join him on a hike. She had gone, expecting a morning walk into the mountains with a new friend.

"I deceived her a bit. She had no idea what the hike would entail." He sat up taller, trying to be strong. "And I had no idea what an incredible woman your mother is. I challenged her to follow me to this waterfall." His hand reached to the framed image. "It's hidden deep within the mountains, away from any trails. I never thought she'd do it." He smiled at the memory. "Think about it. When I met your mother she was an up-tight rich lady whose idea of escape was a plush condo in Estes Park."

With a hint of recognition, Josie's eyes glanced up.

He described for Josie the thoughts that must have fought in Alexandria's mind. If she rappelled off that cliff, it was like you hiking Long's Peak today. She became strong, more confident and capable; her own self worth expanded. If she didn't, she would be admitting some sort of defeat in her life, some acceptance of something deep within her that kept her afraid. Jump and be more, or not and be less. That is what she faced.

"The woman at the top of the cliff never would have walked naked into the lake, into the waterfall. But look at this images, Josie." He stood, Michael's hands rested gently on the back of the rocker. "What do you see in your mother's eyes?"

Josie had already seen it. Serenity, there was peacefulness and joy evident in her eyes. That is what she saw, something she only saw hints of when she was with her mother in the mountains.

Her head down, voice nearly silent, she asked, "But why did she have to be naked?"

"I can't tell you what she needed, why she had to do what she did." His hands rested gently on her shoulders. "Close your eyes for a moment, Josie. Think back to when you were nine, ten years old. Tell me how it was different? What did you and your mother do?"

"We went swimming at The Club."

"How did you dress?"

"In that awful Academy uniform."

"And when you weren't in the uniform?"

"I remember an outfit I always had to wear with my grandparents. It was like a navy uniform. It was dark blue skirt and white blouse with gold stripes and little embroidered anchors everywhere." She shuddered at the memory. "It was pathetic."

"Tell me about school now."

A smile appeared on her face. "I go to public school. It's great, and the kids are so nice and down-to-earth. They lack arrogance."

"Now," he guided her, "when was the first time you remember hiking in the mountains?"

"That fall we went to a ranch by Vail. My mom and I left the group to hike to a waterfall, and I played with the ducks."

"I'm just curious. When did people start calling you Josie?"

Her eyes still closed, she remembered a car ride with her mother. "Mom started calling me that. I remember Daddy got so angry, but I liked it. Only Grandmother and Grandfather Chadwick still call me Josephine."

"You're eyes still closed?"

Slowly, she nodded.

"Your mother changed when these pictures were taken, and it freed your life too. She was so confused with life's expectations, she had forgotten the person she was. And you know who she is, Josie."

He moved back around the chair. Josie had transformed back into a little girl with frightened eyes and flush red cheeks.

"She's a mother who allowed you to choose. To choose between the Club or a hike in the mountains, to choose between an Academy uniform or blue jeans, sweatshirts, and public school."

A slight happiness appeared in her eyes, and Josie looked above Mickey at the images.

"Your mother let you choose. She introduced you to a world of nature; hiking, wildlife and camping, things you might never have known. And she let you choose who you would be, Josephine or Josie." He stooped before her again. "What your mother has allowed you over the past seven years is what reawakened in her when she rappelled off that cliff. You had seven years to adjust. She had seconds when she rappelled eighty feet down into the forest. You have celebrated it as a part of your life for years. Alex only had an instant to prepare for the change. So she reacted."

He searched her eyes, and she looked back at him understanding. It didn't seem so bad when Michael explained it.

"She reacted, Josie." His gestures simplified things. "When that sense of freedom you've built over seven years overwhelmed her in a matter of seconds, she freed herself by walking naked into the lake. Symbolic? Maybe? I believe it was much deeper than that, but only your mom truly knows."

Josie looked at the images before her. There was tranquility. She wanted to believe her mother's eyes. "She's so beautiful."

"Amazing," he nodded. "I just happened to be there with a camera."

She looked into Michael eyes. "Are you in love with her?"

"I'm in love with these images. They are of Alex, but Alex sacrificed this freedom for you and your father, and she has lived the past seven years as Alexandria." Michael acknowledged a slight sadness. "I told the truth at the showing. Your mother left two days after these pictures were taken. I didn't know who she was or where she lived. Until the showing I hadn't seen her since those three days years ago. I only knew she had a daughter she had committed her life to. You are her reward."

Michael stood, lifting her hands, and Josie stood before him.

"I suppose," she tried to be mature, "this kind of eliminates any fantasies I had about you and me."

"That's quite a compliment from a beautiful young lady." His smile spoke as a man to a young girl.

The steady, eerie squeaking of the door handle distracted them. They turned to see the door open slowly, and Alex stepped halfway through, fear in her eyes. Mickey raised his hand, calming. Alex turned to look past the door at the two images. Her head dropped as her hands lifted to cover the slight gasp escaping from her, and she began to cry. Mickey started for her, but Josie held him firm. Then she went to her mother.

"I never wanted you to know." Alex's tears continued, and Josie wrapped her arms around her mother holding her tightly.

Mickey moved by the two women, his hand resting for a moment on Alex's shoulder. With no reaction from Alex, he stepped through the door, leaving them as alone with the images in The White Room.

The rain started on Friday afternoon. Predicted for Saturday, it arrived a day early. Alex and Josie sat on the cottage porch, cool breezes accompanying the torrential downpour. Josie had just begun to talk again. She had never seemed angry, simply sullen and withdrawn. Alex had been waiting patiently giving her time while fearing her questions.

In a childlike voice, her daughter whispered, "Is Michael why you and Daddy are having problems?"

Alex sat on the hide-a-bed facing her daughter, a cup of hot tea resting in her hands. She had committed to being honest, but was her little girl ready? She wasn't sure, but she had to trust her.

"No, Honey," Alex told her. "Your Dad and I, well, we were struggling long before Michael and, I'm sorry, but those struggles have continued."

Barely audible, Josie answered, "I know."

Alexandria began to share with her daughter, talking about her life with William. Not that it was bad, but it was different from what she needed. Image too had its limits. Life had not been happy between William and her for many years, even before she met Michael or rappelled down the cliff. He was not a bad man, and she was not a bad woman, but their needs and expectations were different. He was image and power, she was emotions and relationship, and the two, at times, seemed to be like oil and water. They could fill the same bucket but never truly mix.

Needing surety, she asked again, "So Michael's not responsible?"

Alex reassured her. "No. But he is responsible for the reawakening in my life, and he is responsible for my mind knowing there is more to life than image. Michael didn't create the problems. Meeting him simply made her aware of options, and he did that without deliberate intent." Alex shifted the hot tea. "What you saw in The White Room," she looked at her daughter, but Josie would not look back, "that was a days hike in the mountains seven years ago. Until the showing at The Club, I had not seen or talked to Michael for seven years."

Her daughter continued staring straight ahead through the window toward the mountains.

"Don't blame Michael, honey." She turned the warm mug in her hands. "He could have followed me seven years ago. He could have made a mess at the showing. He could have done so many things, but he didn't. When I walked away, I asked him not to follow. He didn't. There is nothing to blame him for."

Josie sat curled up on the sofa bed watching the constant streaks of rain pour down the window. "I went over there a stupid little girl. I thought maybe he might like me."

The mother in her felt fear, yet Alex leaned forward toward her daughter wrapping her arms around her shoulder and pulling her safely to her. "I know Michael. First, I have no doubts he has great respect for the beautiful, good-hearted woman you will someday be. I also know he is honorable, and he would not have taken advantage of your youth."

"Did I look stupid?" She asked with a sixteen-year-old's fear.

"Actually," Much to Alex's dismay, "you looked pretty hot. In fact, I forbid you to wear that outfit again until you're over thirty."

Josie's confident glance and smile added to her mother's worries.

"Dear," she said in a serious voice. "Know the power of your beauty, but always think with your heart, never your ego. That way good decisions will be made and beauty not misused."

Josie rested her head on her mother's shoulder, sitting silently.

Later that evening after Josie had finally gone to sleep, Alex telephoned Mickey from the bedroom. Through his many apologies and questions of concern, she managed to use the rain as an excuse. She would not see him in the morning. She would not go up the hill to the top of Fall River Road. The next morning she would hug her parents good-bye, and Alexandria and her daughter would drive back to Denver for the Chadwick celebration of Josephine's sixteenth birthday.

The eerie quiet of the drive down to Denver caused Alexandria to feel the pain. Just past Lyons, Josie finally spoke.

"I don't like this." Even though she was looking away, watching the trees through the rain-streaked window, Alexandria knew her daughter was crying. "Michael's great, but you're my mother and Daddy's daddy. I don't like knowing about this."

Josie was quiet the rest of the way home.

Chapter 62

Josie wore the dress she had allowed her Grandmother to select on their shopping outing. It was sweet and mature and made her look like she was a strong girl in black heels with a slight gold trim. Josie thought of her own two worlds, and realized that she'd already developed them. Tonight she was Josephine, a nice girl formally dressed and with a future of money and prestige, but she knew that wasn't her destiny.

The Debutante Ball was all her grandmother wanted it to be. She paraded Josephine around with introductions and embarrassing compliments to people Josephine had known all of her life. With each fully accented smile, she wanted to scream every time someone else told her how grown up she looked. But she did well. Over the years, she had attended other parties put on by other parent's for their daughter's sixteenth birthday. While they had seemed glamorous at the time, she found this embarrassing. Her grandmother only accentuated that feeling, but Josie performed well as a perfect Chadwick woman. She was grace and gracious, all smiles and elegantly sixteen.

At the height of the evening, in her grandmother's glory and her grandfather's joy, they stopped the band and cleared the dance floor, leading the crowd through the foyer to the grand entryway. Requesting that she hide her eyes, her mother smiled patiently and signaled for her to do so. Her father nodded to play along, so she covered her eyes, uncomfortable with the dramatic attention.

Her grandparents led her and the guests through the mansion entrance and down the full front stairs onto the red brick drive that circled the fountain and connected the Chadwick estate to the road a hundred yards away. While the rain had halted momentarily, the bricks were a deep, wet red and puddles sprinkled the drive. There was a dramatic announcement by her grandfather to quiet the crowd, and as the hush fell around them, her grandmother kissed Josephine's check and whispered, "You can open your eyes now."

In the middle of the drive sat a pearl white BMW coupe with a giant red ribbon wrapped fully around it, the bow covering the entire hood. Josephine provided all the squeals and theatrics a sixteen year old has built up anticipating her first car. She bounced in the driver's seat, turned the radio up loud, and opened and closed the sunroof three times. Everybody made a show, hugging her, telling her how lucky she was, and she readily agreed.

When the hoopla had settled, and she had inspected the car with all of the zest required, the guests began moving inside. Josephine hugged her father and grandparents, thanking them for their big surprise making sure she overemphasized both how surprised she was and how much she loved the BMW. Her father hugged her tight, afraid that letting go would be just that.

As she walked up the stairs past the colonnades, she grabbed her mother's arm, leaning close with a sad acceptance in her eyes, "I'm beginning to understand, Mom. This is so manufactured." Then she pulled closer and whispered, "When I'm eighteen, can I trade it for a Jeep Wrangler?"

Still looking straight ahead, Alex nodded absolute approval.

That night behind the closed doors of the den, Alexandria told William about The White Room. He listened quietly, stern anger building in his eyes.

Yes, Josie knew about her and Michael. Apologies seemed to have no effect. He was angry. He held his temper, but she still feared him. She left him with final words, repeating how sorry she was and acknowledged that it was her fault. She was wrong to have brought Michael into their lives. Without a word from William, she walked away to escape the rage not yet released.

That night she slept alone to the restless crashes of thunder. The lightening threatened in ominous white flashes through the windows of her bedroom as the rain poured incessantly.

Chapter 63

Alex could care less if she had to walk in the rain. She wore her hair in a ponytail through the gap in her purple nylon ball cap that matched her new waterproof Columbia pullover with jeans and Gore-Tex hiking boots. When it rains, dress to be in the rain. She walked defiantly from her car to the office building, appreciating the freshness in the damp air and humored at those passing on tip-toed heels under oversized umbrellas.

The mug she picked that day was the Roadrunner, telling Brandon. "William's the cartoon coyote, and the anvil is falling."

Dressed down with little make-up, she sat before him without a hint of the status she held. Her eyes were quiet and determined; her stature tall. So poised, she was a woman Brandon had grown to appreciate.

He mentally shook himself back to business. "That's not the way he sees it. He holds a lot of cards in this game."

"That's his mistake. He thinks I want to win the game. He doesn't realize I just don't want to play anymore." Her look was firm. "He can't win if I don't play."

Brandon sat Yosemite Sam on the coffee table. "Listen Alex. You hired me to represent your best interests, and I feel obligated to do just that. You can come out of this in amazing financial shape. In fact, you'll be incredibly wealthy even if I'm the most incompetent of attorneys, which, by the way, I am not. There's just that much money there, but you have to be patient. Give me time to get you what is rightfully yours."

She turned the cartoon coyote in her hand, staring down into the face of the mug.

"I'm tired, Brandon. I'm tired of waiting, I'm tired of feeling submissive, and I'm tired of living this Chadwick illusion. Work something out." It was simple in her mind, and she was confident in her decision. "You know what I need. You know what I legally deserve. There's a big gap in between the two. Find the magic number in that gap. Negotiate with concessions in mind, and let's end this game."

"I can, but they threw us a curve this morning."

Alexandria glared at Brandon. "So, let me guess. Michael."

"A Michael Cabelli, to be exact."

Alex thought for a moment, knowing she'd brought this on herself. "What'd your investigator find out?"

"In New York?"

Alex nodded.

"I'm afraid she's a high priced call girl." Brandon looked sadly into his cup. "Felicity. We don't know her real name yet, but we know the agency. It's just a matter of time before we get the information."

"Okay," she echoed. "A hooker."

"Call girl." Brandon corrected.

"The agency?"

"Executive Escorts of Manhattan."

Suddenly Alex felt dirty.

He called her back early the next morning. As she listened in on the cell phone, she watched the steady down pour falling against the balcony doors of her bedroom. She heard his words, her head shaking in despair.

"Why is he being such an ass?"

"Leopard's spots," Brandon said. "Claiming adultery gives him power and muddles your reputation in the process."

Anger swelled in her mind. "I'll get back to you," she said.

She hung up, immediately punching the speed dial to William's office. Valerie answered, offering predetermined resistance as William, in all probability, had instructed.

"This is not a request, Valerie." Alex's directness unnerved her. "Put me through. Now please."

There was silence on the wire as Valerie put her on hold. Alex waited, her foot tapping quietly on the bedroom carpet. Finally, a click from the other end and a familiar hush was heard on the line.

"William?" She waited. The next one to talk loses. Why would a husband and wife play such manipulation games? It irritated her. Finally, she heard a heavy breath.

"What?" There was distain in his voice.

"William," she breathed in. "You are too good at these games, but this is not a game. This is our life. More importantly, this is Josie's life. The one thing we've had a degree of success with is an effort to talk to each other. There were a lot of Thursday evenings where we actually did. Now, when we should be talking the most, when our lives are coming apart, we've turned the whole thing over to attorneys." Her voice rose, "They don't know how precious Josie is and are manipulating our lives. God, I hate this William. I hate legal strategy as if one of us is meant to lose."

"You cheated, damn it." Vehemence filled his tone. "You didn't play fair." She could envision the arrogance in his smug grin.

"We've been there, and we both know the truth, William. We both know why you spent so much time in New York and who you spend time with, but I don't want any of this to become a public issue." Her words were unmoving. "William, our marriage is over, so let's end this with a little dignity." She took a deep breath masking the despair. "You know I don't want to strip you of the family fortune. I have no interest in making this a financial mess, so let's you and I sit down and talk this out. Let's get the attorneys out of this and act like two adults who still care for and respect each other and love our daughter. Can't we trust our own good intentions not to make this worse?"

"You fucked that up with Michael Cabelli."

"Oh Jesus, William. You know better than that." She took a deep, calming breath.

"You wiped out eighteen years of trust with your naked jaunt into the waterfalls."

"Yes, William. I made a mistake. I wish I hadn't, but you want to focus on an act when we both know our marriage is the issue. I swam naked, and there's a picture. You can be angry about that, I can be angry about New York and the woman you've spend time with, but that is not why our marriage has failed. Take the waterfall out of our lives, and we're still having a conversation about the failure of our marriage."

"I don't know that, Alexandria." he said obstinate.

"Yes you do, or you wouldn't have paid for a call girl."

His voice rose angry. "I have no idea what you're talking about."

"Okay, keep playing innocent." She spat back. "We can come to a quick settlement, end this agony, and you can pretend Michael's the issue. The other option is I put Executive Escorts of Manhattan, the Executive Town Car limousine driver, the Esquire Hotel desk clerk, and Felicity on the witness stand." She heard his slight gasp. "If that's the game you want to play, then keep playing, but know I have dates, details and witnesses."

The silence was deafening until she finally hung-up.

She heard the scream from down the hall, "Mom!"

Alex sat on the edge of her bed, her phone dangling in her hand where her arms hung limp. A crack of thunder startled her, and she heard Josie calling again. The scream grew louder with Josie's footsteps running frantically toward her room.

"Mom!" She burst through the doors, rushed past her mother, grabbed the remote control, and pointed it at the T.V.

The fear in Josie's eyes frightened Alex. "What's wrong?"

Josie gasp for breathe. "The news," she fought for air. "The local news, a special report on the T.V. There's been a flash flood in Estes."

They both froze, listening to the calm words of the anchorwoman. Information is still coming in, but first reports are an early morning flash flood has crashed through downtown Estes Park sending thousands of residents scurrying up the mountainsides to safety. The picture flipped to a live remote in Estes. A young man in a suit sat with hair blowing disheveled in a helicopter door. The camera shifted from him to a sky view of Elkhorn Avenue.

An emergency call had been made by satellite phone, he said, to the Rocky Mountain National Park Emergency line. The caller, nationally known Wildlife Photographer Michael Cabelli, may have saved thousands of lives when the Lawn Lake Dam broke high above Estes Park in Rocky Mountain National Park just past sunrise. Cabelli, in the park and closest to the lake when the dam broke, has not been heard from since.

The reporter talked on, the whirl of the helicopter pounding in the background as the two women stared stunned at the T.V. The image below was of a black river, raging with the downtown store fronts as its banks. Cars bounced past in the waves; trees, debris, and an RV washed down the mucky sludge of Elkhorn Avenue.

Alex was in her closet, a pair of jeans pulled from a drawer. She grabbed a spandex tank top, t-shirt, her pullover jacket and purple hat. Josie stood in the doorway and reached for her mom's hiking boots under a shelf. Alex dressed frantically, and rushed past Josie in the closet doorway. She stopped in the middle of the bedroom, looking around as if lost, not knowing what to do next. Josie handed her mother her waist pack and boots. Alex stopped and fear filled their stares.

Her daughter pushed her toward the door. "He's all right. I know he's all right. Now go Mom. Go."

"Your father?" She could not think.

"Go," Josie's voice was frantic. "I'll handle Daddy."

Alex stopped thinking with her mind. She had to get to Estes.

Valerie knocked, and William approved her entry with one word. She opened the door, walking across the plush maroon carpet to face her boss, still upset from the phone call.

"I just heard something," she said, "but I haven't verified it."

His irritation grew, not at her but at rumors that always seemed to be about. "What now?"

"Apparently there has been a flash flood in Estes Park. Pretty bad." She waited for his attention. "Your photographer friend, Michael Cabelli. He may have been caught in it. He's missing."

He'd managed to build a solid, distasteful resentment for the man, yet the news set him back. And then he realized, despite his spiteful thoughts his stomach turned in fear for Michael and what this might mean.

He stood, hastened past Valerie. "I've got to go home. Handle or cancel my appointments. If you need me call my cell phone."

Tension clinched his jaw. Even if he didn't survive, it had the same impact. Their marriage was over.

He was out the door and gone.

Before she reached Boulder, Alex called Jennifer's cell phone, but nothing was going through, so she tried the gallery landline. With the flooding, she hadn't expected an answer. She kept calling before she reached the scattered reception in the mountains and then a sudden answer.

Relieved to hear her friend's voice, "Any word?" she pleaded.

"Oh God, Alex." She was obviously shaken. "We don't know what's happened. We're just down off the side of the mountain. We barely escaped. Jimmy and I are fine, but his condo building, the lower level has been wiped out. The gallery is waist deep in muck and the contents destroyed."

Alex stared shocked, looking straight up the highway beginning to rise into the foothills. "You don't know?"

"Know what?"

"Mickey?"

"Oh my God, Michael," Jennifer shuddered in terror. "His cabin's on Fall River." Jimmy held Jennifer close. "Alex, he must have been directly in the path. We'll get out there as soon as we can."

Alex took a deep breath. "On the news. You haven't heard the news reports. Mickey was near Lawn Lake. He called in the dam break. That's why you got above the flood. Mickey was there and called it in when it broke."

Jimmy gripped Jenny's waist as her legs wobbled. He took the phone. "Alex?"

She repeated what she had told Jennifer. "The news reports said Mickey called it in, the dam break on his satellite phone. He must have been working in the park." For a moment both were silent. "Nobody has heard from him since."

Jimmy stopped, holding Jennifer standing deep in mud.

The phone crackled as Alex's car entered a narrow canyon. "I'll be there in forty-five minutes."

The front door flung open as William raced up the steps calling Alexandria's name. Josie met him at the top of the stairs, her eyes red with fear.

"Your mother?"

She blinked against the redness. "She's already gone."

"To Estes?"

His daughter stood strong, tears running down her cheeks.

William gripped the stair railing as his shoulder fell against the wall. He was too late. The anxiety swept through him, feeling the loss as his own eyes fought tears. When was the last time he had cried? As a teenager, he remembered. A friend had died in a vicious car crash. So long, had he become so hardened he'd forgotten how to cry, callous disregard of emotion?

His body twisted, lowering to sit on the top stair. His voice was short of breath. "Any word?"

"You heard?" Josie's voice was soft.

Her father nodded. "Any word on Michael?"

Josie shook her head feeling helpless. She lowered her face into her hands. Emotion was the only thing she felt, fear for her family and Michael. All confused, she stared into her own hands.

"She's gone?" He knew he was wrong to hope that she would not go.

"You waited too long, Daddy." Josie's heart was breaking as she looked at her father. "I love you, and I love that you're my father. But..." tears overflowed her young eyes, "you didn't pay attention. Now Michael could be gone, and Mom's terrified."

He pushed himself to stand, still balancing against the banister. William turned to see the pain in his daughter's face.

"Are you okay, Honey?" He reached pulling her close to him.

"I know you hate him Daddy, but Michael is a great guy. I just want him to be okay. I want Mom to be happy again, and I don't want you to be angry anymore. I hate this, and it's gone on all my life. I'm afraid for Michael and Mom and you, and I don't want to hurt anymore. I want it to stop, Daddy. I want us to be happy, and I don't think that can happen without Michael. I'm sorry Daddy. I love you. But that's what I believe, and that's why I'm afraid."

From the step below Josie, he looked up into his daughter. "When is the last time I told you how much I love you?"

Through the dampness on her cheeks, a smile spread across her face. "I think that's another thing you've forgot about."

His eyes diverted from her. "Sometimes I get so wrapped up in the bank and business." He tried to focus on what he should do. "I love you. Don't ever doubt that, Honey. I know I've lost sight, and I'm sorry. But please, know that I love you with all my heart." His lips pressed against her forehead. "I've misjudged our lives, your mother's life. I'm sorry." He glanced down. "And now this."

Her father looked beyond her, his eyes on the French doors that led to the master bedroom. Never had anything in his life been so out of control.

"I let it all slip away," he said, "and she's gone."

"Daddy?" Josie wrapped her arms around her father's neck. "For Mom's sake, Michael has to be okay."

He nodded, his face next to hers. "What should I do?"

Josie pressed her hands over his face.

"What should we do?" Her words were even more helpless.

William stared at the unique blue in her frightened eyes. Below him, the marble foyer stood empty, the front door still standing open. He shook his head. "Jennifer?"

Josie shrugged, "I haven't heard."

"He's that important?" The emotion swelled in his eyes. "That's why your mother went there?"

Josie stared down the staircase. "She went to help. It's Michael, yes. But it's Jennifer and Jimmy and Estes Park. She's alive there, Daddy. She went to help, to save her friends and herself."

"Not just for Michael?"

Tears again welled up in her eyes. "Yes, for Michael, definitely for Michael and for Jennifer and for Estes Park. You don't know what it means to her. This is Michael, but it is so much more than Michael. She's not running from you, Daddy. She's running to Estes Park. It's been the most important place in her life since she was my age. It's her home, and it's been destroyed." Her eyes filled with fear. "Mom rush home to help her friends."

"If I had your mother's qualities, we'd go too?"

"Mom was out the door before she could think."

He nodded, "Okay."

Suddenly, she stood, turning to run down the hallway toward her bedroom, calling back. "I'll be ready in five minutes."

William watched her wondering how many times he hadn't been there for Alexandria and his daughter. Guilt pressed deep in his chest. Where were his boots? Determination rushed through him, to do something right among so many wrong feelings. The boots, not worn in years were surely still hidden somewhere in his closet. What else would he need?

Chapter 64

Alex was able to get to the fairgrounds south of Lake Estes. Immediately, the damage was evident even in the wider expanse around the lake. Hotels and buildings on the north side showed watermarks of mud halfway up their siding, trees not already taken down or ripped from the ground held debris high up in the branches, and the lake was twice it's size filled with floating objects meant for someone's garage. Small boats were trolling the lake, pulling out trees and rubbish, keeping the wreckage from damaging the Lake Estes dam, she thought, saving the canyon from a greater flood that would wipeout everything from Estes to Loveland.

The eight blocks to Elkhorn Avenue was a run of devastation. Alex slogged through the ankle deep mud on the sidewalks past people fighting away the shock. Some had already, determinedly, begun to clean the foot thick layer of dense muck from their stores. Using snow shovels, they swept the mud, slime, and rocks from the ruined linoleum. Others stood by in helpless shock, bewildered tears in their eyes as they tried to conceive where to begin the clean up of their defiled lives.

Alex stopped long enough to look through the doorway of Lonigan's. The sunken bar area was a wading pool with a carpeted bottom of settling silt. She moved on, hesitating at what she might find. When she stopped, she peered through where the window had been in Nature's Way. The gallery was a mixture of mud, broken glass, and twisted frames ripped from the walls and slammed around the room in what must have been a swirling hurricane of water. Everything in the room was total devastation.

Jennifer was standing in the middle of the gallery, a broken picture frame in her hand, staring as if she didn't know what to do. Jimmy was the first to hear Alex call her name, and she rushed to greet him needing to hold him.

"It was a flash flood, a wall of water from Lawn Lake and a lake in between," he said. "Our condo's three stories up, so it was spared but the lower part of the building, well, the whole place may have to come down."

Alex turned, and she and Jennifer embraced.

"Any word?" she asked.

Jennifer held tighter, her head swaying back and forth.

Jimmy put his hand on Alex's shoulder. "The road's still blocked, and we have no word from the park. Rumors are he called in from part way up the mountain. Probably taking pictures of the bighorn lambs just being born. Who knows what's happened to him. He could have been well away from the actual surge. He's probably just caught between where he was and Horseshoe Park. The bridge is wiped out, and the rangers might not even be in there yet. He's a survivor. We've just got to remember that."

Just south of Estes Park, the State Patrol established a roadblock to turn back the long line of cars. Some were sightseers or demented adventurers, a few probably thieves looking to loot, but most were seeking a chance to help. William pressed his finger to his lips, silencing Josie. He put his car in park as the person in front of him turned their's around and headed back down Highway 36. William stepped out, walking forward to the officer. He reached out to shake the man's hand, handing him his identification.

"Trooper," he looked at the nametag above the badge. "Trooper Abbott, I'm William Chadwick."

His eyebrows raised as the officer looked at the identification, recognizing the name.

"Is the State Patrol Director in Estes Park?" He asked, adding the director's name, emphasizing they were on a first name basis.

"I don't believe so," the officer stated, "but we're in contact."

"Trooper Abbott, I certainly understand your need for safety. In actuality, I appreciate it because our bank has several high profile holdings in Estes Park. In fact, some of those may have been directly in the path of the flood." He looked past the officer, his face exaggerating his concern. "It's of such importance that I decided I had to survey the damage myself and provide any help I can. It's vital that I get into town to secure the property as well as protect our bank assets."

Trooper Abbott, blond and still showing hints of pimples, seemed to agree. "I understand, Mr. Chadwick, but at this point we're not letting anyone in."

"Of course," William looked even more forlorned. "If you would please, just have the officer in charge contact your director by radio. I'm sure he'll approve my entrance. He's aware of the Chadwick financial holdings in Estes and as an owner, I must be allowed access. I'm sure you understand as the director will."

The young officer nodded, returning the identification to Mr. Chadwick. He reached his hand for the radio, trying to decide which of his superiors to contact.

"You are letting property owners in, aren't you?" William taped his license against his palm.

The young trooper fiddled with his hand on the radio as William stared at him, his lips pressed together. His eyes held the trooper's, unmoving with an intensity of expectation.

Trooper Abbott nodded his understanding. "Move your car quickly through the barricade, sir."

"Thank you," he reached out to shake Trooper Abbott's hand. "You are a man of good judgment."

William jogged back to the Lexus, and Josie watched amazed as they drove past the trooper holding the barricade.

Jimmy and Alex were just rounding the corner up Bighorn Drive when she heard Josie calling. Turning, searching for her daughter's voice, she first saw William lumbering across the muddy street in a half wading run, splattering mud with each step. Then she saw Josie close behind waving frantically.

Before she could speak, William, breathless asked, "Any word on Michael?"

When her eyes turned down, William reached out his hand to Jimmy. "I'm William, William Chadwick." He shook Jimmy's hand. "We're here to help."

Alexandria stared at her husband in disbelief. Josie nodded to her mouthing the words *It's okay*.

"William, we can use all of the help we can get. I'm Jimmy." Nodding hello to Josie. "We're heading up to a friend's house to see if we can get a four-wheel drive, possibly get closer to the park or at least Michael's cabin."

William nodded concern.

Jimmy motioned for them to follow, and he headed up the hill. "If we have to search, we may need you."

On Highway 34, the borrowed SUV moved without comment from the occupants. They studied the destruction, the scenic beauty, homes and businesses now in flat and muddy ruin. At Nicky's Restaurant and Resort, a hairy man was clearing the road with a Bobcat. A pile of mud oozed and fallen boulders sat spilling out onto the highway. A moment later the Bobcat stopped in the parking lot muck, and the hairy driver ran toward the Cherokee putting his tattooed arms on the open window.

"Is Michael okay?" He ducked his head down, his eyes looking directly at Alex.

William's face twisted at the disheveled, unpleasant man.

"No word," Jimmy said. "We're trying to get as close as we can to begin searching."

Ralph reached back opening the door next to Josie.

"Scoot over." He gave a toothy grin, jumping in as the girl scooted toward her father. His boots splashed a stench of mud on the carpet and seat. "The rangers have been through from the park entrance to the bridge at Horseshoe Park with snow plows. The bridge is out there, and the turn to Fall River Road is completely blocked by boulders. My guess is we can get within a half mile of the Lawn Lake Trailhead."

Just before Fawn Valley Inn, Jimmy began to slow the Cherokee. William watched the other occupants lean toward the driver's window, straining to see into the valley below. The Jeep stopped in the middle of the road, and Jimmy stepped out as did Ralph. Alex sat, her eyes blankly watching the windshield. Jimmy and Ralph stood on the other side of the road, pointing as they talked. When they returned to the SUV, they did not speak.

As the park entrance came into view, Jimmy reached over resting his hand on Alex's thigh. "The cabin took a direct hit. The patio and kitchen were gone. Being at the curve of the river, the kitchen took the blow first. The rest is probably just water damage. We'll stabilize it, clean it up, and build a new kitchen." Then quietly, he added, "No sign of the Jeep."

William turned to Josie, leaning close.

"Michael's cabin," was all she whispered, her head down.

At the park entrance, the ranger huts were wiped out. There was nothing there but foundation and ripped up sections of blacktop. Jimmy tried to make light. "I guess I don't need my park pass." Nobody laughed.

"This is where the second dam broke." Ralph pointed his tattooed arm out the window toward the campground.

Alex turned, and William and Josie could see the shocked expressions. "The second dam?" Distraught sounds filled her words.

"There was a lake there and a small dam." Ralph continued, pointing into the meadow. "Freeland Stanley built it to power his hotel before the park was a park. About a 12-acre lake, the dam couldn't handle the pressure of the flood from Lawn Lake. It crumbled in mass. It's water and the Lawn Lake water released into the valley all at once."

"That was a lake?" William said seeing the muck, glacier boulders, and debris now cluttered over the black meadow.

"It was," Ralph acknowledged.

The s-curve climbed to Horseshoe Park. Jimmy slowed, while the others did not understand. The meadow of Aspen sat largely undisturbed. Jimmy envisioned one of Michael's earliest limited editions, the first one to be retired. He took it at Easter his first winter here. A fresh snow of eight inches had blanketed the Aspen grove. From this spot on the road, Michael had taken the picture. Jimmy had tagged along, standing, watching, and thinking to himself what a nice little picture it would be. He had not seen it, not until Michael had released the image to the public. The grove of white trees had created a depth, drawing the viewer's eyes down a magnificently pure tunnel of snowy Aspen to the radiance of morning sun gathering in the distance.

Jimmy drove on, a water line of wreckage on the nearby trees. Then Alex grabbed his forearm. Jimmy hit the brakes, and Ralph pushed his head through the open window. From his seat on the opposite side, William could see it. The yellow Jeep rested mangled, forced into the wedge of lodge pole pines on the edge of Horseshoe Park. In silence, the SUV stopped, and they all knew it was Michael's. Tears rolled down Josie's cheeks, and William reached his arm around her, pulling her closer. Impulsively, his hand reached forward and held Alexandria's shoulder.

The rangers had the road blocked just past the wildlife observation pullout. Jimmy turned the truck into the pullout where national park emergency vehicles were gathered. Ralph hopped out, jogging over to the group of rangers. The others stepped out, looking across the normally summer meadow, a grazing land of green and winding streams used by the bighorn sheep. Now a deep, ugly brown, it was washed flat and desolate with the carcass of a young bull elk caught between two trees.

The curve that divided Horseshoe Park from Fall River Road was mostly washed away, and the concrete and timber bridge had disappeared replaced by a gaping, empty hole three times as wide as the bridge had been.

William walked to the interpretive display, looking at the diagram of the meadow. A second map showed the mountains behind him. He scanned the image, finding Lawn Lake. With his finger he traced the path of the stream down to where it flowed into Fall River and the meadow of Horseshoe Park.

Ralph walked back to the group. "There's too much damage to drive on. Boulders and shit all over. Besides, the bridge is gone. They're leaving in a few minutes to take a survey and rescue team up through the flood path. They'll search for Michael as they go. There's no other word."

Josie stood quietly, looking back up the mountain on the other side of the road. Their eyes followed hers. Seventy-five yards up the mountainside, the herd of bighorn sheep began to appear. Stopping, nervously prancing about their rock perches, the sheep looked down upon the transformed meadow. Rams stood boldly, chest pressed forward over the stone ledges. Ewes echoed sounds of distress, their lambs beside them imitating their mother's call. There was nowhere for them to go. Their meadow was now a desert of mud, and the sheep ponds had become bowls of muck and silt.

With the others watching helplessly, William walked back to the tourist map. He waved at the tattooed man, and Ralph walked over to see what he was pointing at.

"What's this?"

Ralph shrugged. "Looks like a cut off stream."

"It's halfway up to Lawn Lake." William's finger followed the map. "Did it flood?"

Ralph brushed his mud-caked hand through his beard. He turned and looked back up the mountainside. "Must have caught some of the gush." He pointed down toward where the curve in the road began. "It comes out down there."

William pointed back toward the sheep still pacing disturbed on the rocky slope. "If Michael was trying to get their pictures, and he was close enough to hear the flood? Maybe he wasn't in the direct path. Maybe he was somewhere along here." He ran his soft hand along the parallel line of the stream on the map.

"Possible," the hairy face bobbed up and down.

"Where's the rescue team going up?"

Ralph pointed on the map, his finger running up the mountain along the direct path of the flood.

William turned toward the peak, pointing again at the map. "If the rescue team is going this way, we can take another route up toward where the sheep came from. Maybe we'll get lucky."

Ralph shrugged, "There's not much chance."

"A chance then?"

"What the hell?" Ralph thought. "We'd be a second search group meeting the rangers here." He stabbed a dirt caked fingernail on the map. "It's the only other way, so it's worth a try."

William called back to the others. "You go ahead with the search team. Ralph and I are going this way," he pointed toward the sheep, "and we'll meet you halfway up."

The two men walked toward the ranger group. One wearing khaki designer slacks and a golfing shirt in contrast to the other's disheveled hair and holey, mud splattered jeans; his body covered in artwork. Ralph stopped at a ranger support vehicle, and when he stepped away, he carried two small bottles of purified water. Somewhere in his mind, William knew water was essential.

William was shocked at how quickly his lungs failed him. As Ralph hiked straight up the terrain, William struggled behind him to keep enough breath to move on. Every few feet he seemed to stop, and when he did Ralph moved farther ahead.

By the time he reached the turn in the stream, his legs were wobbly, and Ralph was long out of sight. It was rugged walking without a trail over mountain terrain. Every few steps he stopped, replenished his oxygen with deep breaths, then trudged on.

Hints of damage began to show along the edge of the stream. Bunches of wildflowers lay flat on the ground, all swept in the same direction. The stream William knew must normally be pure was now a dull, milky-brown. He stumbled, his foot slipping into the ice-cold flow. He yanked it back from the cold surge, pushed his hand against the bank to stand. His hand was covered with bits of sharp rock, wood fragments, and indentations drawing hints of blood. Brushing the flakes away, he wondered if he was lost. He couldn't breathe and had no idea where he was going.

Out of his element, he seemed to be a clumsy misfit. Ralph, the muddy, tattooed man had long disappeared. There was not a trail, just a steep stream bank to follow with the beginning remains of splintered pines, twisted Aspen, and displaced boulders. His hand was cut, his boots heavy and wet. He stopped again. He was always stopping, wanting to breathe. Fatigued in the altitude, he had always thought himself to be healthy.

The rescue crew allowed them to follow to the base of the stream. Insisting that it was not safe for civilians to go on, none were prepared for what they saw when they reached the point of impact. Herds of bull elk had traditionally gathered here following the fall rut, wintering until the snowmelt allowed them to return to the summit. The meadow was now a spacious lake.

At the stream base, a quarter mile wide, yellowish-brown scar has been washed out from the Lawn Lake surge. The hundred-foot crevice was immense, left empty from where ten-ton boulders had once guided the stream. Swept away, Jimmy realized the massive rocks had been piled in a leviathan deposit at the base of the mountain. He could only imagine the damage above.

An alluvial fan, Jimmy called the geological feature. After days of rain, Lawn Lake had suddenly broken from the dam ripping a massive scar down the mountain and into the meadow, leaving the fan-shaped mound of sand, boulders, and uprooted trees over acres of the meadow. The towering pines, splintered to fragments by the severity of the surge were turned upside down and buried head first among the goliath boulders.

Alex sat helplessly back against a rock as the others stared in quiet reverence. Nothing in it's path could have survived.

It was slight, the noise William heard. He balanced himself against the stillness. Again, he heard a slight sound from somewhere. Stumbling over rocks, the dirt slid from beneath his feet as he rushed forward tripping over the terrain. Hearing the sound again, he cleared the next slight ridge. Ralph stood waving frantically and yelling, his arms motioning to hurry.

What lay before William was an intimidating mass of wreckage blocking the mouth of the offshoot from the main tributary. Behind it, a canyon ripped through the mountainside, running straight down and away from Ralph to the fan-shaped boulder mass barely visible a mile below. The flood had decimated the landscape, flushing the earth in an immense crevice where the meandering stream had once been.

Ralph waved again, and William scrabbled up the slope over unsteady rocks and shifting rubble. At the heap, the debris settled against the natural landscape. Ralph was reaching under a large stone, fighting for the strength to move it. William fell down beside him, and as he reached to add strength, the rock moved slightly. Through the shadows, buried in among the mass of debris, the body looked pale white, tattered clothing, lifeless. Ralph grunted more effort. William shifted for leverage and all of his strength. Slowly the rock began to move, and both men pressed harder until it cleared the ridge rolling off to the side.

The opening showed a slight lighted space and the soiled face of a man, his chest and one bloody arm.

In the shadows, Michael opened his eyes and stared up at William. He blinked, his tongue moving across his dried lips. "If that's William," he coughed, his face grimacing with breathy words. "This must be hell."

"Maybe for you," William's word echoed from above.

Michael's head nodded understanding.

Ralph was looking down into the rubble. "He's trapped from the waist down."

William started to lift a log. "Are you in much pain?"

"Some," Michael's shallow voice came from the debris. "I can't tell...how bad I'm hurt. The circulation... too much pressure. Legs are numb...my back."

William looked down at the pile to the base of the scar. Michael had nearly beaten it, probably inches from escaping the wave of crushing water, when it had reached up and grabbed him, pushing smaller boulders and splintered wood to encase his body. William dropped to his chest, turning upside down and wiggled head first into the hole beside Michael.

His voice echoed, calling to Ralph. "Move so I can get more light."

Ralph stepped around the opening, and light pouring down from above.

In the dimness, William looked at the position of Michael's body. He reached and struggled a few inches closer, turning his head away for a longer reach. "Can you feel that?" he asked.

Michael spit the words in a gasp. "Pressure ... on my foot."

They looked eye to eye in the shadows. "You've got feeling." William released Michael's foot and wiggled back to the surface. "This is too big for us." He watched Ralph, looked down the deep scar. "He's got feeling in his feet, but no telling what damage the pressure could cause. Is this where the rescue team is coming up?" William pointed down the boulder-riddled scar.

Ralph acknowledged, pointing too.

Michael lay still, barely able to see William, his mind warped with twisted confusion. He grimaced in pain.

William directed Ralph. "You go. Get help. I'll clear what I can to relieve the pressure. We need more manpower to get him out."

Alex paced after the rescue crew had disappeared. "This is stupid," she turned to Josie. "Any sign of your father?"

Josie looked as lost as Alex felt.

"I can't wait here." A determined look shot from Alex to Jimmy.

He could not wait either. "Okay, but we've got to be patient as we climb. The entire crevice is unstable." Jimmy grabbed her arm. "Are you listening to me? You follow me. Go at my pace." He turned to Josie. "Wait here, watch for your father. This is a big area. Carefully, check the entire alluvial fan for signs of anything. Who knows what's among all of these boulders. We'll go part way up. If we don't find anything, we'll be back within an hour."

By the time Jimmy turned to attack the crevice, Alex was already fifty yards out ahead.

William began to remove the smaller debris. Lifting fifty-pound granite boulders carefully from the top of the pile, he tried to find a place to set them, a place where they would not roll into the crevice and down onto Ralph or the rescue team. Each step had to be judged so the pile didn't shift knowing the slightest movement could crush Michael's legs.

Michael felt the grogginess returning. He looking up through the opening now big enough to see the blue sky and squinted. Often the silhouette of a man would block the blue, moving through the light. The man moved as if in slow motion, sometimes gentle, sometimes lifting a backbreaking load; but the pressure did not lessen the numbness of his legs. The man stopped, took deep breaths, and looked up into the sky. The sun peaked through the tall trees spared by the raging waters.

Michael stared groggily at the man. William? Yes, William had crawled down and grabbed his foot. He knew he was not paralyzed. William had grabbed his foot. The wooziness in his mind complicated any thoughts. What was William doing here? Why as he moving boulders? Michael felt his mind drifting away and the blue sky seemed to fade until he heard his own voice.

"Water," his voice echoed from somewhere among the rocks.

William stopped, looking for the bottle Ralph had left. He leaned across the top of Michael and grabbed it from the ledge. Bending carefully, he lay on the rocks above the trapped man and reached the bottle to his lips. Slowly, he poured until the water ran out the edges of his mouth. When he pulled back, Michael gave a slight nod.

"What are you doing here?" Michael mouthed the words.

William looked at Michael's bruised face with cuts across the right side. "I don't know."

"Friends?" Michael could only manage one word.

"You and I?" William twisted the cap back on the plastic bottle. "I'm not sure. Alexandria is here because of you. I'm here because of her."

Michael's eyes shut as he drifted away, then they opened again, "Alex?"

William did not answer as he tested the looseness of a wedged-in rock. Shifting his body for better leverage, he rolled the rock sideways from where it was wedged until it was free enough to lift with both hands. Moving three steps down the pile, he placed the rock and anchored it next to a protruding tree.

Michael grimaced as he pushed his head back. He took a breath. "Pain...My left side."

William looked down into the mangled rocks. "There's a tree pressed by a boulder against your leg." He pushed himself up, his head a foot and a half from Michael.

Michael moaned. "I never wanted...to hurt anyone."

William looked around for a lever, something long, a movable log. "Well," his voice echoed, "maybe it was inevitable."

Michael could hear the foot movement as William stepped from rock to rock. The sound lessened then strengthened again, and William reappeared above him, forcing a long, thick pole down into the hole beside him. William struggled, forcing the timber deeper. The pine pole moved in just a bit farther, and William adjusted his balance. With determination, he leaned fully into the pole, pushing. The green timber bent, yet he sensed some movement.

"More," Michael's voice seemed less pained. "That helped."

"Can you move out?"

Michael shook his head.

"But if I hold this the pain is gone?"

"Lessened," Michael nodded, still trapped. He tried to move his legs. "Tolerable. There's feeling in my legs."

William pressed into the timber, trying to look down the crevice. How much longer Ralph? His hands were sticky with sap and bloody raw. He kept leaning, kept looking for the rescue team. He tried to see down into the hole past Michael. It was too dark. In the loose dirt, his foot slipped inches. Michael tensed in pain. William forced the pole again, and the pain lessened.

"Alexandria says," he did not look, all his weight pressed into the pole, "says I'm too into power."

Michael stared up at the silhouette above him.

"From my..." he mumbled, "perspective." Michael gasped shallow breaths. "I hope you're powerful..." he gasped again.

"The pain back?" William called down to him.

Michael nodded.

William forced greater pressure against the timber. "Better?"

Michael nodded again. "Good. Just enough...power."

William kept the pressure from crushing. He quit trying to look at Michael, his focus on even pressure against the pole. This is what Alexandria had been talking about. If it were he trapped by boulders, no feeling in his legs; would anyone come to help. Alexandria would. Yes, he could count on Alexandria just as Michael could count on Alexandria. Josephine too. Josie would rescue him. The pole pressed deeper into his shoulder, and he felt the raw pain of bark molding into his skin.

Michael's voice was strained, hollow. "How do you...usually...situations like...this...handle them?"

"Not this well." William answered, gasping with oxygen depleted words. "My nature would be...to let go of this pole."

"It's good...to go...against your nature."

William's body was now at a full forty-five degree angle, pressing his shoulder into the rough timber bark. "Sometimes...I wish this were my nature."

"Now..." Michael took a deep breath, pain beginning to grow with the absence of numbness. "It's a good...time...to change."

His grin was almost a grimace against the harsh wooden pole. With all of his might, all his energy, he forced more strength against the wood. With each little bit more he gave, he could hear Michael's breathing easing. He balanced against his own pain, and pressed his shoulder deeper into the pole. "Deep down inside, Michael...I must be one hell...of a guy."

Michael's voice was soft, echoing from the boulders. "Hell...of a...guy." His face twisted as he fought for the words. "Yes."

William's grimace turned to a painful smile, pressing all of his weight forward. The sun continued to beat down between the few passing clouds. William could feel the heat as salt burned his eyes. He watched his hands, red against the timber. The blood had dried in a caked line around the edges of his fingers. Sweat poured from his brow, falling drop after drop on his forearms. As the shadow of a cloud moved across the debris, he began to worry about the damage to Michael's legs. Where was the rescue party?

Turning his head toward the crevice, listening, he thought he heard something. Michael called out in pain, and William pressed again on the pole.

"Sorry," he glanced down. "Thought I heard something."

He listened again. Without moving, without looking, he listened for the sound. Suddenly, voices became clearer, but William did not call out for fear of lessening the pressure again. A moment later, Ralph appeared in the flooded ravaged crevice followed by the rescue team.

They moved cautiously up the flood field, first two people then the rest following when it appeared secure. The first one up, leaned into the pole with William, his own pain relieved slightly. The second dropped down, her hand patting Michael's shoulder for comfort. The two, nearly face-to-face, talking.

Michael described his pain, and the female ranger looked deep down to where the pole leveraged to reduce the pressure. She called out orders, and Ralph and another ranger found thick pine poles. Guiding them around his legs and under the curvature of the boulders, the two pressed the timbers securely into place.

Two other rangers placed the backboard under Michael's shoulders, and waited to slide him upward and onto it. They worked like a well-practiced team, each knowing their role in life saving measures. Everyone in place, the ranger gave her go ahead.

All three poles bent under the strain, and there were crackles and the grinding of stone. Pulled by the other rangers, Michael slid onto the backboard, freed, and William relaxed the pressure on his shoulder. He sat back on the mountainside, reaching his hand over to grip Michael's. Michael squeezed his tightly, and William could feel the raw blood of his own hand against Michael's. They slid the neck brace under Michael's head, securing the Velcro straps.

Michael gave a squeeze. "Thank you...Hell of a guy."

As Michael released his grip, William felt his own pain disappearing.

The ranger was on her portable radio calling for air rescue when William saw Alexandria scrambling dangerously up from the crevice, Jimmy close behind her. As she reached them, she leaned across William's lap, her face close to Mickey's.

"Are you okay?" Softly, her lips pressed to his cheek.

"Think so," Mickey whispered, his mouth dry and crusted. "My legs...better already."

Jimmy stepped past them, reaching for one corner of the backboard. Alex moved back, allowing the rangers and Jimmy to lift the stretcher, Michael securely strapped into place. William stood between them, taking hold of the corner opposite of Jimmy. Alex gripped her husband's arm, and William nodded. No words were spoken as she leaned her head on her husband's shoulder.

The doctor was smiling when he found them sitting quietly in the waiting room. Jimmy and William sat together, William quizzing him about music. Alex and Josie were across from them, sipping sodas through hospital bendy straws with Jennifer beside Alex holding her hand. Ralph was picking the remains of a tuna fish sandwich from his teeth with a square toothpick. They all stood, surrounding the doctor in a semi-circle of concern.

"Things look good," the doctor began. "The worst are three cracked lumbar vertebra and deep bruises over both thighs and his left hip; his right leg had a clean break which will heal nicely. He's got feeling, so it doesn't appear there was severe damage to the spinal column or other nerves. Besides that his body is typically one big bruise or scrape. It appears with rest and patience the bones will heal, and he will recover fully. He's amazingly lucky. We've got him in traction for his back, but that's just precautionary. In a few days when his bruises allow him to walk, we'll fit him in a back brace and send him out of here. He'll have to wear that for a time. There are cracks in the bones but no displacements. Like any broken bone, in time they will heal."

The doctor was gone as quickly as he had appeared, so many more patients to attend to in the trauma unit. Alex stepped across, her arms wrapping fully around William's neck.

"Thank you," she held him tightly so he could hear. "I'm so sorry."

He returned her hug, looking over his wife's shoulder at Josie. She was a beautiful girl, and her strength had shown. Somehow, she had become all grown up and capable. In her eyes, the same eyes as her mothers, she smiled proudly. How wonderful it felt to have his daughter proud of him. He reached out his hand for Josie, still holding her mother with his other. Gently, Josie took his hand, and put it to her lips.

Alex was hugging Jimmy and thanking Ralph when William walked out the waiting room door and down the hallway to the emergency room entrance. He walked across South Saint Vrain Avenue and into a residential area. The street was lined with small, well-kept homes. Unaffected by the flood, they seemed not to have any people around. Probably helping friends, he thought. At the fair grounds, he found his Lexus, and drove out of the parking area heading southeast on Highway 36. More boats were on Lake Estes working to free the lake of the unwanted run-off.

7:48, the clock on the dash glowed a luminous blue. He picked up his cell phone and punched in the preset number before he lost a signal. Calling her cell, Valerie answered within three rings.

"I'm in Estes but heading home," he told her. "Any issues today?"

"Nothing major here. The crisis was there. Everything okay?"

William gazed at the passing hills. "Lots of damage, but we found Michael. He's pretty beat up, but he'll recover nicely."

Valerie didn't know how to respond. "I'm glad he's safe," she finally said. "I've left a list on your desk. Nothing vital."

It was reassuring to hear her voice. Something about the familiarity was comforting.

"I'm going to stop at The Club and clean up. I'm not quite ready to go home."

"You okay?" She asked.

He laughed, wondering if this was what *okay* felt like. "I'll tell you about it tomorrow." The passing mountains seemed peaceful.

"Really?" The surprise in her voice sounded pleasant.

"There's much to share." He answered.

Chapter 65

Michael woke in his own bed for the first time since the flood. It was quiet, and he feared the quiet. Then he heard sounds drifting up from the kitchen.

Alex worked in the bare framework of studs and plywood rebuilt as the frame for the kitchen. New pans and dishes were stacked on the bare floor where the stove would eventually be. She emptied a can of Campbell's Chicken Noodle Soup into a virgin pan, carried it through the living room, and out the sliding glass doors, still difficult to open against the grit. On the slight remains of the washed away patio, the new gas grill was flaming. She put the soup pan on the grill, and waited for it to warm.

The pines stood still in the breezeless morning, the sun flashing warmth across the valley from the horizon. The familiar scent of pine reminded her it was a crisp mountain morning. All seemed right again in the valley backdrop as Fall River rushed comfortably past, the ripples reflecting the clear rocks below.

Upstairs, Michael pressed his hands against the bed, raising slightly, his back stiff against the pillow behind him. When she appeared in the bedroom doorway, her eyes scolded him for moving on his own.

With a glance, he ignored the scolding. "Soup?"

"A mother knows best, and this is what my mother would feed you." She sat the tray on his lap. Leaning close to his face, she smiled and kissed him gently on the lips.

"Good morning," she whispered, her breath warm.

"Good morning," he kissed her again.

She sat on the bed next to him, offering to feed him, lifting the soupspoon from the bowl.

"You're kidding me," he laughed.

Alex touched the spoon to his mouth, his lips separating slightly as she pouring the broth. Grinning, he took the spoon from her hand and began to feed himself.

For a moment she watched him. Even fragile in the bed, he seemed so capable.

"Jennifer will be over in just a bit to take care of you."

He set the spoon down. "You're sure you have to go?"

Alex touched her hand softly over his cheek.

When he looked at her, he watched her eyes before he spoke. "I'm scheduled to go to Denali in Alaska in September," he said. "With my back and legs, I'll need an assistant, someone to help with the equipment, set up shots, and share the load. Have you ever seen the massive migration of Caribou in the fall colors against the white of Mount McKinley?"

"So," she laughed, "this is temptation at its best?"

"Absolutely," he said seriously. "I want you with me."

She kissed him again. This time with tender passion, and he felt the soft intensity he remembered so well.

"It's a date." She was cheerful like a young girl, her hand still pressed to his cheek. "Jennifer should be here soon." At the doorway, she stopped and turned to him. "It's different this time, Mickey. It might not feel different, but you can trust me." Then her eyes dropped, rising back up to smile at him. "I know you understand. Just for a time, I need to go back."

"I know," he tried to smile, "but don't make it seven years."

She swayed slightly offering a seductive pose. "Have you ever made love in the open air on an Alaskan mountainside?"

"Personally? No," he laughed. "I watched two moose do it once. Looked like they truly enjoyed it."

"Not as much as you will," she winked. As she turned and walked down the stairs, Alex gave Mickey a reassuring glance back over her shoulder. "I'll call you tonight."

Mickey felt the fear of watching her walk away. He looked at the soup. A few days, he repeated to himself. He heard Jennifer's car in the driveway. Listening, he could not make out their words. Then a car left. Setting the soup aside, he heard the front door open.

"Honey, I'm home."

He smiled at the sound of Jennifer's laughter.

Chapter 66

Valerie closed the door behind her, moving toward William. He looked up, admiring her.

"She's here." There was disappointment in her eyes. Then she blinked it away. "Alexandria is here," she repeated.

"Good." William gave her a reassuring smile. "Show her in."

Alex was dressed in slim tan jeans and running shoes. Her tee- shirt showed a bold elk, bugling to the mountains. Her hair hung straight and tucked back behind her ears, the style of a woman without worry. From each ear hung dangling stones of turquoise. William stepped around the desk, and she was surprised to see he was working without his suit coat on. His tie was pulled neat and tight, but his suit coat hung on the seldom-used coat rack in the corner of the office. When he reached for her, his hug was strong and it felt reassuring, if only for a moment.

"Michael?" he asked.

"They released him yesterday."

"Full recovery?" William said.

Her eyes were bright, as was her smile. "Yes, thanks to you."

"I'm glad." His expression was genuine.

Then he turned to the seriousness of the moment. He knew why she had come.

"Well, onto our own lives." He offered her a seat and sat in the chair next to her. "I've learned a lot over the years and especially these last couple of months, even days. We both have." He acknowledged. "I know now that there's no going back. I'm sorry for that, but for both of our sakes, I've accepted it." He shrugged, sad in what he was saying. "I couldn't do this completely without involving lawyers, of which I remind you I am one of the despicable group. Divorce, unfortunately, is muddled in the quirks of legal maneuvering and asset protection."

She laughed a sad smile of apology. "That's why I asked to do this just between us. I never considered our marriage to be based on assets."

"Anyway," he looked less convinced, "I want this to be fair."

She started to speak, but he reached a tender, reassuring touch to her knee. It seemed genuine.

"Please," his eyes surrendered. "I've been trying to discover a new attitude, so please, for a moment let me speak. I want to put the ugliness behind us."

There was kindness in his words. His terms were not terms but offered as ideas for her to consider. It wasn't the Chadwick empire, but she didn't want the empire. Still, it was more than generous, much more than she would have expected. She would be well taken care of. He gave general concepts, and they discussed details.

Josie, he believed she could make many of her own decisions. He hoped she would stay with him and finish high school in Denver, but he would not make her an issue. Josie could determine what was best.

Agreements seemed to be easy to come by. They even agreed to let their attorneys finalize the details. Once done, she and William would have dinner together to review the final documents and make sure the attorneys hadn't messed anything up. Thursday night, William offered, would be a nice evening for dinner.

Alex had to say it, but how do you thank your husband for such things?

"I don't quite understand everything that has happened, William. In fact, some of it has confused me beyond imagination, yet among the confusion, things seem to have cleared. I'm thankful for all you're doing and all you've done. It seems every time I think I know you, you do something unexpected. What you did in Estes, what you did for Mickey knowing what he means to me, William, I'm so thankful."

"Yes, every now and then I do go against my nature." He laughed to himself, feeling comfort in the ease of a difficult conversation. "Sometimes, I surprise even myself. But let me ask you this." William's confidence showed. "What do you think I did that evening when I got back from Estes?"

"I assume you came here to work."

"Ah, yes. My nature." He raised his eyebrows. "But I didn't. I went to The Club to clean up. Didn't feel like going home. Home?" A frown turned his eyes serious. "Funny word. Anyway, at The Club, Ben and a couple of others were just coming off the back nine, and they asked me to join them for a drink." A silly smile returned to his face. "You know? I don't really like golf. Never have. It's a frustrating game, but every time I play, toward the end of the round I sink a thirty-foot putt or maybe drive the green for a birdie putt. On rare occasions, I might chip in. Goofy, frustrating game, but every time I make one of those rare shots, it makes me believe I'm getting better, so I keep going back expecting every shot of to be like that one shot that convinced me to play again."

Alex watched the subtleties in his expression.

William leaned back in his leather chair. "Damn game. No matter how long I play golf, I just don't get any better. I broke 75 once, thought I was better. Surprised myself. Turns out I was only better once. Haven't seem the 70s since."

"But didn't it feel amazing that one time?" she smiled thankful.

"Yes, very good. Fantastic, in fact," he agreed. "Good enough to keep going back and trying to break into the 70s, but I guess it's not in my nature. My best this summer is an 82. You see; I'm just not very good at golf. I have my moments, but basically, I'm not very good."

Alex understood. "But you keep playing, hoping that someday you'll again go against your nature."

"I think it may be time to quit playing golf." He looked large, in control. "That's also my nature. I'm determined and goal driven, maybe to a fault, but part of being successful is knowing when it's time to change."

He tried to imagine how their lives were changing, knowing they were not really changing. He looked beyond his wife out the glass wall of his office at the busy maneuvers of his dedicated employees. Everybody was in motion, and Valerie sat at her computer typing with amazing agility as her finger flew.

"Alex, if I may ask one more question," he smiled calmly. "All of these social functions, these events my family finds so charming," he rolled his eyes slightly. "They're an obligation. Politically, for the business I am obligated to participate." He looked a bit lost with his words. "For some, I can take Josie. I need more time with her, and she has much of her mother's charm and social graces. Other times, well you're so good at such things, and I hope very much that we still care about each other. Could I call you now and then, if I need your style and grace to accompany me at social functions or to consult with the Foundation?"

Almost as if he were asking her for a date, they both giggled a giggle from a long time ago.

"I've always and will always care for you, William. Yes, of course, call if you need me. I'll even be nice to your mother."

A silly smile spread across his face. "You are a woman of patience."

Alex raised her eyebrows. "What about Valerie? She'd do nicely at those social events."

Flushed, his cheeks turned a slight red. "Yes, she would. That's a good thought."

Alex grinned at her perceptiveness.

"Alexandria," he straightened, still dashing in his stuffy cotton oxford and conservative striped tie, "I don't want anybody to go through any more pain than necessary. Can we keep this as private as possible? No need to start a frenzy in the press. I don't believe our divorce or the details of our lives are necessary for anyone else to know."

"I'd want it no other way," she reassured.

For a long moment there was silence. William looked down at the floor between them knowing in the next few moments she would leave his office, and that would be it, the first major failure in his life. Josie had been right. He'd waited too long to fully appreciate the qualities of his wife.

Only now did he realize what he was losing.

"Are you going right back?" he asked.

"I need to spend some time with Josie. Then I must get some things organized at the house and upstairs in my office. Maybe a few days, a week at most, then I need to get back to Estes. For a time, I can help with the Foundation transition from there." Her brow wrinkled, questioning. "Is that okay, that I stay a few days?"

He reached his hand to hers. "Of course."

She wrapped her arms around him, and for moment they held each other. When he finally felt her releasing, he too let go.

As she walked to the door, his memory flashed back to a time when he was in law school, and he'd seen her walking across campus. It was more than the slimness of her hips or the composed posture of her shoulders. It was the playful bounce of her hair, the elegant finesse of her sway that captured him. That day, he had chased after her. With some silly flirtation statement, he had stopped her. He remembered her beauty, the arousing radiance in her smile, and the extraordinary blue in her eyes. She had been more than he had ever expected.

She still was.

Chapter 67

It had been nearly three weeks since the flood and her frantic rush from Denver. This morning the quietness of the Chadwick Estate had been eerie. The door of the guest room was left open, William having already begun his day at work long before she awoke.

When Alex was ready to leave, she found Josie eating breakfast on the sun porch. Continually, she had reassured her mother; yes, she was okay. Yes, she would be up to visit the next weekend. They were only a short drive away. Besides, the next summer would be amazing, living with her in Estes and hiking every day.

Daddy needed her now, and she had volleyball camp and her junior year coming up. Would she bring Michael to watch her play volleyball in the fall? Yes, her mother had guaranteed, as soon as they got back from Alaska, they'd come to every volleyball game.

Josie's hug goodbye brought Alex's tears, stronger than she had expected. She held tightly to her daughter.

"I'm happy for you, Mom," Josie whispered. "I'll be up Friday night for the weekend. I heard there's a great hike to Sky Pond."

Alex pulled her closer. "It's magnificent," she said. "I'll set Saturday aside for us." She stepped back to see how grown up her daughter had become.

"Give Michael a hug for me?" Josie asked.

Her mother blinked the tears away. "Of course."

When the highway turned west out of Boulder, Alex watched the growing mountains. This was the moment she loved, when you first enter the foothills and realize you are in the mountains. The scent overtook her, and visions of terrain rose up to the sky firing the anticipation of going home.

Epilogue

William didn't really know where he was going. He felt out of place, embarrassed that he had never been here before. The halls were empty and all seemed quiet. He stepped up to a sliding glass window where a lone secretary sat in the office.

Her demeanor was pleasant. "May I help you?"

"Yes," he looked down the high school hallway. "I'm looking for my daughter. She's at the volleyball camp. Josie Chadwick."

"Of course," the secretary stood. She pointed directions down the main hallway and to the left.

They exchanged nods of thank you.

Josie was shocked to see her father standing in the school's gymnasium doorway. She broke from the circle of girls in a setting drill as the volleyball popped high in the air one player to another. Her coach waved an okay as Josie jogged across the gym pointing toward her father.

"Hi," she stopped, bouncing before him. "Is everything okay?"

She was at that age that a sweaty tee shirt and boxer shorts with the fly sown shut were perfectly natural to her. Her father found it a bit disconcerting. Quickly, her smile made him forget. He watched as her blue eyes deepened in concern.

"Absolutely," he said, shifting in his suit coat. "Everything's fine. I thought I'd watch a little practice, then take you to lunch."

"Daddy, you've never even been to a game?" she leered at him. "You're sure everything's okay?"

"That's been my mistake. This year, I promise to be at your games." William lowered his eyes. "Do you mind if I watch, then maybe we can grab a pizza." He looked at his watch. "I've got a couple of hours before my one o'clock meeting."

"Pizza?" Josie had never seen him eat pizza.

"Pizza," he said, as if it was the most natural thing to do.

She shook her head, amazed. "What's your favorite topping?"

Her father looked up toward the steel girder gym ceiling. "Can't say. I heard pepperoni is good."

Josie grinned to herself. "It goes best with Italian sausage."

"Spicy?" he answered. "I guess you can give me a pizza topping lesson over lunch."

She laughed like his daughter should. "We've got fifteen more minutes, then I have to change."

"No problem," William winked at her. "I'll wait."

"You'll wait?" Her eyes rolled in disbelief. "Okay, good," then she added, "and Daddy, I'm glad you're here."

"Me too." He pointed back toward the girls practicing. "Go on. I'll just watch for a bit."

She skipped back across the gym, rejoining her friends. The circle of girls stopped as one player caught the volleyball. They all turned looking in his direction, and his daughter waved playfully at her father.

Alex woke naked under the warmth of cotton sheets and a heavy wool blanket. The chill of the mountain morning, slight breeze from the open balcony door, and Mickey excited her. How gently they had made love the night before, careful to avoid any pain from the lingering effects of his injuries.

"Good morning." His kind whisper came from beside her.

She curled, cuddling closer, allowing the covers to fall and leave her naked.

"Morning." She rested her face on his shoulder.

So comforted, she lay allowing the touch of his fingers to gently trace the patterns of her shoulder. When she finally stirred, he watched her stand naked and walk to the bathroom door, closing it behind her. It was one of his pleasures, to watch her walk naked across his bedroom.

When she emerged from the shower she was wrapped in a large, fluffy towel, beads of water still dotting her chest. Sitting at the edge of the dresser, waves of steam curled from the clay mug of hot tea he had left for her. Pressing the towel to her chest, she sat for a time brushing her hair until it hung straight beyond her shoulders. From the corner pedestal of their bed, she took her tattered Denver Bronco sweatshirt, slipped it on, and allowed it to fall over her shoulders hanging just below her bare bottom.

Her hands warmed by the hot mug, she moved through the hallway, past The White Room, and down the stairs to the newly remodeled kitchen. He was where she knew he would be, and she moved to join him on the oversized couch. When he looked up to see her, he lifted his arm raising the digital reader and allowing her to duck under and sit beside him. Leaning fully against him, she snuggled closely with his arm securely around her.

He had accessed the Denver Post and was reading the comics. It was always his nature to read the comics first in each morning's paper. Start the day with a chuckle, he said. Then together, her head resting on his strong shoulder and the tea warm in her hands, Alex and Mickey read the morning news.

ABOUT THE AUTHOR

Brad Manard has been a writer and educator his entire life. In 2008 his first book was published. *Life Lessons of a Legend* is the memoir of Key West, FL legend Captain Tony Tarracino. *The White Room…A Photographic Love Story* encompasses romance and adventure in his love for Estes Park, CO, Rocky Mountain National Park, and nature and wildlife photography. With degrees from the University of Nebraska and a doctorate in education, Brad currently lives with his family in Iowa where he continues to serve as a school superintendent and pursue his passions of writing and photography.

Visit Brad's website at www.bradmanard.com.

www.ingramcontent.com/pod-product-compliance
Lightning Source LLC
Chambersburg PA
CBHW050915250626
47155CB00001B/237